AFTER THE END

Trapped Days

Fractured Days

Final Days

RELAY PUBLISHING EDITION, OCTOBER 2024
Copyright © 2024 Relay Publishing Ltd.

Grace Hamilton is a pen name created by Relay Publishing for co-authored Post-Apocalyptic projects. Relay Publishing works with incredible teams of writers and editors to collaboratively create the very best stories for our readers.

Cover Design by Deranged Doctor.

www.relaypub.com

AFTER THE END BOOK THREE

FINAL DAYS

GRACE HAMILTON

BLURB

In the shadow of a fallen world, law and order are just memories. Only survival remains...

Shannon Grayson had made it through the brutal early days of the EMP apocalypse. Despite suffering a bullet wound in her shoulder, she's managed to reunite with her daughter, Kim. And she's found a safe haven at the Wander Motel.

But tensions are rising in her group of survivors. Kim struggles with the aftermath of Dennis's death and the brutal trials she's been forced to endure. She needs to be at her best to survive and lead in this harsh world, but her past haunts her every step.

Shannon, Kim, and their newfound community aren't the only people fighting to survive in the post-EMP world. Andre, Shannon's ruthless ex-husband, is out of prison. He's rebuilding his motorcycle gang. And he's coming for Shannon and Kim.

Both mother and daughter have paid a heavy price for survival. They need time to heal, physically and mentally. But with Andre closing in, the Wander Motel is no longer a refuge—it's a trap.

CONTENTS

1

KIM NAKAMURA

"I swear, Mutt, it's like my mom thinks I'm still a child—like the kid she used to try and protect from my dad, or the teenager she left behind." With a grunt, Kim Nakamura straightened up from where she'd been digging through a pile of debris.

Beside her, Mutt woofed encouragement. The large mixed-breed dog butted her head under Kim's hand in silent demand for a scratch behind the ears. Kim grinned ruefully and obliged, ruffling the dog's short fur. Then Mutt licked her hand and went off to nose about another tangle of cars and trash, looking for food or something that smelled interesting to her, though Kim couldn't imagine what that might be.

It had been a week since she'd faced down her psychotic father and been reunited with her mother outside the remains of her aunt and uncle's bombed-out scrapyard. That week had only served to make her life more confusing than before the disaster had wiped out the United States power grid and driven her to seek out her family in Memphis.

She'd thought being reunited with her mother, Sarah, would make the world seem…better, she supposed. But it hadn't been that simple. Nothing was.

To start with, her mother now went by Shannon, the new name she'd been given in WitSec.

To make it worse, thinking of WitSec only reminded Kim of the man who'd given his life to try and reunite her with her mother. Like the gun she carried on one hip, the knives she had stashed in her boots and the small of her back, and the worn, military-grade backpack on her shoulders, the name Shannon evoked memories of Dennis Sullivan.

She still saw his face in her nightmares most nights. Sometimes it was scrunched with pain, the way it had been when he'd been trying to detox. But most often, she remembered the way she'd seen him last: sprawled lifelessly on the grass with a neat red circle in his forehead and a puddle of red around his head and shoulders like a macabre halo.

Her feelings about Dennis had been complicated, but she mourned him and missed him with an intensity she never would have imagined a month ago.

Unlike her mother, Dennis would have trusted her instead of feeling the need to watch over her and coddle her. There were so many times in the past week she'd wanted to scream something like that at her mother and her aunt, but every time, she found herself unable to speak, because then she'd have to tell Shannon what had happened to Dennis.

She shook herself out of those thoughts before she could drown in them.

Kim watched Mutt go and sighed. "At least someone in my life is easy to please." She hefted her pack higher onto her shoulder and jogged after the dog.

After a week of wariness, arguments, and far too much tension on both sides, she'd finally managed to convince Shannon and Carol she would be safe searching for supplies on her own. Her mother had driven with her to the area around Horn Lake but finally relented enough to let her slip away to search another section of the highway by herself.

It's not like I don't know my father's still out there and still dangerous. I do. I'd never have made it this long or this far if I was as naive as she thinks I am.

Kim paused to take a deep breath and loosen some of the tension coiling within her. It wasn't entirely Shannon's fault she was so stressed these days. The events of the past few weeks aside, she just wasn't used to being around so many people all the time, and she needed space to breathe.

Like now. She knew Shannon and Bill were only a shout away, but it was still a relief to have some time alone, without other people hovering around her. She'd grown used to being mostly solitary over the years, and the constant presence of others at the motel the Black Rats were using as a temporary base had started to grate on her nerves. The walls were thinner than even the walls in her college dorm room had been. The privacy of her motel room didn't keep her from hearing far more than she wanted regarding the lives of her great-aunt's crew of bikers—men and women alike.

Her mother's constant hovering didn't help either. Especially now, when she didn't want the older woman to know what she was really looking for—besides cars with partially filled fuel tanks and basic supplies.

She was looking for cake ingredients. Anything that could serve to help produce an appropriately sized sweet pastry. Shannon's birthday was less than a day away, and Kim wanted to celebrate it. After all, it had been five years since her mother had gotten to enjoy any birthdays or holidays with her family, and Kim wanted to change that. They might all be struggling to cope with the disaster that had struck almost a month before, but to Kim, that made the celebration *more* important, not less.

She'd started her search four days ago, going out on scavenging missions with whoever was on the prowl at any given time. So far, she'd found more frustration than she had anything else. There was no milk because anything that might have remained in a store or someone's home had spoiled ages ago. Eggs were less perishable, according to Bill Wheeler, but also in short supply. If you weren't a farmer and didn't have access to livestock, you were pretty much out of luck on either front. Things like flour and sugar were rare. Most of it had been looted, and some of what she'd found had been infested with mold or bugs.

When all was said and done, she'd managed to locate enough flour for a moderately sized cake—of sorts: water, some sort of fake egg mix someone had missed or left behind, and maybe a cup or two of sugar. She'd also scrounged some frosting, mostly because it was less practical than many other food items, along with ginger snaps and ginger flavoring.

Her mother loved ginger. Kim figured she could slather vanilla frosting and powdered ginger over the ginger snaps, if all else failed. It wouldn't be great, but it would be better than nothing, as far as she was concerned.

"—elp!" The faint sound jolted her from her thoughts and made her straighten. She stopped searching and listened carefully.

"Help!" This time she heard the word clearly, spoken in a voice that was definitely not her mother's or Bill's, or anyone else's she could recognize.

That didn't mean it wasn't someone from the Black Rats. Even if it wasn't, Kim couldn't bring herself to ignore a cry for help. She slapped her thigh twice to get the dog's attention, using one of the signals she'd been training Mutt to respond to. The dog looked up at once, then loped toward her. Kim grinned fondly at her. "Come on, Mutt. Sounds like someone's in trouble."

She jogged toward the source of the noise and found a man leaning against a burned-out shell of a car. He was doubled over with his arms wrapped around his gut like he had a stomachache. The man looked up at her approach. "Help me, please! I've been...been..." He coughed sharply and hunched further in on himself.

Kim hurried forward, ignoring the way Mutt stopped and made a low growl in the back of her throat. Mutt didn't like strangers.

She was just out of arm's reach when a sense of unease caused her to falter. A voice oddly like Dennis's whispered in her thoughts.

Something's not right. Look at him.

She wanted to dismiss the thought, but years of having to watch out for her father's uncertain temper, along with the lessons she'd recently learned on the road, made her hesitate.

The way he's standing says it's a gut wound. But there's no blood. Can't be a shooting or a stabbing. And a blunt-force wound bad enough to need help would make it near impossible to talk, let alone shout for help loudly enough to get your attention. He doesn't look sick enough for that to be the problem, and there's no sign of him throwing up. He's not acting like he's got cramps either. It doesn't add up.

5

Kim stopped and watched the man carefully as she addressed him. "Sir, where are you hurt? What happened?"

"I...I've been..." The words sounded forced, but now that she was paying attention and close enough to hear him more clearly, Kim noticed the lack of wheezing that would indicate difficulty breathing. "...attacked..."

"By who, sir? And how are you hurt? What are your injuries?" Kim stayed where she was, her muscles tensing and her hand dropping to the weapon at her belt as the man's behavior raised more red flags.

The man looked up at her. "I was..." He trailed off, and his expression changed, from one of pain to one of annoyance and mild disgust. "I knew I should have gone with a broken arm or a head injury." He scowled. "Whatever, just don't give me too much trouble and neither of us has to leave here injured."

Then he lunged at her.

2

SHANNON GRAYSON/SARAH NAKAMURA

"Shannon, did you find something promising?" Shannon—known to her family as Sarah Nakamura before a stint in WitSec had gotten her in the habit of answering to another name—glanced up from her inspection of yet another car wreck. Her close friend, Bill Wheeler, was watching her with poorly hidden concern.

"Might have. Looks like this driver had some tools and an emergency med kit." Shannon worked her way through the gap in the battered door frame, dropped to her side on the seat, and wriggled her way closer to the small white metal box near the floor of the battered SUV they were investigating. "You check the tools, and I'll just grab this."

"I can grab that. I've got a longer reach." Bill moved forward hopefully, and Shannon glared at him.

"I'm not an invalid, Bill. And you wouldn't fit, not unless you forced the door open wider." Shannon pressed forward another inch and managed to catch hold of the handle of the box. She scrabbled her way back out of the SUV's interior and straightened with a look of triumph, which became a grin when she opened it to find several pads of gauze, small scissors, and a partially full tube of antibiotic ointment. It might not be a fully stocked ambulance, but it was better than nothing.

Bill made a noise of appreciation from where he'd started going through the small bag of tools he'd hoisted carefully through the broken back window. "There's some handy things in here, especially for fixing bikes. Nothing big enough for the larger truck parts, but that's all right."

Shannon went to load the kit into her pack. Bill followed behind. "How's your shoulder?"

"No worse than it was when you asked me an hour ago. I'm not picking anything heavy up." She gave him a sideways look. "It's been weeks since I was shot, and you took good care of the wound. You know that, so why are you acting like you think I'm going to fall over?"

Bill hesitated a moment, then sighed. "I'm just worried about you. You've been jumpy and restless ever since we left the scrapyard. You're even worse than you were when we were dealing with Barney Langmaid's murder rampage back in the supercenter. And I know you haven't been sleeping well, either."

Shannon rolled her good shoulder uncomfortably. "The scrapyard got bombed, and a lot of good people got killed. It's not unreasonable to be a little nervous after something like that." She bent to eye the next car, then straightened. "But we've got more important things to think about, like whether this car has any fuel worth salvaging, since there isn't anything inside worth taking."

"I'll take a look at it, if you tell me what's really got you spooked." Bill's voice was annoyingly reasonable.

Shannon directed a halfhearted glare in his direction. Then she sighed and waved for him to take a look at the tank while she slouched against the side door. "It's Andre. My ex-husband. I know I saw him at that attack, and then that boy you rescued confirmed he was the one behind it."

"Lee." Bill nodded to show he was listening as he dropped down to shimmy around so he could shine a light in the body of the vehicle. "I recall he said something of the sort. But why's that got you as flustered as a cat in a room full of rockers?"

"Because Andre's a vindictive, temperamental, violent monster who'd sooner lose his left hand than let go of a grudge. From what he did to the scrapyard, it's obvious prison has made all those traits worse. I'm terrified of what he'll do next."

Shannon grimaced, eyes roaming over the landscape of broken cars and trash-strewn concrete. "That's not the only thing that has me worried. Kim said she had an altercation with him on the road. They ran into each other when he fled, and words were exchanged. Along with bullets. Before that encounter, he might have thought she was someone he could turn into an ally. But now that she's shot him and driven him away, he'll try to punish her too."

Bill pushed himself free of the car. "Good couple gallons or more in here. I reckon we could find a use for it."

Shannon fished a broken screwdriver from her pocket and used it to scrape a sign on the door. To anyone else, it would look like damage from the crash, but anyone from the Black Rats crew run by her Aunt Carol would know it was a marker for viable fuel salvage. She'd tell Carol to send out a siphon team in this direction when they got back to the motel they were currently crashing in.

Bill's hand came to rest on her shoulder. "You know Kim's a tough young lady, just like her mother. And she's already handled him once —I bet she can do it again, easy as eating pie."

"I wish I could believe you. But she took him by surprise that time. He won't be caught off guard a second time. Now that he's lost the

9

element of surprise, he'll come back with reinforcements and a mountain of viciousness on his side." She shook her head. "It scares me."

A rattle of shifting metal made her jump and reach for her blade, only to relax when she realized the wind had blown a bit of debris across the road. She scanned the area again and shook her head. "Speaking of Kim, she's been off on her own for a while. We should go find her, make sure she's okay."

"I'm sure she is. Like I said, she's a tough girl."

Shannon gave Bill a sour look as the mechanic swung both their scavenging duffels up onto his broad shoulders. "Tough isn't always the best thing to be, though." She fell into step beside him as they picked their way down the road to the old pickup Bill had managed to wrangle from the wreckage of the scrapyard and get working. "My being tough, as you put it, is what got Andre all riled up in the first place. He never could stand it when someone pushed back against him and his temper."

I thought that was charming back when we first hooked up. Why didn't I realize his protectiveness was really possessiveness? Or that his defensiveness was the sign of a bad attitude with a hair-trigger temper?

Shannon shook the thoughts away as Bill spoke again. "Maybe, but those are the same traits that kept you alive. And helped keep me and a whole bunch of other folks alive too, back in the supercenter."

"Sure. They're also the reason I got a lunatic's bullet in my shoulder and nearly died in a filthy, dark storage aisle in the back of that same supercenter." She shook her head. "Besides, Kim's young. She's never seen the worst the world has to offer, even if she's learned some hard lessons here and there. I worry about her being unprepared for what's out there—but I don't want her to learn the hard way."

They reached the truck, and Bill tossed the bags into the back. Shannon was just about to suggest they split up to look for Kim when familiar barking caught both their attention—followed by a shriek of pain and fear.

3

KIM NAKAMURA

K im dodged the man's first lunge with a gasp and just barely avoided his grabbing hands. Her eyes darted around, assessing the landscape. The ground was uneven, and there wasn't much room to move without bumping into broken vehicles. The man had chosen his ambush spot well.

She needed to get to her gun or draw one of her knives, but her weapons were secured to prevent loss, and she didn't have a lot of space to move away. In such close quarters, she couldn't risk not having both hands free to fend off his next attack—at least, not long enough to undo the strap. Kim grimaced at her own foolishness. Such a simple mistake, not freeing a weapon the second she'd realized something was off.

"Quit struggling!" The man grabbed at her again. Kim found herself backed too close to a car to move freely or completely avoid him. Still, she was able to block his arm in a rudimentary move she'd learned as a teenager, then she clawed at the man's face.

He lurched back with a yelp of pain as her fingernails scored across his cheek. But even angered and in pain, he managed to grab hold of her sleeve.

Mutt growled and darted forward to sink her teeth into the man's leg. His grip loosened as he let out a yowl of pain, and Kim wrenched herself free. She tried to back up but stumbled over a section of the pavement. She twisted awkwardly, trying to avoid an injury. A shout told her that either Mutt had gotten in another good bite, or her attacker had succeeded in preventing further attacks for the time being.

The backpack was throwing off her balance, and she couldn't get the gun free of the safety strap she wore. She grabbed for a knife instead and drew it as she turned to face the man.

He was holding a metal chunk, and his expression was grim and determined. Not her knife, the rake marks across his face, or the bloody gouges from Mutt's teeth were enough to deter him.

Mutt, on the other hand, was curled up on the ground and whining softly. Kim thought she might have been kicked in the ribs, from the way she was lying. Then the man charged her again, and Kim had no more time to check on the dog.

Kim swiped at the man with the knife, but he dodged her attack with a snarl. Kim stumbled a bit on the uneven ground—helped in her fall by his foot in her path. Before she could regain her bearings, something hard slammed into the back of her head. Stars exploded behind her eyes as she toppled forward onto the pavement, where they were joined by the sting of scrapes on her hands as she landed. The knife skittered away from her grip.

Kim blinked away the blurring of her vision and rolled over. The man was coming closer, and she acted instinctively, the way her mother had taught her to respond to assaults as a child. She lifted her foot and rammed it upward and forward with all the strength she could muster.

Her aim was good, and the blow landed square in the man's groin. Unfortunately, she didn't have as much leverage as she would have liked, and he hadn't been close enough for maximum effectiveness. The kick made him stagger and grab at his crotch with a string of curse words that would impress the Black Rats, but it didn't drop him in his tracks the way she'd hoped.

The pain in her head and the weight of her backpack hampered her as she tried to scramble away, but she didn't dare roll over so she could get to her feet properly. She knew he'd be on top of her in a second if she did that.

The man stalked toward her, manic rage in his eyes. He was still walking oddly, but she knew he was seconds away from another attack. She wasn't sure if she would be able to hit him again. He was guarding himself now, wariness mixed with his determination to complete whatever his goal was. Robbing her, at the very least.

Kim felt along the ground for the knife, or a large rock, or anything she could pull free and easily use as a weapon. Her head still ached, and her vision was slightly blurry. At the very least, she'd taken a bad blow, and she knew the chances were good that she might have a mild concussion.

The man's legs tensed, stance coiling in preparation to spring forward and either kick her or pin her down. Then there was a dull *thunk* from behind him. The man collapsed like a puppet with cut strings.

Shannon stood behind him, makeshift club in hand and a grim expression on her face. A few yards away, Bill was picking his way through the wrecked cars. His larger frame and age slowed him down, but not by much.

Shannon nudged the man with her foot. The result was a groan, and she kicked him in the head for good measure. Then she looked up. "Kim, you all right?"

Her head hurt, and she felt like an idiot for having lost her grip on her knife. But she was still alive, and that was what mattered. "I'm okay."

From the look on her mother's face, Shannon didn't believe her. Kim retrieved her knife and sheathed it, then hauled herself to her feet and began the process of dusting herself off.

"That looks like a heck of a goose egg on the back of your skull," Bill said as he caught up.

Kim scowled. She liked Bill, but sometimes he saw—and said—things she'd rather he didn't.

Shannon marched forward, determined to take a look. Kim stayed where she was and let her. She knew resisting would only cause her mother to treat her even more like a child.

Shannon's fingers prodded carefully over the back of her head. Kim winced when she found the place where the man had hit her. "That's a good-sized lump, all right. But you're not bleeding a lot, so it probably only rattled your brain a little bit. It'll ache for a while, but I think we can scrounge up some pain meds when we get back to the motel."

"As long as it's something like Tylenol." Kim wasn't about to risk taking anything stronger. She still remembered the consequences of Dennis's addiction all too clearly.

"Probably will be, if we've got anything at all." Shannon said. She looked between Kim, the downed man, and Mutt, who was getting to her feet with gentle assistance from Bill. "But before we get on the road, perhaps you'd better tell me what happened here and how likely it is that we're going to run into a few of this fellow's friends on our way."

Her mother's expression was tight, and Kim winced at the raised eyebrow and the stern way her lips pressed together.

Here we go again.

4

AUSTIN

Austin glared at his bike despondently, still clutching a dirty rag to his bleeding face as he tried to ignore the clawing in his gut, along with the throbbing pain of various bruises. After a moment, he bent to heave the bike upright, swearing under his breath as the movement made his nose hurt worse.

The bike might take him back home, but it wouldn't be an easy ride, and getting repairs would be even harder. Austin cursed again as he levered himself gingerly over the seat and pinched the bridge of his nose hard to stop the blood flow enough that he could start the bike and get back to the Rat Trap—the miserable little hole in the wall he'd called home for the past week.

He hadn't planned to hurt Keith. But he was broke, in need of a fix, and hoping to score a little something to entice some female company to his place. He'd asked nicely, but Keith had turned him down. He'd refused to help out unless Austin could pay him—as if he had jack to use for payment or trade.

That was why he'd pulled a knife and tried to make Keith give it up. Well, that and the fact that he'd been mad as a wet cat. Brothers of the road were supposed to help each other out, and Keith had been treating him like a nobody.

He'd forgotten Keith had been taught street fighting by some of the old guard, Black Rats who had run the show back before Austin himself had joined. Back when the Black Rats had really been all they were reputed to be instead of the pansies they'd become under the Gardenas.

Keith's first blow, a sucker-punch to the gut that took his breath away, had reminded him how Keith had earned the nickname Bull-dozer. The beating that followed had been a stark warning of how stupid he'd been in trying to fight someone with Keith's reputation.

The broken nose and the trashed bike though—that was adding insult to injury. He might've earned the thrashing—though he'd deny it—but destroying a man's bike was taking a lesson too far.

Austin took a cautious breath, stuffed the cloth up his nose as an added deterrent to any more bleeding, and started the engine. He winced at the scratched and dented handlebars in front of him.

At least the bike still ran. It would have been the ultimate humiliation to be a biker without a ride. With a grunt, he got the bike going and began to guide it toward the Rat Trap. There was a wobble that suggested either the frame or a wheel had been bent out of alignment, and he grimaced. That would be harder to get fixed than the dings in the paint.

Ten minutes of uncomfortable riding later, he'd made it back to the Rat Trap. It wasn't much—the place was so worn down and badly maintained that calling it a dive bar was generous—but it was the closest thing he'd had to home since the scrapyard exploded in flames. The bed he'd scrounged was lumpy with busted springs, and the rest of his setup wasn't much better. However, he had access to cheap booze and crappy little snack items the former owner had stocked. Plus, no one cared if he did his business outside in the alley instead of trying to use the indoor crapper, which had probably been busted even before the world went crazy.

Austin shut the bike off, set it carefully upright—the stand was a little bent too, but it held—and staggered off the bike. His nose throbbed, along with his ribs, the wrist Bulldozer Keith had stomped, his knee, and a couple other places. He felt worse than he had after his first crash, and that was saying something.

Austin staggered toward the door, then froze. He knew he hadn't left it open. He wasn't that much of a fool, and he sure wasn't going to invite people to just waltz in and take over his squatting place or rob him blind. But there it was, gaping open like the new gap in his teeth.

After a second, he realized the door was freshly splintered, and the frame was cracked and broken. Someone had kicked the door in rather than picking the lock or something a little less conspicuous.

He'd just gotten a solid beating, and he wasn't sure he could handle another one. Common sense suggested he grab his bike and find another place to settle in. But his pride, and a gritty, scrambling, tight-fisted determination to keep what was his, stopped him from running. The Rat Trap was a dump, but it was *his* dump. If someone thought they could just take it from him, then he'd show them otherwise.

He pulled out his knife, mustered the toughest expression he could with a purple, swollen nose and bruised jaw, and stalked inside. "Don't know who you are, but you've made your last mistake, breaking into my place like this!"

"Have I now?" A figure at the bar unfolded from his seat with leisurely grace and stepped smoothly into the light.

Austin's mind went blank in a wash of adrenaline and fight-or-flight reflexes. The guy was big, well over six feet tall, and muscled like a football player. There was something in his eyes that told Austin this guy was way more dangerous than Bulldozer Keith. Keith was sullen, but okay till you pressed him.

Austin didn't think this guy was "okay" in any sense of the word. Even the smile on his face looked predatory, kind of like he thought a shark would look right before it bit someone in half.

The man stepped forward, and Austin jerked the knife in his hand up so it was pointing at the stranger. His fear intensified as he recognized the man from the scrapyard explosion a week before. The one who'd nearly shot him.

"Don't you come near me! I ain't gonna let you kill me! I'll gut you first!" His voice was high-pitched with terror and muffled by the stuffed-up condition of his nose, but he didn't care much about that. He was too terrified to worry about how pathetic he sounded. "I'm warning you!"

The man stopped, then laughed. The sound rolled through the room, deep and dark and not at all comforting. "Do not be foolish. Why on earth would I want to kill you? For this?" He waved a massive arm. "I can find better, if I so choose."

"What you want then?" Austin didn't dare drop the knife. It could be a trick. "Why'd you kick my door in?"

"Because I was looking for you, and not inclined to wait outside." The man's smile widened. "I have been watching you, Austin. You see, I am looking for comrades, and I rather think you and I could work quite well together."

Austin blinked. "What?"

The man laughed again, and this time it didn't sound quite so ominous. He held up a bottle of alcohol Austin knew hadn't been behind the bar when he'd left this morning. "It's really quite simple,

Mr. Wallace. My name is Andre, and I've come to offer you a job, along with a better home, and the opportunity of a lifetime."

It wasn't enough to make him put the knife away, but Austin found himself shuffling forward, drawn by the bottle in the man's hand. "What sort of job?"

Andre fished out two glasses and filled them, then passed one to Austin. "I'd be happy to tell you all about it. But first, perhaps a drink? You look as if you could use one."

Austin considered, then leaned forward warily and snatched the glass furthest from him, instead of closest, and swallowed a large gulp of the contents.

The alcohol was pretty good, better than Austin was used to, and it helped with the pain of his busted nose. Austin finished it and held out his cup for another. By the time he finished that, he felt a lot less terrified and far more appreciative of Andre's presence in his home.

He looked up at the large man. "So, what's this big opportunity you said you wanted to offer me?" Andre's proposition hadn't sounded bad before, but with two glasses of good liquor in his gut to numb his bruises and his sense of caution, it sounded a lot more intriguing.

Andre waved his hand at the interior of the Rat Trap in a vague gesture. "It's very simple. I have noticed a number of our brethren of the streets have been left without the support—and the accommodations—they are used to since the disaster a few weeks ago. I have been gathering them together to give them a place to live and enjoy the comforts they deserve. However, I have been away from Memphis for some time, and I find myself in need of someone who knows the streets as they are now. I thought you might be a worthwhile individual to assist me."

"Yeah, maybe." The drink was making him warm and more comfortable, but he wasn't about to offer up his help so easily. "What's your plan for these bikers, huh?"

"Again, it is quite simple. Those who are under my command will be expected to assist me in asserting my authority in the area, along with a few other tasks. In return," Andre smirked, "well, that really depends on what they want. I feel men should be well rewarded for loyalty and service. And I am prepared to be very generous."

"You mean, more booze like this?" Austin waved his glass at the bottle.

Andre chuckled again. "That's the least of it. So long as you do what I ask when I ask, you may have as much liquor, drugs, and women as your heart desires. Or, if weapons and bikes are more to your interest, I have ways to acquire whatever you might wish. Drink from dusk to dawn, snort a mountain of cocaine, deliver mayhem to the area around our territory—truly, the possibilities are endless."

Austin found himself nodding. He'd always dreamed of living like a king, with top-notch drink, plenty of coke, and a hot and willing woman at his side. Serving under a guy like Andre could be his ticket to the top.

He couldn't imagine anyone would want to mess with a guy like Andre. Not if they had any sense. The man looked ten times tougher than Bulldozer, and he'd already managed to torch a major base and get away clean.

He grinned and offered Andre a sloppy toast. "I like the sound of that. You got yourself a deal. I'll follow you and do what you need."

"Excellent." Andre smiled and refilled both their glasses. "So then, where do you suggest we begin with our efforts to clean up and unite the streets of Memphis?"

Austin thought about it for a moment before an idea formed. If Andre had a beef with Bruno and Carol's type, or their folk, that might represent an opportunity for him to get a little payback.

He pointed his free hand at his swollen nose. "The guys that did this to me. They're loyal to the former Black Rats prez and his old lady. And they're mad as poked bears about the explosion of the old clubhouse. Me, I don't care. Me and the old prez didn't get along. But they'll remember your face, and if you leave them alone, they'll come for you, sooner or later. Might be best to clear them out now." *And I'd like to see Bulldozer Keith try to handle this guy the way he handled me!*

Andre nodded. "That does sound like the proper place to start." He rose and stretched. "Shall we?"

Austin blinked. "Now?"

"Why not?" Andre bent to lift a bag behind the bar that Austin hadn't noticed before. He opened it to reveal an assortment of knives and other weapons. "I have a method for dealing with small groups of malcontents, and as you can see, I have plenty of tools for the both of us."

He offered Austin the bag. Austin grabbed a makeshift club and a couple of the bigger knives. The gun looked interesting, but he wasn't a great shot at the best of times. He wasn't about to risk hitting his new boss with a stray bullet.

Andre removed some knives of his own and a set of brass knuckles before he zipped the bag up again and slung it over his shoulder. "Come. I believe I know where the men you speak of make their home. And where better to confront them if we wish to show them their own powerlessness?"

Austin followed the big man out. He started for his bike, but Andre shook his head.

"We don't want the noise to announce our arrival prematurely." Andre raised an eyebrow as he explained further, "Besides, why take it with us when there will likely be much better machines available at our destination?"

Bulldozer's running mate, Sparky, had a rig Austin had been coveting since he'd first seen it. The thought of getting his hands on that sweet ride and making it his own was enough for Austin to fall in beside Andre without a word of protest.

They walked down the streets together. Austin let a rare, cool early summer breeze soothe his bruises and clear his head. After they'd traveled a few blocks, he looked up at Andre. "Can I ask you a question, boss?"

"You may, so long as you don't question my plans."

"Nah. Ain't that. I was just wondering why you got a grudge against the Black Rats—the rest of them, I mean. 'Cause you look like the guy Sprocket said trashed Black Roads, and I saw you back at the scrapyard shooting folks. That's why I thought you was there to kill me, when I saw you at the Rat Trap."

Andre sighed. "I suppose that is a fair question. Tell me, did Bruno Gardena or his old lady ever mention Andre Atkinson?"

"Sure, loads of times." Austin's mind connected the dots. "That's you?"

"Indeed. I'm sure you have heard many unsavory stories about me, but they are misleading." Andre shook his head. "I joined the Black Rats in my youth, back when they were true one percenters. Our MC members were kings of the roads back then, doing what we pleased, and accepting no opposition. We were powerful, and we took what we wanted, when we wanted. Then Bruno Gardena and his old woman took over and brought in their niece from New Mexico. Everything went downhill from there." Andre's lip curled. "Why anyone called that man 'Brute' Bruno, or trusted him to be a proper president of the Black Rats, I will never know. It was all too clear, even in the beginning, that he was a weak-willed fool led around more by his wife's nagging than any understanding of what the Black Rats ought to be." He snorted. "If ever a man was gelded by his woman, Bruno Gardena was."

Austin snickered. "Yeah. I've thought the same, a bunch of times."

Andre smiled thinly. "I originally planned to take over and restore the Black Rats through peaceful means. I managed to claim Gardena's niece as my woman. But then she turned on me and turned me into the police. Worse, Gardena and his supporters let her do so. Even when she collaborated with the feds and went into Witness Protection, the Gardenas never fully renounced her as they should have."

Austin grunted. "Heard about that. Should have thrown her out in the cold the second she spoke against you. A woman ain't supposed to go against a brother who takes her in."

"Exactly. I knew then that the Black Rats had fallen far from what they were meant to be. Instead of kings of the road, they had become a bunch of weaklings and squares pretending to be men."

"I've been saying that!" Austin bobbed his head.

Andre turned his head to look at him. "That is why I sought you out. The two of us may well be the last of the true Black Rats still roaming the streets. It is also, to answer your question, the reason I attacked the scrapyard. I knew that before I could restore the Black Rats to their former glory, I would need to eliminate the influence of the squares. The Gardenas, their niece, and those who are loyal to them. Only then can we return the Black Rats to true one percenters."

Austin had a vision of himself rolling down the road behind Andre on a bike like Sparky's, dressed in expensive leather and chains, with a pretty girl perched on the bike behind him and watching him with an adoring expression. That sort of vision was the entire reason he'd come to Memphis and joined the Black Rats in the first place.

"Sounds like a great plan, boss."

Andre tipped his head. "You do not feel remorse or regret for going against your brethren?"

"Heck no! Like I said, me and Prez Bruno didn't get along. I was always telling him we were getting too soft. If those fools can't see you're offering them something better, that's their problem." Austin shook his head decisively, then winced as it made his nose throb. "Nah. I'm with you all the way."

"Good." Andre waved him to a stop. "There, I believe, is the place where your former compatriots have holed up." He pointed to a bar across the way.

"That's them all right." Austin eyed the front curb. There were over a dozen bikes parked in front, including Sparky's rig and Bulldozer Keith's. "We gonna go in now?"

Andre shook his head and settled back against the wall. "No. Why risk such odds when we cannot be sure of turning any of them to our side? It is better to be patient and wait for some of them to leave." Andre gestured to the wall across from him. "Take a seat and make yourself comfortable." He smiled. "I have the rest of the bottle with me, and some food, so we can wait in relative comfort. I believe I even have some painkillers to help ease the ache of your injuries."

Austin accepted the bag eagerly and dug until he had the bottle of meds in one hand and the drink in the other. He slugged down one pill with a shot, then capped both. He wanted more, but he knew it was better to wait until after the raid. He didn't want to miss the fun, after all.

Anyway, what was the hurry? After this, he'd have all the drugs and drink he wanted to celebrate, and maybe something more fun than pain meds. Andre might even be able to help him score some good coke or LSD.

He grinned at his new boss. Things were finally looking up for him.

5

SHANNON GRAYSON

The air inside the truck was thick with tension as Shannon guided the beat-up diesel down the road, back toward the motel where they were staying. She could feel the stress building in her shoulders, and she knew it was visible in her face. Bill looked wary, and Kim looked sullen and angry. It was a good thing Mutt was in the bed of the truck. The tension in the air would have had the big dog pacing and growling, ready to bite someone.

Shannon could sympathize. Part of her wished *she* could bite someone.

There was another part of her that knew she might be overreacting. That she was wound up over Andre's escape and the danger he represented. But knowing that didn't stop the churning in her gut.

And then there was the little whisper in the back of her mind that wanted desperately to set the whole incident aside, to avoid jeopardizing the fragile relationship between her and Kim. But she was too wound up, too upset by the thoughts of what could have happened, and might still happen, and the devastation she'd feel if that relationship was permanently cut short by her daughter's death. The mingled terror, distress, and anger that filled her made her almost sick. The words inside her mind escaped despite her desire to keep the peace.

"What were you thinking?"

"I was—"

"Don't answer that. It's clear you weren't thinking at all. Just running up to a strange man without a care in the world. I didn't raise my daughter to be so stupid about diving into danger headfirst. I would have thought you'd learned by now—you can't just charge into things blindly! And you can't trust strangers, especially not now that the world's gone crazy. Half the people out there would knife you for the supplies in your pack, and the other half might do it for nothing at all. Don't you have any sense in that head of yours, or did going off to college drain it out of you?"

Bill spoke up hesitantly. "Now, Shannon, the girl is—"

"The 'girl' is not a child, and I can speak for myself, thanks," Kim snapped. "As for what happened out there—yeah, I got a little banged up. But I thought he was injured, and I wanted to help. That's the reason I was going into medical school before this happened. I could have handled him. I know how to hold my own in a scrape, and if you'd come a few seconds later, I'd have had one of my knives, or even the gun, in hand. I could have stopped him."

"Sure you could. Or maybe he'd have wrestled that weapon away from you and used it against you. I've seen it happen to plenty of people who were sure they could 'handle' someone." Shannon's hand tightened on the wheel. "This world isn't a place for acting carelessly. It wasn't even before the power went down and chaos erupted. If you don't watch yourself, Kim, the next person who manages to get you on the ground like that will do a whole lot worse than leave you with a bump on your skull and some bruises."

Kim scowled but didn't say anything else. Bill looked between them then sat back, clearly intent on staying out of the way. In fact, he looked like he wished he could be riding in the back with Mutt.

They crept along for a few miles in silence, anger filling the air. They were about two miles out from the Wander Court Motel when they spotted a family staggering along the side of the road. There was a mother, a father, and two kids. One looked to be a teenager, or close to it. The other was young, not long past the toddler stage. All of them looked worn out, hungry, and two steps from collapsing. There was old blood on the father's shirt.

Kim frowned. "It looks like they're hurt. Maybe we should stop for a second, make sure they're all right."

"Why? So they can try to kill you too? You want to try four-on-one odds now? I don't think so." Shannon deliberately pressed the gas and sent the truck darting past the family.

Kim twisted around in her seat. "Mom, they're hurt—"

"That's what you thought about the last guy. I don't care, and we're not stopping. If you try to do something stupid like jump out of the truck, I'll have Bill stop you, and you can spend the rest of the trip tied to that seat."

Kim's expression twisted into a glower she might have learned from Carol or Dennis—wherever he was. "They don't look armed. Anyway, it wouldn't be four-to-one odds if you, Bill, and Mutt came with me. I'm pretty sure we'd be fine. If you'd just stop for a few seconds."

"I said no. Besides, we're past them now, and I'm not about to try and turn this truck around. Even if I were inclined to risk another ambush, you've still got that goose egg on your skull that needs to be looked at properly. If you've got a concussion, the best place for you is back at the motel, resting, while your head recovers from the thumping." Shannon shook her head. "Put them out of your mind, Kim."

Kim collapsed into her seat, a scowl on her face. Bill gave Shannon a remonstrating look, which she pointedly ignored. Maybe she was being harsh, but between Kim's injury, the healing scars on Bill's side and arm from an encounter in Stuttgart, and her own shoulder, she had plenty of reminders why trying to be the good guy was just a bad idea, especially these days.

After another moment of silence, she sighed and stopped the truck. "Toss them a bag of food," she said. They were far enough away from the family that they were safe, and by the time the family got to the bag of food, they'd be well out of range from any planned attack.

Kim grabbed a plastic bag and shoved some of their supplies inside before she rolled down the window and looked behind them. "For you!" she shouted at the family, then tossed the bag into the roadside ditch.

Shannon started driving again before Kim was even fully back inside.

Ten minutes later, they rolled into the parking lot of the Wander Court Motel. The area to one side was full of motorcycles in various states of repair. The back lot was mostly occupied by the eighteen-wheeler she and Bill had coaxed all the way from Oklahoma to Memphis. She parked the battered black pickup she was driving next to it, and the three of them tossed the tools and other scavenged non-food supplies into the back.

Bill eyed Shannon and Kim as they finished loading stuff into the truck, then waved a hand at the motel. "How about you two go rest, and I'll see about getting things organized out here?"

Shannon nodded. "Thanks, Bill." She and Kim exchanged a look, then headed toward the archway leading to the central court of the motel.

Kim paused as they entered beneath the arch and took a deep breath. "Mom, I know we don't agree on some things, but thanks for coming to help me out. Even if I could handle that guy, I know it could have been worse than it was. So thanks."

Shannon sighed. She was still jittery from the adrenaline and the stress, but she tried to set it aside. She didn't want to make the rift between them any larger. She gave Kim a one-armed hug. "You know I'd come to help you anytime, Kim. I just wish you'd be more careful and think a little more before jumping into harm's way."

Kim made a face, but she didn't say anything more as she returned the embrace. After a moment, the two of them separated and continued into the main part of the motel.

Most of the Black Rats were out on scavenging duties of their own, but Aunt Carol was sitting in a rickety chair by a weather-beaten outdoor table, playing solitaire. Bill's newest foundling and adopted hard-luck case, Lee, sat nearby, reading a book and hunched in on himself as if he was trying to hide.

Shannon wasn't sure how she felt about Lee. He was a kid, and he seemed like the quiet sort, not much trouble at all. On the other hand, he'd been with Andre at the scrapyard, and he'd admitted to setting the explosions that sent the bikers running for the front gate, where Andre had shot several of them, including her Uncle Bruno.

Carol hadn't turned the kid out, mostly because she liked Bill, and the mechanic had vouched for the boy. She was also of the loudly stated opinion that it was better to have a viper where you could see it if you weren't going to shoot it. Lee, for his part, had the good sense to stay out of Carol's way when he could. He spoke very little, mostly to Kim and Bill, and wandered around like a lost shadow the rest of the time.

He was probably only in the court so Carol could keep an eye on him.

Carol looked up at the sound of their footsteps, then abandoned her game to come meet them. "Welcome back, you two. You have any luck?"

"Some." Shannon nodded. She would have said more, but Carol's sharp eyes landed on Kim's newest bruises and scrapes.

"Kim, you're hurt! What happened to you, girl?" Carol held out one hand and started toward her, but Kim sidestepped the gesture of concern with a quick motion.

"I'm fine, Aunt Carol. Just a bit of a tumble." Kim gave her great-aunt a quick hug and darted away toward the community food storage area.

Shannon met Carol's gaze with a sigh and shook her head as she dropped her own bag of scavenged supplies on a nearby table. "It's been a day."

She repeated Kim's quick embrace, then made her way toward a door on the far side of the enclosure. The last of the adrenaline was fading, and she wanted nothing more than to go to her room and collapse for a spell, perhaps even take a brief nap.

Maybe when she woke up, she'd be able to find a way to speak to Kim about her recklessness that didn't involve the two of them being at odds with each other. It was either that, or she'd have to come to terms with her daughter's determination to be independent, and Shannon wasn't sure she could manage that just now. Not with Andre on the loose and how recently they'd been reunited.

The bed in her room was worn, the pillows thin and the mattress in marginal condition, but to Shannon, it might as well be a feather bed. She kicked off her shoes and stretched out with a sigh of contentment, then let sleep carry her away.

6

KIM NAKAMURA

Putting up the food supplies she'd gathered didn't take Kim much time. After she'd finished that, washed the dirt off her skin and the small amount of blood out of her hair, and changed to a semi-clean shirt, Kim found herself at loose ends. She was too restless to go to her room and sleep. She wasn't interested in enduring more of Aunt Carol's or her mother's fussing.

She didn't feel like talking to Lee either. He didn't seem like a bad person, honestly, but he'd still been involved in blowing up the scrapyard and getting a member of her family killed. Plus, he'd been helping her father. That was reason enough to be wary, even if she suspected Andre had manipulated the poor guy the way he'd tried to manipulate her.

Frustrated and slightly bored, she took Mutt and wandered out into the parking lot, watching as the dog sniffed random objects, poked at others, and did her business. The familiar, simple motions were soothing to watch, a reminder that in a world gone crazy, some things could still be counted on.

"Hey, Kim." Bill's smooth bass rumble made her look up. He was wearing his battered work clothes and holding a beat-up clipboard in one hand. "I was just about to do some work on the truck. Want to join me?"

Helping Bill was more productive than pacing around and brooding. "Sure."

Kim followed the mechanic over to the rig. It was huge and ungainly, and it stuck out like a neon sign, as far as Kim was concerned. She knew it was useful, and it had served as shelter for some of the Black Rats right after the scrapyard went up in flames. It still looked like a rolling target to her. But that wasn't her concern. "What are we doing?"

"Just a quick check of the fluids, the connections, the fuel level, and the tires." Bill waved a battered checklist he'd retrieved from the cab, then slipped it into the clipboard.

Kim frowned. "I thought we did all that recently. A couple days ago."

"We did, but it doesn't hurt to double-check, especially if you have a rig parked for long periods of time. It's the same with the bikes, but I wouldn't dare touch them without asking permission." Bill gave her a brief grin as he tugged the engine cover up and out of the way. "Besides, I like working when I've got something on my mind, and the truck's the best thing to work on, what with all the jerry-rigged components I put into the thing."

"Makes sense." Kim stepped up beside him and began checking gauges as he directed her to. When he handed her the clipboard and started to poke around in the tangle of engine parts, curiosity finally got the better of her. "You said you've got something on your mind?"

Bill hesitated, then heaved out a sigh. "Sure do. I've been trying for days to smooth things down between folks, but it's been hard. I'm at my wits end." He waved a distracted hand at the motel. "Your aunt's bound and determined to hold a grudge against that boy, Lee. Mean-while, he's jumping at shadows, including his own, and acts like every harsh word means he's about to get whipped. Which makes him awful twitchy, with the way your aunt's been."

"And he's your roommate." Kim knew Bill had taken Lee in to share his room, as much to keep Lee safe as to keep him out of trouble.

"Yes he is. And Shannon's my friend, which makes it pretty uncom-fortable to see her at odds with family. Which she is, what with you two butting heads over near everything, and she and Carol only just starting to work out the hurts between them."

"Aunt Carol's grieving. And Mom leaving the way she did really upset Aunt Carol and Uncle Bruno both." Kim couldn't help the defensiveness in her voice.

"I know, I know, and I respect that. But it still makes things awful tense between folks, and I have to admit, I'm a bit out of my depth. Don't know enough about everyone involved." Bill hesitated, then looked at her. "I was going to wait till you seemed a little less stressed, but I was hoping you could help me."

"You know Mom won't listen to me. And I don't think Aunt Carol will either." Kim swallowed the edge of bitterness in her voice. "They don't understand where I'm coming from."

"Fair enough. But maybe I'd be able to help bring them around if you felt like telling me what's on your mind."

"Did my mom ever tell you about the federal marshal who sent her into WitSec?"Kim took a deep breath, then leaned against the truck. She hadn't meant to say those words aloud, but at the same time, she couldn't be sorry she had. A part of her wanted to walk away from the conversation now. But Bill was a good listener, and she knew he'd be easier to tell about the experience in Humboldt than anyone else. She also couldn't deny the incident still haunted her nightmares, and she'd heard from friends at college that talking about nightmares sometimes helped. She let her mind drift, trying to find a place to start explaining what bothered her most in the tangle of issues that plagued her thoughts, waking and sleeping.

"Can't recall that she did. She mentioned he was supposed to look out for you, once or twice maybe, but I don't think she ever said much more. I don't think I even know his name."

"Dennis Sullivan. His name was Dennis Sullivan. He showed up at my dorm about a week after the EMP exploded. He looked awful. Real messed up." Kim folded her arms around herself. "Dennis was... He was a retired Marine, but he'd been hurt really bad a couple of times, bad enough to cripple him, and being hurt had turned him into an opioid addict. But he still came to find me, and he still agreed to help me travel to Memphis so I could be with my family."

"But he didn't come all the way with you?" Bill's question was gentle.

"He couldn't." Kim heard her voice crack and felt the sting of tears in her eyes. "When we stopped in Humboldt, we met a friend of his who suggested we stay while Dennis went through detox. And I," she swallowed hard, "I told him it would be a good idea. I convinced him to stay. But then they found out I had medical schooling, and they refused to let me go. Dennis came to rescue me. And the man we thought was his friend..." Her voice broke, and tears slid down her cheeks. She forced herself to finish the story. "The man Dennis trusted like a brother beat him bloody, then stood over him and shot him in the head. He just dumped Dennis's body on the ground like a piece of garbage. All because he wanted to control me, and Dennis refused to let him."

"Oh heck, girl. Come here." Bill helped her down off the truck wheel and tucked her close to his chest, then enfolded her in the circle of his arms. "I'm sorry that happened to you."

"I was twenty yards away, watching from the woods, when they shot him. I saw him die for me." Kim's throat ached with grief. "He helped me figure out the supplies I needed to survive on the road, and he showed me how to travel, how to shoot, and how to dress game. When I needed him, he was there to rescue me. And I couldn't save him. I couldn't do anything but watch him die, then run away."

She didn't know if anyone had buried Dennis. Had Joan Danville given him a grave, or was he just another body left to the mercy of the elements and scavengers?

Bill's hands were comforting as they stroked her hair. "You never told your mom."

"I don't know how to. She knew Dennis better than I did. They were friends, I think. How do I tell her I watched her friend die and did nothing?" Kim gulped in a ragged breath. "I couldn't do anything about the attack at the scrapyard either. I got here too late."

"That's a hard thing to live with. Both things, I'm guessing." Bill's voice was soft, and his hand never stopped its soothing motions, even as his other arm held her close.

"I keep having nightmares. I see Dennis die again. And Uncle Bruno…Andre shot him almost the same way Dennis got shot, did you know? Right in the face. The way they died, the way they fell, it was so similar." But at least Bruno Gardena had gotten a proper burial. Aunt Carol had insisted on that, after they'd found shelter and returned to the ruins of the scrapyard to salvage what they could.

She breathed in Bill's comforting scent—motor oil, metal, and deodorant he must have scavenged from somewhere—and kept talking. It was easier now. "I know Mom gets mad at me for running into things, but I can't…Ever since then, it's been this feeling I have. That if I can get to the danger first, then it means everyone else I care about will be safe. It's okay if I get hurt. Just as long as no one I care about does."

"There's no question you've had a hard road, Kim. I'm sorry you've been through so much. That's a heavy load to bear, maybe too heavy for anyone to carry alone." Bill's voice was a deep murmur above her, and its vibrations, along with his steady heartbeat, were soothing. "But much as I understand what you're thinking and why, I also have to tell you that you aren't quite correct."

His embrace kept her close even when she wanted to pull away. Not that she struggled very hard as he continued speaking. "You see, Kim, if you get hurt, the people who love you also get hurt. No one likes to see their loved ones in pain." Bill's voice was heavy. "I had to watch my wife die not long before the EMP, and it just about killed me. I would have given up if I hadn't met your mother."

Bill paused. "I think if something happens to you, the same thing will happen to Shannon. But I don't think anything in the world will be able to save her, the way she saved me. Do you understand?"

Kim tried to swallow the sudden lump in her throat. She'd been so focused on her own perspective and her frustration at her mother's insistence on protecting her that she hadn't thought of that. She looked up at Bill. "I understand." She pulled away so she could turn and pet Mutt, who'd sensed her distress and was now whimpering at her in concern, her head pressed against Kim's thigh. "But it's hard."

Bill sighed as he reached up to get his tools and secure them in his bag. "Of course it is." He offered her a wry smile. "I reckon it would be even if you were a normal girl growing up under normal conditions. But you're a tough girl, like your mom—"

"And the world went insane a few weeks ago," Kim finished. "Yeah." She scrubbed the last traces of tears from her face. "Anyway, we need to finish checking the truck."

"Done most of it. Just need to check on the trailer mostly, especially the brakes." Bill wiped his hands on a rag and turned to make his way toward the first set of wheels that supported and transported the fifty-two-foot trailer.

Kim started to follow him, then stopped as a thought occurred to her.

"Bill."

The mechanic turned back around. "Yes?"

"The trailer—it's not full, not by a long shot." She knew that because she'd seen how empty it was when they were depositing supplies. "I know we have some of those sturdy storage crates we salvaged and a few more we've looted from various places."

"Yeah. I know. What are you thinking?"

"Why are we hauling the trailer along? I mean, it's great for storage, but it eats, like, five to ten times as much fuel as any regular car, and way more than a bike. It's easily the slowest vehicle any of us are riding or driving. Plus, it's like a giant target on wheels."

Bill frowned thoughtfully as his eyes slid over the expanse of metal siding closest to them. "You're not wrong."

Kim pointed at the long axle, or whatever it was, that connected the trailer to the cab of the truck. "If you take the trailer off, you've still got a lot of space to put things there, especially if you add some slats of wood or metal to stabilize the base. We could set it up kind of like a mini flatbed. We could unhitch the trailer, put as much as we can on that pickup truck we scrounged and in the back of my car, then use cords to tie the rest of it to that section there. The cab of the truck is still pretty conspicuous, but not nearly as much as a fifty-foot trailer."

"It'll improve the mileage as well." Bill grinned. "Heck, it'll be easier on the whole engine, and we'll be able to go faster without the load and the risk of it jackknifing on the highway." Bill bent to examine

40

the spot where the trailer hooked up to the truck. "Might need some tools to get all the lines uncoupled, but Shannon told me a bit about the way the procedure is supposed to go, and she already had me engage the landing gear."

"Landing gear?" Kim stared at him in confusion.

"What they call the brakes, or maybe it's more like a built-in jack-stand. That's how I always thought of it, at least, after she told me what they were for." Bill pointed to two metal posts that extended from the base of the trailer to the asphalt of the parking lot. "Either way, it takes the load off the cab section while the rig is parked."

"Okay." Kim moved closer. "Do you think we need to tell Mom what we're doing?"

"I know Shannon will be as relieved as we are to get rid of the giant flag saying, 'Rob me.'" Bill chuckled. "It was different when we had supplies to deliver, and she wasn't sure what might be useful and what wouldn't be."

Kim watched as Bill worked through the steps of unfastening various parts of the trailer. First, he unplugged some wires and a hose or two. These he tucked neatly against the trailer. Then he grabbed a heavy looking handle and pulled carefully on it. With a slight creak and a soft grinding sound, some sort of giant latch hook came apart. Bill grunted in satisfaction as he stepped away from the handle. "Sounds like it came free."

He pulled a set of keys out of his pocket and stepped up into the cab. "All right, Kim. I'm gonna pull forward to free the fifth wheel and the back of the cab section. You keep watch. Let me know if it looks like the mechanism isn't fully free. We don't want to damage anything."

"Gotcha." Kim paused. "How will I know?"

"It'll try to come forward with the cab. Or you'll hear sounds like some of the weight is still sitting on the wheels. Mostly it'll produce a really loud grinding sound."

The truck started up with a growling snarl, louder than normal since Bill had left the engine hood up. Kim watched as he carefully edged the cab forward. The metal creaked, but it didn't grind or strain as if pulling.

Bill paused, and Kim called out, "Looking good!"

"Give it a minute to settle, and we'll try to get the rest of the way free," Bill called back.

After a minute had passed, Bill pressed the gas a little further. Air hissed, and the long base of the cab section slid free. Kim whooped in excitement.

Bill moved the cab completely clear and parked it nearby. Kim went around to the back to raise the door and drop the ramp in the back of the trailer while the mechanic shut down the engine and closed it up. She'd hopped up into the cargo space and was dragging the first of the storage bins forward when Bill joined her.

"Hold up, Kim."

Kim paused. "Why?"

"You've got a good idea when it comes to leaving the trailer here, but thinking on it, maybe we don't want to leave all our supplies visible on the truck and the back of the cab."

"Good point. But if we don't want to leave them visible or in the trailer, then where can we stash everything?"

"We'll stick it in one of the empty rooms." Bill indicated a nearby door. "It's far enough from both the truck and the occupied rooms that no one would expect us to put supplies there. If they started checking rooms to find the stash, whoever is here would probably find them before the thief found the supplies."

Kim grinned. "You're pretty devious."

Bill shrugged. "I'm an old man who used to have to hide my wife's birthday presents from her. Sometimes I'd have to hide my lunch or my tools from the mischief makers I worked with at the garage, too, so I learned a lot of useful tricks."

Together, the two of them started moving boxes. It was heavy, tiring labor, but between Bill's formidable strength and her own stubbornness, the task was soon done.

Once the last box was shifted, Bill waved her off. "You go change clothes, get some rest and maybe some food or water. I'll finish up."

Kim was tempted to argue, but her muscles were aching, and her shirt was soaked through with sweat and streaked with dirt and oil from leaning against the truck. She nodded and headed back into the courtyard.

Aunt Carol met her at the inner doorway. "Saw what you and the mechanic were doing. You're thinking to leave the trailer and pack the boxes elsewhere?"

"Yeah. We're planning to tie them down on that sort of flat part over the extra wheels. Bill said we'd be able to move faster and use less fuel."

"Good thinking." Aunt Carol hesitated. "Your head feeling better?"

"Yeah. It looked worse than it was." Kim tucked her hands deeper into her pockets to resist the urge to touch the lump on the back of her head. "I've got a tough skull."

"Like your mom—and everyone else in our family." Carol sighed. "I know you're an adult, and tough as nails. But the world out there isn't safe, not for anyone. And it's getting worse, not better."

Kim bit her lip. A part of her wanted to sigh in exasperation at yet another well-meant and unnecessary warning. But another part of her remembered what Bill had said, and it was with his words in mind that she responded. "I know. I'll try to be more careful."

Carol grimaced. "I know you will, but your mother ain't the only one that worries. I'd never sleep again if something happened, and I didn't do anything to prevent it. That's why I want you to have this."

The blade she turned over was a long hunting-style knife with wicked serrations on the back and an edge so sharp it looked like it could cut air and leave a vacuum in its wake. The handle was worn and had clearly been leather wrapped and renewed once or twice. It was a beautiful blade—sharp, functional and well-used, deadly and eye-catching all at once.

Kim sheathed it carefully and looked up at her great-aunt. "Where'd you find this?"

"I didn't. It was your Uncle Bruno's favorite blade. Never left his rig or his hip, unless he was showering, sleeping, or making love. And during the last two, it was usually under his pillow."

That was more information than Kim wanted to know about her great-uncle, but she didn't interrupt as Aunt Carol continued.

"I know Bruno would want to watch over you if he could. Since he can't be here, this'll have to do. You know much about using a knife?"

"Sure. Mom taught me some before she had to leave. I learned more from…" She swallowed and tried to keep her face impassive as she finished "…from a friend who traveled a distance with me on the road from Murray."

"Wish your friend had come the rest of the way with you. We could use an extra set of hands to defend and help out."

Kim bit her lip, trying not to laugh as she remembered her great-aunt's feelings about any sort of law enforcement type—and Dennis in particular. She was saved from having to respond when Aunt Carol shook her head, visibly dismissing the thought.

"But it is what it is, and folks all got their own problems. In the mean-time, it's good you know how to use that. But with any luck, you'll never have to."

"Yeah. We can hope." Kim carefully hooked the knife sheath to her belt, opting to set it two inches behind the butt of the pistol. "For now though, I'm going to go get something to drink and change shirts."

"Good idea. Get some rest while you're at it." Carol waved her off.

Kim went toward the food storage area, then past it toward the room she'd claimed as her own. Her thoughts were as heavy as her footsteps.

I wish Dennis had come with me too. Even if Aunt Carol would've probably tried to shoot him. With her father on the loose, they could sure use the help of someone who had earned the name of Super Soldier Dennis Sullivan.

She missed him. She missed Uncle Bruno. And she couldn't help but think she was going to wish she had them both at her side before everything was over.

7

AUSTIN/ANDRE

Andre stared down with contempt at the sleeping man he'd recruited as his newest follower. The fellow was even more spineless than his former cellmate, and that was precisely what he was looking for. Men like Cardoza and Austin were weak-willed and utterly pathetic, but they did have their uses.

Better still, they were easy to manipulate. He'd hoped for someone who could serve as a proper subordinate—someone who was ruthless and intelligent enough to act as a proper right hand, but Kim and Lee had both proved disappointing at best. He'd come to the conclusion that he'd have little luck finding such an individual unless he found a woman to bear him a child he could mold into the proper personality. And that he had no time or interest for. Not when there were other ways of gaining loyal, able-bodied recruits.

That was why he'd chosen Austin. A drunk, lack-witted drug addict was the perfect tool. If Austin failed, Andre would hardly have wasted any time, effort, or resources on the fool. There were also plenty more of his sort around, and from them Andre could build the foundation of his empire. Then he could conduct a more leisurely search to find the gold hidden among the dregs of humanity.

Eventually, he knew he would need someone a bit more violent and bloodthirsty. By then perhaps some of his earlier plans, laid while he was still in prison dreaming of escape, would bear fruit. In the meantime, Austin had at least pointed him in the direction of an excellent target. As a recruit, the man who'd beaten Austin bloody would make an excellent foot soldier.

And if he wouldn't be recruited, the man would make an even better example.

Austin was enjoying a dream about shacking up with his favorite girl —a pretty redhead—amid feather pillows and mountains of money when a sharp jab to the ribs jolted him back to reality. His head shot up and he blinked, looking around.

Right. He was in an alley, with his new prez, Andre, who was currently giving him a slightly exasperated glare.

"Really, Austin, if you cannot even stay alert and pay attention—"

"I'm paying attention. Just had me a little moment, with the pill and the booze. Sorry, boss." Austin scrambled to his feet and did his best to look awake and energetic, though his head felt stuffed with cotton. "What's up?"

"It appears that most of the bikers have left on errands of various sorts. There are only three left, including, I believe, the man who accosted you."

Austin looked. Andre was right. There were only three rigs left— Bulldozer Keith's, Sparky's, and another nondescript but functional bike that could belong to anyone. "Oh, cool. We gonna go take care of them now, boss?"

"Of course. What better time?" Andre drew a wicked blade from his belt. Austin hurried to do the same with one of his borrowed blades. It was heavier in his hand than his usual blade, and deadly sharp—a real fighter's weapon. Austin gripped it tight as excitement began to replace the leaden weariness caused by the meds.

Andre took the lead as he strode confidently across the street. Austin followed, trying to look tough in Andre's wake. As much as he wanted vengeance, he wasn't exactly eager to get another dose of Bulldozer Keith's fists, not when his face still ached as a reminder of the last time they'd crossed paths.

Andre didn't bother to knock on the door to the bar. He simply kicked it in with a crash that made the three residents of the building look up in alarm.

Austin studied the three from his position behind Andre. Bulldozer Keith was the clear leader, with Sparky hovering at his elbow like a nervous puppy. The third biker looked both irritable and drunk.

Bulldozer Keith lurched up from the bar, a snarl on his face as he overcame the shock of the door breaking. "You got a lotta nerve, punk, busting into my place. You're gonna regret it."

"I hardly think so," Andre sneered back. "And do be polite. I've come to make you an offer."

Part of Austin wanted to protest. He didn't want Bulldozer Keith getting the same offer he had. *He* was Andre's second-in-command! Still, he wasn't going to argue against the new prez. He kept quiet as Andre continued.

"I am assembling a new crew of the Black Rats. Join me, and I will give you access to everything you've ever wanted—food, booze, drugs, women, and weapons. Refuse me and," Andre smiled another of those sharklike smiles of his, "well, it really is better not to refuse."

"Screw you." Bulldozer Keith shook his head dismissively, contempt in his eyes as he took one aggressive step forward. "I don't answer to any wannabe tough guy, and you ain't no Black Rat." He glared at Andre, and his gaze raked briefly over Austin. "Get out of my bar, pissants, unless you want me to squash you like the bugs you are."

Austin was already bracing to take a step back when Andre moved. The large man exploded into motion, his knife a blur as he lunged at Bulldozer Keith. Keith might have been a decent brawler, but he was drunk and not ready for Andre's attack. He didn't even have time to try and protect himself before the knife sank into his chest and ripped out again in a spray of crimson. Bulldozer Keith staggered back. Andre followed, his free hand clenched firmly on Keith's jacket, and stabbed him again.

That was all Austin had time to see as Sparky and the remaining biker pounced on him. Outnumbered two-to-one, Austin found himself backed into a corner, barely keeping the two bikers at bay with his blade. If Sparky hadn't been such a runt, he might not have even managed that.

But Sparky was a runt, weak, and in a drunken rage. It made him careless and stupid. His third attack brought him into Austin's striking range, and Austin clubbed him in the temple with the butt of his knife. It was a lucky shot more than anything else, but Austin didn't hesitate to use it to his advantage. He cut Sparky hard across the face as the younger biker staggered, then punched the kid again to send him to the ground with a whimper.

Austin lifted a foot to stomp Sparky some more, but he'd gotten too focused on his target—he'd forgotten the third biker. He was made painfully aware of that mistake when the man slammed into him and took them both to the ground. The biker's larger hand grabbed

Austin's wrist with bruising strength and bashed his hand into the floor. The impact forced him to let go of the knife.

Austin punched at the man, but he wasn't in the best position, and fighting barehanded wasn't his strong suit. He yelped as the man delivered a hard blow to his already bruised chin.

Aw heck...I'm in for it...

The biker froze with a gurgle as a huge, bloodstained hand closed around his neck and wrenched him backward. With a snarl, Andre threw the man to the side and kicked him hard in the gut—hard enough that Austin thought he heard ribs crack. The biker doubled over, breathless and gagging from the pain.

The punch Andre delivered as a follow-up shattered teeth and possibly the biker's jaw. By the time Andre finished with the guy, Austin might have felt sorry for him if he hadn't been part of Bulldozer Keith's crew. As it was, he was in awe of Andre's savage strength. The large man finally dropped the barely breathing biker to the floor with a dismissive gesture and turned to him.

Andre was splattered—no, he was practically painted—in blood from the roots of his hair all the way down his front. His hands and arms looked as if he'd gone diving in a vat of red paint. Behind him, and past the battered body of the biker he'd just beaten, Austin saw Bulldozer Keith, whose face was twisted in pain. His chest was a red ruin of stab wounds.

Drenched in blood and surrounded by his fallen foes, Andre looked to Austin like a god of war from those myths his teachers used to make him read, a long time ago.

Then the god of war offered him a hand up from the ground. Austin took it, and Andre heaved him effortlessly to his feet.

Andre was smiling, his teeth startlingly white against the gore. "Well done."

Austin blinked, then looked down at Sparky bleeding at his feet. A sense of elation and pride filled him, sweeping away his fear as if it had never existed. "Yeah. I got one. Not as impressive as you, boss, but I got one."

"All he owns is now yours, as we agreed." Andre clasped his hand, his expression fierce and bright with the pride of a victorious warrior. "You fought by my side, and that means we are now brothers in truth, bonded in bloodshed. We are ride-or-die partners now, Austin."

"Yeah." Austin grinned back as he basked in Andre's expression and the heady aftereffects of the fight. Andre could take on the world, he was sure. And he'd be right there beside him. He clasped his own hand tighter around Andre's larger one, ignoring the sticky blood between them. "Ride or die, boss. I'm with you all the way."

8

SHANNON GRAYSON

S hannon dragged herself out of bed wearily and scrubbed a hand over her face. She hadn't slept well, thanks to visions of what might have happened to Kim dancing through her brain. She was worried, too, because she knew something else had happened to Kim out there on the road to Memphis, and her daughter refused to tell her what it was.

Just like she refused to talk about Dennis Sullivan. But Shannon thought she recognized the pistol she'd seen Kim cleaning and inspecting once or twice. It looked like Dennis's, and Shannon had to wonder how her daughter had come to have the marshal's pistol—if it really was his. Even if it wasn't, there was definitely a story behind how she'd come to be carrying a gun. Shannon was concerned about her daughter's new familiarity with firearms, but she couldn't think of a way to ask about it without sounding intrusive and possibly angering Kim further. Besides, she wasn't entirely sure she wanted to know.

If Dennis really had met up with Kim at some point, in Murray or elsewhere on the road, something had to have happened. Something bad, because she didn't think anything else would cause a man like Sullivan to abandon his responsibilities.

On the other hand, Kim was an adult in every sense of the word. She knew her daughter was smart and capable of taking care of herself in most circumstances. She'd been hurt a bit in the scuffle with that thief yesterday, but she'd also been far from helpless when Shannon intervened. She knew Kim resented her overprotective attitude, and in some ways, she might be right to do so, especially since Shannon hadn't been a part of her life for the past five years.

Shannon also knew how bad it could get when you tried to be a hero. The barely healed bullet hole in her shoulder was a constant reminder of that. Kim's insistence on trying to help anyone and everyone they came across worried her. She couldn't help fearing that her daughter's determination to try and fix everything would end with her getting a bullet wound of her own, or worse.

She shook her head and sipped some of the water in a bottle she kept with her. This wasn't the time to be thinking of such things. There was too much to be done, and they couldn't stay in their current lodgings forever. Another sip of water, and she tied her hair back and went to the door, intent on grabbing a bite to eat before she got to work on whatever the day's tasks were.

"*Surprise!*"

Shannon stopped dead, blinking at the sight before her in disbelief. Carol, Kim, Bill, Lee, and the rest of the Black Rats were gathered in the courtyard. A battered banner made of printer paper and tape read "Happy Birthday!" in spray-painted letters. Beneath it, one rickety table held a small pile of loose items and a couple of lumpy and poorly wrapped parcels. Another table held some food and plenty of beer.

Kim came forward to hug her. "Hey, Mom! Happy birthday!"

Shannon swallowed hard, trying not to let her shock show. She'd forgotten, with everything going on, that she even had a birthday coming up, much less which day it was. In all the chaos, especially after her days spent unconscious in Stuttgart, she hadn't bothered to keep track of the date. But someone apparently had, likely Carol or Kim.

She wrapped an arm around her daughter. "You set this up?"

Kim grinned as she pulled away. "Me and Aunt Carol. We've been planning it for a few days, getting stuff together."

Shannon blinked. "I haven't had a party in—"

"Years. We know." Kim dragged her forward. "But we could all use some time to unwind and just celebrate being alive. You deserve a party, especially since a lot of the supplies we used for the meal are things you hauled across the country."

"Girl's right. We could use an excuse to lighten the mood and remember the coming of the apocalypse ain't the end of everything, not so long as we're still alive." Carol appeared at her elbow. "What do you want first? Food, presents, or entertainment?"

That was an easy question. "Food."

The food wasn't much compared to what it might once have been, but it was a feast to the Black Rats. Baked beans, Vienna sausages, and canned vegetables, all inexpertly heated over a fire or gas stove and kept warm by the virtue of some Sterno a man called TimFist had provided. There were chips of all kinds in an awkward pile. There was even cheese, of a sort, that looked like it had been scrounged from a bunch of combined Slim Jim packs.

The drinks consisted of off-brand sodas, lots of beer, and a few bottles of hard liquor. Shannon ate and drank until she was completely full, though she avoided the stronger alcohol in favor of cola. Once everyone had eaten their fill, Bill brought over a chair and sat her down so she could inspect her presents.

The Black Rats in general had gotten Shannon small practical things, like clean shirts, clean socks, extra hair ties, and the like. A woman called Hannah even found her a hairbrush to replace the comb she'd been using for a while. Bill and Kim showed her what they'd done with the truck to make travel much easier while still allowing her to keep the truck cab that had been her home on the road for five years.

Bill had also gotten her a new bag, sturdier than the duffel she'd snatched on a whim during their last day at the supercenter.

Carol had somehow found the materials and tools to give her a new club jacket, one that wasn't full of holes and stiff with dirt and blood. It was a little big, but it had the patches she cherished, and it felt good when she slipped it on. The size reminded her of when she'd gotten her first jacket as a teenager.

Lee, the odd, quiet kid Bill had more or less adopted, gave her a picture he'd drawn of her little family. It was well done, and Shannon respected the time and skill it had taken to make it, even if she wasn't sure what she thought of the boy himself.

Kim handed Shannon a lightweight boot knife in a well-worn leather sheath. Her eyes were a little sad when she passed it over. "It's from me, and kind of Dennis too. He would have given it to you if he could."

Shannon studied her daughter's face, a little bemused by the unexpected answer to one of the questions she'd been considering earlier. "I didn't know you'd met up with him."

"He checked up on me just after the EMP. He helped me when I was getting started. But he couldn't come all the way to Memphis. He didn't make it." There was a heavy shadow in Kim's eyes that made

Shannon want to ask more questions, but her daughter only smiled and stepped aside.

Shannon looked at all the gifts spread out around her. "Looks like I'm all set for wherever we go—if we ever decide to leave this nice motel."

The group went quiet as all of them considered the matter. Then Carol spoke up. "I was thinking we could rest and collect supplies for another day, then head toward Tupelo. There's a chapter of the Black Rats there, and last I heard, Toad was still the president of the chapter. He and Bruno were good friends, and he'd help us out, I think."

Shannon frowned before she remembered. "That'd be Johnny Cameron. Got his name for the deep, croaky voice?"

"That's him."

Bill coughed. "I hate to contradict, but are we sure any Black Rats chapter is safe after what happened to the last one?"

Lee twitched. "That was different." He hunched in on himself as the rest of them looked at him. "Scrap yard only got burned because of me and Andre. Mostly because Andre's got a grudge against his..." He gulped. "Sorry. It's just, I'm pretty sure that was a one-time thing."

"Not necessarily," Bill said. "If he's got a grudge against Shannon strong enough to bring him all the way here, there's no telling what he might do. If he's still after causing trouble, then he might expect us to seek out other Black Rat chapters." He shrugged. "I think going to your friend might be a little too predictable."

"But Toad would help us fend him off." Carol growled out the words.

"You don't know that, Aunt Carol." Kim spoke up. "He might have been your friend before the world pretty much ended, but disasters like this can change people. Places that seem safe and people who seem friendly might not be. I've seen supposed friends at each other's throats and supposedly nice people willing to shoot their own brothers in the back."

Shannon opened her mouth to ask when that had happened, but Carol interrupted her. "You think we should stay here then, Kim?"

"No. It's not really safe to stay anywhere." Kim took a deep breath. "Motorcycle clubs are supposed to be the brotherhood of the road, right? So why not? Why not just go on the road, travel wherever the mood takes us? We can find supplies wherever we go, and we can trade for other things and shelter when we need to."

"Not sure that's practical." Shannon interjected. She could see Kim's reasoning, but five years as a trucker had taught her life on the road as a nomad wasn't as easy as it sounded.

"It could be." Kim glanced around. "I mean, we've all got our skills we could barter. Look at us. Bill's a mechanic. I've got medical training. You know about managing vehicles and supplies, and keeping track of what we've got available, Mom. Aunt Carol knows how to organize people, set up housing, and write out the best travel plans for the resources we have. We could do a lot of good, and being on the road might make us less vulnerable."

"It sounds nice in theory, but what you're talking about ain't realistic, Kim. Folk, even nomads, need a place to call home and come back to. Sometimes you need to be able to rest in a safe space, and we'll never get that with what you're talking about. Besides, how would we get enough fuel to keep that up?" Carol shook her head. "Sorry, girl, but that's your naivete talking. Take it from someone who knows."

Kim glared at her great-aunt, eyes filled with a now-familiar blend of hurt and frustration. "You don't know for sure that it's impossible."

Carol's lips thinned, and her hands went to her hips as her own temper started to rise in response to Kim's. "I'm sure running around without having a safe place to go back to is a good way to get yourself stranded in an unfamiliar place—and most likely killed."

Shannon watched and listened as everyone contributed their two cents. Her own mind was spinning. She understood where Kim was coming from, but she was sick to death of life on the road, always on the move and looking over her shoulder. Like Carol, she couldn't see any way it wouldn't be an eventual disaster.

If it came right down to it, she was tired of loneliness. She'd come all this way to settle down with whatever was left of her family. What if they got separated? She wasn't sure she could find them a second time, especially if they were wandering nomads.

Bill had a point too. Andre was a vindictive man. And he knew most of Carol's close friends and contacts within the Black Rats. They'd been his friends and contacts too, once upon a time. Whether he continued to hunt her or decided to do something else, he'd likely try to build a network. Even if he didn't actively pursue her, she doubted he'd leave her be if she came within his grasp.

On the other hand, Carol was right that their friends among other chapters were their surest allies. They were family of a sort and were more likely to help than complete strangers. Most of them knew Andre for what he was, which meant there was a good chance they'd side with her against him, if it came to it.

That was what decided her. She stood. "Enough. This is supposed to be a celebration."

Everyone fell silent. Shannon took a deep breath. "Honestly, I'm with Aunt Carol. Even if we decide to take a different road after that, going to Tupelo to try and hook up with the chapter there is a good move. We could use some friends and allies, and a proper place to rest up. Tupelo and Toad are as good an option as any other."

There was an awkward silence, then Kim heaved herself to her feet. "Well, if that's all, I'm getting dessert."

"I'll help." Lee followed after her, most likely relieved to escape the glares he'd been getting since the burning of the scrapyard came up.

Shannon waited, curious. It was a birthday party, so in theory there would be—

Kim and Lee reappeared, and Shannon had to bite her lip to keep from laughing. The thing they carried between them was a cake only if one were being very, very generous. It looked more like someone had made a very large biscuit as the base, then layered it with far too much frosting and what looked like sugar snaps or ginger snaps, and more frosting, topped with candied ginger and—was that ground ginger?

It looked like it had been made by a five-year-old. It was also the most amazing thing she'd ever seen and far more than she'd expected to get, even after Kim had announced the party.

Little slivers of wood served as candles, and Shannon found herself laughing as she blew them out, accompanied by an incredibly off-key and out-of-tune version of the birthday song.

The cake was surprisingly good as far as Shannon was concerned. It was more frosting than anything else, and the amount of sugar was incredible, but there was enough ginger flavoring in various forms for her to enjoy it. She didn't eat all the frosting on her plate, but these days, if you left something alone, it was going to get scavenged. No one wasted food, and sugary treats like this were rare. Sure enough, within seconds, someone with a bigger sweet tooth scarfed the left-over frosting.

The party devolved into conversation and demonstration of various skills, like juggling, knife throwing, and arm wrestling. Then people started playing games using whatever could be found. Card games and a few battered board games appeared, including a Monopoly board that had half the pieces missing. Carol and Kim joined that game.

Shannon took an opportunity to excuse herself and snag a fresh bottle of beer. Bottle in hand, she looked around to be sure her absence wasn't noted, then made her way to the roof access stairs they'd discovered for the lookout station when they'd first arrived. From there, she could see the entire party. She wasn't surprised when Bill joined her, a quiet, steady presence at her side.

"You don't enjoy games?" she asked without turning to look at him.

"I like them fine. But it didn't seem right the birthday girl was up here all alone."

"You know I do fine on my own."

"Sure. But I also know if you wanted to really be alone, you'd hide in your truck or your room." There was a soft sound as Bill took a swallow of his drink.

"There's that." She sat for a while, sipping her beer and watching the ruckus below, including the skinny little figure who hovered on the edge of the chaos, present but not really joining in.

Her whirling thoughts settled after she'd drunk about half the bottle, and she spoke. "I'm not sure about Aunt Carol's plan. I think you might be right to be concerned."

"But you agreed with her." Bill didn't sound surprised or irritated. Mostly, he just sounded curious. Shannon was glad. It made it easier to explain her thoughts without feeling defensive or uncertain.

Shannon nodded. "She knows how to lead. She's been the prez's wife since I was a kid. She's got a solid plan and a concrete goal, which is more than the rest of us seemed to have."

"But?" Bill's voice coaxed the words out of her.

"But she's also newly widowed, and she's just lost her home. That can be jarring. She's not used to not having control over her life. I'm afraid she's so focused on making things feel right to her that she's not thinking things through."

"You think your ex-husband might think about going to Tupelo?"

"Going to Tupelo's the logical next step for us. He knows that, especially if he knows Carol survived the fight at the scrapyard. Whether he cares about that or not, Andre likes having influence. Hauling the surrounding Black Rats crews and whoever else he can into a little gang of his own is the kind of thing he'd do. If he's after taking over the Black Rats to make a point to me, then Tupelo's his next goal too."

"Think it'll be a question of who gets there first?"

"I think we don't know enough about the sorts of resources Andre can marshal. Or what his next move might be. He's dangerous, and only predictable in the fact that he's an egotistical, vendetta-driven maniac with delusions of grandeur."

It felt good to say all that. Good to be listened to as well. She couldn't say things like that in front of Lee, and she wasn't sure she could say them in front of Kim either. Carol only scoffed and acted like she was giving Andre too much credit, in spite of the scrapyard incident. Bill, on the other hand, trusted her judgment.

Another minute passed in silence as they drank their beers. Finally, Bill spoke. "I have my reservations for sure, but you're right that we can't stay put. Your aunt's got a good idea of where to head next. But I think we need to keep our eyes peeled, and if we see anything going wrong out there, we need to book it like there's a cattle stampede on our tail."

Shannon spluttered in laughter. "I have no idea what that looks like."

"Fine. Like a whole posse of trailers lost their brakes on a hill, and you're at the bottom."

Shannon winced. "Now there's a nightmare. But a good way of describing Andre, I guess."

"So now we have a plan for moving forward and a plan for what to do if things go wrong." Bill grinned at her. "So we can rest a little easier."

"Sure." Shannon sighed. "Except now I need to find that map with the fuel dump locations. The cab and the pickup both need more fuel before we get to running."

"I can do that," Bill offered.

Shannon shook her head. "No. Carol will want you to make sure the bikes are in good shape. I can manage fuel retrieval." She looked down at the small party, which was now a loose gathering of people clustered around different games. "But I'll go tomorrow. I want to just enjoy the rest of today."

"Sounds good to me." Bill smiled and offered her a toast. She clinked her bottle against his, and the two of them settled in to watch the antics of the crew below in comfortable silence.

9

AUSTIN

"Well, well. Look what the rat dragged in. Austin! I thought it was a joke when I spotted the call-out sign with your mark on it by our flop!"

Austin grimaced as Sharp Trager—his real name was Bobby, but he'd ignore or hit anyone who called him that— threw an arm over his shoulder.

"Look at you, with your hot new ride!" Sharp said.

Austin shoved at his friend halfheartedly and watched as the others filed into the room. Sharp might be a loudmouth, but he was a decent buddy, and he'd brought the whole cadre with him—Art Zito, Chip Zebrowski, and Christine Marstien, called Cherry. They were more obnoxious and fun-loving than a lot of the toughs on the street, but they were loyal friends and could hold their own. Especially Cherry.

Austin let his gaze linger on Cherry for a moment. She was the only girl in the little group, named for her fiery red hair and her cherry-red lips. The past weeks had made her a little thinner and dimmed a little of that vibrant color, but she was still a pretty girl, with nice hips and a rack that could fuel a man's fantasies for days. She'd always been more inclined to go for the bigger guys, like Sharp or Chip, but now that he was big-time... Austin pushed the thought away. He had business to deal with first.

Art popped up beside him. "You know, Austin, your face looks like someone's been using you for either a punching bag or a canvas." Art was a tagger who liked his work and liked showing off his skills. "Black and blue don't go with your skin tone though, brother."

Austin growled at him. "Ah, back off. I got on the wrong side of Bulldozer Keith."

"Yowch." Chip shook his head. "I always knew you were a bit dim when you were drunk, but how drunk you gotta be to try and take Bulldozer Keith, Austin? You gotta be able to handle Cherry first at least."

Austin sneered back and stuck his chin out. "Doesn't matter. Bulldozer Keith won't be anyone's to handle no more. My new prez took care of him."

"New prez?" Sharp blinked. "You leave the Black Rats? I heard the base got demolished, but I thought plenty of 'em made it out."

Austin shrugged. "Doesn't matter who made it out and who didn't. Come on, you guys know they were all squares."

Art frowned. "Squares and wimps like you, sure. But I didn't take you for being a runner."

"I ain't. My new prez was a Black Rat before the bosses betrayed him and sold him out to the feds. He's looking to remake the club the way it used to be, the way it should be."

"Yeah? And what's that supposed to be? Cause if it's all bootlickers— no offense, Austin—that's not my idea of a good time or a good club." Art shook his head.

"I ain't a bootlicker, Art. Andre likes guys that can manage themselves. Heck, when he took out Bulldozer Keith, I took out Sparky. Now I'm the boss's second-in-command." Austin lifted his chin again and stared down his nose. "You keep smack-talking me, I won't tell you why I sent the call-out. And maybe I tell the boss you need a lesson too."

"Hey, no need for that. Don't need to get so sore over a few friendly comments." Sharp held out his hands placatingly. "We didn't realize you'd been promoted, that's all. We were surprised. You know what we're all like without a bit of a snort to take the edge off."

Austin relaxed. It was true that Sharp had earned his nickname by being sharp-tongued when he wasn't stoned into politeness. "If it's a good hit you're looking for, Andre's got it all. The new prez of the reformed Black Rats is a total hardcore one percenter, and he knows how to get stuff—and get stuff done. He's consolidating what's left of the Memphis gang scene, bringing them under his banner. His rule is real simple—join and obey, you get everything you want: booze, bikes, drugs, guns. It's a gangster's paradise with him. Defy him, you get squashed like Bulldozer Keith—and like the Gardenas."

"Any idea what he's planning after he gets done consolidating?" Art tipped his head, but there was a gleam of avarice in his eyes Austin recognized. Art was already hooked, and the others were listening.

"Expansion. Take over the other nearby territories. Might make a play for all Tennessee, Mississippi, and Kentucky, but we'll start small. He wants an empire under the Black Rats banner, where we're the kings of the road, and we can do what we want, when we want."

"Sounds ambitious." Chip still looked uncertain, but he was the only one. Austin knew he'd come along if the rest of the cadre joined up.

He smirked at his friends. "Nah. He says it'll be easy. We only gotta deal with the remainders of the squares, like Bruno's old woman, and their niece. Especially the niece—she's a proper backstabber, that one. We clear them out, and the rest of the territory will fold easy enough."

There were some looks exchanged, then Sharp spoke up. "Free drugs and a good time, living like kings? Sure. I'm with you."

Mutters of agreement followed, and Austin led them out toward the bikes. He was about to climb on his new rig when Cherry stopped and smiled at him, leaning over in a way that put her assets right where he could best admire them.

"And what do you think my place could be, in this new empire? Does the king need a queen, do you think?" She batted her eyes and pursed her lips at him invitingly.

"Well, I dunno." He knew better than to act desperate, no matter how much he wanted to drag her closer to explore her charms further. "Lots of girls want to have a taste of the king, or the power beside the throne." Since he'd become known as Andre's second, plenty of girls were willing to share his bed, his booze, and his drugs. Some of them had introduced him to interesting ideas he wouldn't mind trying out with Cherry.

"But Austin, we've been friends for such a long time…" Her voice was breathy, coaxing.

Austin grinned. "Why don't we discuss the possibilities back at the new base?"

Cherry pouted but went back to Sharp, who gave him a side-eyed look of warning he ignored. Austin hopped on his bike and kicked it into gear, revving the engine before he took the lead and showed them the way to Andre's new safehouse.

It was a big place, one of the nicer hotels in Memphis, with its own classy bar and everything, and rooms fit for kings. Not that most of them didn't sleep off their drug-induced haze or drunken stupors in whatever space they found. And why not? Even the couches were soft and better than the cots Austin was used to.

Andre greeted them in a large room off the lobby. "Austin! These must be the compatriots you spoke of seeking out." His cool gaze flickered over them.

"Yeah. They're my buds. Good riders, good people to have at your back." Austin grinned, proud that none of the others said anything. They clearly knew who the boss was and their place in relation to Austin's. "I can vouch for that, prez."

"Good, good." Andre waved. "New stashes were delivered while you were gone. Please, help yourself. I understand there's some Bacardi Gold in the new batch. It is quite excellent."

Liquid gold. Austin barely managed to keep from salivating at the thought. No one in the seedy bars he usually frequented could afford that sort of booze. "I could try some, I guess."

Andre waved a dismissive hand. "Take the whole bottle if you wish. I have already made my own selections. As for the rest of our supplies, you know where they are. Please, do show your new lieutenants where they can be found so you may all enjoy yourselves." Andre turned and strode away.

Austin waited until Andre was gone before he turned to smirk at his friends. "See? That's how a real prez acts. You stick with me, and we'll be living the life. You'll see."

"Sure, Austin." Sharp nodded, his eyes wide. "Say, since you've got permission from the prez, could we try some of that Gold with you? I mean, if it's not a problem."

Austin pretended to consider. "Well, I'm not sure. I guess we could come to an arrangement if you were to go fetch the stuff while Cherry keeps me company. Grab me three or four hits of coke too, dime or quarter bags if they got it."

Three or four hits—let alone three or four dime or quarter bags— would keep him high as clouds for days, but it wouldn't hurt his rep any for them to think he'd be able to snort it all in a sitting. He could hide the rest.

It was like the Gold. He hadn't had anything more than cheap beer, and not much of that, until he was an adult, and that's what he drank most days. Didn't take much to leave him mellow. He knew well enough going from beer and low-grade scotch to Gold was like a kid trying to go from a tricycle to a Harley in one riding lesson. But it didn't matter. All he had to do was down the first shot like a boss, and they'd think he was as hardcore as any of them.

Never mind if the first shot would likely put him on his back faster than Bulldozer Keith had. No one else needed to know it. He might be a lightweight—a fact he could thank his overbearing, stuck-in-the-mud, dull-minded preacher of a father for—but he'd learned a long time ago how to bluff and swagger with the best of them.

Austin had done that to become a Black Rat, despite his small-town, blue-collar, all-work-and-no-play upbringing, and he'd keep doing it until no one, not even himself, would believe he'd ever been anything other than a hardcore biker and a *true* one percenter.

Sharp, Chip, and Art scrambled as soon as Austin pointed them in the direction of the storage rooms. Austin sauntered over to a large chair and sat down, patting the arm of the chair. "Now then, I think you wanted to discuss what sort of place a girl like you could have in the new regime." He didn't bother to hide his appreciation of her.

She didn't hesitate to sit beside him, leaning close so he could take in the view. "That's right." Cherry's smile was pure seduction. "I would."

The boys came back with the booze and drugs. Austin watched with satisfaction as Sharp poured out a glass for him and Art prepped the drugs while Chip hovered, waiting for any orders Austin might give.

The booze was smooth going down, and the drugs lifted him to heights he'd never enjoyed before. As he sailed away on his second glass and a good hit of high-quality coke, Austin felt Cherry settle in his lap and snickered drunkenly to himself.

The pleasant haze held him for a while, until the needs of his bladder dragged him back to the real world. Cherry had moved off him, and Austin took a moment to mourn the loss before he staggered to his feet and wobbled drunkenly toward the nearest door to do his business.

He was busy taking a leak when Andre appeared with quiet steps and nearly startled the life out of him. He hurried to zip up. "Hey, boss. Stuff you gave us was really top notch. I enjoyed it."

"Good, good. I came to find you for a reason." Andre moved closer. "I was wondering if you knew the status of the other chapters. I have talked of Tupelo to you, but I neglected to ask you if they were even active."

It took Austin a moment to sort out what the words meant, but then he nodded. "Yeah. Sure. Prez there is almost as old as Brute Bruno, supposed to be a bit of a stick-in-the-mud. Course, that's what squares under Gardena said. I don't know if that's accurate." He snorted. "Not like it matters. Can't be worse than my old man."

"Your old man?" Andre's voice was cool, but he didn't stop Austin from talking.

"He was a minister. Small-town. I left him behind a long time ago." Austin shrugged. "Anyway, I've heard Toad's a stiff, but he can't be that bad."

69

"It remains to be seen. In any case, I intend to bring the chapter into our own, as part of the new Black Rats. I trust I can count on your assistance?"

"Sure, boss." Austin nodded.

"Then I will leave you to enjoy the rest of your evening. Do tell your compatriots to do the same." Andre turned and stalked off.

Austin watched him go, then went back to taking care of business. Once that was handled, he went back to the group.

Half a glass of Gold later, and he was drifting away on an alcohol daze once more, into dreams that, for the first time, felt within his reach.

10

KIM NAKAMURA

K im woke to the all-too-familiar sound of arguing in the motel courtyard. She groaned, then rolled out of bed and collected her clothing and equipment for the day. Shannon had already left with Mutt and a crew for fuel recovery, Bill was going to be doing maintenance, and she was in the mood to practice her hunting skills a little more. But that would come after she kept her Aunt Carol from shredding whichever poor soul had ignited her temper now.

It was probably Lee again. Lee was her great-aunt's favorite target when she wanted someone to snap at. Kim understood her reasoning, but she still found it frustrating. Lee might have made mistakes, sure, but he was far from the only one. Hadn't Aunt Carol and Uncle Bruno been the ones to let her dad join the Black Rats and marry her mom? Without that, none of the rest of it might have happened—though of course that meant she wouldn't have existed either.

She exited her room to find Lee huddled in a doorway looking miserable, with Bill standing between him and Carol. Bill was trying, as usual, to soothe Aunt Carol's temper. And, as usual, Aunt Carol wasn't having it. Bill was getting steadily more frustrated as the argument continued.

Kim shook her head. Bill was always trying to help, and she admired him for it, but after a week he ought to have realized the best thing to do when Aunt Carol was in a mood was get out of her way until she calmed back down.

She slipped around the two combatants until she reached Lee's side. "Hey. You know anything about hunting?"

Lee blinked. "Sure. I used to hunt a lot, back home in Tunica."

"Great. You want to come with me? I'm going out to get some meat for dinner, and Mom will kill me if I don't have a buddy."

Lee grimaced. "Pretty sure your mom will kill us both if you take just me. She…doesn't like me." His gaze went back to Aunt Carol. "Nobody really does."

"Bill does. I don't know you well enough to like or not like you." She'd heard about Lee being with her dad in the attack on the scrapyard, but it wasn't like she'd actually seen him hurting anyone there. "Come on, let's get out of here. At least they'll stop arguing when they realize we've gone. Look at it this way: if they get mad at us for going together, at least they'll be shouting at you for something new and something you did on purpose."

Lee winced, but after a moment, he nodded, relief clear in his face. "Yeah. Okay."

Together, they sneaked out of the courtyard, then out of the motel lot and into the nearby woods. Once they were far enough away to avoid unnerving folks at the motel, Kim checked her weapons.

"You prefer guns or knives?"

Lee shrugged. "I can use either. I'm a pretty good hunter."

Kim unholstered the backup pistol she'd picked up in her flight from Humboldt. She usually carried it low on her leg in a makeshift calf holster, the way Dennis had shown her. "How good a shot are you?"

Lee took the weapon, and Kim felt a brief stab of envy at how comfortable he appeared with it. He held it with casual ease, barrel pointed away from her as he checked the chamber and the clip. "I can hit what I aim at most of the time."

Kim pointed to a branch. "Hit that, where the branch connects to the tree."

It was a skinny branch, and the junction point wasn't that big. Lee didn't hesitate. He raised the pistol, sighted down the length, and fired. He pulled the trigger in a smooth motion, Kim noticed, rather than jerking it the way she still did most of the time. The branch cracked and fell to the ground.

Kim stared. "You are good." She flushed and looked away. "I'm still a beginner."

"Oh. Well, I didn't mean to show off." Lee rolled his shoulders, embarrassment and apology clear on his face.

Kim waved it away. "I asked."

"Yeah, still. I know most people don't like getting showed up." Lee hesitated. "I know lots of people don't like guns, and I saw your face when I fired. If you'd like, I can show you how to rig a snare trap. They're better anyway, since they aren't as loud or likely to startle you or your prey."

Kim nodded. "I've read about them, but the person who was helping me, he didn't get a chance to show me how to set them."

"I...it wasn't..." Lee hesitated.

Kim shook her head, guessing the question he wanted to ask and was afraid to. "It wasn't anyone at the Black Rats compound. It was a friend I was traveling with for a while."

"Well, you can make them out of just about anything." Lee gestured. "Maybe we could set some up here, at the edge of the woods, before we head out to the open area."

They made their way to the edge of the woods. Kim had some cords in her pack—part of Dennis's preparations for anything—and Lee showed her how to bend a sapling, tie a bit of rope or cord in a simple loop with a slipknot, and pin it down with a rock or any nearby material. He also pointed out a stand of yaupon holly.

"The roots on that are pretty good for using as snares in a pinch, though they can be hard to dig up. So's knotgrass, though it's tricky, and it dries out pretty fast."

Setting snares turned out to be easy. After they'd covered over the third one, Kim noticed Lee was making a mark on a nearby tree. "What's that for?"

"To remind me where the snares are so I can check and dismantle them before we leave." Lee eyed the trap. "Some hunters leave permanent traps, but that's no good unless you can check them regularly."

Kim frowned. "Why?"

"Because snare traps are quiet and easy, but they don't kill gently. A lucky animal might get its neck snapped when the trap goes off, but if that doesn't happen, it'll be trapped by a foot and panic, or it'll be caught in a way where it can suffocate slowly."

Kim grimaced. "I didn't know that."

"Most people don't if they aren't hunters. But it's still true." Lee sighed. "I prefer shooting, when I can. Seems fairer, somehow."

Put like that, Kim had to agree. She watched Lee make another mark. "You seem like a decent guy. I'm sorry my great-aunt is giving you such a hard time."

Lee shrugged. "She's got a right." He returned from his marking, and the two of them headed out into the open scrublands, looking for a place to set up and wait. After a moment, Lee continued. "I got her partner killed. I don't blame her for wanting to give me a thrashing. Her or the others in the gang."

Kim frowned. "It's not like you actually killed my great-uncle."

"Nah. I didn't have the guts to shoot people. But I set off the fires that made them run that way." There was enough guilt to choke a man in Lee's voice, and Kim shook her head in sympathy as she answered.

"That doesn't make you a bad person. Just someone who made a stupid mistake that got people hurt. Most of us have done the same at some point."

"Doesn't make me a good person, either, and it was a bad mistake." Lee flopped down near a small stream. Kim joined him and splashed a little water into her face to cool off as Lee continued talking. "To be honest, I'm less surprised at her anger than I am by the fact that Bill dragged me along. I'd have left me there, standing in the fire."

"Bill's a nice guy," Kim pointed out.

"Yeah, but I still don't get it. And I don't know why everyone else hasn't chucked me out or thrashed me to a pulp." Lee stared over the waving grasses. "They should."

"No. They shouldn't. Aunt Carol may have a right to be mad, but being real, any of them who remember my dad know what kind of guy he was. They've *all* fallen for his smooth-talk at least once, including my great-aunt and my mother."

Lee blinked. "Your dad?"

Kim scowled. She didn't want to talk about it, but Lee deserved to know. If nothing else, it might give him some perspective about the situation. "Yeah. Andre's my biological father. I know now that he's a monster, an abuser, and a liar, but when I was your age, or a little younger? It was a lot harder to tell."

She folded her arms around her legs, remembering those years, long ago. "Andre…he convinced my great-aunt and great-uncle to let him join the Black Rats. And he wooed my mother, convinced her to marry him, even though I've heard there were already warning signs that he wasn't the best person. Even before they married, he was into shady stuff. Drugs and weapons. It was bad enough that he got black-listed and barred from the MC eventually."

"I didn't know that."

"Most people don't. Andre could be incredibly good at convincing you not to notice stuff or to decide it wasn't that bad. He did it to everyone. Including me." Kim shook her head, a bitter smile tugging her mouth. "I loved my parents as a kid, you know? And my dad, he encouraged that. He was always bringing me treats, giving me compliments, letting me get away with stuff. He was the 'fun' parent, I guess? He made me feel like I was…"

"Like you were an adult. Like the stuff you said mattered." Lee spoke softly.

"Exactly. My mother was the disciplinarian, the one who made me do my homework, come home at night, stay away from drugs and alcohol. I mean, she could be fun too. She helped me with homework, took me on her bike, let me hang out with the bikers when she could. But if I wanted to go somewhere, I'd ask Dad. Especially if she'd already said no." She shook her head again. "It was so easy to like him, to believe he was the best person in the world. To want his approval. But sometimes, I'd see a darker side of him. When I was a kid, it was these brief flashes of temper. Then he'd apologize and smile again, and we'd pretend it never happened."

"Did he ever hit you?"

The question made her look at Lee. From his expression, he'd gotten on the wrong side of Andre's fist at least once.

"Not until the end." Kim heard her voice crack a little and winced. "But he hit my mother. And he threatened her. I think he threatened me too, just not where I could hear. As a kid, I didn't understand, but the older I got, the more obvious it got. Too many bruises and too many excuses. I started watching the TV shows and seeing the commercials. The ones that talk about domestic violence. And there were the school programs about bullying, and abuse, and stuff like that. Eventually, I couldn't pretend I didn't see it anymore. I knew what he was doing."

"He was abusive." Lee said the words with a quiet conviction that came from far too much experience. "Yeah. I've..." He took a deep breath. "I've been there. Before Andre." His face was miserable. "I thought he wasn't like that at first."

"That's Andre for you. He's good at convincing people he's a savior when he's the demon that drags you into the dark. I think everyone falls for it the first time they meet him. Unless something happens that makes him forget to keep up the act."

"I thought he was going to protect me."

Kim nodded. "I did too, once. Until I realized the truth about all my mom's 'accidents.' Then he killed a guy in cold blood."

"I didn't know that either." Lee sounded lost and more than a little confused. Kim could sympathize.

"No reason you would." Kim reached out and put a hand on his shoulder. "Look, I didn't mean to vent a whole lot of family business at you, but I just wanted you to know, Andre's manipulative. I think Aunt Carol is just trying to stay mad because admitting you made a mistake means she has to remember she did too, once upon a time. Her mistakes are how Andre entered our lives to begin with. She doesn't want to think about it."

"Can't blame her. I don't like thinking about how easy I fell for it either." Lee grimaced.

"But you'll know better next time. And Aunt Carol will get over it eventually."

"Maybe, but—" Lee stopped, his gaze focusing on something out in the grass.

Kim turned to look. They'd been talking in soft voices the whole time to avoid disturbing the wildlife. Lee's change in focus turned her attention to the landscape and the movements she'd mostly been ignoring as she tried to console him.

A few yards off, a large rabbit was hopping slowly and softly through the grass, nose twitching and ears flicking back and forth as it moved. It was being cautious, but they were downwind of it, and they'd been sitting fairly still.

A quick exchange of glances, then Lee shifted position and raised his gun. Two hands on the grip and both eyes open, just like Kim had been taught. He'd had a good teacher in that, no matter what else he'd been through. One deep breath, then he exhaled and fired, all in one smooth motion.

The rabbit dropped at once, red blossoming over its head. Kim stood and followed Lee over to the small body. "Good shot, Lee." She grinned at him as he pulled out a blade to start dressing the rabbit. "Keep providing meat for dinner, and I guarantee you'll have everyone won over before another month is out, including Aunt Carol."

"I dunno about that." Lee paused. "But thanks for talking to me. It helps, I guess, knowing I'm not the only one who fell for Andre's talk."

"Not even close." Kim squatted down beside him to help with cleaning the meat and packaging it to take back. "Honestly, while it's been kinda nice getting in touch with people I haven't seen in a long time, like my mom, sometimes I dream about just taking my stuff and heading off on my own again. Not even saying goodbye, you know? The whole world is different. Could be a chance to completely start over."

Lee was nodding along with her words. "Not even saying goodbye…" he repeated, and Kim could tell from the color in his cheeks that was an idea that appealed to him, too.

"Anyway," she continued. "Try not to beat yourself up too much about falling for Andre. We all did. And much as we all wish otherwise, you're probably not going to be the last person to believe him either."

11

SHANNON GRAYSON

"I swear Mutt, sometimes I just want to shake some sense into her. Other times, I realize she's all grown up and I need to give her space. Then something happens that reminds me there's so many dangers out there I never prepared her for, and I worry again."

Shannon shook her head at the dog, who was sniffing a random section of pavement while she talked, happily oblivious to Shannon's monologue. "Then there's the fact that her father escaped from prison, and who knows what he's up to? He's had a week to plan, and Andre's not stupid, much as I wish he was."

Shannon sighed and stretched her back. She'd been tasked with relocating the marks for the fuel reserves while the more experienced siphoners did their work. They'd tried a gas station, but getting into the underground tanks wasn't easy, and it was impossible for any of them to identify which tank held diesel versus gasoline. Pulling from cars was easier, and more in the skill set of most of the bikers.

She kept walking, checking cars for the marks she and Bill had left as she rambled on at Mutt about her worries for her daughter, her fears concerning Andre, and her thoughts about the small family unit she'd gathered in general.

A soft whoof interrupted her. Mutt had gone on alert, stiff-legged in a way she never was around any of the residents of the motel. All the bikers there had learned she was a softy and easy to win over with a little petting and a treat or two. Kim and Shannon were still her favorite people, but she'd go to anyone she knew who looked willing to feed her.

A skinny figure was stumbling toward her, barely upright and clearly not in the best state. He was also wearing a vest with a Black Rat patch on it. Shannon edged closer, then hesitated as she recognized him.

Austin. The man who'd been the most vocal about his distrust of her and Bill when they'd arrived at the Black Rats compound. She knew he'd fled during the shooting, and she hadn't seen his body when they went back to salvage what they could, but she hadn't heard anything else about him. Honestly, with everything else she had to worry about, she hadn't much cared.

He'd obviously survived. The bruises on his face gave her some concern, especially what looked like a broken nose, but as he staggered closer, her concern changed to barely controlled disdain.

He might be hurt, but his real problems lay in the stench of booze and drugs that hung around him like a miasma. He was drunk, wasted, or both.

She was about to turn away and leave him to whatever he was doing when Austin blinked reddened eyes. "Hey, I know you." His words were slurred, but basically intelligible. "You're Carol's niece."

"I am." Shannon nodded and moved closer to him, though she was careful to remain out of reach and close to Mutt. "You're Austin. I haven't seen you since the scrapyard burned. You look like you've had it rough."

"Nah." Austin grinned sloppily at her. "I mean, yeah, got a little roughed up, but then I found a new crew to roll with. New crew, and a *real* prez. Someone who knows how to get stuff done and provide for his guys."

"You don't say." Shannon kept her voice even, despite the surge of anger that threatened to boil over at the insult to her uncle. Bruno was dead, and she was irritated to hear a lowlife like Austin speaking poorly of him.

Then the anger drowned under concern as the rest of his words filtered through her mind. She hadn't heard about a new crew taking over the Black Rats. True, the state of the world and their current location left them out of the loop, but it was still disquieting that they hadn't even heard rumors.

"Yeah. He's great. Everybody gets what they want. Past day I've drunk top-shelf booze, snorted more coke than I ever knew you could get in one haul, and the girls! I got women lining up to show *me* a good time! All thanks to the new boss."

"I see. Well, I wish you luck." She didn't trust the type of person he was talking about, and she wasn't sure he was even telling the truth, rather than rambling on in some drug-induced delusion.

She turned away, but she hadn't gone more than two steps before she heard Austin stumble after her. "Hey! Wait a second. I wanted to ask —how's the old prez's old lady? Did she make it out? I never did hear."

He actually sounded distressed, enough so that she turned back. What he said next, though, froze her in her tracks.

"I've been wondering about Carol a lot. And your daughter, Kim. Did she make it to meet you? Heard she was in the area, but no one knows if she got to the base before you and the others lit out."

Shannon took a deep breath, holding herself still as fear and fury pounded through her. Her voice was a rough growl when she managed to speak. "Who told you about my daughter? I never mentioned her, let alone her name."

Austin blinked, then a slow, smug leer crossed his battered features. "What's it to you?"

"I want to know who told you the name of my daughter or her whereabouts."

"Bet you do." Austin smirked. Shannon throttled her temper back with an effort, though she'd much rather have throttled the answer out of him instead. "Well, I told you I have new friends. Real good friends, and some of them know you and your daughter *real* well. Talked about Kim, and I'm looking forward to getting to know her a lot better too."

"I want the name of the person who told you about my daughter." Shannon shuffled closer, and Mutt made a low growl at her side.

"Not telling you. Not unless you come crawling on your knees to swear loyalty to the new prez. Or maybe you swear to be my woman. My piece. Might consider it then if you gave me a good enough ride and talked pretty to me." Austin's voice was a mocking sing-song, his eyes gleaming with avarice and amusement as he taunted her.

Fury swept over her, and Shannon acted without thinking. She lunged forward, fist lashing out in a move Bruno had taught her as a teenager. Her aim was true, and her fist connected solidly with Austin's cheek and eye.

Austin staggered back with a howl of pain. "You little...you..."

Shannon advanced, and he backed off with a yelp, especially when Mutt growled at him. His face was crimson with hatred and fury as he glared at her out of his good eye. "You'll pay for that, you and everyone you know. I'll see you do." He staggered backward, eye fixed on her. "You'll see. I'll have you beg on your knees like a dog to have the privilege of even licking my boots, let alone anything else. You'll wish you'd showed me proper respect then!"

He turned and staggered away at the closest approximation of a run he could manage, still howling curses. Shannon watched him go, her chest heaving.

She didn't regret losing her temper, but she wished she could have shaken some answers out of him before she'd decked him.

Shannon swallowed hard as fury drained away and panic began to take its place. There was only one person she knew of who knew Kim had come to Memphis, aside from the Black Rat survivors who'd gathered at the motel. There was only one person she could be sure would know Kim's name and what she looked like after so many years.

Andre. Which meant at the very least, he was now part of whatever crew Austin had gotten involved with.

Shannon feared it was worse than that. Andre had never hidden his ambitions to be a big boss or that he thought he'd do better than Bruno. She also knew a crew under her ex-husband's leadership would be little more than lawless marauders held together by Andre's manipulative and dangerous charisma.

A new prez who let his riders do what they wanted? That sounded like Andre when he was trying to charm people into his sphere of influence.

Crap on a weevil-ridden cracker. Andre hasn't been quiet this whole week. He's been building an army.

12

KIM NAKAMURA

"Aunt Carol!" The frantic shout, laced with fear in a voice she usually considered fearless, made Kim look up in alarm. She and Lee had been fully butchering the rabbit—a task she still hated—when the truck her mother had taken out came roaring into the lot and screeched to a halt. The engine was barely off before her mother toppled out of it, her eyes wide as she shouted for Aunt Carol at the top of her lungs.

Kim and Lee followed her into the courtyard, and bikers came boiling out of their rooms, drawn by the frantic calls for their leader. Bill joined them a second later from the back lot where he'd been working on the vehicles. He was the first to reach Shannon, Aunt Carol not a breath behind.

"What's the matter, Shannon?" His calm voice visibly settled Kim's mother, at least enough for her to take a deep breath. "You don't get rattled often."

"I know I don't." Shannon gulped in another breath. "But I ran into that punk Austin while we were scavenging." Another heaving breath. "He asked about you, Aunt Carol. And then he asked for Kim, by name. Said he knew she was in Memphis because friends of his had told him."

Kim frowned. "I don't know any Austin."

"But I do." Carol's voice was cold.

"Isn't he that weaselly skunk of a man who ran with us for a while?" TimFist asked.

Carol nodded. "Sure is. Ran like the yellow-bellied cur he is when the scrapyard got bombed. I figured he got out, but I also figured he was halfway across the country by now."

"He's not. Said he's with a new crew, led by a new prez who gets stuff done. Then he started asking after you and Kim, and he said his 'new friend' told him about her." Shannon's eyes were wide. "There's only one person who knows Kim is in Memphis who isn't here with us."

Kim felt like she'd been dropped in the middle of a lake in winter. "My...you mean..."

"It has to be Andre. I'd bet a month's food rations that he's the new prez. Making a power play in times like this—it's got Andre written all over it." Shannon's voice was shaking and so were her hands. "He's been building an army while we were trying to regroup here."

"Knew I should have shot him." Carol snarled the words. "That man's worse than a plague-ridden rat."

Bill reached out and put a hand on Shannon's shoulder. Kim moved to hug her mother from the other side. She could see the shadows of old fears and terrible memories in her mother's eyes and knew that learning Andre was gaining support had shaken her mother badly.

"What do we do?" Kim recognized the voice as Hannah's, somewhere amid the gathered bikers.

Carol spun to look at the men and women around them, most of them barely recovered from the disaster at the scrapyard. "Pack up and get ready to move out. Get everything we can scavenge onto the truck and bikes, and all the supplies onto the back of the big rig. Get ready to ride."

Kim looked at her mother, still shaken and pale. She moved to intercept her great-aunt. "I know we need to move, but can't we at least have a minute to catch our breath? Mom's just had a shock. She needs—"

"She needs to get as far away from that maniac as possible. That's what she needs." Carol snapped. "We don't have time to hang around thinking about the problem or waiting for trouble to find us."

Kim wanted to argue, but a hand landed on her shoulder. She turned to find her mother behind her, eyes huge and face pale. "She's right. We need to get out of here." She shuddered. "I need to pack up my things."

"I'll help you." Bill wrapped an arm around Shannon's shoulder and led her away.

"Can I help?" Lee appeared at Kim's side, his face tight with a fear she recognized all too well. "I don't have much, and I never unpacked it, except for my sketch pad. Kept expecting to get kicked out."

She didn't want help. She wanted to go comfort her mother and take a minute to think about what it meant that her father was building an army and likely to come after them. But Aunt Carol had given her orders, and Kim knew she'd better keep up and get ready or risk being left behind or tossed into her mother's truck with nothing but the clothes on her back.

Kim took a deep breath to fight back her own fear and anxiety. "Sure. I could use some company."

Lee followed her to her room and began handing her things to pack into her bags. He didn't try to talk about Andre, or Shannon, or anything else. He was just there. Kim appreciated it more than she would have questions or attempts at soothing her.

Maybe that was why her mom had gone off with Bill. Bill could be soothing too.

Her hand fell on a shirt. Kim picked it up and began to fold it, only to falter to a stop as she recognized it. Large, with a faded Marine logo on it. It wasn't hers, but Dennis's. She'd been carrying it in her pack all this time and just never realized. She'd been too busy with one thing or another to go through his packs after she'd grabbed them from the forest and escaped from Humboldt.

"That belong to one of the others? I can take it to them." Lee's quiet question startled her out of her frozen state. He started to reach out, and she pulled it back, holding the t-shirt close.

Kim shook her head. "No. It's...well, it's mine now, I guess. But it used to belong to a friend of mine." She started to fold the shirt carefully. Her throat hurt, and it was hard to keep her hands steady.

After a moment, Lee perched carefully on the chair. "Was it the guy who taught you to hunt? The one you were talking about earlier?"

Kim nodded. "Yeah."

Lee's voice was carefully neutral, demanding nothing as he spoke. "What was his name? If you don't mind me asking."

Kim shook her head. "I don't. His name was Dennis Sullivan."

Lee nodded. "You said he came part of the way with you?" He paused. "I heard you mention him to your mom yesterday. You said he couldn't come all the way, but you didn't say why."

"Because I can't tell her the truth." Kim hunched around the shirt. "Mom was Dennis's friend, even though they argued a lot, because he was also the federal marshal assigned to her in Witness Protection. How am I supposed to tell her he didn't make it to Memphis because he got shot halfway between here and Murray?"

"He got shot?" Lee's eyes were older than his years, and his expression was gentle. "Like, by thieves or something?"

"I wish." Kim flopped on the bed, eyes stinging as she remembered. "He got shot by a man he thought was his friend. The jerk wanted me to stay in his crappy little town to be their doctor, because he'd gone and got the previous doctor killed. When I refused to stay, he tried to keep me prisoner. Dennis got me out, but then he got caught, and his 'friend' executed him. For being a decent human being."

"Oh man. That's all kinds of wrong." Lee shook his head. "Is this why you were arguing against staying in any one place?"

Kim nodded. "Yeah. How can you trust people not to try and cage you?"

"Dang. I can see why you'd feel that way."

Kim huffed and sat up so she could stuff the shirt into her bag. "It's just—it was so stupid, the way he died. I hate it, and I hate that I can't bring myself to tell my mom, and most of all, I hate the fact that I couldn't save him."

"You shouldn't." Lee's soft but firm declaration made Kim look up.

"What?"

Lee stepped closer and took the shirt to fold it with swift, careful movements. "I don't know much about the circumstances, but I do know it wasn't your fault he died. You didn't pull the trigger, and trust me, there's a big difference between watching someone die and doing

89

the killing. It's one of those things I learned around Andre I wish I didn't remember."

Kim almost asked him about it, but the tight set of his shoulders was a clear indicator he didn't want to talk about it. She was willing to respect that.

Lee took a deep breath. "It's not your fault. And you know what's amazing? Even with that happening to you, and how it makes you feel, you still keep moving forward. You still want to help people, like you talked about yesterday. That is incredibly awesome, and I bet your friend would say so too." Lee's expression suddenly turned sheepish, and on anyone with a lighter complexion, she'd have sworn he was blushing. "At least, that's what I think."

Kim swallowed. It still hurt, but she couldn't deny Lee's words helped a little. "I just wish I could have helped him."

"You might always wish that. There's stuff I wish I hadn't done, and more I wish I had. But you'll keep going, and you can help the next person. Someone like me, or your mom, or Bill, or Carol. Or someone we don't even know yet. You'll save them." Lee's voice was full of quiet conviction.

After a moment, Kim leaned over and bumped his shoulder with her own. "Thanks."

They finished packing in silence, then took their stuff out to be loaded. Carol was supervising the packing and stacking of the storage crates. She eyed Lee balefully but didn't say anything to him. Instead, she turned to Kim. "How attached are you to that car of yours?"

Kim shrugged. "It's a car. Why?"

"'Cause we can fuel six bikes for what we need to fill that car. Of the rides that aren't bikes, it's got the least to offer in terms of storage space."

Kim eyed the car. It had gotten her safely out of Humboldt, but she wasn't attached to it the way most of the bikers were attached to their rides. It didn't help that sometimes when she looked in the rearview mirror, she had flashbacks of seeing Dennis dead on the ground near the body of the man who'd murdered him, getting smaller as she drove away.

She looked back at her aunt. "Strip it down as salvage and leave it here then. I'm okay with that." If she absolutely had to, she could probably find another car or relearn how to ride a motorcycle. "What about the pickup truck?"

Carol made a face as if she'd stepped in one of Mutt's messes. "Keeping that for our tagalongs and to store some of the supplies we might need easy access to on the road."

"Okay. I guess I'll ride with Mom in the cab." Kim made her way over and tossed her bags into the space behind the seats. Once her gear was stowed, she stepped back and looked around.

Bill was doing last-minute checks on the bikes, hovered over by whichever biker owned the rig he was looking at. Lee was assisting where he could and trying to stay out of everyone's way. But she couldn't see Shannon.

"Where's Mom?"

"Working in the storeroom, sorting things into containers and getting a count of what's what." Carol waved her in the direction of the room where she and Bill had stacked the boxes.

Kim found her mother inside writing up a makeshift list of various containers and their contents with Mutt lying nearby. She picked her way over, dodging the guys picking up the boxes and loading them. "Hey, Mom. How's it going?"

Shannon looked up from her list. There was a smile, or something that was supposed to pass for one, on her face, but her eyes were full of fear and wariness, like a hunted animal's. "Not bad. We managed to salvage plenty of food and fuel. We've got a good selection of tools and medical supplies too, more than I would have expected. If you and Lee can hunt a little more, we'll even have a good amount of meat."

Kim wrapped an arm around her mother's shoulders. "That's good, but not what I meant. How are you holding up?"

"I'm doing all right." Shannon's response was quick, and unconvincing. "You know, we've got a plan and allies now, so…" She trailed off, and Kim hugged her close.

Kim took deep breaths, determined not to make her mother's fear worse with her own uncertainties. "We'll be all right, Mom. He's run once, we can make him run away with his tail between his legs again."

"I'm sure we'll be fine." Shannon took a deep breath. "Help me with the boxes, will you?"

Kim nodded and started packing and shifting things around under her mother's direction. But even as she worked, she couldn't help the thought that followed her around, popping up every time she spotted the tension in her mother's shoulders and the tightness around her mouth and eyes.

I'm scared too.

13

KIM NAKAMURA

K im scowled as she dragged herself out of her room for the last time. Because of the time it had taken to pack up, Aunt Carol had decided to wait for morning to get on the road. Aside from safety reasons, it allowed them to eat some of the more perishable supplies and lighten the load a bit.

Kim had been hoping that a last night of sleeping on a bed would make them all feel more alert and ready for the trip ahead. Instead, she'd found herself awakened sometime late at night—or very early in the morning—by roaring engines and manic shouting. From the dark circles under everyone else's eyes, she wasn't the only one.

As if to confirm her thoughts, Lee staggered over, munching on a stale granola bar that had been set out for part of the morning meal. He washed it down with marginally drinkable apple juice. "Man, did you hear the racket last night?"

Kim grunted as she picked out her own breakfast bar and some form of generic, off-brand cola she didn't look at too closely. It had caffeine, which was all she cared about. She wasn't generally a coffee fiend or caffeine addict, but for this morning she needed the pick-me-up. From the way the stock had diminished, she wasn't the only one. She took a long gulp before responding to Lee's question. "Who didn't?"

Lee grimaced. "It's the first time I've been woken up like that. It's almost like the world's just getting crazier."

It probably was. Kim recalled a long ago reading of *Lord of the Flies* from her school days. With minimal resources, no established government or law enforcement, and everyone trying to survive, chaos was bound to happen. Most people would be trying to simply get by, but there would be tyrants rising to create their own little enclaves by gathering like-minded people to them. Or collecting whatever maniacs they could get to join them.

Somewhere out there, one of those tyrants was probably her father. Kim scowled.

"You okay?" Lee sounded worried, and Kim pulled herself out of her funk enough to answer him.

"Yeah, just thinking. It's probably going to get worse before it gets better."

"Worse?" Lee winced as he glanced around. "It's already pretty frickin' bad out here."

"Well, all we can do is our best. But man, I really wish I could relax and watch a movie or something."

"A movie sounds great. Something light and fun. Maybe animated."

"Yeah. With a happily ever after."

Chattering about movies allowed Kim to relax a little as she ate. By the time they had packed up the last supplies and trooped out to the vehicles, she was a little more awake and a lot more settled. She was glad of that as she swung up into the cab, because it was clear her mother had slept even worse than she had and was cranky as a result.

The crew was a ragtag bunch, Kim had to admit. Her mom's big rig cabin—Shannon called it the tractor, which made sense of the phrase "tractor trailer," Kim thought—sat in the middle of a biker escort of sorts. Carol rode in the lead, followed by a couple of her men. Then the tractor, followed closely by Bill and Lee in the pickup truck, and Mutt riding in the space left in the truck bed. They were followed by the rank-and-file bikers—mostly men, but with a handful of women as well, riding one or two people to a bike. It was a small convoy with TimFist and Hannah driving in the lead, but at least it was company on the road.

They left Memphis in a slow but steady procession. Kim watched the landscape slide by with the window rolled down so she could enjoy the cool morning air.

They followed the map and the route Aunt Carol and Shannon had arranged the evening before as they wound their way over to Interstate 22/Highway 78. They planned to take that down southeast to Tupelo in what was pretty much a straight drive, unless they encountered a serious obstacle they needed to drive around.

At first the drive was easy. By now, all of them were old hands at skirting wrecks and avoiding roadblocks. Even Shannon's huge tractor wasn't much of a hindrance, especially now that they didn't have to contend with the fifty-two-foot trailer as well. It was even easier now that she had outriders to call back warnings about obstructions and extra hands to clear the road as they went.

About an hour or so down the road, Kim began to smell smoke. Everyone went quiet and tense as the smell got stronger. It was joined by the smell of burning upholstery, melted rubber, and chemicals. It was sharp enough that Aunt Carol called a stop while all of them pulled bandannas over their noses and mouths to filter the acrid stench.

Kim shared a look with her mother. "What do you think happened?"

"I don't know. Shouldn't be anyone out there to create a pileup that would smell like this. Not anymore. Wrecks from the disaster burned out a long time ago." Shannon's voice was muffled by the face covering, but Kim could still hear the worry in it.

Kim swallowed hard. "Maybe someone had a salvaged vehicle and it overturned. Blew a tire or something?"

"We can hope."

Kim tried to hold onto that hope, though a whisper in her mind told her it wouldn't—couldn't—be so innocuous.

The smoke got heavier until it was an actual haze in the air. Then they came around a bend in the road. Kim gagged, and not just from the smell.

It looked like a war zone or something out of a hellish nightmare. Wrecks had been pillaged, overturned, and set alight. Pieces of cars were strewn over the road, and the nearby buildings had been broken into with extreme violence. Doors gaped open along with the shattered glass that remained in the frames of destroyed windows. Fires still burned here and there among the wrecks and over the nearby ground until the stone and gravel of buildings and parking lots stopped it.

Kim's voice caught as she spoke. "What happened here?"

"Looters. Bandits. Ruffians. Take your pick, but it was nothing like natural forces, and it was nothing good." Shannon's voice was grim.

"How could anyone...?" Kim gulped. She'd done her fair share of looting and felt bad enough about that. How could anyone be so heedlessly destructive?

"I don't know, and I don't want to. The type of person who'd understand the motivations behind this is no type of person I want to be." Her mother's response was quiet. "I just hope there weren't any people around when whoever did this came through."

Kim could wholeheartedly agree. She knew as well as her mother did that the type of people who could cause destruction like this probably wouldn't leave much by way of survivors. And anyone who lived through this kind of carnage would probably wish they hadn't.

She and Lee had joked about the *Mad Max* way of the world over breakfast, but there was nothing funny about it now.

There was no conversation outside the tractor, and no one said a word in protest as they drove through the scene of the disaster then past it. Kim wanted a break to stretch her legs and relieve herself, but she'd far rather hold it than stop anywhere close to the grim scene they'd stumbled onto.

They drove until they were on the edge of the Holly Springs National Forest, and the smoke was a fading memory in their nostrils. It was only then that Aunt Carol directed the convoy to a small picnic area to take a break. Kim barely waited until the brake was engaged before she bolted from the truck and into the woods.

She was far from the only one. A lot of the bikers were staking out spots to do their business, and Mutt had bounced out of the truck bed and raced into the woods before the truck even finished rolling to a stop. Kim didn't blame her.

Kim made her way to a place close enough to see the trucks, but marginally out of view, and took care of her own business. Once she'd relieved herself and stretched, she made her way back to the convoy. Most of the bikers hadn't gone far, but there was no sign of Shannon or Carol, or any of the other women who'd ridden with them. Kim watched the woods for a moment, wondering if she could spot them, then meandered over to where Bill and Lee were digging out drinks and food for everyone to snack on.

"How we doing?" she asked.

"Not so bad," Bill said. "We've made good time as far as I can tell, and we're not hurting for any supplies, though I reckon most of the bikes could use a top off."

"Good thing you've got all those extra five-gallon fuel containers then." Kim grinned and hopped up onto the back end to help Lee dig out rations.

Carol and Shannon came back while they were distributing food and took their own portions, followed shortly thereafter by the rest of the women.

Kim studied the woods as she ate her nutrition bar and drank some water before loping over to her aunt. "Hey, Aunt Carol, do we have time to do some foraging?"

Carol snorted. "I wouldn't know what to look for, and neither would most of us." She glanced over the assembled bikers. "And I don't want to be off the road too long."

That was fair enough. Kim had learned about wild edibles during her time in Humboldt and on the road with Dennis—Survival 101, he'd said, was to not starve—but it made sense that the city-based motor-cycle club members didn't know about edible plants. When it came down to it, she was still learning. She'd probably take longer than she needed to while she double-checked to make sure she wasn't picking nightshade instead of choke berries or something. There might be wild blackberries or other easily recognized fruits and nuts growing in the woods, but she wasn't sure if they were in season yet, and there was no way to find out. Not out here on the road.

The time consideration left out hunting as well. Lee was a better hunter than she was, but even she knew they'd probably scared away nearby game, so it would take hours to even have a chance of shooting anything. Kim shrugged and set the thought aside for later. Maybe they could hunt and gather to shore up their supplies after they reached Tupelo.

But it did bring up an interesting idea. "Aunt Carol, I learned some things about hunting and foraging while I was on the road between Murray and Memphis. I've got some information in my packs as well. Do you think, after we get to Tupelo, we could get a crew together for food duty? I could show them how to get food that isn't prepackaged. It might be good to learn it before the store stuff runs out."

"Might be at that. Though getting those boys to chase anything that ain't booze or a woman, or a miserable attempt at hunting…" Aunt Carol shook her head.

Kim grinned. "It might be easier than you think. See the dandelions?" She pointed. "Just get them to gather those. I know how to fry 'em up like flatbread using some of the fat we got from the rabbit. It actually tastes pretty good, especially if you can add a bit of seasoning."

"Fried dandelions?" Carol raised an eyebrow.

"Yep." She spotted another flower at her feet, a small purple one that reminded her of a miniature honeysuckle. She picked it and held it out. "In one town where I stopped, they called these alesfoot. You can use them to brew beer."

"Huh. Some of the boys been pining after a good beer. Ain't much left out there." Carol took the flower with callused fingers. "You think you could teach these boneheads that sort of thing?"

"If I can't, I can find a bookstore or library that hasn't been too badly ransacked, or maybe something at a park visitor station, where I can get the information." Kim shrugged. "I can't promise the results will be great, but they'll be food. And beer."

Carol considered that. Kim let her think in silence. She might not be able to convince Carol that going nomadic was the right choice, but maybe her great-aunt and her mother would be more inclined to listen to her and trust her judgment if she could prove she had good suggestions for taking care of the crew.

Carol sighed. "I want to get to Tupelo before I make any decisions, but I'll think on it. Meantime, you talk to your mom and your tagalong friends. I can't deny it'd be good to have folk riding with us who know about getting food from somewhere other than a cheap diner or a grocery store."

Kim grinned and trotted away to where Shannon and Bill sat at a table, talking softly.

They rested for about an hour before Carol directed the crew to pack up and load up. While the men were packing, Shannon scanned the group, then went to the edge of the parking area. "Mutt! Mutt, get back here, you crazy dog!"

There was a moment where Kim feared the dog had gotten lost. Then there was a soft noise, and Mutt came bounding out of the woods with a scrap of fabric in her teeth. She ran over to Shannon and nudged at her with her massive head, demanding attention. Shannon scratched her ears for a moment before she reached down and tugged at the cloth. "What you got there, Mutt?"

The dog huffed and reluctantly let go of the cloth, allowing Kim to see it better. Underneath the drool, the fabric was a drab green with a patch of faded lettering on the very edge, where it had obviously been torn from a larger piece of cloth. Shannon frowned and moved to a table to lay the fabric out flat, so she could see the letters. Kim followed.

There wasn't much, just ragged edges and the letters *te Pen* stenciled in dirty white paint on the fabric. Shannon sucked in a sharp breath and went so pale Kim darted forward to make sure she didn't fall.

Kim stared at the fabric. It didn't look like anything special to her, let alone as terrifying as her mother found it. "What is it?" Shannon didn't answer, and after a moment, Kim gave her mother's shoulder a little shake. "What's wrong?"

"I thought the color looked familiar." Shannon traced the letters with a shaking hand. "If I had to guess, I'd say that's part of a label that says *Mississippi State Penitentiary*. They had uniforms this color for some of the work-duty convicts."

"State Pen." Kim took a breath, vaguely aware of activity around them ceasing as Carol, then Bill, then Lee and the rest of the bikers became aware something was wrong. "Dad?"

"Yeah." Shannon swallowed hard. Bill came up and put a hand on her shoulder. Carol stepped to the other side of the table to look at the fabric while Lee hovered near Kim's elbow with consternation on his face. "Has to be Andre, or someone connected to him, to be up this far from the prison instead of taking over down there."

"Andre doesn't wear prison uniforms," Lee said. "He had a couple shirts to use as rags for stuff when I traveled with him, but he didn't wear them."

Kim gulped. "Any chance he passed through here before and left it behind?"

Shannon shook her head. "No. I mapped the routes when I was trucking in case I ever got word he was out for some reason. Didn't want our paths to cross. This isn't a path he'd have taken traveling between the prison and Memphis, not unless he went well out of his way."

"He didn't. He came up the highway through Tunica." Lee hunched in on himself as everyone turned to him. "I only know because that's where I used to live. I met him while I was out trying to get some stuff." He rubbed one wrist in an absentminded fashion.

Silence fell over the group as everyone contemplated the words none of them were willing to say aloud.

At best, escapees in the area meant more enemies or more dangers to guard against. But the worst-case scenario, and the one they had to be aware of, was that the escaped convicts had joined Andre.

Kim had always known her father had connections among criminals. Ever since she'd been old enough to question the world around her, she'd known that. But it had always been a sort of abstract knowledge. In the aftermath of their first encounter, she'd assumed his contacts and networks had collapsed when he went to prison. If they hadn't, the disaster had accomplished that task anyway. She'd thought he'd attacked the scrapyard with Lee because there was no one else available to get dragged into his mad plans.

She hadn't thought about the fact that if one person could get out, more people could escape as well. Or the fact that five years was plenty of time for her father to find allies, or toadies, inside the prison. Just because they hadn't come with him initially didn't mean they'd never planned to follow him.

Kim felt a little sick at the thought. *How many escaped convicts are there? And how many of them joined my father?*

Carol finally broke the paralysis that held all of them with a huff. "Well, standing and worrying isn't gonna get us anywhere safer." She turned to the men gathered loosely around them and shouted, "Mount up and roll out!"

Kim nudged her mother out of her state of stunned terror and hurried to obey.

They left the fabric on the table, lying like a bad omen on the surface as they rode away. Kim was willing to bet that Aunt Carol, her mother, and Lee were all trying to avoid thinking of the same thing and having just as much luck as she was.

What's going to happen if Andre has convicts and maybe real psychos under his control, as well as a few minor gangsters and drug lords?

It was too bad the answer was as clear as the question, and just as hard to avoid thinking of.

There was only one thing guaranteed to come from Andre being allied with the darker criminal element—and it was nothing good.

14

AUSTIN/ANDRE

Andre hummed a little as he waited on the outskirts of Memphis. Today was the day at least one of his plans would come to fruition, if he'd judged his prison mates correctly, and the thought was enough to put him in a good mood. Even if he didn't achieve the desired results, the day was fine, and his empire was coming along nicely, with plenty of hangers-on like that new lackey of his, Austin.

The man was a barely passable excuse for a human being, but he was loyal, and he was obedient. He'd clearly been feeling worse for the wear when Andre had sent him out to scour the city for news, or any sign of Sarah, Carol, or Kim, but he'd gone nevertheless. He didn't even need any of the lessons so many men of Andre's acquaintance generally required.

A pity, but then there was little satisfaction to be had from pounding a weakling like Austin into submission. Far better for his talents to be used on some of the less compliant members of the criminal underworld in Memphis, such as the youngster who'd claimed leadership of the Crypt Kings. Beating him into shape and taking most of his weapons and drugs as tribute—that had been fun.

But that was the past, and though the memory was an entertaining one, he had other things to think of. It was unfortunate, but for all his prowess and skill, he was only one man, and his resources, while much improved, were finite.

But now it was time to see if his prison plans had materialized results.

He'd not been idle those five years. And though he'd not taken much time to explain matters before leaving the penitentiary, he had long since established plans among the inmates who were loyal to him, and even some of the more erratically tempered ones who were not. He'd always planned to return to Memphis to settle the score and build his kingdom on the ashes of his enemies.

That was why he'd told those who were interested, and worth cultivating, that there were opportunities if ever he gained his freedom and they theirs. Opportunities to have everything they wanted, and for some of them to exercise their darker appetites for carnage under his banner. The disaster he'd exploited for his escape had been unexpected, but the day before walking out, he'd told his followers to look for him in Memphis.

He'd hoped to be further along, with Sarah and the Gardenas dust under his heels, but no matter. If those he hoped to see came, they might find the hunt enjoyable—a good way to slake their bloodlust.

"Oi. Andre. That you?"

Andre smirked as a man in a torn green uniform with a pack on his shoulder and a gun in his hand emerged from the shadows of a nearby building. "Indeed. Welcome, Miguel. You are the first. I hope you are not the last?"

"Nah. There's others." Miguel grinned. "Got almost a whole block's worth o' crew for you, if you'll have 'em. Some from our wing, some from the *real* high security. And a couple from Special Quarters."

Andre smiled back, a thrill of delight humming through his veins like a song. "Excellent."

By the time Austin got back to the hotel, Andre had taken over. Austin had a wicked headache, worse than his hangover, and his left eye was swollen shut. Carol's brat of a niece had a nasty right jab, the little witch.

Cherry met him in the lobby and snickered. "Look at you. What, did you fall into your rig again?"

"Shut up." Austin scowled as he went to look for something semi-cold to put on his eye.

Cherry stopped laughing like a switch had been flipped. "All right, Austin, all right. Didn't mean to be disrespectful." She shuffled in place. "You want a hit or something?"

"Nah. Just want my bed." Cherry got out of his way, and he staggered toward the rooms he'd claimed as his own. Two minutes later, he was drifting off amid pleasant fantasies of payback and good living.

He was awakened a short time later by what sounded like a stampede going through the lobby. Barely coherent, he grabbed his blades and his guns and staggered out to see what was going on.

Bikers from every crew, from Black Rats to Crypt Kings, were scrambling out of the way as men Austin had never seen before took over the lobby. They were wearing what looked like ratty uniforms Austin couldn't place. Even that wasn't nearly as noticeable as the air of danger all of them exuded. There was a sense of casual violence the men carried with them, the kind that sent danger signals through Austin's booze-addled brain.

"Austin! There you are! I have a mission for you." Andre appeared, eyes bloodshot and face distorted by a warped and manic smile.

Austin blinked, trying to get his mind to work properly. He still had a headache and the lingering remnants of his hangover. "Uh, sure, boss. Who're the new guys? Don't think I've seen them around here."

Andre's smile was dangerous, and his laughter made some part of Austin's brain want to run screaming into the darkness and never come back. "Oh, these are my associates from the penitentiary. They elected to follow me and join my new empire."

"That's cool." Austin gulped and tried to sound enthusiastic. Inside, his stomach sank, and a sick apprehension snaked its way through him.

These guys were convicts like Andre. He was pretty sure these weren't the types of guys who went to jail for tame stuff like grand theft auto or robbing banks.

"Is it not? They make fine warriors."

"Hey, Atkinson. Where are we bunking?" one of the men called out. He was a big fellow, not as big as Andre, but still large and muscled enough to snap Austin in half like a chicken bone.

"Oh, wherever you like. Make yourselves comfortable. I'm sure the others will be more than happy to accommodate you." Andre looked at Austin then made an offhand gesture in his direction. "Speaking of which, this is Austin, my liaison with the local gangs, and my second-in-command. I may ask you to accompany him on jobs for me from time to time. I trust that won't be a problem."

The convicts muttered agreements, and Austin clenched his jaw to prevent himself from shouting out a denial, knowing anything he wanted to say would make him look weak.

Oh, heck no! I don't wanna have anything to do with these guys! One wrong move, and I'll be toast!

After a minute or so, the new arrivals dispersed to find rooms. Austin watched them go, then turned to his boss. "You said something about a job for me?"

"Yes." Andre smirked. "Tonight, we shall begin my plans for expansion."

"You mean like taking over some of the outskirts of Memphis?"

Andre chuckled. It sounded a little unhinged. "Nothing so banal and limited. No. You recall our discussion about the Tupelo chapter?"

Austin thought. His mind was still clouded from the booze, but he did recall something along those lines. "Yeah, sure boss."

"Tonight, I want you to take some of the men and ride to Tupelo to speak with the president of the chapter there. Give him my ultimatum: join our new order, or perish."

He'd rather stick his head in a sewer, especially if Andre was thinking of sending the convicts with him. He took a deep breath and winced at the stabbing pain in his head. That gave him an idea. "I'm all for it, boss, but I gotta admit, I ain't at my best. That beating I took from Bulldozer Keith and all…not sure I'm good for a longer ride just now. I don't want to disappoint you."

"Oh, you won't. As for your condition, I have just the thing." Andre dug into a pocket and tossed him a dime bag of coke, followed by another. "A little bit of this should help you feel ready for anything. You get that into your system while I select the men to go with you."

Andre strode off. Austin watched him, then plopped at the nearest table. He wasn't thrilled about spending a night on the road with a bunch of lunatic escapees from prison. He'd rather see if he could lure

Cherry into his bed, but orders were orders, and he wasn't going to risk his position or his skull by disobeying.

At least he got some coke to smooth out the aches and give him a pleasant ride. Austin tapped out a little powder from a bag onto his hand and inhaled it with a deep, satisfied sniff, then tucked the rest away for later.

By the time Andre returned with the cadre of men who were going with him and got the supplies sorted out, Austin was high as a kite and ready to ride. He didn't even mind when Andre took one guy aside to give him orders in a low tone he couldn't hear. Andre was the boss, after all. If he wanted to give someone extra work to do, that was his right.

Together, he and the newly armed convicts trooped outside and grabbed bikes. There were plenty, including Austin's beat up old rig, which he'd kept around as a spare. Austin waited for all the men to get settled, scornfully noting the ones who seemed uncomfortable. Clearly, they were newbies to the brotherhood of the road. Too bad for them if they thought he was going to ride easy or play nice. They'd just have to keep up and keep the whining down.

Austin raised a hand and revved his engine. "Let's ride, boys!"

Roaring engines answered him, and the ragtag group peeled out and burned rubber into the night, laughing as they went.

Three hours later, Austin rolled into the parking lot of The Spoke and took a deep breath as he kicked his kickstand down. The night ride had been invigorating, and they'd had plenty of fun stopping to cause mayhem on the way. Between that and the cocaine he'd huffed any chance he got, he was feeling good. Even the bruises felt more like a badge of honor, proof that he was a tough guy.

There was no one there to greet them as he and Andre's chosen crew pulled up to The Spoke, but that didn't bother him. He knew this watering hole was Toad's favorite, and the rigs parked by the door showed that the Tupelo chapter prez was in residence.

Austin gestured for the convicts to fall in behind him as he swaggered up to the door and shoved it open. He smirked as every Black Rat in the place turned to look at him.

Some of them relaxed when they saw his patches. Austin made note of them. This might be an easier job than he expected. But even if it wasn't, he had the muscle to get the job done, and these fools were already off guard, expecting him to be one of them.

They were in for a rude awakening, in that case, because he was a *real* Black Rat—a king of the road. They'd see the difference soon enough.

He strode forward and eyed a nearby Black Rat. "Hey. I need to speak to your prez, Toad."

The biker sneered. "Who says Toad wants to talk to you?"

Austin pulled out the large, gleaming gun Andre had encouraged him to take from the arsenal he'd collected and pointed it at the biker. "I say Toad wants to talk to me. I got a message from the leader of the Memphis chapter."

"Horse crap you do." A gravelly voice made him turn to see Toad standing in the back doorway, gray hair under a bandanna and the beginnings of a beard on his jaw. His dark eyes were bloodshot and filled with ire as he glared at Austin. "Bruno knows better than to threaten me and mine. He wouldn't send a punk like you down here with any message." Toad was fingering a knife at his belt, a not-so-subtle reminder that he had wicked aim with a throwing blade. "You drop that gun, brat, before I make you regret it."

Austin shrugged and lowered his arm. "I wouldn't use it unless your fools forced me to. I respect you well enough, Toad."

"If that were true, you wouldn't be waving guns around in my territory." Toad spat on the floor, close enough for Austin to bristle at the blatant disrespect. "Give me your message and get out. And don't think Bruno won't hear about this, punk."

Austin sneered. "You could send him word, but it won't matter none. Bruno's dead and buried, unless he burned along with his base. Memphis has a new chapter prez." He moved closer, staring at Toad. "He sent me here to tell you the Black Rats need to be united under one banner and one leader. He wants to invite you to join up with him and ride under his leadership."

"And if I don't?"

"Then there's consequences, and you won't like them." Austin could feel his nerves singing, itching with the need for action. He kept himself still.

"Hmm." Toad raked him with a faintly contemptuous look. "Why don't you tell me the name of this new president? And don't try to give me yours, Austin Wallace, 'cause you don't have the chops."

Austin felt his skin flush with anger, but he kept his voice steady and tried not to rise to the bait. He tilted his head in pride. "New prez of the Memphis chapter is Andre Atkinson."

He was expecting Toad to frown, maybe flinch and show a little fear, if he knew Andre. He wasn't expecting Toad to break into scornful, mocking laughter. "Andre? That obsessive, creepy, fussy weasel? I never saw such a useless waste of space and bad temper before or since. He was always running around behind our backs, trying to sell drugs, guns, and jackets to kids to buy their loyalty. I never knew what Bruno saw that made him think it was worth taking the punk into his crew. Sure as heck didn't think his girl'd marry the cur. Figured he must have got her drunk or drugged to get her to agree to be his old lady."

Austin's lip curled in a snarl. "Don't insult the boss."

Toad laughed again. "He ain't my boss, boy, and he ain't ever gonna be. You can tell him that. I wouldn't bend my neck to anyone, but sure as heck not a rough-necked, bad-tempered, limp-between-the-legs piece of chicken crap like him."

The mirth faded as Toad regarded Austin again. "I'll be honest, boy. You look like a yellow-livered scrap as far as I'm concerned, and Andre's welcome to keep ya. But if you've got any sense in that drug-crazed skull of yours, you'll get out and find somewhere else to do your drinking and someone else to do it with. Andre's a delusional madman with pretensions of leadership. If he's calling himself the prez of your chapter, then soon there won't be any chapter left. He'll destroy it, and everyone with him. That's what he does."

Austin clenched his jaw. "You're wrong."

"You wish I was wrong. There's a difference." Toad shook his head and started to turn away. "Dig your own grave, brat. I won't be part of it."

The clear dismissal was enough to push Austin into a boiling fury. "Hey, Toad."

The Tupelo chapter prez looked at him. Austin raised his gun and fired. He was too close to miss, and the back of Toad's head exploded as a neat circle of red blossomed above his eyes. The former head of Tupelo fell dead at Austin's feet.

He sneered and kicked the body. "Guess I'll be digging your grave instead." His gaze flicked to the thugs waiting with barely concealed anticipation behind him, then to the stunned bikers around them.

Triumph and a sort of heady feeling, a lot like being drunk, swept over him, and he grinned savagely at the men who'd accompanied him. "Grab the women. As for the men..." His gaze slid over the horrified faces of his former compatriots under the Black Rats patch. "Time to join or die, boys. Your choice. You can tell my associates which one you choose."

The man nearest to Austin lunged at him, swinging a pool cue with a wild scream of fury. One of the convicts intercepted the biker and plunged a nasty-looking hooked blade into his gut. The biker folded in half, gurgling for breath, eyes wide with pain as he tried to clamp his arms over the wound. He collapsed with a choked scream as the convict ripped the blade back out.

Austin stared, feeling strangely numb as he wiped blood off his face. "Guess he decided to die." Then he continued to the door and stepped outside.

He pulled one of the cocaine bags out of a pocket and took a hit, listening with morbid curiosity as screams erupted from inside The Spoke, along with the sounds of fists striking flesh, blades colliding, and the occasional gunshot. Violence didn't excite him much, not near as much as a good drink or a good shag, but there was no reason not to let the lads have their fun.

Eventually, it went quiet. One of the convicts stepped outside, blood-splattered and grinning wildly. "Decisions have been made, Second. What do you want us to do?"

Austin shrugged, then strode back inside. A line of women and some men were kneeling at the bar under the watchful eyes of Andre's men. The rest of the room was drenched in blood and gore, with bodies everywhere.

He looked over the survivors with a dispassionate eye. "You know the rules. Swear your oath to the Black Rats, and to Andre. You serve, you ride, and you die at his command from now on. Your women are his to do with as he pleases. So are your spoils, your gear—whatever he wants. Serve well, and you might rise in the ranks. Serve poorly, or try to argue with the prez, and you'll be punished."

He walked up to the first man in the line. "Kiss my boot and swear your oath."

One by one, each man bent his head and promised to serve Andre. Every woman swore to serve the Black Rats as needed.

Once the oaths were done, he waved his men over. "Grab the booze and whatever else you want. We'll have us a little refreshment before we head back to Memphis. Get them to load their bikes with the spoils, but make sure they don't try anything funny, like making a run for it. When we're done drinking, we'll set this place on fire and burn it to a husk—with one exception. We need to make an example." He saw appreciation in the eyes of the thugs and felt a swell of pride.

It really was easy to lead men properly if you did it the way Andre did.

His eye fell on the body of Toad. He grinned coldly and pointed at it. "Get two of the boys to haul that outside. I got an idea that will make sure *everybody* knows Andre means business."

15

KIM NAKAMURA

When they finally reached the outskirts of Tupelo, it was afternoon, and Kim was restless. Shannon hadn't been in the mood for conversation ever since the stop where they'd discovered the scrap of prison uniform.

Kim tried to tell herself they didn't know for sure that it was part of a uniform from Mississippi State Penitentiary. The color and the lettering could be coincidental. Or it could be a convict who had nothing to do with her father.

Suppose most, or all, of the prisoners held in the same place as Andre had escaped. Surely, they had come from all over the country, or at least the state. It was only reasonable to think they'd scatter in all different directions. Why shouldn't some of them have headed somewhere that meant they'd have to move through the Holly Springs National Forest? They were on a major road, so it made sense for anyone traveling this way to pass through the same area.

Anyone could tear a shirt. Maybe there was some high-level white-collar criminal who'd come in this direction.

Kim grimaced at her reflection in the window. The words sounded good in her head, but she couldn't convince herself to believe them. She didn't really believe in coincidences, and finding a scrap of shirt from the same prison that had housed Andre was too close to a coincidence for her. She knew her mother and her great-aunt felt the same way.

Besides, Andre had spent five years in that place, and all of them knew he could build up a following held together by admiration, avarice, and fear far quicker than that. Bill was the only one who wasn't aware of what her father was truly capable of. He'd only encountered the man that one time, at the scrapyard. The incident had been violent, chaotic, and destructive, but it was nothing compared to the devastation Andre could cause when he combined his penchant for violence with his innate charisma and incredible persuasiveness.

He was also vindictive, something Kim and her family had known even before he went to prison. It was obvious, at least to her, that he'd always planned to return to Memphis to take his vengeance whenever he escaped. The question was how far he would take it. And what sort of help he might have amassed in prison.

At least Tupelo was quiet, with no sign of the chaos and noise that had filled Memphis. They might actually get some sleep tonight instead of being woken up by lunatics roaring around.

Kim's thoughts stuttered to a halt as the deeper meaning of them hit her. Tupelo was quiet.

"It's too quiet. This can't be a ghost town, can it?" Shannon voiced the very thought that had just occurred to Kim.

"People could just be inside their houses," Kim ventured. "Maybe they're staying indoors for some reason?"

"Maybe, but that's a whole different kind of ominous if they are." Shannon's voice was grim. "This long after the EMP, most people won't have supplies laid in. They don't have air conditioning, so by this time of the day, they should be looking for a breath of fresh air. They should be out foraging and scavenging for whatever it is they need, or whatever they can find. They should be out defending their spaces or trading what they've managed to find or make that might be of use to someone."

That was true. Kim had seen it in every town she passed through on the way to Memphis, and most of the towns between Memphis and Tupelo. The only exception had been the burned-out town. The thought made her swallow hard. "You don't think...?" She let the rest of the words die away.

"We can hope not, but if this place has been sacked like the others, we'll see signs before long."

About two blocks farther along, Kim spotted a few people ahead. She was just about to point them out and suggest they stop and ask if there was trouble in town when one of the individuals looked up, presumably at the sound of their vehicles.

Even at a distance, Kim saw the fear in their postures. All of them turned and bolted away from the street as if they'd spotted the devil himself.

Kim exchanged a glance with her mother. Even if the silence hadn't made them both suspicious, the behavior of those people would have. The tractor and the truck with their loads of boxes were clearly visible, and even in the dangerous times they lived in, it would have made more sense for residents to flock to the bikes and ask for assistance. Instead, it looked like they were too scared to do so.

A few blocks later, they turned into Tupelo's downtown. Kim caught her breath in horror.

There weren't any fires this time, but the shops and buildings around downtown looked as if they'd been caught in a battlefield. There wasn't an intact window to be seen, most of the doors had been violently smashed open, and the interiors had been completely destroyed. Kim was certain she saw bullet holes in some of the walls and doors, along with suspicious splashes that could be blood.

The sight was grim. They stopped briefly, and Aunt Carol pulled her bike up to the window with Bill on her other side so they could communicate. "We gotta get to The Spoke. I can't imagine why Toad would let this sort of thing happen in his territory."

"Are we sure your friend is still in charge?" Bill's question was quiet and respectful, but Aunt Carol bristled like a cat faced with a strange dog.

"No way would Toad step down in the face of a disaster like the one that hit a few weeks ago, no more than my Bruno would have. He was prez when I was last able to contact him, and he's still the prez as far as I know. I don't know how this happened, but I'm thinking that Toad's response to this kind of stupidity is what has folk so skittish." Carol huffed. "Foolish of him, but we gotta keep order somehow, I guess, and every crew has a few loose cannons."

After a moment, she revved her bike back up and kicked off the brake. "Let's just get to The Spoke. We can sort it all out there." With that, the convoy started up again.

The rest of the ride to the clubhouse for the Tupelo Black Rats was quiet and filled with tension. Kim knew her mother was thinking along the same lines she was—either Toad wasn't the man her great-aunt thought he was, or something was wrong.

She just hoped it was something simple. Maybe the bikes had run out of gas and the loss of their rides meant the Black Rats of Tupelo couldn't keep order like they did in Memphis. In that case, the Memphis convoy could help out, and they'd be able to restore some order to the town.

They turned down the street to The Spoke, and Kim noted the number of bikes parked there. It looked like it might be most, if not all, of the crew, assuming that the Tupelo chapter was around the same size as the Memphis chapter. Maybe things were all right after all, and they just needed a little support to get everything straightened out.

That thought lasted until they pulled into the parking area and Kim caught sight of Aunt Carol's expression. The sudden, sick look was all it took to make her shove open the door and jump out.

The smell hit her first. Sickly sweet and metallic all at once, overlaid with a scent like meat starting to go bad and the smell of an uncleaned portable toilet. She gagged and shoved her hand over her mouth and nose. She wasn't the only one to do so, and Lee staggered away to retch violently a few yards from the truck. Behind her, Mutt whined and hunched down behind the seats instead of jumping out of the sleeping space and dashing away to stretch her legs like she usually would. The women riding with the bikers huddled together, frightened and on the verge of fleeing. The men didn't look much better, though several of them were attempting to look grim and stoic instead of sick and scared. Everyone who had a weapon was reaching for it, eyes wide and wary.

The door of the bar was open, and through it Kim could hear a low droning sound and see half-dried pools of something red.

Please be wine, please be wine. This is a bar. Please let the bikers have gotten drunk and broken a few bottles before passing out.

Then one of the men from their convoy—she thought he was called Sprocket—swore in a strangled voice. "Son of the devil and a rabid dog...who'd..." His voice choked off as he joined Lee in puking off to one side.

Aunt Carol's eyes weren't on the mess inside The Spoke. They were looking off to one side. Kim started to follow her gaze, but Shannon dove in front of her. "Kim, no, you don't need to see this. Get back in the truck and don't look any closer."

If her mother had been a taller woman, she might have succeeded in keeping Kim from seeing what had them all so unnerved. If Kim hadn't lived through the events in Humboldt, she might have joined Lee, Sprocket, and a few of the other men in throwing up everything they'd eaten at the rest stop.

As it was, all she could do was stare in mute horror at the sight before her.

Bill had been right. Toad was no longer the prez of the Tupelo Black Rats. From what she'd glimpsed inside The Spoke, there might not be a Tupelo chapter left. But it didn't matter whether there was a crew left or not.

Hanging from the nearest telephone pole, like some macabre sign or a sick reenactment of the Wild West, was Toad's body, his sightless eyes staring in silent accusation and rage from beneath the bloody hole someone had put through his skull.

16

SHANNON GRAYSON

S hannon had seen a lot of things that made her feel queasy, most of them having to do with her ex-husband. This was easily near the top of the list.

Someone had shot Toad execution-style and strung him up as a warning. That was bad enough. They'd trashed The Spoke too, from the look of it. So it wasn't some lone lunatic running around. Doing this much damage took manpower, and she didn't think it came from someone in Toad's crew looking to stage a coup. They'd have done it properly, not like this.

Any rat, Black Rat or not, could tell you not to foul your own base.

That made the bikes parked out front a lot more ominous. Either the whole chapter had been present and was now dead, or there was someone still here. Whether they were the people who'd done this or not, they weren't likely to be friendly.

Shannon swept her gaze across the bikes, and her heart skipped a beat. Some of them looked far too familiar, particularly a tricked-out rig near the door. *Mouse droppings but that looks like the rig that scumbag Austin was riding.*

Aunt Carol grabbed the gun she always rode with and stormed toward the door of The Spoke. "You yellow-bellied scum! That man was one of ours! You get out here and you answer to me for what you've done, or I'll set this place alight and make it your funeral fire!"

She fired into the building. Once, twice—she got off seven shots before Shannon could grab her arm.

There was no time to think any further, and this was no place to linger. Shannon whirled around. "Everyone get back to your rigs! We need to leave now," she shouted as she pulled Carol to some cover.

Shannon made it just in time. No sooner had she yanked Carol back than whoever was inside the bar recovered their wits and fired back. From the hail of lead that came toward them, there were a lot of people shooting back.

Members of the convoy returned fire, but their attack was thin and scattered compared to what the occupants of The Spoke were sending their way. Shannon spared a moment to wonder where they'd gotten their weapons and ammunition, then decided to worry about more important matters, like getting out of their current predicament alive.

Shannon dragged Carol back to where Kim was tucked close to the truck. "We need to get out of here. We don't know how many there are, but they've got a better position inside and better firepower. We need to regroup elsewhere."

Carol's jaw was tight. "Those scum—"

"Are gonna do to us what they did to Toad if we don't get outta here." Shannon scowled at her aunt, then turned to Kim. "Can you get folks moving? Get them back on their bikes and get the bikes in the shelter of the tractor and Bill's truck so they're a little safer."

"Sure." Kim nodded then pulled out her pistol and fired toward The Spoke before she darted away, moving like a rabbit running for a warren.

Shannon met Carol's eyes. The older woman still looked ready to kill someone, anyone, and Shannon shook her head. "Can't avenge Uncle Bruno or Toad if we die here."

Finally, Carol nodded and turned to head back to her bike.

Kim was already coaxing the rest of their crew back into safer positions, and for a moment, Shannon dared to hope it was over and they could get away without further incident.

There was an indistinct shout from inside the bar, and seconds later, men started pouring out of it. Shannon took one look and swore. Some of them were dressed like bikers, but all of them looked like thugs. One of them was wearing a familiar green-colored shirt. And there were more of them than she wanted to face in a shoot-out or a brawl.

"Back on the bikes and let's ride!" Carol's shout echoed over the din.

"Get 'em boys, and make 'em pay!"

The voice sounded like Austin's, but Shannon wasn't about to look closer to make sure. She was too busy watching out for Kim, who was headed back toward her; Bill, who was hanging behind the door of the truck and holding it open to provide a better shield; and Carol, who was bulldozing her way toward her bike with grim determination.

"Look out!" To Shannon's surprise, Lee darted out from cover and straight toward Aunt Carol. He cannoned into her, and both of them crashed to the ground not two feet from Carol's rig. Lee yelped in pain and grabbed at his shoulder.

Shannon's breath caught as she saw red spreading across Lee's sleeve where he'd been hit. If he hadn't tackled Carol when he had, her aunt probably would have taken a bullet to the chest or gut.

Carol rolled and got into a crouch, partially sheltered by the bike. She hesitated a moment, then hauled Lee up and slung him onto the back of her bike while somehow managing to get herself in the seat at the same time. "Hold on, boy." The engine cranked, and Carol gunned it, pulling her bike around in a tight arc to race for the road. Lee clung to Carol for dear life as the bike roared out of the parking lot. The rest of the crew hurried to follow her lead. Bill was barely two seconds behind the bike carrying his rescued stray.

Kim was in the tractor by that point, so Shannon hauled herself in and cranked the engine. She backed up in a tight quarter circle that allowed her side of the cab to become an improvised shield for the rest of the bikers as they scrambled onto their rigs and headed for the road.

The attacking men didn't waste their bullets after the first few shots. Instead, they headed for their own bikes to give chase. Shannon's last sight before she spun the tractor around and followed her aunt was Austin's pasty face glaring at her as he clambered onto the shiny bike she thought she'd recognized.

Less than a minute after they'd taken to the road, the tractor rejoined Aunt Carol's posse in flying down a stretch of some highway or another. Shannon thought they were safe.

The thought lasted until a bullet zinged past her door and cracked into her side mirror. Shannon's stomach flipped.

Austin and his lunatics were actually in pursuit, trying to drive them off the road or gun them down. *That crazy, misbegotten son of a weasel and a wharf rat!*

Bullets flew haphazardly, and Shannon could barely tell who was firing in which direction. She did, however, notice when a bullet shattered the glass on Kim's window. "You okay?"

"I didn't get hit by the bullet. Nothing else is serious." Kim's voice was short as she brushed glass from her hair and clothes. Behind her, Mutt made an unhappy woof. Some distracted, semi-hysterical part of Shannon's mind made a note that they'd have to be careful of cleaning the glass up so Mutt wouldn't cut her paws—assuming they survived the next few moments.

Shannon was turning her head to double-check that neither of her passengers was hurt when she saw the biker—not a biker, she realized a moment later, but a convict still in Mississippi State Penitentiary green and riding a bike—pull up alongside and aim a .45 at her daughter.

"Kim!"

Without thinking, Shannon threw the truck wheel to the side, whipping it into a hard right swerve that tossed both of them hard against their seat belts. The truck jumped like a startled horse and the tires protested as she used an engine meant for hauling multi-ton loads in a manner better suited for a bumper car in a melee.

The thug never had a chance as the full weight of the tractor sideswiped him hard and sent him flying.

Carol came up on that side a moment later to act as a shield. Some of the other riders followed her. The maneuver gave Kim a measure of protection, but it also opened up a hole in their convoy. Some of the pursuers took advantage of it and went straight for Bill's truck.

Shannon swerved back to try and cut them off, but two of them got past her. Bill sped up, obviously trying to shake them, but the bikes were faster and lighter than the old diesel truck, and their riders were a lot less careful than he was.

Seconds later, a lucky shot hit Bill's back tire and blew it out, sending the truck into a wide swerve before it flipped and rolled. It went through a full rotation, spilling fuel and supplies all over the road before it skidded to a stop in front of them, turned at a ninety-degree angle to the road.

His two assailants hadn't expected that, and they crashed hard. One lost control trying to avoid the madly twisting truck, and the other smashed into the back end when he couldn't slow down in time.

Shannon hit the brakes hard to avoid joining the small pile up. She heard several crunches and screams as the men who'd been hot on her tail failed to brake or evade the back end of the tractor. She grimaced at the sound. Hopefully they hadn't damaged too much of the equipment or the framework back there.

The sudden loss of a number of their comrades was enough to convince the marauding force that the pursuit wasn't worth the cost. There was a shot like a signal from farther back, and the whole group turned away in a ragged pack and swept back the way they'd come. Shannon didn't know if they were headed back to The Spoke or back to Memphis.

She also didn't care. For the moment, they were gone. The convoy was safe, and that meant they could stop and take a breath. They had a little time to figure out what the damage was and where they would head next.

She shut the tractor off and turned to Kim. "You hurt?"

"Scratches from the glass, maybe a couple bruises. Nothing serious. But we'd better check on Lec and Bill at least." Kim was already digging for the small pack full of medical supplies she kept on hand. Shannon felt a surge of pride at her daughter's levelheaded response to the situation. Her own hands were starting to shake as the rush of adrenaline faded.

They exited the cab, and Shannon hurried toward the overturned truck while Kim went to Carol's bike to see to Lee. Mutt bounded back and forth between the two of them, whimpering and clearly unsettled by the smells of blood and burned rubber around them. Shannon found Bill levering himself out of the battered driver's side door with a grunt, one arm tucked close to his side.

"You all right?" she asked.

Bill grimaced. "Feels like I might have torn or dislocated something in my right shoulder. But I think I'm all right otherwise." He finished dragging himself free of the wreckage with a scowl at the damage. "Truck's pretty bad off. Don't know that I'll be able to get her on the road again." He looked closer at the twisted framework of the truck bed, now empty of most of the boxes it had carried. "And the supplies—"

"We'll deal with the supply recovery later. Get your shoulder looked at first. Kim's over by the big rig tending to Lee."

Bill's eyes widened with worry. "I saw him go down. How bad is he hurt?"

Shannon shook her head. "I don't know. Let's go find out."

They left the ruin of the truck where it was sitting on the road and went back to where the others had clustered around the tractor in various states of shock and dismay.

Kim was just finishing up with Lee's arm when they arrived. Shannon let her finish before speaking.

"What's the damage?"

"Mostly bruises and scrapes on our side. Lee got clipped by a bullet, but it wasn't bad. Didn't even need stitches in the end, just butterfly tape and a wrap." Kim's gaze flicked upward. "Bill?"

"Just some bruises and a shoulder that could use looking at when you've got a moment."

Bill sat down on a proffered bike seat while Kim poked at his shoulder along with his head, torso, and both legs. "I'm all right other than the shoulder, Kim."

"I'm sure you think that. But something I learned getting certified as a first responder is that most people think they're all right just after a major incident, and they might not be. Shock and adrenaline can hide the first warning signs of serious injuries. For example, did you know you've got deep bruising from the seat belt?" She prodded a section of Bill's chest.

Bill winced. "Guess I do now."

"Yeah. But it probably saved you from worse." Kim came back to the injured shoulder. "Okay, try and move this for me. Start by trying to lift your arm above your head."

Bill complied but dropped it with a wince before it reached halfway. "Don't think I can."

Kim guided him through a few other movements while her fingers poked at the joint. "Yeah. It's dislocated. We can try and rotate it back in so it'll heal, but you're going to be hurting for a few days."

"Go ahead. It isn't my first popped joint, and it probably won't be my last." Bill nodded agreeably, but Shannon saw the sheen of sweat and the slightly pale cast to his face.

Kim prodded at the joint a few more times, then directed two of the bikers to assist her as she carefully rotated the shoulder back into alignment. Shannon couldn't quite see what she did, but there was a push from Kim, and a sharp pull from the bikers, and a low crunching sound. Bill's shoulder popped back into the socket, and she wasn't the only one to wince at the sight and sound as the bones settled back into place.

Bill grunted as if he'd been kicked in the gut. "Lord have mercy but that does hurt." He sighed and shifted the shoulder in a testing motion. "Still, feels better than it did. Thank you, Kim."

Kim fished in her bag for some bandaging and growled when she came up short. "I need more tape and gauze."

Shannon nodded. "We need to check the supplies anyway. Rig him up a splint till we can find your medical stuff."

She and Carol went around to look at the back of the tractor first. She thought she remembered a bullet or two impacting the supplies, but she hadn't had time to investigate.

Two boxes had holes, and one had been blasted so thoroughly the side wall looked like it had exploded. It was a miracle they hadn't lost the entire contents of the box all over the road. A quick inspection showed they'd lost some of their food and some of the spare parts, as well as a few gallons of fuel. They'd also lost part of one of her tires, though as a truck tire it wasn't as bad as it could have been.

Luckily, their medical supplies were still intact. Shannon dug out a length of bandages for Kim and antibiotic ointment for scrapes that might have been acquired. Kim finished tending to Bill and the bikers while Carol and those who were mostly uninjured looked over the vehicles.

Most of their bikes were a little dented and scraped, and two or three had bullet marks, but they were intact and running. The same was true of Shannon's tractor, though that had a few more bullet holes from where she'd acted as a shield during their flight from The Spoke. A quick check showed that if there was any damage to the engine or suspension, it wasn't severe enough to take the rig off the road.

Bill's truck was a different story. The tire that had been blown had shredded completely, and the inner rim was bent. Most likely, so was the axle, if it hadn't been broken by the jolting. The supplies he'd been carrying were scattered all over the road, despite being tied down. None of the full gas cans had been hit by gunfire, but most of them were damaged and had leaked the contents all over the road and the dirt by the wayside.

All in all, they'd lost about twenty or thirty gallons of stored fuel, three-quarters of a box of ammo and parts, about three meals' worth of food, and the truck itself. It could have been worse, but it was still a fair amount of losses. And that didn't count what they'd lost in terms of spent ammo at The Spoke or the fuel they'd burned in their escape.

They'd also lost any hope of allies or shelter at The Spoke. The presence of criminals and Austin made it clear there was no safety there, and probably nothing left of the Tupelo chapter of the Black Rats.

On the plus side, their convoy had taken out at least half a dozen of their opponents. The riders who'd wrecked hadn't survived the impact, leaving their gear for members of the Memphis Black Rats to salvage. That meant extra guns and some food they'd been carrying. The saddle bags also carried booze and drugs. TimFist took the alcohol to drink or trade. Kim took some of the pot and opioids, which she said could be used as emergency painkillers. The stronger drugs, especially the cocaine packets, Carol glared at in disgust before dumping them with Hannah's help into the nearest and deepest puddle of gasoline to render them useless.

Aside from the bike that had plowed into Bill's pickup and the one that had hit Shannon's tractor, the bikes were usable. They could be ridden, or they could be stripped down for parts later as needed.

Carol stared at the reclaimed rigs, her expression stoic. "Guess we'll need to take a couple for the kid and the mechanic, once they're good enough to ride solo."

Shannon was about to voice her agreement, over Bill's denial, when Carol's mask cracked. "God above, I was so stupid. You warned me. You all warned me. You and the kid and the mechanic and Kim—you all told me not to depend on Tupelo, not to risk coming here without a backup plan. And I went ahead and plowed ahead like a boneheaded fool."

Shannon swallowed hard and bit back the recriminations on the tip of her tongue, even as the other women in the crew gathered around their leader. It was easy to chastise Carol now, but it was clear her aunt felt the weight of her mistake all too heavily on her shoulders, on top of her grief for Bruno and now for Toad.

"We didn't know it'd be like this," Shannon said.

"But we knew Andre was a snake, and that he knew about the MC, and where the different chapters were. Knew he could guess we'd come this way. So he got here first, and now Toad—"

"Toad isn't your fault. Andre's power-hungry. He'd have tried to take over Tupelo eventually, and Toad never would have let him." Shannon moved forward to wrap an arm around her aunt's shoulders.

"We could have lost more than some supplies today on account of my foolishness. I was gonna charge that bar head-on if you hadn't stopped me. I could have got us all killed."

"But you didn't."

"But I could have. Could have got you shot, dragging me back, and Kim shot trying to get everyone to safety. I did get the kid shot, saving my fool hide." Carol's voice cracked, and tears began to drip across her weathered cheeks. "I screwed up. I screwed up bad." The rest of her words disappeared into a soft choking sound as she started to cry.

Shannon pulled her aunt close and let her cry. Carol had needed to get it out of her system since the scrapyard burned. Maybe this wasn't the best place or time, but she wasn't going to refuse her aunt any comfort she needed. Even Mutt crowded close and licked softly at Carol's hand before butting her head up under it, as if attempting to soothe her distress.

Kim and Bill started organizing the repacking of the supplies, both of them standing a sort of informal guard while Carol broke down in Shannon's arms. Lee helped as much as he could with that, though once or twice he glanced over in their direction, as if he was contemplating offering support but suspected it wouldn't be welcome.

Shannon sighed and leaned against the truck. They needed a plan. They needed a safe place to regroup at the very least. Ideally, they needed a place to set up a home again. The problem was that none of them had any idea where that should be.

They couldn't stay where they were. Sooner or later those psychos—and she would have been willing to bet the tractor's entire load of gas they were Andre's psychos now—would probably return. They'd be in a lot of trouble when that happened, unless they were elsewhere.

Where could they go and hope that Andre wouldn't follow, or find them immediately?

17

KIM NAKAMURA

G etting on the road took a while, but eventually everything was repacked. What could be salvaged had been gathered up and loaded, including some of the parts and supplies that had flown out of the damaged boxes in the fight. Two of the bikers, Sprocket and a well-built fellow called Jackalope, had gone back and searched out some of the lost equipment and brought it back.

Sorting out what to do with Bill and Lee was a tad harder. Neither of them knew enough to drive a motorcycle on their own, and even if they had, Bill's shoulder meant he wasn't up to the strain of controlling a bike on rough roads.

Shannon and Kim eventually decided Bill could ride in the cab of the tractor with them. It would be crowded, but not as bad as cramming all three of them into the pickup had been, not even with Mutt in the sleep space of the cab.

Carol, surprisingly enough, provided the answer to the issue of Lee. "He can ride with me. I can start teaching him the bike on the road. Once he's a proper rider, we'll have one less tagalong with us."

The offer startled all of them.

"Aunt Carol," Kim began.

Carol snorted. "I know what you're thinking. I've been riding the kid hard. But today taught me—again—that everyone can make a stupid mistake. At least he's got the excuse of being young and not knowing any better."

Carol's gaze shifted to Lee. The young man gulped, but held his ground, and Carol nodded. "You got spunk in you under that meek attitude of yours. Nerve's part of what a good rider needs out on the road. More than that, I owe you for taking a bullet instead of me, even if it was only a graze. You spilled blood for a Black Rat, and I'll admit, you've pulled your weight fair since the mechanic brought you in. So you ride with me, and we'll see if you've got what it takes to be an actual Black Rat instead of just a ride-along."

"You mean..." Lee's voice trailed off.

"Consider yourself a prospect, unless you don't like it or someone else has a problem with it." Carol glared at the men and women gathered around her. "I know it ain't usual, but it is what it is, and I'd be dead in the dirt but for Lee."

There was a rumble of voices, then Sprocket spoke up. "Ain't normal, sure, but does that mean the kid's still a gopher? We ain't gonna put aside all the prospect rules, are we?"

"Nah. Just the ones that might be bad for the crew, and the one saying he oughta have his own ride and the skill to stay on it before he becomes a prospect." Carol faced Lee. "If you pan out, you can pick a salvage for your own. You up for it?"

Lee cast a quick look at Bill, who nodded in approval. Lee grinned. "I like the sound of that."

"Then let's get going. We'll find materials for your jacket later."

Kim wondered if Lee knew what he was getting himself into. She'd seen how prospects were treated. They were everyone's dogsbody, more or less, gopher and maid and whatever else they were wanted for. After a moment, she shrugged. Lee could probably handle it, and if he couldn't, they'd probably let him fall back on being Bill's assistant mechanic.

Once that was decided, it was a matter of mounting up and getting back on the road. The smell of freshly burned rubber, spilled gasoline, and blood was disconcerting, but they left it behind as quickly as they could, and soon enough, they were back to the pace they'd maintained for most of the day—a steady glide down the road.

In their wild flight, none of them had paid much attention to where they were going. As it turned out, they'd wound up on Highway 45, southbound. With no other direction in mind, they kept going the way they'd started. They no longer had a set destination, and choosing a random route might throw off any pursuit by Andre.

Kim turned to ask her mother how long she thought they'd be on the road and caught her staring. "Mom?"

"Just thinking. About the attack." Shannon turned her gaze back to the road.

"That was a heck of a thing." Bill said. His eyes were troubled. "I never figured folk could act like that. Read about it, seen it on TV, sure, but I've never seen people hunting or hurting other people like that. Let alone—" He stopped, his throat working as he tried to clear it and remove the distress from his voice. "I've never been involved with that sort of thing before."

Kim grimaced in sympathy. "It's scary the first time. Scary every time, I guess. But we survived, and no one got too badly hurt, so that's a win, or at least as close as we can get to one." She patted his good shoulder sympathetically.

Bill shook his head. "We scraped six bodies off the road and the truck, and I don't know how many we left behind in that bar. Don't know I'd call that a win."

Kim was surprised when her mother spoke up. "It isn't. But it's like with Langmaid and Connor. Sometimes there is no better way to handle things. You get a person who's got nothing in their eyes but viciousness and greed and spite, and you have to put them down hard, or they bite you again."

Bill nodded. "I understand. Just wish it weren't true." From the back, Mutt woofed softly, as if she was agreeing with the mechanic.

"I know."

Kim looked between her mother and Bill, wondering about the story behind that exchange. It sounded like she wasn't the only one who'd had some adventures on the road to Memphis. But before she could ask, Shannon spoke again.

"You did well out there, Kim."

Caught off guard, all she could manage in reply was a startled, "What?"

"You did good. Getting folks to safety, staying out of danger as much as you could, then helping out with the wounded—you handled yourself well. Kept a cool head. I'm proud of you and how you took care of yourself and others in that situation."

Kim gaped. She'd expected to be fussed at for not being careful or told to watch her back more carefully. Maybe even scolded for not ducking further when the window got shattered. Instead, her mother complimented her.

It took a moment, but she mustered up a weak grin. "Yeah, well, I do my best, even if my mother is driving like an utter madwoman. You do know this is a tractor for an eighteen-wheeler and not a stunt car made for a movie or something?"

A small corner of Shannon's mouth twitched, and Bill snorted, as if trying to hold back laughter. "I'm pretty sure I know what I'm driving, yes."

"Are you sure? Because those were some pretty crazy moves. I mean, going broadside on a shoot-out, then that hard turn onto the highway," Kim imitated the turn with a swooping motion of her hand, "and then you sideswiped that guy with the gun, and he went flying! It was like you were in an action movie."

"I don't watch a lot of movies." Shannon wrinkled her nose.

"Mom!" Kim glanced at Bill with a pleading look. "Bill, help me out, here. Action movies are great, right?"

Bill grinned. "I don't know, Kim. I never was much for going to the movies."

Kim groaned. "Oh my gosh, I cannot believe you. Why? What do you people do with your time?"

"Read a book."

"Work on my projects."

She was about to throw her hands up in disgust when Bill started snickering. Shannon's mouth curved up in a wicked grin, the likes of which Kim hadn't seen since she was a child.

Kim huffed. "Very funny."

"I thought it was." Shannon gave her a quick glance.

Kim gave a melodramatic sigh and flopped back in an exaggerated manner. "Sure. Whatever. Just tell me you have at least heard of Vin Diesel?"

"Sure. I like action movies."

"Oh thank goodness." Kim relaxed fully into her seat, and the cab lapsed back into a more comfortable silence.

It was strange to think it had been a month since she'd last watched a movie of any kind. Even stranger to think she might never watch one again. These days, surviving was the most important activity. On any given day, there were about a hundred things that needed to be done and barely the time or resources to accomplish half of those tasks. That was on a good day. On a bad day, getting food and shelter to stay alive were pretty much the limit of what people hoped for. Things like finding a way to watch movies weren't high on anyone's list of priorities.

But what about a year from now? Five years? Maybe ten? Would it be like some of the survival movies she'd seen, where people used tricks like rigging projectors to bring back little pleasures like movie nights? Or would everyone just adapt to a world without luxuries like film? Assuming they were alive in five years, would people walk past old stashes of DVDs or television sets and smile at the quaint relics of the past, the way people her age laughed at boom boxes and vinyl record players before the blackout?

It was kind of a depressing thought. She looked for something else to think about.

Up ahead was a weather-beaten sign showing a man with a toothy smile. The text beneath the image stated GOD SHALL BEHOLD YOU, then, in smaller print, extolled the virtues of the "Righteous" Reverend Jeb Butler. Kim snorted in bemusement and disgust. The man looked like one of those sidewalk street preachers or TV evange-lists who cared more about saving your money from your pocket than anything else, at least in her opinion. Even if he was a legitimate man of God, she'd had her fill of "righteous" people back in Humboldt.

She'd almost rather deal with her father than another so-called righteous leader.

At least with Andre, she knew the attack was coming. She knew he was an evil psycho and had no delusions he might ever be anything other than a rabid monster who needed to be put down for everyone else's sanity and safety. Righteous people, however, were sometimes decent human beings with a little bit of a stiff spine, and sometimes vipers waiting to stick a knife in someone's back.

As far as Kim was concerned, both types of people were dangerous lunatics who could wipe each other out. She'd be happy to spend the rest of her days dealing with plain ordinary people like Bill, Lee, and the members of the Black Rats.

They passed the sign and drove into the town of New Wren, and Kim winced at the sight before her. She'd known, logically, that Tupelo and the nameless small town they'd encountered wouldn't necessarily be the only places the marauders had hit. But she'd had the impression that they were some gang allied with her father, and some part of her had hoped they wouldn't have gone and caused mayhem any farther south than Tupelo.

She'd forgotten her father's prison recruits, if that's what they were, must have come over from the west. The devastation that greeted the convoy in New Wren suggested the prisoners had stopped to have some fun along the way.

It could have been another gang. There were probably plenty of marauders out there to choose from. It could even have been some sort of reaction by the townsfolk to the disaster that had engulfed the world nearly a month ago—a wildfire of bad feelings or a fight over resources that got out of hand. People could get crazy when their entire world got upended. Kim knew that. Even so, her heart insisted it was most likely the doing of Andre's thugs as they made their way to Memphis to meet her father.

Whoever had destroyed New Wren had been thorough about it. They'd set fire to large sections of the town. The places where the buildings weren't burned-out husks all had missing windows and shattered doors. In a couple places, Kim thought she saw bodies. She looked away fast.

They drove through the town in silence. Bill looked sick. Her mother looked grimly stoic, as if she'd expected to see atrocities but wished she'd been wrong.

The other end of town had another one of those stupid billboards with the same guy's face tacked on it. Kim wondered if the idiot whose face was displayed had been here when the attack happened, then decided she didn't care.

There was a car on the side of the road, right next to the billboard, with a bundle of something thrown across it. It was such a common sight these days that Kim almost ignored it completely, until she spotted a thin curl of smoke rising from the hood. Then the "something" moved and resolved itself into a woman who waved a hand at them.

Kim pointed. "Mom, look. We need to stop."

"Again with this?" Shannon stared at her for a moment. "I told you before, we can't be stopping for every person you see. It's not safe."

Kim huffed impatiently. "Yeah, but maybe she's a survivor who can tell us what happened to the town. Isn't that important information? Plus, Bill needs a place to do repairs to the bikes that got damaged and to check the truck out. She might be able to guide us to a good place to set up."

Shannon frowned. "I don't know. You remember what happened with that man in Memphis."

Kim restrained the urge to try and take the wheel herself. "Come on. Even if she is some sort of crazy, there's only one of her. We've got the entire convoy on our side. She wouldn't be able to do anything before someone flattened her."

Shannon eyed her for a moment, then sighed and tapped the horn in the signal for "stop" they'd agreed on with Aunt Carol. "All right. But I'll be keeping a careful eye on her."

Shannon pulled the truck over to the side of the road and turned it off. The bikes circled around to form a perimeter as Shannon opened the door.

Mutt immediately shoved her way out of the sleeping area, scrambled awkwardly over the seats and their occupants to exit the cab, and bounded forward. To Kim's surprise, the woman showed no fear at the large dog racing toward her. She stood stock still and allowed Mutt to run a small circle around her, sniffing and huffing madly. When Mutt came closer to sniff her directly, the woman held out one hand to be sniffed and used the other hand to scratch the dog's ears.

"Aren't you a sweet girl? Good dog! Yes, you are a very good dog, taking care of your people." Her voice was mellow, somewhere in the alto range, with just a hint of roughness to it, like she'd been breathing smoke and hadn't quite got her lungs clear yet.

Kim watched the woman sweet-talk Mutt into a slobbering puddle of goodwill. She looked like she was somewhere between Kim's age and Shannon's, with light-brown hair just starting to show the first signs of gray and pale skin liberally dotted with freckles rather than tanned. She was dressed sensibly in jeans, shirt, and good walking shoes. She had a backpack on her back and a small, friendly smile on her face.

After a few moments more of petting Mutt, she looked up and gave them an abashed grin. "Sorry, sorry. I know I flagged you down and all, but when I saw this pretty girl come running, I got a little distracted." She patted Mutt on the head, "I had a dog a lot like her. Died recently, and of course there's been no chance to find another one, even if I wanted to replace her."

Kim could see the honest sadness in the other woman's eyes. It was apparent that Shannon could as well, because her voice was less hostile than Kim would have expected when she spoke.

"Sorry for your loss. My name's Shannon. You?"

"Rebecca Holden. Used to live in New Wren until a few days ago." She sighed. "I was trying to make a salvage trip, but it's a long road, and I didn't get as far as I hoped." She glared at the car she'd been sitting on and kicked one foot back to thump her heel against the tire. "Thought this old clunker would be worth a few miles more, but I guess not."

Carol spoke up. "Didn't look like there was much to salvage in New Wren."

Rebecca shrugged. "I could always hope. Most folks left without anything but the shirts on their backs, not even the basic necessities. That includes my father, and he needs his heart meds, which is why I made the trip." She hefted her pack. "But I'll admit, I could sure use a ride back to where we're staying, if you don't mind."

Kim stepped forward to take over the conversation before anyone could say anything too distrustful or awkward. "There's space on my mom's rig. But we were hoping you could answer a couple of questions for us before we get back on the road."

"Sure. Whatever you want to know," Rebecca said.

"Well, we were wondering what happened to New Wren. It looks like a huge fire went through part of it, but the rest…" Kim hesitated.

"Wasn't a fire, not like a natural disaster or an accident with someone's natural gas, if that's what you're thinking." There was a sharp note of bitterness in Rebecca's answer. "A bunch of thugs came through a few days ago from the west. Escaped convicts from Mississippi State Penitentiary, from the uniforms some of them were wearing."

Kim sucked in a sharp breath at the confirmation of her suspicions. Beside her, Shannon stiffened and went pale, her hands clenched in fists as Rebecca revealed that her worst fears had come to pass. Andre had indeed made allies in the prison and convinced some of them to spread out across the state and secure his territory.

Rebecca continued speaking, oblivious to the consternation her words had caused. "They rolled into town, maybe a dozen or more of them, and started demanding whatever they wanted. Food, beer, clothes, drugs, weapons—there wasn't a thing those monsters didn't demand. Didn't take." Her voice was sharp with an anger verging on hatred as she spat the words. "Then three of them cornered a couple of our girls. I saw the results—the wrecks they left behind. So did a lot of the town. That's when our town council—we had set one up to keep the peace three days after the blackout—attempted to bring the hammer down on those reprobates."

"Attempted?" Shannon's question was quiet.

Rebecca nodded, her mouth a grim slash and every trace of her previous good humor gone. "They tried to drive them out of town with the guns we had on hand. But we're a small town, and our town council were mostly elders. They didn't stand a chance. After they were dead, the scum went crazy and wrecked the rest of the buildings and anyone they could get their hands on."

"So you hightailed it for the hills," Carol said.

"Yeah." Rebecca looked defensive. "We don't have a lot of fighters, or a lot of weapons."

"You did the right thing. Those guys are dangerous." Kim said. "I'm sorry you had to go through that."

"The world's been getting more dangerous since that EMP event." Rebecca sighed. "We were just kind of hoping the worst of the danger would pass us by since we're such a small community."

"Ain't anywhere that's safe," Carol said.

Kim, however, was interested in something else. "You said everyone fled. Did you all go in separate directions, or did you set up a new community somewhere?"

Rebecca tipped her head to one side. "Most of us stayed together. We went back to 278 and east a bit, set up near the old Ed Grady sawmill a few miles out from here. We've been trying to establish a new settlement in that area. We're calling it Watchdog."

"Is there a place there we could get spare parts for the truck? And for some of our other vehicles? We had a run-in on the road with some of those same guys. They tried to force the truck over." Kim figured it was easier to say that than to try to explain the whole situation.

Rebecca frowned in thought for a moment, then her eyes brightened. "Oh, sure! I didn't think of it at first, because we don't have any vehicles, especially not now. But over on the southwest edge of town, there's a place called Big Ed's Gas and Auto Barn. It probably has everything you'd need to do repairs. Might even have fuel for your big rig." She grinned. "Big Ed's a friend of my dad's. If you want to come to Watchdog, I'll introduce you, and he can help you out with anything you need in that department."

That sounded almost too good to be true. Kim exchanged glances with her aunt and her mother, reluctant to commit to anything without seeking their approval first. After a moment of thought, both of the older women nodded. Kim turned back to Rebecca. "Could we trade a ride back for a guide to Big Ed's?"

"Sure." Rebecca grinned. "Heck, you could join us in the Watchdog community if you like. We're not large, but we're pretty good at taking care of ourselves, and we'd welcome some more hands to get everything running and keep it going. Plus, more vehicles to help with salvage, scavenge, and foraging efforts would be a huge help." Kim hesitated, and Rebecca continued. "You could also get a lot of good-will from the folks in Watchdog if you could help them recover things they were forced to leave behind. Medicines they need, clothing, keepsakes..."

Keepsakes. The word made Kim think of the oversized shirt in her backpack, as well as the guns and knives she carried, and the pack itself. All keepsakes of the companion, sometimes teacher, and protector she'd lost. She turned to her aunt and her mother. "Think we should give setting up a new place in Watchdog a try?"

"I'm willing," Carol said.

"I don't mind," Shannon nodded as well.

Kim offered her hand to Rebecca. "I didn't really introduce myself or anyone else earlier, but my name's Kim. Shannon is my mom. That older lady is my Aunt Carol, the big guy is Bill, and the younger guy riding with Carol is Lee. The rest of these guys and girls are friends and members of my aunt's club, the Black Rats. It looks like we're headed to Watchdog, and we'd be happy give you a ride and ask you to show us the way."

"Pleased to make your acquaintance, and I'd be happy to give you whatever directions you need." Rebecca shook her hand. "So, where am I riding?"

"Got your choice." Carol said. "We've spare rigs that are rideable, even if they aren't in the best condition. Or you can take your chance riding with someone who's got a free space on the back of their saddle. Same for riding on the back of Shannon's rig or squishing yourself into the front cab."

Rebecca eyed the various spots. "I think if you folks don't mind, I'll squish myself into the cab. I'm not much good on a motorcycle. Haven't ridden one except for a couple wild nights when I was in high school."

Bill smiled. "It might be tight, but we can make it work."

It was tight, especially with Bill in the cab, but with Kim and Rebecca in the center and Bill leaning out the broken window, it was tolerable, at least as long as Mutt kept to the sleeping compartment and didn't try to stuff her head over the seat to get her ears scratched.

The bikes circled back up as the truck rumbled to life, and they were on their way to their new destination—Watchdog.

18

SHANNON GRAYSON

S hannon's first impression of the newly formed community of Watchdog was not a favorable one. She might not know anything about the inhabitants of the ramshackle little town the survivors of New Wren had cobbled together, but she knew the signs of a group in dire straits.

The town buildings and homes were old, battered, and in need of repairs. A few had some paint clinging stubbornly to the weathered siding, but most were barely functional structures made of cracked bricks, worn concrete, and warped plastic or metal. Most had windows that were opaque with years of grime, broken, and inexpertly patched or not patched at all. The door of an antique store looked ready to crack under one good push, and most of the others were lopsided and had serious gaps between the door and the frame. If she didn't know better, she would have called the place a ghost town.

For that matter, the people who started peeking out of doorways and window frames as their vehicles roared down the narrow street weren't much more than ghosts. Everywhere she looked, she saw pale, wary faces and tired expressions. By the time they parked and turned off their engines, a few of the more adventurous people had started to emerge, but most were hanging well back.

Rebecca was the first to climb from the cab after Shannon, which prompted a few more people to come closer as the rest of them clambered out of the tractor or swung off their rigs. "Hey folks! I brought some new friends I found on the road."

The first to approach was an older man who shared some of Rebecca's features. "You were gone a long time. I was afraid you'd been waylaid."

"I wasn't, but the car finally gave up the ghost. I thought I was gonna be stuck walking until these guys gave me a lift." Rebecca dug into her bag. "But I found some heart meds for you. Not a lot, but a few pills should last you a couple days." She handed over a small pill bottle.

"This isn't my usual prescription." The man glowered at the bottle. "I don't know the dosage for these."

To Shannon's surprise, Kim pushed forward. "Sir, I have some medical training. Can I ask what you were taking?"

The man frowned, but he rattled off a long name Shannon couldn't make any sense out of. It must have meant something to Kim, though, because she brightened. "Oh, I know that one! We studied it in pre-med." She looked at the bottle in the man's hand. "If this is labeled right, one pill twice a day should work, especially if we can get you some red wine and aspirin to go with it."

"Red wine and aspirin?"

"Sure. They're both blood thinners and pretty easy to find or make. In a pinch, you can use willow bark for the aspirin. It just has to be boiled down, and it tastes horrible." Kim grimaced.

"Well, all right. If you're sure." The older man frowned and looked at Rebecca. "Rebecca?"

"Kim's a good person, Dad." Rebecca looked up with a slightly embarrassed grin. "Sorry, I should have made introductions. Folks, this is my dad, Rufus Holden. Dad, this is Kim, her mother Shannon, her Aunt Carol, and friends. They're traveling together." Mutt whined, and Rebecca grinned. "Oh, and this here is Mutt."

"Pleased to meet you." He didn't sound pleased, but Shannon didn't blame him. No doubt he was recalling the last time his community had encountered strangers.

"Don't be a curmudgeon, Pop." Rebecca made an affectionate swatting gesture at him.

"I'll be how I like, young lady." The words were growled, but Rufus's shoulders relaxed a little bit.

Their conversation had drawn others out of the buildings. Rebecca named each person as they came close, starting with a man about her own age with shaggy, short, salt-and-pepper hair and a medium build. "So, that's John Deckon, who used to be a manager at our local mart. And that's David Skinner, who used to work part time at the gas station and part time doing odd jobs for different folks, including some construction work. He's been trying to get the houses in better repair, but it's slow going." He was a balding fellow of indeterminate age with wide shoulders and a belly that had probably been a lot rounder a month ago.

"Margaret Tarrow," Rebecca continued. "She used to teach in the school, but now she runs a sort of daycare for the youngsters who are too small to help with town efforts." That was a tired woman with hair that had once been dyed blond and was now colored a dirty blond fading to light brown.

"Sam Simmons. He's a plumber, been trying to get some decent water flow, but that's even slower than the repairs." A skinny fellow with messy hair and a heavily stained shirt gave them a nod.

"Suzie Mullen. She had a store in the town square and did sewing for people on the side. Been keeping people's clothes in good repair, and it turns out she's got a good head for farming, foraging, and salvage." That was a lean woman with her hair tied back from her angular face and a no-nonsense air about her. Her expression was particularly grim and distrusting, and Shannon didn't blame her. A store in the town square meant that, at the very least, she'd watched years of hard work and most of her livelihood be destroyed at the hands of the marauders.

The next arrival made Rebecca grin. "Hey, that's Ed!" She waved over a man with a solid build to rival Bill's. "Guys, this is Big Ed Connolley. His is the shop I was telling you about." Her attention switched to the new arrival. "Ed, these guys have some repairs to make on their vehicle. I told them you might have some parts they could trade for, maybe give them a hand."

She might have said more, but a strident tenor voice cut through the crowd, the tone making Shannon's back tighten up with near instant dislike. "What's all this? What's all this? Rebecca, who do you think you're bringing into our town?"

The crowd parted to reveal a figure in a cheap, badly worn, and somewhat stained suit. Shannon stared at the man in bemusement as he strode up to the group, chest puffed out as if he thought he was a mayor. His hair was white, his face jowly, and his chest and stomach were semi-rounded with the look of a man who, up until recently, had been well fed and living the good life.

As he came closer, Shannon recognized him. It was none other than the Righteous Reverend Jeb Butler, whose face graced the signs outside the wreckage of New Wren.

Rebecca proved her right a second later. "Evening, Reverend. These are some new friends I found on the road. They were kind enough to give me a lift back after my car finally died."

"Kindness? You call it kindness? Oh, Rebecca, you poor innocent, do you not see how the wolves have attempted to convince you they are lambs? You say these are friends, but what proof do we have that they are anything of the sort? Just look at these rough characters, and these machines they ride." Jeb's patronizing tone set Shannon's teeth on edge, and his smug "I know better than you" expression inspired the urge to slap it off his face.

Jeb either didn't notice her reaction or didn't care. He carried on speaking as he made an expansive gesture to the motorcycles. Another wide, sweeping gesture pointed to the tractor, with its broken windows and bullet holes. "Look at these signs of violence! Surely, they are but thieves and brigands who have been driven away from other pastures and now seek to steal into our midst and take what belongs to us!"

There was some muttering at that. Shannon could see suspicious glances being exchanged and angry expressions on different faces. Even Big Ed and Rufus Holden looked like they were reconsidering their earlier welcome.

Rebecca spoke up hotly. "Hey now, don't treat me like a child or an idiot, Jeb Butler. I wouldn't bring in more devils to our midst. Anyway, if they were the type of people you think they are, why would they help me out?"

Jeb Butler clucked his tongue and shook his head, his expression suggesting he was humoring a simpleton. "Is it not obvious? For why should thieves take by force that which they can take by sly tricks and deceitful actions?"

"Then why not have one of their number hurt me and come back here pretending to rescue me?" Rebecca glared back. "Or come limping in here without their vehicles and pretend to be injured themselves? Although from the looks of those two, it wouldn't be much of a pretense." Her finger stabbed at Lee and Bill, whose wounds from the tangle at The Spoke were clearly evident.

Shannon exchanged a glance with her aunt. It went against her nature to give away supplies, but even with what they'd lost on the road, they had enough to put out a decent meal for folks. They might need to do some serious scavenging and foraging tomorrow or the next day, but they'd have needed to do that eventually anyway. And the food had to be eaten by someone. Even the longest-lasting food would eventually go bad if it wasn't consumed.

Aunt Carol nodded. "Go ahead."

"There! See! Now that they are discovered, they begin their nefarious plans to steal all we have!" Jeb's voice was gloating.

Shannon snorted. "All you have isn't much, according to Rebecca." She ignored the outrage on nearby faces. "If you want to call it a nefarious plan, you can, but I don't see what's so evil about offering to share our provisions with you."

"Provisions?" That was a hoarse question from a man followed by a woman and two children near the edge of the crowd. "What do you mean?"

Bill stepped in, his expression open and friendly as he took up the explanation with an easy manner Shannon could never have imitated. "Shannon here was a long-haul trucker with a full rig of food she was driving when the power went down. We've had some mishaps and given some food away in other places, but we've got a lot left, along with what the rest of us salvaged while we were in Memphis earlier this week."

"We've already made plans for foraging and hunting to replace it, so we're not worried about starving too much in the near future," Kim interjected. "We've got food we can spare."

"And it does look like you folks could use a good meal." Bill stepped forward, managing to look calm, confident, and friendly, despite his arm being in a sling. "Plus, we've got other supplies to help with building efforts, and my friends here have their bikes and the truck here to help you with some salvage efforts." He smiled. "I might not be much help with physical labor at the moment, but I can help Mr. Connolley with some of the mechanical work as well. We might even be able to patch together a few more working vehicles for other folks to use."

At Carol's wave, the Black Rats crew began climbing over the back of the tractor, offloading the crates marked for food and cooking tools. As the boxes opened and the supplies came out, Shannon saw relief and even joy sweep over several faces.

She'd been right. These people were on the edge of starving, and they desperately needed the food. Promises were one thing, but the sight of actual food was enough to win a lot of people over to being, if not friendly, at least cautiously trusting toward them.

Someone brought out battered, ancient utensils, and a couple of women from the Black Rats convoy set up an improvised cooking area so they could have hot food. Shannon took over basic meal preparations while Carol and one of the local residents supervised the actual cooking. Kim offered her medical services to those who needed them, and Bill engaged with Big Ed in a friendly discussion about cars and repairs that could be done. Before long they'd drawn in the plumber and the odd jobs guy as well, and Bill was explaining how he'd rewired the truck to run. From there, they started discussing other things that could be made to work, and Shannon tuned them out.

Mutt started off wandering between Shannon, Bill, and Kim before some of the children cautiously approached her. The big dog wasn't exactly friendly toward them, but with a little encouragement from Bill and Kim, she was willing to stand still while the children petted her. She didn't even bark or fuss. She just stood or flopped on the ground and made soft huffing noises every once in a while, to the obvious delight of the youngsters.

Reverend Butler was reduced to skulking on the sidelines, watching through hooded eyes as the Black Rats crew and the people of Watchdog came together over their improvised meal.

"Sorry about the reverend." Shannon turned as Rebecca came up beside her to help with the food prep. "He likes to talk big, but he doesn't mean much by it."

Shannon shrugged to show she took no offense, even as she voiced her thoughts. "Seems awful distrusting. I guess I can't blame folks for feeling that way, but he was pretty adamant about it. He lose someone?"

Rebecca grimaced. "No. Nothing like that. It's just—before the disaster, the reverend was a big thing in New Wren. He ran the biggest church in town—Mount Sinai. He had a huge congregation, and people would come from several towns over to listen to his sermons, especially on holidays. Then the blackout happened."

"And folks stopped coming." Shannon thought she was beginning to understand. In a way, Jeb was a bit like Andre, if less violent and maniacal. He liked attention and being placed on a pedestal.

"That was part of it. But he tried to sell everyone on 'God's just testing you' and saying things like 'and the righteous will be saved and restored to glory.' Stuff like that. People bought it for a while, but platitudes and promises don't fill stomachs or keep people healthy and

154

safe. Now most people don't bother listening to his sermons or his speeches. We've got better things to do."

"You'd think he'd welcome new potential converts."

Rebecca smiled weakly. "You'd think so, but not when you have the potential to take people's attention away from him even further. He wants to be everyone's beacon of hope, and you're a distraction from his messages and all."

Shannon shrugged again. "He needs fewer messages and more action."

Rebecca chuckled. "Can't argue with that."

Twenty minutes later, dinner was ready, and Shannon collected a plate and went to join Bill, her daughter, and their new friends. Kim looked around between bites, her eyes alight with curiosity. Finally, she turned to Rebecca. "I have to ask. This town looks really old. The buildings look like they've been standing forever. How'd you wind up settling here, of all places?"

Rebecca laughed. "I guess it is a little strange to pick a deserted place like this. But I think we were drawn here by the local history and legends."

"Sounds like there's a story there." Bill smiled encouragingly. "I'd like to hear it."

Rebecca grinned back. "It isn't much, but if you're interested, here's what I know."

She took a deep breath. "Around about the 1840s, a group came in and set up a lumber company and a sawmill near where this town was built. It was a thriving town for about a hundred years. I hear it was even booming, back in the 1920s, when all the lumber transporters were also running moonshine through here. But then, of course, they established the Holly Springs National Forest, back in 1936."

"Sure, part of the preservation efforts and all." Shannon vaguely remembered something about that, though she remembered more about the Great Depression, which had started a few years before.

"Yeah. Between the reduced amount of lumber they could take and the loss of money and jobs all across the country, the town started to go downhill. People started drifting toward cities in search of work and money to live on."

"So the town became a ghost town, like a lot of others."

Rebecca's mouth quirked in a rueful grin. "You'd think so, but it didn't happen quite like that. See, there was this family, descended from some of the first settlers and mill operators. A family called the Gradys. They stayed, and when the Second World War happened and more resources were needed, old man Edgar Grady managed to revive the town, even expand it, which is why we have places like a hospital and Big Ed's automotive parts yard out here. The former's a little run-down, but it's still sort of stocked, even."

"But then..."

"It wasn't sustainable. Too many people wanted to be closer to Memphis. Plus, New Wren was already a town, and it was closer to the highway."

Shannon could guess what had happened from there. "Businesses started to build up near the highway, and so did the jobs and the homes. Fewer people wanted to live or work away from the modern conveniences and the profitable work zones."

"You got it. Plus, the old sawmill hadn't been upgraded in forever, and the new lumber clearing methods are a lot easier and more convenient. They're also more in line with forestry regulations and standards. Grady's sawmill just couldn't compete." Rebecca looked out across the weathered buildings. "By the 1970s, no one was coming out here except to Big Ed's, and sometimes to the health center if they had an accident nearby. The sawmill closed down, and everybody moved away. Eventually, there was only one resident left."

"Who?" Kim sat forward, her eyes wide. "Who'd stay isolated in a ghost town?"

"Edgar Grady's grandson, Edgar Grady II." Rebecca shook her head. "I met the man a few times in town. I don't know if it was the isolation or if he always was a little out of touch with the rest of the world, but a more paranoid, stubborn, and fatalistic man you'll never meet. To hear him talk, the end of the world was nigh and everything from communists to aliens to a new ice age was poised to sweep us away."

"Or a plague." Big Ed spoke up. "He told me once that scientists were going to engineer a plague to wipe out most of the population as a way of claiming all the resources for the privileged few."

"That sounds like him too."

It also sounded uncomfortably like Barney Langmaid. Shannon shifted in her seat. "He still around?"

"Nope. He died a couple years ago. Old age and orneriness, I think." Rebecca shook her head. "Rumor has it, he had secret caches all over Watchdog to prepare for the end of days. Food, medicine, and enough weapons and ammunition to make the entire United States Army jealous."

"You're hoping to find them?"

"I guess so. We found his generator and some other stuff, but nothing like the legendary supplies he supposedly left behind. Don't know if they were exaggerated, or if he lied to make people cautious, or we just haven't been lucky yet."

Rebecca scraped the last of her food out of her bowl and stood up to take it to where some people were setting up a cleaning station. "It's kind of ironic, isn't it? Old man Grady spends all that time preparing for an apocalypse only for it to happen after he's dead and gone. Now all the weapons and supplies he might have had are going to molder away in their hideaways just when we need them most."

She left then. Seconds later, Big Ed finished his own meal and rose, nudging Bill's good shoulder as he did so. "Come on. As thanks for the meal, I'll help you fix up the worst issues with your truck, like that damaged tire you've got. You and that kid—Lee, right?—can help me gather parts and do some of the lighter lifting and easier tasks."

Bill and Lee hurried to follow after the local mechanic. Kim took Shannon's plate and her own to the cleaning station, leaving Shannon alone.

The idea of more food and medicine was intriguing enough in its own right. You could do a lot with full stocks of food and medical supplies, even if they only lasted a short amount of time. At the very least, the time you weren't spending looking for those things meant you could get more done, like repairs and establishing a stable infrastructure for the community.

Still, as nice as the idea was, it wasn't the idea of medicine or food that held her attention.

Rebecca had said there was a cache of weapons large enough to outfit an army. The idea of Andre and his madmen getting ahold of something like that made her shudder. The idea of finding it first, on the other hand—that was interesting.

With enough weapons, they could stop even Andre and whatever lunatics and stooges he'd gathered to follow him. Even if she didn't normally care for guns, when it came to Andre and his followers, she was willing to make an exception. A bazooka-sized exception, in the unlikely event that she found one of those lying around with both the gun and the ammunition in good condition.

There was no question Andre would continue coming after her. No doubt he'd hunt her the length and breadth of the land, and eventually he'd find her, even in an out-of-the-way place like this. She was as sure of that as she was of her love for Kim. But that stash could level the playing field between them.

Assuming the stash existed, and if she could find it, perhaps she could convince the people of Watchdog to let her have enough firepower to stop Andre. Or if they really succeeded in putting down roots here, maybe she could convince them to help her mount a defense against him.

The question was where those weapons might be hidden. And, more importantly, what would she—*could* she—do if the Black Rats found them?

19

AUSTIN/ANDRE

Austin returned to Memphis torn between fury at having been shown up by Bruno's witch of a niece and concern at how Andre would take the news that they'd encountered her yet hadn't managed to wipe out her group.

Heck, he wasn't sure they'd managed to kill *anyone* she'd been traveling with. Not that old mechanic, or that kid they had as a tagalong, or even Carol. He'd taken a shot at her from the bar, once he'd gotten his wits about him, but he'd missed.

The smell coming from his clothing made him wrinkle his nose. He wasn't some priss who needed a bath and to smell like roses every day, but he'd gotten liberally splattered with blood and booze, and the smell was definitely strong.

None of the men riding with him seemed to mind, so he'd kept his thoughts to himself. But he couldn't help noticing the look Cherry gave him when he came through the doors of the new base. She looked disgusted and horrified.

Worse, now that his buzz was wearing off, there was a small part of his mind that didn't blame her. Just a few weeks ago, he'd have avoided anyone who looked and smelled like he did now.

Austin shoved that thought aside. He was the prez's man. He didn't shirk the heavy lifting or the dirty work. He'd done for Sparky, hadn't he?

But fighting Sparky hadn't been like the wholesale slaughter at The Spoke, his mind whispered. That had been brutal. And hanging Toad from a phone pole? He'd wanted to be a tough guy, but that wasn't his style.

He just needed to get a fresh hit, and he'd stop thinking stupid things like this.

"Austin, how did you fare?" Andre came out from wherever he'd been lurking to greet them. His eyes drifted over their bloodstained clothing. "It appears they were not as welcoming of our proposal as I had hoped."

"'Fraid not, boss. Toad refused outright, and I had to put a bullet in him. Then your boys took care of the rest. We brought back a handful though."

"Very good." Andre looked at the men straggling in behind Austin and frowned. "You seem to have brought back fewer of my men than you left with. Did the Tupelo chapter put up such a fight?"

Austin tensed. This was the part he wasn't looking forward to telling his new boss. "Nah. The Tupelo guys went down pretty easy once Toad was dead. But while we were there, Carol and your ex showed up with a bunch of ragtags. Riffraff from the old Memphis chapter, and some lame tagalongs I didn't know, though I think one was the mechanic she was stringing along. Other two were kids, a girl and some dark-skinned kid."

Andre's remaining good humor faded into a cold intensity that made Austin want to back away quietly, the way he would from a sleeping mastiff. "I trust you dealt with them."

"We tried." Austin cringed as that icy glower intensified. "We shot at 'em, nearly got Bruno's old lady, but that kid saved her, and then they took off. We chased 'em down, fast as we could, but they," he gulped and forced the last words out, "got away."

"Got away?"

"Yeah. The chick, Bruno's niece, she sideswiped one guy, knocked him a good fifty yards. And the mechanic did for two. Then a whole bunch of them got run over by that truck of hers. And we cut our losses there, 'cause—well, I figured we oughta come back and report."

"Come back and report your failure, your utter incompetence in dealing with a few women, children, and weaklings?" Andre's face darkened. Austin stepped back and braced himself for the explosion he could see coming.

"You complete and utter fools! Weaklings! I send you on a simple mission to subjugate a bunch of drunk, useless idiots and take out a couple of women and cockroaches, and you fail?" His words cut like glass and were meant to slice to the bone. "I thought you were *true* road warriors. True one percenters and fighters. Men who could and would do anything. Instead, I find a bunch of childish incompetents who pretend at strength when they'd be better served drinking milk out of sippy cups! You are all worthless cowards!"

Austin was ready to make a run for it. But one of the others, braver or stupider than the rest of them, stepped forward. A second later, Austin recognized it as one of the new guys from the prison. "Hey! Stuff it, Atkinson! I came up here to live the good life, and in exchange I said I'd help you off your ex, sure. But you didn't tell us she was a lunatic who drives like she's in a war zone. That woman was nuts! She did things with that truck no sane person would consider trying. I thought she was gonna kill us all with that monster rig of hers."

Quick as lightning, Andre lunged at the man and grabbed him by the shirt and one shoulder. The guy yelped as Andre wrenched him forward hard enough to have dislocated the joint. His scream cut off in a choking gurgle and a sharp crunch as Andre delivered a vicious headbutt that broke the man's nose.

Andre dropped the limp body with a disdainful sniff, stomping the guy's hand for good measure as he turned. "Would anyone else care to argue with me?"

Everyone else was absolutely quiet. Austin wasn't sure most of them were even breathing.

He'd known Andre was a fighter and had a vicious streak, but what the heck? What kind of leader dropped his own crew—people he'd personally recruited—just for making a statement? Sure, maybe the guy hadn't phrased it the best or picked the best time, but still, that was just a bit far.

Andre raked them all with his gaze, then nodded. "Fine. Resupply yourselves, and get back out on the road. Take two-thirds of the rest of the crew with you back to Tupelo. From there, they'll have to go on Highway 45 or Highway 278. Find them, and report back."

Most of the men scattered. Austin stayed where he was, confused by the orders. Sure, they had a score to settle, but the state was huge, and even the full crew wouldn't be enough to search for the escapees properly. One turn, and they'd be off the main drag and could be headed anywhere.

"What are you waiting for, Austin?" The sharp question brought his attention back to his new prez. Austin winced at the expression in his eyes.

"Just waiting for the boys to come back is all, boss." He should have shut his mouth, but some latent streak of crazy that only seemed to hit when he was sober spoke up for him. "Boss, I know we've gotta find the chick and deal with her, but I was wondering…That is, we'd have more manpower if we took over a few more towns, conscripted more guys to search with. Expanded our base and our information networks and stuff like that."

"Are you questioning my orders?" Andre's fists flexed.

Austin saw the guy on the floor and remembered the way Andre had torn into Bulldozer Keith. He held up his hands quickly in a gesture of surrender. "No! No way, boss. Nothing of the sort. Just thinking, we could maybe kill two birds with one stone by doing some more takeovers. Tupelo didn't go so bad, except for the last bit. I could even maybe convince people to capture her and turn her in."

"Stop babbling, and get out there and *find* Sarah, along with all her useless allies. That is all I require." Andre stalked toward him. "Go, or I will find a new second-in-command."

"Going, boss!" Austin jerked his head in a nod, then turned and bolted for the storerooms. He grabbed all the stuff he could carry, shouted at a few guys to hurry up, and raced back to his rig.

Twenty minutes later, he was back on the road, still sober, and in an increasingly foul mood. All that work, and he hadn't even gotten a chance to relax. Plus, it wasn't like he'd failed at his job. All Andre had told him to do was conscript or wipe out the Tupelo chapter. Dealing with the broad had been the orders for those toughs Andre had brought in.

He understood vengeance. He did. That was why he'd pointed Andre at Bulldozer Keith. But still, chasing over the whole state for one woman, to the exclusion of doing any real empire building, seemed a little excessive. And, though he'd never say it aloud, let alone to Andre's face, a little stupid.

With more towns under their control, and more manpower, finding one woman would be easier. Even if it wasn't, it would show that Andre was a proper leader. Besides, if the man conquered Mississippi and maybe Tennessee, then who was going to care if one woman escaped him?

Nobody, that's who. And even if someone did say something, Andre and his loyal underlings could take care of the fools who dared to bring it up. Plus, as their reach expanded, Carol and her niece would have fewer places to run, and eventually they could put her down like the useless mongrel she was.

Andre should have been smart enough to know that. Austin had thought he was. But he obviously had a blind spot when it came to his ex. A blind spot, an obsessive need to deal with her, and a too-quick temper.

Austin wondered what he'd signed up for, because he agreed with the guy who'd got clobbered. He'd signed up for living the high life and being kings of the road. Not the kind of crap Andre focused on, chasing down one woman.

Still, he was the prez's man, and he'd sworn to ride or die.

They reached the place where the confrontation had happened. He paused the group to search for clues as to where Carol's crew might have gone. He heard the men with him muttering, looking at the scene of the carnage with wide eyes and uncertain expressions.

Finally, he had enough of the sidelong stares, the whispers. He turned on his heel to face the riders. "If you pansies got something to say, say it."

To his surprise, it was Art who spoke first. "Austin, man, I get you thought this guy was a good leader, the real deal. But we aren't seeing it. And the way he destroyed that guy—"

"Yeah, really," Chip chimed in. "Who beats their own conscripts into a pulp like that over a little disagreement? Guy's dangerous."

Austin snorted. "Of course he's dangerous. He's a true one percenter. King of the road. And how he enforces discipline ain't our concern. We do what the prez orders."

"Prez? What kind of prez is he?" Someone else shouted out. "Bringing in outsiders who barely know how to handle a rig? And all this chasing after one woman—for what? She did him wrong, and instead of leaving her in his dust, he acts like catching her is the most important thing in the world. It's crazy. And I say he's crazy."

Austin sneered back. "How'd you handle someone who got *you* sent to prison, huh? Betrayed the brotherhood *and* marriage vows to go crawling to the feds and sell you out?"

"I'd make the brotherhood good enough that they'd come crawling back on their knees to me, not chase them around like a dog after a bone."

Cherry slipped from the crowd to stand in front of him, and Austin cursed that he'd been too preoccupied to notice she'd come along. He could have had her riding with him, and it might have made this trip a lot less irritating.

Cherry came close and looked at him with wide, pleading eyes. "Come on, Austin. You know the boys are only telling the truth." She twined an arm around his neck. "That man's obsessed with a woman, and there's nothing else to it. We don't need to be a part of it. We can just go somewhere else, start again. Make our own Black Rats gang. You could be the new prez, and we could all live the good life without chasing after some loser at the orders of a maniac."

For a few moments, he was genuinely tempted. It made an attractive picture. Being the head honcho, with Cherry as his woman, his old lady. Then reality reasserted itself.

He'd been living in a broken-down crap hole, beaten up by the likes of Bulldozer Keith, when Andre had come along. Could he really believe anyone would follow him without a strong leader backing him up? Even if he could, he didn't have Andre's connections to get the good stuff, so they'd be back to hardscrabble life in no time.

They were so ready to turn on Andre—how long would they tolerate him? For that matter, how long before Andre decided he was next on the hit list? He needed to end this crap before that happened.

He pushed Cherry back and addressed his companions. "Look, I get it. Andre's tough. That's cause he's a real boss, and we ain't had one of those before. He's just flexing his muscles, like we all have a time or two. And maybe he's a little obsessed with his ex, but she did him wrong, and a real king don't take no kind of crap from anyone. We get this done, he'll reward us. Then we can start building a real empire to thrive in. We all know the prez can put his money where his mouth is —look at what all we got! How many of us can say we had access to half the food, booze, drugs, or gear we do now, before the boss came along?" As expected, no one raised a hand. "Right. So we do this job and get back to the way things are supposed to be. Once his issues with this broad are settled, Boss Andre will cool down, and he'll lead us into a golden age, just like he promised."

"You don't know that." Someone in the group spoke.

"Who are you to be calling the boss a liar?" Austin retorted. "I dare you to say that to his face, or mine." He put a hand on his gun. When no one stepped forward, he snorted in contempt. "You talk big, all of you, but you can't even face me square. And you want to rebel against the prez? Buncha lunkheads and ingrates is what you are, all bark and no bite. So I'll leave you with one last thought before we get back to searching."

He looked long and hard at Cherry, then Sharp, Art, and Chip. "Andre clearly don't tolerate traitors. You wanna be next on his list?"

That got a bunch of shudders, but no more grumbling. He turned back to the mess in the road. "Let's keep going south, see what we find." He ignored Cherry's reproachful look as he climbed back on the bike.

They swept on down the road, and Austin kept his eyes peeled for anything that might give them a clue to where the ragtag group had gone.

They split the group at a small town whose name Austin didn't bother to register, where US-45 split with the Alt US-45, and rode for an hour, maybe two, until both Austin's tank and his stomach were starting to grumble at him. His head had been aching for ages for a fix.

They'd just passed through Pine Grove, and Austin spotted a used car dealership on the right side of the road. He signaled, and they all turned into it. It wasn't much, but it might have a vending machine or a fridge with something in it, and car dealerships usually kept the vehicles tanked up so customers could test drive them. Perfect place to do a little siphoning.

He hauled himself off his rig and picked out two men at random. "See what you can drag outta these cars to fill the bikes. Rest of you, spread out and look for anything usable or any signs of people." He sauntered toward the office building, intent on digging around for some food.

The door was unlocked. Austin blinked. Most people didn't leave doors unlocked. During the first days of the blackout, anyone with the bad luck to be away from home and working locked the shop or hunkered down. Nowadays, people were too worried about having their stuff stolen to risk it.

His thoughts were interrupted by a high-pitched scream, almost a squeal. "No! Wait! Please!"

Austin made his way toward the source of the sound to find three men menacing a cowering man with a badly defined combover, oily hair, and a beat-up suit that looked like it had been a chew toy for dogs at some point.

Austin waved at one of the guys. "Hey, hold up. Lemme talk to him." They dragged the guy to his feet, and Austin looked him up and down. "What's your name?"

"R-R-Robert Kelton." The guy's teeth were chattering, and Austin spat in disgust. He was pathetic. "P-p-please don't kill me."

"Well, Robert, that kinda depends on you." Austin gave him the nastiest smile he could manage, and the guy cringed again. "See, I need some information. You give me what I need, maybe you walk away intact and with whatever you've scrounged. You don't and—well, the boys are tired and bored."

"Whatever you need!" Kelton's voice was barely more than a whimper, and Austin figured he'd have been curled in a ball on the ground like a kicked dog if the men hadn't been holding him up.

"I'm looking for a woman running with a buncha wimps on bikes, and some other folk. Broad I'm looking for drives a big old truck, cab of an eighteen-wheeler, but without the trailer. What do you know about her?"

"Uh…" The man cringed. "Don't really know anything but—Wait!" He yelped as one of the toughs raised a fist. "Wait! I was gonna say, I was out scrounging, for food you know, and maybe some other stuff, yesterday. Was coming back from checking out some of the abandoned houses roadside. It ain't stealing if it's abandoned, right?"

"Get to the point, before I let them beat it out of you."

"Right. So, I was coming back, and I thought I saw a truck like that turning on the south branch of 278." Robert shuddered. "I didn't get too close, thought they might attack me, but I saw 'em. Looked like they were on the road to Amory or thereabouts."

Route 278. Amory. It was a slim lead, and given by a cringing coward who might be lying as easily as telling the truth. Austin considered that. Then he realized something else. "How'd you get all the way out there and back, huh?"

Robert gulped. "Uh, some of the older cars still run. Like, the vintage ones, or the ones from the 1970s."

Most of Andre's toughs weren't the best on their bikes, and bikes, cool as they were, were a pain for hauling loads of salvage. Austin grinned as a plan came to mind.

He looked at the two thugs. "You boys happy with your bikes?" He knew the answer was probably no, since one of them was riding Austin's old rig with all the dents. Sure enough, he got a couple head-shakes.

"Great." He kicked Robert in the leg. "Make sure this guy ain't lying, and make him point out some of the best cars to take. Give him a good thrashing if you have to." As if he didn't know they'd planned to do that anyway as soon as he wasn't looking. "Then let him go, take some cars, and head back to report to the prez."

"What will you be doing?"

"First, I'm gonna rustle up some booze and food. Then, I'm gonna take my ride and see if this guy's given us good information or if he's blowing smoke out his rear end. Tell Andre I'll be back to tell him what I found in a day or two."

Robert spoke up again. "P-p-please, I stocked some stuff in the back office. Just don't—" He yelped as one man tightened his grip. "Don't hurt me!"

Austin grinned nastily. "Ain't you heard, Robert? Misery loves company. Me and my boys have had a tough time, and we're all about sharing the feeling."

He turned and walked away, smirking at the sound of whining and begging and the pained screech that followed it.

First, food. Then he'd find that witch and her friends, finish them, and get back to the life he wanted to lead. A life at Andre's side as a king of the highway.

20

KIM NAKAMURA

Watchdog looked like a pre-blackout slum. There was no other way to put it, as far as Kim was concerned. But the people seemed to be the honest, hard-working type, just down on their luck.

The morning after their arrival, most of the residents of the ramshackle little place greeted the members of the convoy with smiles of welcome. Part of that was probably the food they'd been given the night before, but Kim couldn't help but respond in kind. A part of her distrusted those smiles, but another part of her wanted to believe she'd found a good community who just needed a bit of help.

As she and Lee helped out with the breakfast chores, she said, "You know, they seem like nice folks."

"Yeah." Lee nodded. "I was talking to some of them—mostly Big Ed, 'cause he had Bill and me helping him with the truck—and I feel bad for them. They pretty much lost everything. They had to leave it behind when they fled."

It was a familiar story. Kim looked around at the kids who were forlornly trying to make do with the few toys they had, or trying to coax Mutt to play fetch, and the adults who all looked weary and heartsick. She knew about leaving things behind. She'd left her favorite blanket, her music collection, and a lot of other stuff sitting in her room when the marshals had come for them when she was a teenager. She'd never recovered most of it.

Normally, she'd have said there was nothing they could do. But they had a truck. And with two meals served, they had a lot of newly emptied boxes.

She met Lee's eyes. "We could find out what they want and need most. Take the rig back to New Wren and gather stuff up. Not just supplies, but little stuff. Keepsakes, and maybe some necessities you don't normally think of."

Lee nodded, his whole face lighting up with enthusiasm. "That's a good idea. If we could convince Shannon, that would be great."

"You leave convincing Mom to me. First, let's find out what people might want rescued, besides the obvious. We can make a list." She dug in her bag then blinked as Lee produced his sketchbook and extra pencils. "Great."

Together, she and Lee plunged into the breakfast crowd, making conversation and gathering information. Most people were interested in a fresh change of clothing above all else, but Margaret Tarrow wanted more books to read to the children, Don Garvey—a former cook in the local diner—said he'd like a Bible, and Suzie confessed that some fabrics and thread to work with would be welcome because she was trying to patch rags with rags, as she put it.

The kids universally wanted toys, ranging from a generic "I wanna play cars again" to specific favorites like "Mr. Mittens. He's my plushie cat" and everything in between. Electronic toys were pointless to try and bring, but Kim and Lee made note of everything else.

Then there were the people who were in dire straits and in need of things like specific medications. Rufus Holden was only one among many who was reliant on certain drugs to keep him going. Kim wasn't sure what they could do about the diabetics who needed insulin, but she promised to try her best. Even if any insulin they found hadn't been refrigerated since the blackout, there was still a chance it might help. She'd learned that in one of her classes. It wasn't the best idea, and it might be far less effective, but it was better to take the chance than try to get by with nothing at all.

By the time breakfast was over, she and Lee had amassed a four-page list in addition to the generic supplies people needed. Kim herself added items as she thought of them, like the more generic medicines, socks, and cleaning supplies to try and stave off the sicknesses that would likely come if the current living conditions remained as they were.

They might not be able to bring all of it back in a day—probably wouldn't be able to, given the specifics of some of the requests—but even a little would help ease the stress on the people of Watchdog and prove the Black Rats' goodwill.

She went to her mother. "Mom, we've been talking to some people. There's a whole list of things they need and want, and I was thinking we could run a quick recovery trip, now that the rig's patched and we've got empty boxes."

Shannon nodded. "Don't see why not."

"What are you planning? I hear you! Planning to steal from our homes, are you?" Reverend Butler pounced on the conversation.

Before Kim could react, he'd seized the list and was waving it above his head, calling out to the nearby people in his loud, sharp voice. "See how the devil works amongst us, tricking us into revealing our valued possessions so they can snatch them away from us! Clearly this is a ploy to rob us blind, and they have attempted to make all of you complicit by asking for what you most want so it can be taken from you!"

Kim nearly hit him as he took the list she and Lee had spent an hour or more making and stomped it underfoot.

"That's not true!" She folded her arms and glared at him. "What the heck would we even do with kids' toys or gall bladder medicine?"

"The wicked always find ways to use what they have stolen from the righteous." Jeb intoned, looking down his nose at her. "It could even be a trick to mask your true goals."

She'd seen better acts, and she matched him sneer for sneer. "Sure, keep telling yourself that. Like I'd bother if all I wanted was to loot the town. We're the ones with the running vehicles here."

Lee elbowed her, and Shannon rolled her eyes. "Not the best way to make your point, Kimmy."

Sure enough, there were a few troubled looks going around. Kim blushed.

Shannon stepped forward. She bent to pick up the list and handed it back to Kim. "You folks got your reasons to be worried, I don't dispute that. But we've done you no harm, and I'd like to think we've done fair by you, sharing our food and all." That got some shame-faced looks. Shannon continued, "Now, my daughter wants to help you out, and really, what have you got to lose? Not much, I'm think-ing." That swayed a few more.

Reverend Butler thrust his chin out. "I won't let you rob these people blind. I insist on precautions being taken, for the good of us all!"

"Fine by me." Shannon's easy agreement clearly caught him off guard. "I'm tired of driving, and Kim knows the basics of handling the rig. I'm betting Big Ed knows as much or more."

The man nodded. Shannon smiled briefly at him before her attention returned to Jeb. "You don't trust us? Send some of your folk along with my Kim, and whoever wants to go with her. Rest of us will stick around town and see what we can do to help out. Simple as that. If Kim doesn't come back, you'll have someone to address your displeasure toward."

It was a perfect solution, and Kim could have kicked herself for not thinking of it sooner.

Jeb Butler looked as if he wanted to chew on lemons. "I insist on a salvage team of New Wren residents. And I will be going with them to ensure nothing untoward happens to my citizens."

"Suits me. As long as Kim has someone to watch her back and the tractor, I can live with that." Shannon turned to her. "Kim?"

"Lee was going to come along with me. You've seen his hunting skills, and he's good at finding things."

"Good enough. Prospect's supposed to do the heavy lifting and hard labor, so that'll please the boys." Shannon nodded.

It was strange to see her mother being so agreeable to her plans, so willing to let her make her own decisions and go off on her own. Kim was tempted to ask if Shannon was feeling all right, but she didn't dare make her mother think twice.

She took a moment to make sure the list was still legible while Lee told Carol and the rest of the Black Rats crew what the plan was. Jeb and Big Ed rounded up a couple of others.

In the end, the salvage party consisted of herself, Lee, Big Ed, Suzie Mullen, Sam Simmons, and Jeb Butler.

Kim eyed the group. "We are not all going to fit in the tractor cab."

Big Ed agreed. "We can rig some straps and handholds around the edges of the back. You youngsters and Sam could sit on the struts there. As long as you keep your feet up and we go fairly slow, it shouldn't be too dangerous."

Kim wasn't so sure. "Or Lee and I could borrow one of my aunt's bikes. I'm not a great rider, but I can manage." She'd learned how to ride a motorcycle before college, and though she wasn't the most comfortable rider, she could handle it.

"You really think that's gonna be safer?"

"I think I'll take my chances."

Carol had come up to listen. "You might as well. Lee needs to learn to handle himself too. We've got the spares, so there's no better time."

Sam opted to try riding on the back of the tractor, while Kim and Lee found rides that suited them and did a few practice laps up and down the road. Once they were confident enough not to crash, the truck crew joined them.

By the time they'd gotten a few miles down the road, Kim felt a bit better about the ride. The muscle memory of her long hours learning with her great-aunt and uncle was coming back to her, and her body had started to remember how to move with the rig as it turned, sped up, and slowed down. Lee was still a little awkward, but he had good balance and good instincts, and he was doing better than she'd have expected of a beginner.

By the time they pulled into New Wren, Kim was invigorated by the ride and ready to do some serious salvage and recovery.

By prior agreement, they started in the town square. It was a wreck and still kind of stomach-churning to look at, but it was where they'd be able to recover the most stuff in the shortest amount of time. Depending on how fast they worked, they could start looking through other areas and individual houses once they finished. What they couldn't get today, they'd come back for tomorrow, or next week. What mattered was doing the best they could with the people they had.

Kim was surprised to see Jeb Butler was the first to leave the tractor cab. She was less surprised when he immediately scurried away, abandoning the salvage efforts before they even began. She stared after him. "Where's he going?"

"Probably the church, to collect something or other. Maybe a new suit or two. The reverend likes to keep up appearances," Ed grunted. "You'd think he'd see there are more important things to worry about, and think more about the state of our stomachs and our health than our righteous souls, but I guess preachers have different priorities."

"I guess." Kim frowned at the square. "So, I was thinking we ought to try the pharmacy, the hardware store, and Suzie's shop first, for basics, and whatever clothing or general supply stores you have here. We can set aside one crate to fill up at the end of the day with treats and maybe some toys for the kids?"

"Sounds good to me." Sam nodded. "I can start in the hardware store. I know what all we need the most."

"I can start in my shop," Suzie said.

"I can move between groups, help with heavy lifting and shifting debris," Ed volunteered.

"Cool. I was thinking I'd go to the pharmacy, since I know what kind of medicines we need and what we can substitute for different things, like Mr. Holden's heart medicine. Lee can pick a general store or help someone else." She swallowed, thinking of Jeb's suspicions. "If you'd rather we stayed with you, I can go with Suzie and Lee can help Sam." It would cut down on their effectiveness, but it was better than more accusations of theft.

178

The three former New Wren residents exchanged looks, then Suzie shook her head. "I'm not as paranoid as Jeb. You've not been dishonest this far, and at least you're helping."

Sam nodded. "I'm of the mind that if Jeb wanted you kept under watch so badly, he ought to have stuck around to do the job himself. We'll collect more of what we need, and faster, if we divide up like you said, little miss."

"I agree. Let's split the task as suggested and get done what we can." Big Ed slapped his hands together. "Time to get to work, ladies and gentlemen!"

Kim grinned as they all scattered for their various destinations. Sticking around in Watchdog might work out after all.

21

SHANNON GRAYSON

W atchdog turned out to be bigger than it looked. That wasn't saying much, but as Rebecca showed them around, Shannon had to admit it was in better shape than the houses might lead one to believe.

There was a medical center, like the one she and Bill had holed up in while she was recovering from being shot. It wasn't fully stocked by any means, but it was staffed by Glenda Evans, a retired doctor who'd taken up caring for people once again in the wake of the blackout.

The sawmill had a water wheel, and it was clear that someone, probably Sam Simmons and a man named Vernon Grover—a water treatment officer—had made efforts to get it working again to produce cleaner water and maybe even power for a generator.

Bill stopped to take a closer look at the stream when he heard that. "Doesn't look like you need the purifier. Just some coal, maybe."

Rebecca stared at him. So did Shannon and Carol. "You can't drink river water straight. It has to be purified or boiled."

"Most times, sure. But there's no signs of cows upstream, or chemical plants. Look at that nice moss." Bill pointed.

"Moss. What about it?" Carol gave the green growth an unimpressed look before turning back to the mechanic.

"Aside from being food, according to my granddaddy?" Bill raised an eyebrow. "Out in the country, we learn things a little differently. Wells are popular where I grew up. But when it comes to streams, my grandfather used to take me camping, and we always filled up our canteens straight from the river. But he was always pretty particular where, so I asked him about it."

"What did he say?" Carol folded her arms. "That if you drink it often enough, you'll stop getting dysentery, or whatever?"

"No. He told me you always look for a clear, quick-running stream with nice healthy moss. He told me, 'Bill, when you've got a good-flowing stream that you can see the bottom of, and nice, bright-green moss, then you've got clean water, clean as God and nature intended, and just as safe to drink.'"

"How?"

Bill shrugged. "Was a good many years ago, but he said the moss and the stone served as a natural filter and cleanser. A little bit of charcoal from the fire in a cloth bag to keep the ash out of your food, and you couldn't find better for drinking."

"Moss and charcoal? That's all it takes? We've been trying to stock up iodine and work out the proper chloride ratio, and all it takes is moss and charcoal?" Rebecca looked as if she wanted to call Bill out for a liar or sit down hard and breathe for a spell to get over the shock.

"A good-moving stream with the livestock on the other side of town. Do that, and so long as the mill doesn't dump too much debris, this water should be fine."

"Of all the…" Rebecca shook her head. "Any other advice for us, Mister Wheeler?"

Bill shook his head. "Not much. You've picked a good place to settle down." He waved a vague hand at the surrounding area. "The buildings could use some work, but they've got sturdy framework. There's plenty of land for growing crops, and for hunting. You're far enough off major roads that trouble will have difficulty finding you, but close enough you can run salvage and foraging missions fairly easily. If Big Ed and I can fix up a few of your cars and get a little more of the infrastructure in place and the buildings weather-proofed, Watchdog could be a good place to live, even the way the world is now."

Rebecca sighed. "I don't doubt you're right, but the thing is, we don't have a lot of folks who are skilled in the types of things that need to be done. And we don't have a lot of people who know how to organize the town to make sure it runs smoothly."

She gestured to the run-down buildings. "Big Ed, Sam Simmons, Vernon Grover, and David Skinner are the best we've got for handymen, and Big Ed has more experience with cars than anything else. Glenda's our only medic, and she's got arthritis. As for running the place, John Deckon's the only one with any management experience, now that most of the town council is dead. And he tends to defer to Jeb."

Shannon raised an eyebrow in surprise. "Jeb? The preacher?"

Rebecca grimaced in reply. "Yeah. He's about as good a leader as you're thinking. Every time anyone comes to him with a problem, he has one of two answers. If he's sober, he says 'I'm working on it'—as if that's any help when we don't see results. And if he's drunk, which is more often than you'd think, he'll say something like 'God will provide.' That's worse."

Bill sighed. Shannon shook her head. "I'm surprised he didn't try to claim we were the hand of God instead of trying to run us out of town."

"Probably would have, if he hadn't seen you as a possible challenge to his authority." Rebecca took a deep breath. "I'll admit, most folks are wary of outsiders, and with good reason these days. But as sad a shape as we're in, any help we can get is welcome. You folks seem pretty well organized."

"We have our moments." Bill said. "Part of being a convoy, I suppose."

"I imagine that does make it necessary." Rebecca smiled. "On the other hand, if you decided to stop here a while, even settle down, I don't think anyone would mind."

Shannon's first instinct was to refuse, but one look at Bill's face was enough to curb the impulse and make her think about it.

There was no question the members of the Black Rats would want to be on the road frequently, but none of them had denied it when Carol had said that even nomads needed a home base. Why not somewhere like Watchdog, where they could be an integral part of the community and not just outsiders?

A mobile team like a motorcycle club could do a lot of good in terms of foraging, scouting, and salvaging. Most of the members either had odd skills or could learn them. If nothing else, they'd proved in Memphis that they could be good scouts and defenders of their chosen area.

Shannon knew Kim wasn't eager to be tied down to any one place, but she hadn't taken much time to think about what she wanted. She'd been so focused on finding her family, and then on dealing with Andre's attack and the aftermath, that she'd taken no time to consider the matter.

She'd spent almost all of the last five years on the road, or in a place she knew would only be a temporary home. If she was honest with herself, she was tired of always being on the road and on the move. She wouldn't mind having a place to call home again. She also knew she couldn't let herself hope for a stable place too long, not as long as Andre was still around and focused on finding her.

"Shannon?" With a start, she realized she'd gotten lost in thought. Bill and Rebecca were both waiting for her response to Rebecca's welcome.

She shrugged her uninjured shoulder. "I can't speak for everyone. I know there's some among our convoy who wouldn't mind settling down. On the other hand, I'm not sure you'd want us sticking around here. You might have noticed the bullet holes in our rig."

Rebecca nodded, a wry smile on her face. "Kind of hard to miss."

"We ran into some trouble on the road here, and we're not sure if it will follow us this far," Shannon said. She knew Andre was looking for her, but she could hope their unexpected turn off the highway and out to this little formerly abandoned settlement would throw him off their trail. If he couldn't find even a trace of her, perhaps he'd give up.

There were plenty of abandoned buildings, and the parking bay at the old medical center was big enough to hide her tractor. If she could just lay low for a while, she could evade Andre, or at least give herself a chance to decide how and where she encountered him next. Having more allies and friends around would help, especially since she was sure Andre was building an army. But that didn't mean she wanted to drag the people of Watchdog into her mess.

Rebecca frowned thoughtfully then shook her head. "I know I can't speak for everyone in Watchdog when I say this," she said to Shannon, "but I think we're likely to face danger no matter what happens. The world's just like that these days. But you folks have done well by us, and there's no reason we shouldn't welcome you, as long as you're willing to continue supporting our community."

"That's fair," Bill said.

"I only wanted to give you fair warning," Shannon said.

"And you have," Rebecca said, "which is better than we had when those ruffians rolled through town. Like I said, you keep taking care of Watchdog, and if you want, Watchdog will keep taking care of you."

Shannon exchanged a long look with Bill and Aunt Carol. The idea sounded good in theory, but so had going to Tupelo.

Eventually, Shannon gave Rebecca a cautious nod and the only honest answer she could. "We'll consider it."

Rebecca smiled. "That works for me. In the meantime, there's some housing over here that isn't too bad. Once the salvage team comes back, we can see about making it more comfortable for you." She started toward a cluster of buildings, and Shannon followed her.

Rebecca's invitation meant they all needed to consider their situation carefully. Even so, Shannon knew one thing for certain: Bill was right. Watchdog had the potential to be a nice place to live—if Andre and his thugs didn't burn it to the ground.

22

AUSTIN/ANDRE

The Mt. Sinai Baptist Church of New Wren was nicer than a lot of churches Austin had been in, but he found little comfort in that fact. Sure, there was stuff he could possibly loot, but that wasn't going to help him with his biggest problem.

He'd followed Route 278 all the way to Amory and back several times, but there was no sign of the truck or its cadre of bikers. Somewhere between the dealership in Pine Grove and Amory, it had vanished.

The problem was, there were a lot of back roads and side roads and little towns tucked back off the main roads, and the truck could have gone to any one of them. It was impossible for one person, or even an entire posse, to search everywhere. The last place anyone had seen the truck was New Wren, but there was no sign of it now, and Austin hadn't found anyone to shake information out of.

Andre wasn't going to be happy to hear that, and Austin didn't have anything else he could tell his boss to take the edge off his failure. Somehow, he didn't think the cars he'd sent back with the convicts would be enough to calm Andre's temper.

That was why he was hiding out in a church and waiting for Andre to come to him rather than returning to the base in Memphis. Anything to delay the moment when he had to tell the prez that once again, his ex had disappeared. That he'd failed.

Andre had bashed a guy's nose in just for asking questions. He'd also said he didn't tolerate failures. Who knew what Andre'd do to him for losing the trail again?

Plus, he was out of food, out of booze, and almost out of coke. He was sober and uncomfortable, and he hated it.

Austin slumped into the pew nearest the altar and tried to distract himself by looking around. Churches had always been his safe haven of last resort, the place he'd go if he was down on his luck and desperate. He'd grown up shuffling between different towns and different churches, moving to a new sanctuary and new congregation every time his father got the call. He'd resented it when he was young. Later, when he'd become a biker, he'd come to appreciate how well his father had built his tolerance for travel and life on the road. It was one of the few things he did appreciate about his upbringing.

Austin snorted. The old man would have a fit if he knew all his lessons had come to this. His only son, a one percenter. He'd have been mortified and demand Austin—David, back then—repent and be cleansed of his sins.

Then again, his father wouldn't have thought much of New Wren's Mt. Sinai Baptist Church. It was too flashy, had too many little touches his father would have called "decadence." The pew cushions felt like they were covered in velvet, and the banners looked like they were made of satin. There were lots of lights in the ceiling and an expensive-looking sound system.

Lots of fancy things, but nothing that might help Austin pacify Andre. Nothing he could even consider good loot. And no alcohol that he'd managed to find. He'd hoped for some communion wine to take the edge off.

He found himself looking up at the picture of Christ. The eyes stared at him. Austin hunched his shoulders at the feeling that he was being silently judged and found lacking.

Who cared what some long-dead guy thought? And God—Austin was pretty sure he'd never seen any proof God existed. And if he did? Well, that wouldn't matter to Austin till he died. No reason to worry about it now.

Austin huffed. He didn't like being sober—didn't like having thoughts like this. Didn't like the little itch in the back of his mind that asked if maybe he'd wound up in a church because he knew he needed something a church could provide.

His eyes went back to the picture of Christ, and he glared at it. "Don't judge me. I got a right to do whatever I want. And I like who I am and being a one percenter."

The picture didn't answer, but he felt like the painted gaze was somehow saying, "Really?" He was opening his mouth to say more when he heard the creak of a door opening. Austin quickly ducked out of sight.

He was expecting Andre. The man who came through the door was far less menacing in his rumpled, stained suit. Austin took a moment to study the white hair and the fake tanned skin before he realized he'd seen the face before. It was the guy on the billboard: Reverend Jeb.

Austin might have had his scruples about shaking down a preacher, but this guy—well, any man who put his face on billboards and called himself "righteous" wasn't the kind of preacher Austin had to feel guilty about putting pressure on.

Jeb was busy rummaging around in the front of the church. Austin stalked up behind him and grabbed his shoulder. "Hey."

Jeb whipped around, his face twisting in fear. His hands jerked up to shield his face. "Don't hurt me! Please!"

Austin sneered at him. "You ain't worth my time. Just wanted to know what you were doing here."

"Oh, well, that is..." Jeb's gaze slid back to the alcove where Austin had found him rooting around. "Just a little libation."

Austin shoved him roughly to the side and dug deeper into the recesses. His fingers found a bottle, and he dragged it out. Bourbon. "Hey. Got some nice booze."

Jeb flushed. "It's just a little something for personal use."

"Sure." Austin reached in and found a second bottle. "And here's one for me. Come on, preacher, let's sit and talk."

He gave Jeb his best intimidating glare, and Jeb gave him a quick nod. Austin slouched back to the pew and sat down, alcohol at his side. Jeb sat down a short distance away.

"So, why's a preacher need the bottle? I'd have thought you'd be in your element with this end of days stuff." What Austin really wanted to do was drink himself stupid, but he wasn't about to pass up a source of potential information.

"I do my best to guide my flock, I truly do, but people are so easily led astray." Jeb flushed, frustration on his face. "Since these tribulations began, they have been reluctant to follow my lead, and now..." His flush deepened, and he glanced at the bottles Austin held.

"And now?" Austin pointedly moved the bottle a little farther away. "Come on, preacher, don't stop there. Unless you want me to go looking for any other good stuff you might have."

From the panicked look Jeb gave him, there was probably something to find, but the preacher began talking again. "I have tried to be the voice of reason and guidance for my flock, but only yesterday, strangers appeared—strangers bringing temptations in the form of easy food and promises of aid. My folk have turned deaf ears to my warnings and the warnings of the Lord—"

"Save the speeches about God, preacher. I don't need 'em." Austin could feel his spirits rising, hope taking cautious root. "Tell me more about these interlopers. You said they had food?"

"Boxes of it, yes, on the back of a truck."

It couldn't be. "Truck? Like a pickup?"

"No, no, it was the front part of a large truck, but there was no trailer. Just the driver's cab, and the back loaded with boxes." Jeb's face creased with anxiety and frustration. "I tried to warn people that these strangers were dangerous, that their promises and gifts could only bring trouble, but none would heed me."

"Yeah? How'd you know they were trouble? Might be angels in disguise." Not that Austin believed in angels, but he knew how to talk to religious guys well enough.

Jeb scoffed. "What angels would present themselves riding motorcycles like brigands? To say nothing of the bullet holes in the vehicle. It's clear these people are trouble, and I must convince them to leave, but they have suborned my authority, and I—"

"Yeah, yeah. I get it. Interlopers. Undermined your authority. Sure." Inside, Austin was cheering. He shifted closer and slung an arm around Jeb's shoulders, ignoring the way the other man stiffened. "I got good news, preacher. I know a guy who might be able to help with your interloper problem."

Andre had followed the signs Austin left on the road for him and was now pulling up to Mt. Sinai Baptist Church with three of his men. There was no sign of Sarah or her truck, so he was in a poor mood when he stepped off his bike.

Austin came hurrying out. "Hello, boss. How was the ride?"

"That depends entirely on what you have to tell me." He gave Austin a cool glare. "I trust I will not find that you have wasted my time in making me come this distance from Memphis?"

Austin quailed a little under the glare, but he rallied a moment later. "No, boss. Your ex and her friends—they're somewhere around here. They've been talking to the people who used to live in the nearby town. I got a guy inside says they've been in his community, stirring up trouble."

That was interesting. Andre wondered what could have brought Sarah and her friends in this direction. He dismissed the thought. Doubtless it was only another trick to evade him. He would prove that there was no way she could hide from him forever. In the meantime, he needed more information, and Austin was likely too much of a brute to have truly gained anyone's confidence.

"Introduce me to this new associate of yours, Austin. I wish to know what he knows."

"Sure. Sure. Name's Jeb. He's a preacher—got billboards with his face, you might have seen them—and he says—"

"Austin." One word, but it was enough to shut the man up. Andre smiled to himself. Austin truly was the proper subordinate. Easily cowed and with just enough intelligence to follow orders and accomplish necessary tasks.

Inside the church, he found a man in a rumpled suit that would have been cheap but looked expensive before the disaster. He had white hair, a fake tan, and a manner that reeked of self-importance and inflated self-confidence. Andre smiled. He knew this type of man.

He strode over and offered his hand with a smile. "Good afternoon, Reverend. I wouldn't wish to presume, but you are Jeb Butler, are you not? The Righteous Reverend."

"Yes I am. And you are?" Dark eyes, slightly bloodshot, studied him, and the breath that wafted toward him was sharp with the smell of alcohol. Bourbon. Andre restrained his smirk with an effort. Even better.

"My name is Andre Atkinson. My associate Austin tells me you have a problem with interlopers." He shook the preacher's hand firmly, politely. There would be time enough to crush the man later. For now, one caught more flies with honey. It was a common theme of the books he'd read in prison.

"We do, and it vexes me that the rest of my flock cannot see the danger in them as I can. It is clear they are tempters and thieves, brigands, and yet no one will listen to me." Jeb looked slightly mournful but very frustrated. Andre understood him well. He was a small-minded man who had been important before the disaster and wished to be important again. The easiest way to control him was to sympathize and offer him promises that control would be restored to him—with only a little assistance to and from Andre and his crew.

Andre pasted an insincere, apologetic smile on his face. "I do understand. I've faced such troubles myself. But please, tell me more about these interlopers that distress you. I want to help you, Reverend, but you must tell me all you know."

He ignored Austin, who was giving him odd looks from the doorway, and focused his attention on the preacher.

The man took a swig from a bottle, then his other hand gestured expansively. "It's terrible. They tricked one of my vulnerable members into bringing them to the town where we shelter. I tried to warn people they were dangerous, but they started passing out food and talking about helping with salvage. Since then, no one has listened to me!"

Andre couldn't have cared less, but he nodded and offered the man a sympathetic expression anyway. "I understand. Now, I heard they traveled with part of a large truck." Jeb nodded. "This truck, it was driven by a woman?"

"Yes. A woman—looks a little bit Asian, black hair and dark eyes and an intense stare. She rode up in a truck cab with a young girl, an old man in a sling, and a monster of a dog, and started talking people around with that deceptive silver tongue of hers."

"I can imagine." Andre put an arm around the man's shoulder. "You see, Reverend, I've had the misfortune of dealing with this woman before. She once convinced me to marry her, and then she betrayed me. You're quite right to be concerned about her influence with your people."

"I know! Such people mean nothing but trouble! I keep telling my flock that such gifts come with a price, such a heavy price as they cannot imagine, but they see the immediate gain and pay no heed to the risk."

Andre nodded along with the man's rant. "Indeed. It is a common failing. It is how she gains her followers and influences people. I'm very familiar with her methods." He squeezed Jeb's shoulders. "I believe I can help you with your interlopers, but I will need some assistance from you, Reverend."

"What sort of assistance?" The man's eyes blinked blearily, suspicion in them warring with the desire to believe there was a solution to his problems that would require little effort on his part.

It was just as well that Andre needed little from such a man. A spy in the enemy's camp would suffice. "I need you to be my eyes and ears.

Keep an eye on this woman and her companions. Help me find the best place and time to rid you of them."

"Well," Jeb took another swig from the bottle, then nodded. "All right. I can do that. Is there anything else?"

Andre pretended to think. "Are there any of those interlopers nearby? I'd like to observe them if I can."

He half-expected the answer to be no, but the preacher nodded, wavering a little on his feet. "They came, two of them, they came with some of my flock to gather things from the ruins of New Wren. They call it salvage, but I know they intend to rob us blind." Jeb hiccuped suddenly, then took another swig.

The man was fast becoming too drunk to be of any use. But that was all right for Andre. If he could get Sarah alone and finish her off, he could concentrate on his empire. No one would question him again. "The ones who came to town, was one of them the woman?"

Jeb shook his head. "No. Woman's daughter though, and a boy."

Lee and Kim. Andre considered that. Lee was a lost cause, a coward even if he wasn't a traitor. But Kim—Kim was his daughter. She had spirit. She could be a good ally, if only she could be turned from Sarah's influence. It might be too late, but he was loath to throw away what was his if it wasn't necessary.

He offered Jeb another smile. "I see. Well, perhaps such young people can be persuaded away from the wrong path. But you look tired, Reverend. Perhaps it is better for you to rest while I go see what else I can learn. Austin and I can make preparations to assist you."

It didn't take much to coax the man to flop bonelessly onto a pew. The bottle of bourbon was rescued from his limp hand and stowed in Andre's pocket. He waited until Jeb began to snore, then turned back to Austin and gestured for the man to follow him out of the church.

"I want you to go back to Memphis and gather the crew, both there and along the road. Bring them here. We will use this church as our new base while we deal with Sarah and her friends."

Austin frowned. "So we're gonna help him?"

Andre snorted derisively. "He is going to help us deal with the traitors. After that, this town can become part of our territory. I'm sure his 'flock' will make good servants." He looked down his nose at Austin. "I believe I gave you an order, Austin."

"Yes, prez." Austin scuttled out the door.

Andre watched him go with a smile, then turned to the other three men who had ridden with him. "One of you keep an eye on our preacher. Make sure he doesn't show any signs of changing his mind. You two, look around. We will need food, beds, and other amenities while we are here. I will go into town and see if I can gather information about our quarry."

The thugs obeyed. Andre turned his steps toward town, humming to himself.

23

KIM NAKAMURA

Salvage wasn't the easiest work, but it was rewarding, as far as Kim was concerned. There was something satisfying about being able to pick supplies up and put them in the truck, knowing they were going to people who needed them, and an even greater satisfaction in being able to tick things off the list.

She'd found half a dozen or more of the medicines, either actual prescriptions or things that could be substituted for the prescriptions with a few adjustments. Even better, she'd found a pharmacist's reference book under a counter, which would be an invaluable resource for her and whoever else might be serving as a medic.

In addition, they'd got plenty of clothing as well as fabric to make more clothes or patch old ones. Sam, Ed, and Lee had gathered a lot of building supplies and tools meant for construction rather than Bill's tools for engines.

The New Wren residents might have been suspicious of them in the beginning, but after hours of working side by side, the walls had broken down.

Kim had finished searching out medicines and teamed up with Sam to haul some larger items, including a couple of generators that could be run off fuel from the canisters or siphoned from the tractor. What they found could help provide at least limited power to some of the community areas, like the medical center and perhaps the childcare center.

She and Sam set the last generator on the tractor bed and lashed it down. Sam dusted off his hands and cracked his back. "I'm gonna take a leak and maybe a break to get a drink. You want something?"

Kim shook her head. "I was thinking I'd walk around, maybe scout out some more good salvage sites. And I might pick up some toys for the kids."

"Sure. Have fun with that." Sam waved her off.

Kim grabbed a water bottle she'd found and started down the road. They'd not explored farther than the town square, and she wanted to see if there were any nearby shops that might have things they needed. She also wanted to locate the library, since it wasn't in the town square. The reference books could be invaluable, and she could bring back reading material for Margaret and the children or some of the older residents of Watchdog. Even if they couldn't get everything today, knowing where to start the next trip would save time.

There were a few likely stores, but a lot of them had been vandalized and looted, which meant the salvage would be minimal. They were still worth looking into, but they might not be priorities. The same was true of the library, which she found a couple streets over, its broken windows gaping forlornly open to the elements.

Not far beyond the library, she saw the beginnings of a neighborhood. The houses were simple one-story brick houses, all of them abandoned. She started to turn away when a flicker of movement caught her eye.

A man emerged from the shadows of the buildings, and Kim froze as she saw his face. "You."

"Hello, Kim." Andre smiled pleasantly. "I hope you're doing well."

Kim grabbed for her gun, only to stop as her father sat down on the curb and held out his arms, his hands open and empty.

"What are you doing?" she asked.

"I'm unarmed. I hold no weapon. I simply wish to talk for a moment." Andre shrugged and dropped his hands. "You may shoot me if you choose, but I do have men patrolling nearby. A gunshot or sounds of a struggle would bring them here, and then…" He shrugged again. "I suppose there's no one to keep them in check if I were wounded or dead. Or threatened. I don't know that you or your friends in town would survive the fallout."

She didn't believe for a minute that Andre was holding anyone back. But she could believe he had backup nearby, and there was no telling how many men there were in his group. Or how many weapons. If it was another team like the one at The Spoke, she wasn't sure any of them would survive a confrontation. Kim took her hand away from her gun and edged forward. Andre patted the ground, and she sat down, making sure she stayed well out of arm's reach.

"Okay. You want to talk, then talk."

Andre—she refused to think of him as her father any longer—shook his head in mock sorrow at her blatant distrust. "Kim. Why are you so hostile? I'm your father. Surely, I deserve better treatment than to be greeted with such an attitude."

Kim snorted. "If that's all you want to say, you can take your cheap ploy for sympathy and sit on it. Preferably alongside a rusty knife blade or a loaded hair-trigger pistol."

Andre sighed. "I see your mother has managed to influence your opinion of me. I thought you would understand me, Kim. Understand why I've pursued your mother so far."

"I don't."

Andre gave her another of those wounded looks she didn't trust for a minute. "Kim, she betrayed me. Not just me, but our family. She tore us apart. By going to the federal marshals, she betrayed everything our way of life stood for. How could I not want to call her to account for that? Don't you also want to demand an explanation from her?"

"I already got one. And I'm happy enough. I've made my peace with what happened."

"That is all I want: to make my peace with the past." Andre shook his head. "Your mother took everything from me—my life, my companions in the Black Rats, my job, and you, my daughter. I can't just let that go."

It didn't escape her notice that she was last on his list of things he'd lost, like an afterthought. She was apparently separate from his life. She had no intention of thinking too much about it, not when she had more important things to worry about.

"So? What, you want Mom to do something?"

"Oh, not necessarily." Andre shrugged again, doing his best impression of a reasonable person. "I just want to talk. Ideally, of course, I do believe Sarah should pay for the trouble she has caused and for her betrayal. But all I truly want at the moment is to be able to speak to her and begin to understand why she would betray me and destroy our family as she did."

"You killed someone." Kim didn't have the energy to mince words.

"In defense. Your mother told everyone I murdered that man, but it was self-defense." Andre's expression took on a disbelieving cast, as if he didn't understand why anyone would believe he was a murderer, even with all he'd done. "Kim, do you not understand? Your mother is the one who was wrong. Her actions have cost us all so much time."

He gave her a look that was probably supposed to make her feel sorry for him. Kim wasn't fooled. She stared back.

After a moment, he heaved out a dramatic sigh. "I know I have made some mistakes. I was angry, of course. I wanted to make those who turned their backs on me pay. I may have acted in haste and temper."

"Is that what you call lighting up the scrapyard and shooting Uncle Bruno?"

"That was a mistake. I didn't realize who I was shooting at. I was trying to scare Sarah a little, and I might have gone too far. I really do just want to speak to her, to make her understand how much she has hurt me."

Kim scoffed. There were so many lies in that little speech she could only bring herself to address the most obvious and important one. "Please. You want to kill her."

"If she is not remorseful, then I may have to, yes. She does need to pay for what she's done, after all." His eyes met hers. "I would like to have you back by my side, daughter. I truly would. But I understand your mother has likely filled your head with lies." Andre rose to his feet, and Kim scrambled to hers, waiting for him to lunge at her. But Andre only stuck his hands in his pockets and regarded her with a cool, distant expression. "I shan't force you, Kim. Lee has already proven to me the lack of value in unwilling conscripts. But I do wish you to understand something."

"What's that?"

"I will find Sarah. I will make her pay for all she has done and all she has taken from me. Those who stand beside her and help her will be treated as traitors. Whether I kill her or not, they will share her fate." He gave her a wintry smile, cold as ice. "You decide what fate you will choose, my daughter."

He turned and walked away, whistling what sounded like "You Are My Sunshine" as he did. Kim watched him vanish among the houses, then she turned and ran for the square.

The rest of the group was already gathered, with the exception of the reverend. The New Wren residents looked worried.

Kim jogged up and came to a stop. "What's up?"

Big Ed spoke. "Sam told me you were looking around for other good salvage sites. I thought it was a good idea, so we were all doing the same. I spotted one of those thugs that attacked New Wren before. He was poking around one of the gas stations between here and the church."

So Andre hadn't lied about having reinforcements around. It didn't make Kim feel any better. "Sounds like trouble. I saw a guy as well. A big guy." She saw Lee start at the description and met his eyes, hoping he'd guess who she was talking about. From the way he paled, despite his complexion, she figured he had.

"We could fight…" Sam trailed off as Kim shook her head.

"We don't know how many there are, and we don't have a lot of weapons or a lot of experience. It's probably better if we take what we have and get back to Watchdog," Kim said. She really wished she could go and grab the books she wanted from the library, but it would take too long to collect them. Every minute they stayed in New Wren was another minute they might be attacked.

"She's right," Sam agreed.

Suzie nodded, backing them both up. "We should pack up the last of the stuff and get going."

All of them scattered to grab the last odds and ends they wanted. Kim found some simple toys for the kids and stuffed them in the top of her open, half-full box. Lee did the same with some clothes and shoes while the three New Wren adults grabbed tools, fabric, and anything that looked useful.

Reverend Jeb showed up just as they were finishing, pasty and smelling of alcohol. Kim glared at him as he huffed to a stop.

"What are you doing now?" he demanded.

"Getting ready to get out of here. We saw some of those bandits back again, and we don't want them to steal this loot," Sam answered.

The reverend jumped like a startled cat at the mention of bandits. "Brigands, here again? Well, in that case, we should most certainly leave. At once. Yes, we should return to Watchdog at once." He turned and shuffled to the tractor cab and vanished inside before any of them could say a word.

Suzie groaned. "Wherever he was hiding, I wish he'd stayed there a little longer. Now we're gonna have to smell him all the way back."

"That's no way to talk about a fellow man." Ed shook his head. "You kids be all right with the motorcycles? We can hook 'em up to the back of the truck and find a place for you, if you're worried."

Kim shook her head. "We can manage. If all else fails, we can probably outrun them." She hoped so, at least.

"Then let's go before those thieves find us."

Kim and Lee hurried over to the bikes. Just before they started the engines, Lee leaned over. "Was it him?"

"Yeah. It was." Kim started her bike and turned it around, fighting the urge to crank up the speed and race back to Watchdog as fast as possible.

Andre knew they were here, or at least nearby. Watchdog wouldn't be a safe haven for long, if it still was. Shannon needed to know as soon as possible.

24

SHANNON GRAYSON

After their tour of Watchdog, Carol wandered off, intent on some errand or another. Shannon and Bill spent some time checking out the buildings that would be their new base and helping the bikers make themselves comfortable. The ladies of the crew began setting up the space, and Shannon decided it was best to get out of their way. That done, Bill went to mingle with the community members and make friends, and Shannon went to look for her aunt.

It hadn't escaped Shannon's notice that Carol had been pretty quiet ever since they'd escaped The Spoke, aside from claiming Lee as their newest prospect. She understood why, but she also knew there was no sense in standing about and mourning what had been lost. There was too much for all of them to do.

She found Carol standing by the bikes, staring at them with a bleak expression. Shannon thought for a moment, then went to stand beside her aunt, content to stand quiet for a few minutes.

Eventually, Carol broke the silence. "It's a hell of a thing, what happened to Toad, and to the rest of Tupelo."

"Yeah."

"Worse after what happened in Memphis."

"I can't argue with that."

Carol's face twisted with grief and something else. Shannon couldn't be sure what the emotion was, but it put her in mind of a child lost in a crowd and waiting for someone from their family to come and find them.

"I spent my whole life with bikers—been running with one club or another ever since I was a young 'un. I can't remember when I wasn't part of a crew. I worked my way up to being your uncle's old lady with looks and brains and determination, and I never thought I'd regret it. Never thought the day would come when I'd wish I knew another way of life. And it's the world's worst feeling to think I might have been wrong."

Shannon was a little surprised at Carol's words. "You don't want to be a biker anymore?"

Carol hissed between her teeth, eyes filled with an indecision uncharacteristic of her. "I don't know. I don't know anything anymore. I lost everything I had—husband, club base, closest thing I had to a home, and a good portion of the people I called a family. Where do I go from there?"

That, at least, Shannon had an answer for. "You don't go anywhere. You stay here, with us. With the bikers who are left, and with your family. Me, Kim, Bill—I think you could even count Lee if you wanted to."

Carol snorted. "Lee's a brat with no sense."

Shannon raised an eyebrow. "Sense enough to get you out of the way of a gunshot. You wouldn't have taken him as a prospect if you didn't think there was some grit and worth in him."

Carol exhaled hard and folded her arms, but there was no heat in her voice when she replied. "You might be right. But I don't know that I can settle down."

"It's not like you won't have any chance to ride. If you didn't want to settle down at least a little, then you wouldn't have been so against it when Kim suggested being nomads."

Carol eyed her. "When'd you get so wise, girl?"

Shannon looked away. "I spent five years alone and always moving. I had a lot of time to think about things like that."

The two of them lapsed into a comfortable silence as they watched the children play.

Shannon was just beginning to relax and consider preparations for another meal when the truck rolled in, with Kim and Lee just ahead of it. Kim barely got the bike parked and turned off before she was off it and heading straight for Shannon. Unease filled Shannon's gut as she saw her daughter's frantic expression.

Carol noticed it too, because she pushed off the wall. "I'll go see about organizing the boys to unload."

Kim exchanged an absentminded nod with her aunt, then turned to Shannon, her eyes serious. "He's here."

There was only one "he" her daughter could be talking about, but Shannon had to ask to be sure. "Who?"

"Da—Andre. He's in New Wren, at least. I saw him."

"You saw him? Did he see you?"

Kim winced. "Yeah. We spoke for a minute. He wanted to try and convince me to join him. He said he just wanted to talk to you too, Mom, but I didn't—Mom?"

Shannon couldn't answer. Andre wanting to talk to her made the breath freeze in her lungs. She couldn't draw in a proper lungful of air, and the world went gray around the edges as bone-deep terror assaulted her.

She knew, all too well, what it meant when Andre "talked" to people. She could still remember how many of their "discussions" had ended in bruises and blood on her side, and the face of the man Andre had gone to "talk" to about missing money from a drug deal. The man he'd shot in cold blood. She was fairly certain that if her ex-husband had his way, she'd be asking for the bullet by the time she died.

He'd been near Kim. He'd spoken to Kim. The thought of what could have happened to her daughter was stomach-churning. Shannon wanted to puke, scream, and cry all at once, then huddle in a dark corner and never come out.

"Mom!"

Kim's voice dragged her out of the whirlpool of terror she'd been drowning in and pulled her back to some semblance of sanity and self-control. Shannon forced herself to take a deep breath, then another. "I'm all right."

"No. You aren't." Kim glowered at her. "You looked like you were about to throw up, curl up in a ball, or run for it."

Shannon reluctantly nodded. "That's about how I felt for a minute." She grimaced. "Hearing that your father is so close shook me a bit. I hoped we'd have a little more time."

"Time for what?" Kim asked.

"Time to figure out where to go next, I guess."

To her surprise, Kim shook her head. "That's not the answer, Mom. We can't keep running and hoping to lose him. He's not going to stop."

Shannon bit her lip. "I know that. But what else can we do?"

"We make a stand. Put an end to it. Here, in Watchdog, where we've got a fighting chance." Kim pointed at the town. "If he catches us out on the road, on our own, we're toast. Especially if he's been recruiting the kind of people who destroyed the towns we passed through. Here, we have shelter, we have backup, and we have a better chance of surviving."

Shannon felt compelled to point out the most obvious flaw. "You don't know that the folks here will help us or that they'll accept having a fight on their home turf."

"So we tell them the situation, and we ask them if they'll support us. If not, we can find another place to make a stand. But we have to put Andre down. He's not going to stop otherwise."

The idea sent shivers down Shannon's spine—both the idea of facing Andre and the idea of setting out to deliberately plan to kill a man. Not for the first time, she wondered what had happened to Kim in the five years she'd been gone, and the weeks between the EMP and their reunion. Her daughter was a lot more ruthless, and a lot tougher, than she remembered. She was proud of Kim, but it also worried her.

Shannon decided it was best to say what she was thinking. "I don't want to risk losing you."

Kim's expression softened. "I get it, Mom. But the fact is, I'm at risk either way. If nothing else, today proves that."

She was right. Shannon took a deep breath and forced herself to consider the matter logically instead of through her fear. Andre wouldn't stop. She'd never be safe—Kim, Carol, Lee and Bill would never be safe—until he was dealt with. Even if she could nerve herself up to give Andre what he wanted, he'd find another reason to come after the people she cared about. If there was no one she cared about, he'd find another reason to hurt more people. That was just who Andre was.

They'd tried running, and all it had got them was dead allies in Tupelo and Andre on their doorstep here. Casualties, the same type you'd get if you had a vicious animal running wild and unchecked. You didn't run from a rabid dog and hope no one got bitten. You trapped the beast and put it down.

Shannon took a few deep breaths, then looked her daughter in the eye. "I don't like it, but you're right. If we're gonna do this, though, we're not gonna do it without letting folks know what they're in for. We need to tell these people what's going on."

"Tell them the whole story, let them decide for themselves. That's fair." Kim nodded.

Shannon sighed. The truck was almost unloaded, and folks had started preparing for the evening meal, which looked like it was going to be some variation of cracker sandwiches and beef jerky. "No time like the present, I guess."

Kim went to find Carol and the rest of the Black Rats contingent while Shannon searched out Rebecca.

"There's something I need to talk to your people about," Shannon began. "Is there any way to call everyone together?"

"Sure. I can round them all up in about ten minutes. Is it urgent?" Rebecca's brow creased in a frown. "I heard from Big Ed that the raiders had been seen around New Wren again."

"It might be related. Probably is, actually."

"I'll get folks together." Rebecca hurried off.

Shannon climbed up on the edge of the tractor tongue. She wasn't exactly comfortable being in the spotlight, but she wanted to be seen and clearly heard. She watched as people filtered into the open space. Her shoulders relaxed a little as Kim, Bill, Carol, and Lee came forward to stand close to her, forming a loose line on the ground in front of her. The bikers and their ladies formed a loose cordon around the edges of the crowd, in case things went wrong.

Finally, everyone was there. Rebecca appeared last, along with the reverend, who scowled and skulked off to one side.

Rebecca stepped up to the front. "Our new friends got something to say, and they say it's important, so give them your attention." She nodded to Shannon.

Shannon took a deep breath to calm her nerves. Bill reached up and gave her shin a soft squeeze of encouragement, and that helped. It got the words moving, at least.

"When we arrived yesterday, I'm sure all of you noticed the bullet holes in my rig. The thing is, five years ago, I was married to a man, a very dangerous man, named Andre Atkinson. I helped put him in jail for murder, but when the disaster happened, he escaped. He's been after me and my family ever since. Right now, I know three things about him: he's hunting me for vengeance, he's got friends with weapons and violent tendencies, and he's in New Wren."

She took another breath. "I think the raiders who destroyed your town were part of his crew, or they are now. We're sure some of them are associates of his from prison."

Her gaze flicked over the crowd, seeing concern, confusion, and questions in people's eyes. "My family and I want to put an end to this. Andre isn't going to stop coming after us until we make him, and we've decided to take a stand. We're thinking to make it here in Watchdog, if you're willing."

She looked to Rebecca. "These are dangerous people. I guess you know that, but trust me when I say they're worse with a leader, and especially when they're being led by Andre. Stopping them won't be easy. There's sure to be fighting, and I can't promise everyone who gets involved will live to see the end of it. Still, odds are better with greater numbers. That's why I'm asking for your help."

Silence fell. Shannon wondered if there was more she could say, but she couldn't think of anything.

"You're certain those monsters who raided our town are part of the group that's after you?" Rebecca called out.

"Yes. You said Big Ed saw the raiders back in New Wren. My Kim saw Andre there too, and they seem to be operating under his orders," Shannon answered.

Rebecca's chin went up, anger in her normally friendly gaze. "Then I'm with you folks. I owe those men for what they did to our town. And I'm not the only one." There were some nods and murmurs from the crowd around her.

"Don't be foolish! Surely you can see they mean to trick you into dying for them so they can steal our hard-won homes!" Reverend Jeb pushed his way forward to address the crowd. "If a man brings evil among you, let him be cast out, lest it destroy you all! These people bring danger and divisiveness and war to us! Far better that we should drive them out, send them away, so we can be safe!"

He pointed at Shannon. "She brings danger to us! Once these intruders are gone, will not the danger pass us by, and leave us to live in peace? Is that not better than getting embroiled in a conflict which has nothing to do with us? Why should we risk our homes and our citizens for strangers, to whom we owe nothing?"

"Do onto others as you would have done onto you." Bill's deep voice cut through Jeb's tenor and silenced him. "I don't know about anyone else, but I seem to recollect that being a big part of the Bible too, Reverend."

Bill stepped forward to address the crowd. "You all have your worries, and I won't say the reverend is completely wrong. I will say that I don't think we've done poorly by you, and I don't think you folks are the sort to do poorly by us—or yourselves." His gaze slid over the crowd. "I'm a mechanic and a lifelong small-town man. If there's anything I've learned from either, it's that a community can do a lot of jobs a single person can't. I'm thinking this gang of thugs is one of those things it takes folks working together to handle."

Jeb scowled. "But these thugs, as you put it, are your problem, not ours. There is no reason to involve Watchdog in your altercations."

"There was no reason for New Wren to get wrecked, either." Lee's voice cracked a little, but it was still audible as he stepped forward. "But your town square's wrecked, and people died. These guys—they don't stop. They won't ignore you just 'cause we leave." His eyes were haunted, his hands clenched in fists. "I've seen what Andre does. He won't give you any freedom, not now he knows where you are. Once he sees you, it's join him or die. Doesn't matter if we're here or not. Doesn't matter if you help us or throw us out. He'll run right over you. Anyone who stands up to him will get killed, or wish they had."

Jeb glared at the youth. "How do we know you are any better?"

"Because we're honest." Carol shouldered her way in front of Lee, a hard stare on her weathered features. "If you don't believe words, you can believe actions well enough. My niece was the one who said we should give you all food. She sent the truck with the salvage team today, and she didn't have to do either of those things. And she's telling you this now, giving you a choice about being involved. She could have waited until it was too late."

"Shannon's a good woman," Bill spoke up again. "I was trapped with her for near a week right after the disaster happened, with about a hundred other folks. She helped keep us fed and taken care of when others were trying to get in the way. If it weren't for her, a lot of folks would have starved or died of dehydration, and we might still be trapped."

Jeb started to speak again, but Rebecca stepped forward. "Enough, Reverend. You've said your piece. We all know how you feel. But we could talk till the sun goes down about who to trust and who to help and who to throw out on their ears. Right now, we need to make a decision."

With Bill's help, she climbed up next to Shannon and looked out over the crowd. "Now, the way I see it is, we owe those thugs for what they did to New Wren. But more than that, we owe it to ourselves to stand and defend our new home. As for Shannon and her family, I'm for helping them. Partly because they've been a help to us, and partly because it doesn't sit right with me, the idea of turning them out to fend for themselves. I don't like the idea of people dying because I didn't do anything. That's not how I was raised, and I like to think the rest of you are the same."

There was some muttering, but not even Jeb spoke out against her statement.

Rebecca nodded. "All right. We'll put it to a vote then. All those in favor of welcoming Shannon and her folks, helping them out and teaching these mad dogs a lesson, raise your hand."

A forest of hands went up. Jeb's hand stayed stuffed in his pocket, and Shannon saw a few others here and there who were holding back. But it was a clear majority that voted to help them. Her heart rose.

Rebecca did a swift count. "All right. All those who want us to send these folks packing and hope that trouble passes us by, raise your hands."

A few hands went up, but Shannon could count the number and have fingers left over. Jeb's was the most prominent, and Shannon saw his scowl when he realized he was in the clear minority.

"All right. Looks like we're agreed." Rebecca turned to Shannon. "I've said it before, and I'll say it now: you're all welcome to stay in Watchdog as long as you like. If that means taking up arms against raiders and the people who destroyed our home, then that's what we'll do."

Shannon nodded and clasped Rebecca's hand when she held it out. "Thanks." It was hard to talk past the lump in her throat, but she managed. "We'll do our best for you as well."

"You already are." Rebecca hopped down.

The crowd started to break up then, with some of them going to start preparations for the community-wide dinner most folks enjoyed, while others went about personal tasks. Jeb turned and gave Shannon one poisonous glare before he stalked off.

Bill helped Shannon down, and Kim gave her a tight hug. "Good speech, Mom."

"You all helped." Shannon swallowed her fear as she held her daughter in her arms. She didn't doubt Kim's resolve, or Rebecca's or even Carol's. She knew they'd all fight, just as she and Bill and Lee would. But how many of the others would stand their ground? These people weren't fighters or killers, like Andre and his men. They wouldn't be filled with bloodlust and drugs and alcohol. They'd be filled with fear and uncertainty, just like Shannon herself.

And how many of them could actually kill a man? Shannon knew she could take a life in self-defense. She'd done it before. Bill might be able to kill if he was protecting someone else, the way he'd helped her stop Langmaid and Connor. Carol probably could, especially if she spotted the men who'd wiped out the Tupelo chapter, or Andre. But what about the rest of them?

How were they supposed to defeat a gang of lunatics who thrived on violence? Shannon wasn't even sure they had enough weapons to arm most of the citizens of Watchdog. Most of the Black Rats had at least one gun and one blade on hand. She had the small caliber in her truck, plus two knives. Kim had a couple knives and one, maybe two guns. Bill wasn't carrying anything except a knife he'd borrowed from her during their time in Stuttgart.

If they really were going to make a stand, they needed to figure out a plan of attack and a plan of defense. They needed to decide what critical places to protect, like the med center, and what to do about the noncombatants, like the kids. Andre wouldn't hesitate to use children as hostages. Or worse. They needed a solid plan for making sure anyone who wasn't fighting was well out of the danger zone.

There were a lot of questions that needed to be answered, and plans that needed to be made, and Andre was already on their doorstep. She wished it was someone else's job, but Shannon didn't want a repeat of what had happened at the scrapyard, which meant those issues were hers to deal with immediately. At the very least, they should arrange patrols to keep a watch on the surrounding area.

Shannon took a deep breath, then went in search of Rebecca and some of the other prominent Watchdog citizens, like Big Ed. She also wanted to find Glenda Evans, who'd been introduced as the closest thing the community had to a doctor.

There was work to do, and no time at all in which to get it done.

25

SHANNON GRAYSON

The Black Rats and the people of Watchdog spent their lunch break talking over initial plans and agreeing on what needed to be done. Most of the residents were happy to take direction from more enterprising or experienced individuals, so Shannon and Rebecca formed a planning team.

They needed to start scouting for signs of Andre's crew closer to Watchdog, and they needed to set up some watch posts. Lee, Bill, TimFist, and a few of the others would be responsible for that task.

Fortifying and setting up safe buildings was next on the list. Each of the safe buildings would have a generator with gas either taken from the spare containers or siphoned from the tractor and any cars they came across. The bikes would be left alone for transport of people and materials. Safe buildings included the old medical center, the improvised childcare center, Big Ed's, and the Old Grady Sawmill. Once the walls had been shored up there and basic supplies laid in, individual homes and buildings would follow. Big Ed, David Skinner, and Sam Simmons volunteered to start fortifying buildings, even if that just meant stacking stones and sticking them together with concrete or boarding up the windows.

"Maybe we could set some traps in the street?" Rebecca suggested. "At least the ones that approach Watchdog. If we keep the children away from those locations, dangerous—even lethal—traps could be set." At Kim's suggestion, the planning team set aside that plan for further consideration after the scouts returned.

Kim and Glenda volunteered to gather medical supplies and other basic necessities, like water. Most of those supplies would go to the medical center, but they'd also stash a certain amount at the other safe areas for use in emergencies.

Shannon and the Black Rats volunteered for scavenging and salvage. In addition to food and other basic supplies, they could bring back a lot of the smaller and lighter materials necessary for building and fortifying, like screws and nails. The crew could also find the best places for the truck to gather the larger items needed for construction and fortification, such as extra wood, stone, concrete or sheet metal, or storage boxes for the supplies at each of the emergency locations.

Suzie and Margaret led another group on a cautious foraging expedition. The former schoolteacher had collected some material about edible plants in the area over the years. She'd been studying the books since the EMP, with the help of one or two older members of the community who had decades of experience with the local flora.

Kim took it upon herself to speak to Suzie and Margaret before they left. Shannon only heard part of the discussion, but it involved dandelions, yaupon holly roots, willow bark, and a few other plants. Some of them sounded familiar, some of them didn't.

She vaguely recalled that Kim had mentioned the willow bark as a substitute for aspirin. She wondered if the rest of the items Kim listed were also remedies. Whether they were or not, she was impressed with her daughter's knowledge of wild plants and their uses. Shannon herself could barely tell a blackberry bush from a holly thicket. Much less tell someone what they were used for, beyond the obvious.

Those Watchdog residents and Black Rats who weren't detailed to aid a specific work group took care of the daily tasks, such as cleaning, gathering wood for fires, planning meals, and keeping an eye on the children. One member of each task group started listing the supplies they had available for Carol and Rebecca to track.

A council of sorts, consisting of Rebecca, Big Ed, Suzie, John, Shannon, Kim, Bill, and Carol, set up a command post in the Black Rats' new space within Watchdog. Carol explained to Rebecca and John that it saved having to designate another location as a separate control center, and the crew was used to living in a base of operations anyway.

Rebecca's salvage and fortification crew at the Old Grady Sawmill unearthed a detailed map of Watchdog while they were working and brought it back. She tacked it to one wall of their command base and began plotting strategies for defense, salvage, and further settlement with Shannon's aunt.

Shannon left the two older women to their strategizing and headed out with a few other Black Rats on their salvaging mission. She was more suited to hands-on activities. Besides, it was good to see Carol focused on something other than the grief and anger that had filled her since the fall of the Memphis home base. Her aunt knew about setting up a defensive territory; the Black Rats had done it before when defending their area from other gangs.

Shannon's salvaging expedition had mixed results. There wasn't much in Watchdog, given how long it had been abandoned before the disaster had even occurred. However, Shannon did discover one major find: an old electronics store. It hadn't been looted, since most electronics were useless, and she'd almost passed it by before she remembered the supercenter.

Radios. Not all the radios were useless, and the store might have some of the older-style hand units like the type Bill had used. If so, they could have reliable communications again.

Picking the lock was easy, and she found plenty of batteries available inside. Better still, Shannon found a good dozen handheld radio units in the back of the store, all matching the specifications Bill had given her back in Oklahoma. She had her team pack the lot of them into large boxes to take back to town.

When Shannon and the salvage crew returned to the new command post, she left the unloading chores to the Black Rats. She went to find Bill and Lee, who were locating places on the map to designate as watch posts. An old storefront labeled Carlo's Pizza was the closest suggested watch post to the main settlement and living area. The next was an old general store near the edge of town that had already been thoroughly cleaned out. The last location they'd marked on the map was an abandoned hunting lodge up near Lake Monroe.

Rebecca pulled up some plans she'd apparently had the construction crew bring over while Shannon was out on the salvage run. Either that, or someone had brought them over on the assumption they'd be useful. They were all old, but there were city zoning plans, as well as a thick sheaf of structure blueprints and what looked, to Shannon's unpracticed eye, like plans for the power grid and sewage and drainage systems.

"I'm hoping we can find a basement in town to shelter the children and other folks who can't fight. Worse comes to worst, we could try to sneak them out of town to the hunting lodge, but it'd be safer if they could hide in place."

Bill frowned. "I haven't seen anything like that, but then, we've been looking at stores, except for the hunting lodge. A basement is more likely to be found in a house."

Lee nodded. "Or maybe the medical center? If they've got a morgue or an autopsy area, it might be below ground, right?"

"It's worth a look. In a serious emergency, you could even use the storm drains under the streets, though we'd need to provide lights to make sure no one got lost."

Shannon went to the table they'd set up and joined Rebecca and Carol in searching through the pile of building blueprints for any sign of an underground space to hide. By the time the call came round for dinner, the three women had no luck with finding a basement, but they had decided on a few possible escape routes from the safe buildings to the outskirts, including an underground storm drain that eventually terminated near the sawmill.

Outside the command post, Watchdog was undergoing a rapid transformation. Big Ed and his crew were hard at work sealing windows that had gaped open with boards or makeshift barriers. Another crew led by Sam Simmons worked at reinforcing battered foundations, along with the worst of the wall cracks, using everything from concrete to rubber cement and grout filler. The crates brought back by the New Wren salvage team had been pulled off the tractor and distributed to the relevant work crews or designated supply locations.

The biggest difference, however, was the people. The Black Rats and the people of Watchdog were organized, and they moved together with a sense of purpose and community that wasn't apparent when the club had originally pulled up. The remaining members of the Black Rats were mixed in among the townsfolk, helping as needed, and there was very little sign of discord.

In fact, Sprocket was helping Margaret prepare some edible greens they'd found, and both were smiling as they worked. Big Ed and Bill had corralled two other bikers to help test the radios, and one of the oldest members of the Black Rats was helping mind the children. Mutt was once again wandering between groups, soliciting attention and whatever scraps she could coax people into giving her. She was followed by a couple of the kids, who'd latched onto her with adoring eyes and refused to be shooed or pulled away, except by their families.

Shannon thought it was heartening, even if there was a voice in the back of her mind whispering that this peace couldn't last forever. Sooner or later, someone would stir up trouble that couldn't be ignored, and the solidarity of the community would be diminished or broken.

She was surprised Jeb wasn't around, trying to sow discord and win people back to his side. There was no sign of the disgruntled preacher. After a moment, Shannon decided to be grateful for small favors rather than to go looking for trouble.

"It's a good start, isn't it?"

Shannon started slightly when Rebecca's voice broke into her thoughts. She turned to see the other woman standing beside her, holding out a drink.

Rebecca nodded to the gathered inhabitants of Watchdog. "The circumstances aren't the best, but it's good to see people working together and getting things done."

"It is." Shannon took the drink and sniffed it. It was beer of some kind, and she sipped cautiously. It was lukewarm, but palatable enough.

"Seems like you might be settling in here after all."

Shannon nodded. "I think so."

Rebecca smiled and held out her own drink. "To your arrival—and the community we'll build together."

Shannon tapped her drink to Rebecca's. "To Watchdog."

May we be able to keep everyone safe.

26

KIM NAKAMURA

The day after the salvage operation in New Wren brought a lot of new changes. That morning, Shannon, Rebecca, and Carol wrote out a roster of scouts and lookouts that rotated on six-hour shifts. A duty roster went up in what was now the command post and council office, and everyone was told to put their name up, or they would have it put in for them. Even Mutt had a duty: keeping an eye on the town with either Shannon or Kim.

Kim was unsurprised to find herself on duty at the medical center with Glenda. The two of them were the only people present who had training in more than the most rudimentary first aid, and they worked well together. Kim found Glenda to be a capable medic, but also a good instructor. There were a lot of things Kim hadn't had time to learn, including surgery techniques, that Glenda had at least been trained in. They'd still be in trouble if someone developed appendicitis or went into cardiac arrest, but Kim thought they'd be able to handle most wounds and the more common illnesses, at least for a while.

They agreed that running water was a priority, as well as finding ways to distill alcohol or other disinfectants. In between tending minor injuries and putting up supplies, the two of them brainstormed to prepare for the emergencies that might happen. They also set up a quick-reference list of substitute medications for those who needed them, based on what they were likely to run out of first. Since Glenda admitted to having atrocious handwriting, Kim wrote everything down in a notebook Glenda had found in an office.

Kim was surprised when Rebecca's father came in with a crate of wine scavenged from somewhere and dropped it off with a muttered, "Remembered what you said about the wine working as a kind of medicine. Figure folks could use it."

It was almost lunchtime, so Kim was about to go get some food when Mutt, who'd been lounging in the front greeting area, started barking. Kim and Glenda looked at each other and then toward the noise. Kim hurried to the front to find David and two of the other designated scouts supporting an older man who looked like he'd been in a brawl and a younger woman who was clearly exhausted from helping him. Both the new individuals were dirty, dehydrated, and sunburned, their clothing disheveled and torn.

Kim went to the older man first. "What happened?"

"Farm got attacked by a buncha goons on bikes." The words were slurred through split lips, but there was enough venom in them to make a copperhead envious.

Kim frowned. "Farm?"

"Found 'em out near Dryden Barn," David said. "I know these two. Herb Roberts owns Dryden Barn and the land around it, and Chelsea Jerkins used to work in the post office."

The woman nodded. "I was out on the back roads doing deliveries when the disaster happened. I've been moving from place to place since." She shivered. "I've seen those men on bikes before, but I never let them see me. They look dangerous."

"They are." Kim turned her attention back to Herb. "Herb, I know it's hard to talk, but I need you to tell me if there are any sharp pains or grinding when you move your jaw."

"Just the ache from the bruise, and where I lost a molar."

Glenda saw to taking care of Chelsea while Kim ran Herb through a diagnostic. Aside from the split lip, he had a broken collarbone, three cracked ribs, a busted knee, a sprained wrist, and a lot of deep bruising. Kim set to work patching him up.

"You said you got attacked?"

"Yeah. Buncha men on bikes. I was out gathering wood when they showed. Wasn't gonna stand for it, but some young piece-of-crap in an oversized jacket beat the dickens out of me. Mean as a hornet, he was." Herb winced. "Thought he might do me in, but some girl pulled him off."

"Yeah?"

"Yeah. Seemed friendly, didn't stay that way from what I heard while I was crawling away from the lunatic." Herb's eyes were full of bitter anger. "Family's owned that place since my grandfather, and I got run off by some drug-addled thug. Wish I had a gun to teach that boy a lesson."

"That's a common wish around here," Kim agreed. "Unfortunately, no one knows where to find more guns."

Herb snorted. "If Ed Grady were still alive, you wouldn't have to ask that question, young lady. Ed had enough guns to stock an army, and the ammo to go with 'em. Heck, Ed had it all, anything you could want—pistols, rifles, machine guns. I even saw him with a case of grenades once, and he swore he had landmines and two or three bazookas too. All Cold War stuff, but he kept it in prime condition."

Kim bit her lip to stop her excitement from welling up and causing her to make a mistake. "I've heard rumors about Ed Grady's cache, but nobody I talked to knew if it was real or not."

Herb started to move his head, and Kim stopped him with a touch. "It's real, all right. I can't count how many times Ed would call me up just to tell me about a new gun he acquired or how often I saw him testing out a new rifle. Darn near blew us both up with a box of C4 one time."

"You knew Ed Grady?" Kim asked.

Herb almost smiled, though he winced as the movement pulled his split lip. "Grew up with the man. My folks lived in Watchdog until my granddad passed away and we took over the farm. Ed Grady was a hunting buddy of mine from the time we were young 'uns. Couldn't set a trap to save his life, and didn't like 'em anyway, but if it could shoot, Ed knew how to handle it and could put a mark on a bullseye with it. At least when he was younger. Not so much when he got older, but then I'm no marksman anymore either."

"And you think he really collected a bunch of guns?" Kim had trouble picturing it.

"He collected an armory." Herb went to shake his head again, then flinched and kept it still before Kim could remind him. "Ed always figured doomsday would come—kept saying the Red Soviets would invade someday. He was dead set on being prepared for it, determined to have enough weapons to supply an army, and beat one too. Weapons, food, supplies—man was a hoarder when it came to anything survival related." Herb sighed. "I used to think he had a screw loose."

"We all did." Glenda spoke up from where she was giving Chelsea some water and lidocaine for sunburn. "It's bad luck he died before he found out he was right."

Kim hesitated, then decided she might as well ask the question that was on her mind. "Mr. Roberts, do you know where Mr. Grady stored his weapons cache?"

The regretful expression he wore gave her the answer even before he spoke. "I wish I did. But Ed was paranoid. Didn't keep anything in his home or at the mill. Too easy to find, he said. He hired some equipment and dug out a bunch of bunkers on his land in random locations. He stockpiled everything in those bunkers, and whatever system he had for keeping track of where they were and what they contained died with him."

Kim swallowed back a flood of disappointment. She'd known it was a long shot, but she'd hoped Herb at least had some clues. "He never let any kind of clues slip?"

"Only that the guns were in the woods surrounded by stone, food was in a dry space where nothing could come, and everything else was somewhere close to home." Herb made a sound that might have been a halfhearted laugh if it hadn't made his ribs hurt. "Close to home for Ed meant within a two-hour hike, and he could move fast when he wanted."

Kim's heart fell a little further. A two-hour hike in any direction from Grady's home or the sawmill was a lot of area to search. Who knew how well the bunkers had been hidden, assuming Ed Grady hadn't just been blowing smoke.

She forced a smile onto her face and set to work binding Herb's knee. "It's a pity, but maybe someday one of us will get lucky and find the bunkers."

"Maybe." Herb agreed. "Ed was good at hiding things, but stuff has a way of being found too."

Kim finished patching him up and turned him over to Glenda for a spot check of her work. She was getting more confident with her splinting and bandaging, but Glenda was still more experienced.

As she finished up, one of the town's children came in with a skinned knee, and one of the construction team came in with painful blisters on her hands. Kim took care of both while Herb rested in a cubicle.

The peace and quiet didn't last long. A few minutes later, the front doors erupted inward to reveal Lee, his face cut, his jeans torn, and his wounded arm held close to his side. The bullet graze was bleeding again, but the first thing Kim noticed was the wide-eyed look of desperation in Lee's eyes.

"Where's Shannon?" he asked, his voice cracking.

"Up near the mill, I think." Kim was fairly certain her mother had gone with Rebecca to make the mill more defensible. They also wanted to see if it could be used for water and maybe power.

Lee started to turn away, and Kim just barely caught hold of his good arm before he bolted out the door. "Hey, hold up. Those wounds need to be looked at. And the sawmill's probably full of dust and dirt you don't need to get in open cuts."

"It doesn't matter. I gotta find Shannon." Lee's expression made Kim's stomach clench.

"Why?" She wasn't sure she wanted to know, but she had to ask. "What happened?"

"Bill and I were on scouting patrol, and we ran into some other guys. Think they were from the prison, but I don't know." Tears filled Lee's eyes. "They attacked us—shot at us, and one guy came at us with a knife. There were four or five of them. We tried to get away, but I fell and cracked my knee bad, twisted my ankle. And Bill…"

Lee's voice broke, and a tear tracked down his face. "Bill led them away. He baited them so I could escape. I thought he was gonna rile them up and slip away and come back, but he didn't. He didn't come back. I heard shouting, and I snuck closer." Lee was shaking, his face tight.

Kim's stomach sank to the level of her shoes. "Did they…?"

"They captured him. Those guys…" Lee swallowed hard. "Andre has Bill."

27

AUSTIN/ANDRE

The hardest part was waiting, but he'd always been a patient man. Andre focused on the decorations of the Mt. Sinai Baptist Church as he waited for news from his men. Most of the crew was out searching, and only Austin was still present and standing by for his orders.

Austin. The man really was a weakling. He hadn't even managed to beat up the farmer he'd accosted the previous day before being dragged away by the red-haired woman whose attentions he coveted. Without his drugs, the man was almost useless. But then, most people were. At least with enough cocaine, Austin became marginally useful. And he had gotten them this far, so Andre was inclined to be somewhat lenient about his current laziness.

Sooner or later, his men would find Sarah, whether she was still with that pathetic reverend and his sheep or if she'd fled elsewhere. Sooner or later, he would corner her and make her pay for what she'd done. Until then, Mt. Sinai offered a comfortable enough base of operations.

Shouting at the door to the foyer drew Andre from his contemplation. The men fought—frequently, in fact—but if they'd returned and not come to give him a report before descending into petty bickering, then he might need to reinforce some discipline. That was a pleasant thought.

He emerged from the sanctuary to find four of his men holding down a well-built older man with dark skin and a scowl like a thundercloud. He was on his knees and being restrained with a knife to his throat, but he didn't look cowed in the least. The bruises and blood on his face and hands suggested he'd put up quite a struggle.

Austin was standing to one side, clearly uncomfortable. Andre sighed. A proper second-in-command would have started asking questions. It seemed he'd have to do all the work himself. "What is this?"

"We captured this guy a few miles away. He was traveling with a kid, a boy with skin like his, all skinny and rangy. Kid got away, but we brought this one back for you. Figured he might have some information." He gave a kick to the man's leg.

The man didn't flinch, and Andre found himself intrigued. The face also looked familiar, and he moved closer. Delight filled him when he realized why he recognized the man. "Information, indeed. I do believe you are Sarah's mechanic, aren't you? You were with her at the scrapyard. You stole my protégé."

"Can't steal something that was abandoned, and that boy's better off without you." The man spit blood from a split lip at him.

Andre smiled. "There is no need for such unpleasantness, is there? All I want is some information regarding the whereabouts of my former wife, Sarah." He crouched. "I'm sure you know where she is."

"I know she wants nothing to do with you." The older man stared back at him with contempt in his eyes. "I don't blame her for leaving you either, boy."

Andre felt his good mood fade, replaced by irritation. "I would watch your tone with me." He seized the man's jaw in an iron grip. "I am not a man to make light of."

The man jerked his head free with a mocking expression. "From what I've heard, you're not much of a man. A man understands when a woman tells him to get lost. You seem hellbent on not listening."

"She betrayed me."

"She left you, and you've been nursing that petty, bruised ego of yours ever since." The man shook his head with a derisive laugh. "I've seen playground children who'd be embarrassed by the way you act."

One of the men made a choking sound. Andre rose to his feet and glared but couldn't see who it was. He didn't need to see to know they were laughing. At him.

He turned and brought his boot up hard into the man's gut, and the man doubled over with a grunt, still held up by the guards. Andre grabbed his head and forced it up. "Do not test me. Do not mock me. You will answer my questions, or you will wish you were dead. Do you understand?"

"I understand." The words were a hoarse wheeze, and then the man smirked at him. "I understand you're a schoolyard bully on a power trip."

Enraged, Andre jerked the man forward, out of the guards' grip, and slammed his face into the floor. There was a muffled crunch as his nose hit. "Tell me where Sarah is, and what she is doing, and I will put you out of your misery. If you do not, I will increase it a hundredfold."

"Don't know any Sarah."

"My former wife. You travel with her. Where is she?"

"Long gone and lookin' for someone who's not a loser like you." Andre lifted his head an inch, using a choking grip on his collar, and slammed him back down, which earned him a choked gasp followed by a short sound of laughter. "Boy, I've had cars fall off the jack on top of me. If you think I've never had a broken nose before, you've never done an honest day's labor." A pause. "Which is just about what I expect of you."

Andre wrenched him up and threw him back. The old man landed hard on his side. Andre leaned in, grabbed his jaw, and hauled him back to his knees with brute strength. "This is your last chance. Tell me where Sarah is and what she is doing. Or I will wring the answers from you."

"I've told you everything I've got to say, boy. If you can't let go and face the facts, that spite's gonna be the death of you."

Fury filled him at the older man's dismissive attitude. He looked at the two men standing nearby—fellow penitentiary inmates. "Take him to the room with the long table and bind him to it. Have your fun if you wish it, but leave him alive and able to talk. I will be there in a moment. I need my tools."

Neither man hesitated to grab the old man and pull him away. They knew what Andre meant by "tools" and what it meant when he decided he wanted them. They'd seen the results of the one time Andre had collected his tools in prison.

They knew if they disobeyed, he'd use those implements on them instead.

Andre watched them drag the man through a door, then he went to his bag. He had a number of lovely implements he could use, but a knife suited his mood. He grabbed the hilt of a wicked-looking one with a partially serrated blade.

He would teach that man to mock him and to side with Sarah. Once he had extracted all the information the man had to offer, he might consider letting him die.

Austin watched Andre disappear through the door where they'd taken the old man. He didn't even attempt to follow. He felt sick.

His eyes went to the blood on the floor where Andre had broken the old man's nose. He got it, he did. Andre couldn't let the guy disrespect him like that. The man was asking for a punishment, the way he was talking to the boss. Even so, the cold depravity in Andre's eyes made his stomach churn. The way he'd picked up that knife, and the way he'd talked about needing his tools—that was like the boss was talking about *torturing* the old guy or something.

Austin knew he wasn't a great person. He knew that. He liked being a bad boy. He'd beat up that guy in the barn the day before, and it had felt good. For once, he'd been the one doing the pounding rather than getting whaled on.

But Cherry hadn't liked it, and she'd left. Left him and left the crew. That hadn't made him feel too great. Now it sounded like Andre was going to go beat up a guy who couldn't fight back. That didn't sit well in Austin's gut.

He took a hit of coke, but it didn't settle him the way it usually did. Sure, he got the rush, but he couldn't stop thinking about Andre, and the old guy, and the knife, and what might be happening in that room. It made him feel sicker than having a hangover.

Beatings were one thing. But torture? That was hardcore in a way Austin had never pictured himself. Not even a second hit of coke could silence the part of his brain that kept whispering, *That guy only said what you've been thinking for a while now.*

It was true. The old mechanic had only said the same things Austin had been thinking during the long rides searching for Andre's ex. He'd only said what a lot of the bikers and even some of the convicts were saying—that it was nuts, and it was stupid and petty and worthless, to chase one woman all this distance for something that had happened years ago.

Andre was obsessed with this Sarah, and nothing Austin could tell himself made it seem like anything less than a stupid fixation. It made him wonder, and not for the first time, why exactly he was following Andre. He'd thought he was getting a leader when he agreed to join the guy, but Andre wasn't building an empire or leading the Black Rats like a proper prez should.

He could leave. The door was right there, and Andre would be busy for a while.

Austin had almost made up his mind to hit the road when a scream echoed through the building. A deep voice, howling in pain, rose up the register until it cracked with agony.

A moment of silence, then it came again, another of those throat-ripping screams. This time Austin recognized it as the mechanic's voice. No words, just a sound of pure, desperate pain ripping through the air and stabbing into Austin's brain like a knife.

It froze him in his tracks. All he could think as he listened to that scream was, *If Andre does that to a guy for talking back to him, what would he do to me if I actually left?*

Another cry echoed through the building. Austin dropped to his knees and slapped his hands over his ears. He screwed his eyes closed as he tried not to listen to the sound.

It didn't help. Not even the rush from the second hit of coke could stop the sickness that filled him as the screams filled the church.

28

SHANNON GRAYSON

S hannon had finished up at the mill, so she and Big Ed were supervising the establishment of a lookout post in the center of town. They talked about buildings they could erect a temporary or permanent tower on without too much trouble.

Big Ed gestured toward an already assembled kid's play tower nearby. "We could relocate that to get some height and visibility. Your truck could move it, no problem.

"Not a bad idea," Shannon agreed, "but then how will we get the tower up on top of a building? And which building would be the best choice for planting a tower?"

As they considered the nearest rooftops, Kim and Lee came running up. One look at Lee, beaten and barely patched up, was enough to make Shannon turn to Big Ed.

"Hold up. It looks like something's happened."

"Shannon…" Lee's voice failed him. There were tears on his face, and he looked sick.

"What? You look like you've been in a fight."

"He was." Kim's face was grim. "He and Bill got jumped by Andre's guys out on patrol."

Shannon's stomach lurched. "What? Bill—where's Bill?" There was no sign of the mechanic. "Is he—"

"We don't know. Lee said they took him prisoner."

Shannon swore, using invectives she'd heard from some of the older Black Rats combined with a few words she'd learned from other truckers. "Come on."

The four of them hurried to the command post, where they found Carol and Rebecca working on fine-tuning plans for escape routes.

"We've got a problem," Shannon said. "Bill's been captured."

Rebecca flinched, but Aunt Carol didn't waste the time to look horrified. "Where?" she asked tersely.

Lee answered, "Up near Lake Monroe. We were coming back from sweeping the area around the hunting lodge."

"Right." Aunt Carol grabbed the little car-shaped game piece someone had appropriated from a kid's Monopoly set after a scavenging mission and set it on the map. "So about here. Where's the closest places they could take him?"

"With a roof over their heads and some privacy?" Rebecca frowned. "Borley Farm would be my best guess."

Ed spoke up. "They might head over to my auto barn, my storage site for parts and wrecks that have been cleaned out. I haven't had a chance to check over there lately, and they might have stopped there to look for parts for their bikes."

"There's that too." Rebecca dropped two red dots from some other board game on the farm and the shop. "So we need one, maybe two, rescue teams to get Bill back."

"One team, and they can go both places if they need to. We can cover the ground easy enough on the bikes, but we don't want to divide forces." Shannon voiced the strategy and received a round of nods. "We need to pick a group who are used to fighting and can move fast."

"I'll go." Kim spoke first. "I can take two or three volunteers and head out right now."

"Not a chance." Shannon shook her head. "I don't want you going out there on a rescue mission, Kim. It's too dangerous."

"I can handle danger." Kim's eyes were hot with anger. "I can fight, I have my own gun and knives, and I know how to move quickly and quietly. And, now, how to ride a motorcycle. I'm a perfect choice!"

"No. You need to stay here."

"Why, because you think I might get a scratch or a bruise?" Kim's jaw clenched. "I'm not a child, Mom, and I can handle this. Bill's my friend, and every second we stand here arguing is another second Bill's in danger."

"And you're our medic." Aunt Carol stepped between mother and daughter, her expression stern. She turned to Shannon first. "Take a breath and start thinking instead of reacting with your gut." Then Aunt Carol turned to Kim. "And you—I know you want to help, and that's admirable, but you need to stop and think a moment too. We've got a lot of people who can handle a weapon and ride, but only you and one other who can patch up whatever injuries the rescue team gets."

Kim's mouth snapped shut.

Aunt Carol continued, "Knowing Andre, Bill isn't gonna come out of this unscathed, no matter when we get to him. At the very least, he'll be banged up from his capture. Odds are, whoever goes after him isn't coming back without getting bruised and bloody."

She put a hand on Kim's shoulder. "The best thing you can do, Kim, is lend your gun to someone else and go back to the med center. Start prepping for when we come back with Bill, 'cause we're gonna need you."

Kim still looked angry, but she finally nodded. "Okay." She turned to Lee. "Let me finish patching you up, and I'll give you my gun so you can go rescue Bill."

Lee nodded. "Okay." The two youngest members of the group moved off to bandage his wounds.

Shannon took a deep breath. "Okay. We have Lee. I'm not leaving Bill in Andre's hands, so I'm going. Who else?"

Carol made a derisive noise. "If you think I'm letting you and our only prospect do this without me, think again. I'll have the boys hold the bikes hostage if you try to leave me behind."

Shannon knew Aunt Carol was a good scrapper, and smart. She was also more levelheaded than herself, and Carol could curb Lee as well. "Okay."

Big Ed stepped up. "I can shoot, and I can show you the quickest way to both locations. Plus, I'm not bad in hand-to-hand combat." He held up a fist. "Bill's a good man. I'd like to help get him back."

"Same," Sam Simmons said, and Shannon jumped. She hadn't even heard him come into the building. Sam gave her a tight little smile. "I saw you all come in here with Lee looking very much worse for the

239

wear, so I figured something was up. I'm quiet on my feet. I can scout, maybe even a rescue if you make a distraction. I served a stint in the Army."

"Fair enough." Shannon looked at Rebecca.

Rebecca shook her head. "I'll stay here with a radio in case trouble comes. They might figure on someone trying to rescue him and attack Watchdog while our numbers are down."

That was a valid concern. "Good thinking. We'll leave a couple guns for you as well."

"Leave the rifles. You'll probably want closer-range weapons with you on the rescue," Sam said.

"Good call. And we'll need to take a field kit—there's one in my truck. We might need to do emergency care for Bill." Shannon was making a quick list in her head. "And water."

"And extra antiseptic solution." Kim returned with a freshly bandaged Lee and a bottle of rubbing alcohol. "If you have to place any bandages, clean your hands and splash the wound. That'll be enough to hold him until you get him back. And don't pull out anything that might be stuck in him, even if it's just a splinter in his finger. Don't try to set any breaks or dislocations either. Just bind it and bring him to the med center."

"Noted." CPR would probably be the biggest problem, if it came to that. Shannon really hoped it wouldn't come to that.

"You'll need rope to make a harness too." Carol's expression was grim. "If he's that bad off, he won't be able to sit a bike proper, and that man's too big to be slung over sideways on the seat."

"If need be, I'll take him on the bike with me." Big Ed held up a hand. "I'm closest to his size."

"Sounds like a plan." Shannon swallowed hard to combat the fear boiling in the pit of her stomach. "Is there anything else we need to know or do?"

"Just get our gear together and grab our bikes." Carol straightened from the map. "I'll get the boys to grab the four best for the trips, and get Sprocket to loan me his rig for Ed. It's one of the bigger ones."

"Can't imagine he'll like that," Sam said. "I thought bikers didn't share their rides."

Carol responded with a wry look. "They don't, and he won't, but he owes Bill for some repair work. And unless or until the whole crew votes otherwise and picks a new boss, I'm the highest ranked of this rat pack."

The five rescuers dispersed to gather their gear. Shannon went to the truck to grab her pistol and her emergency medical kit from the cab. The gun felt oddly heavy in her hand. She slipped the magazine into the gun and engaged the safety, then strapped it to her hip. One knife went to her opposite hip, the other to the small of her back. She remembered the hatchet she'd used at the supercenter and wished she'd kept it. But she'd have to make do with what she had.

From there, she went to find some rope. She was digging through the supplies, trying to remember where the rope from tying down the cartons had been stored, when the radio crackled and a scratchy message came popping over the airwaves.

"Incoming riders!"

Shannon bolted out of the building, joined outside by Carol, Lee, and Rebecca. Kim appeared a few moments later. She, Big Ed, and Sam, plus a couple of others, formed an impromptu cordon to keep the rest of the Watchdog residents from coming further forward.

Together, the small group of unofficial leaders hurried out to meet the new arrivals. By the time they reached the edge of Watchdog, Shannon could hear the engines. Her jaw clenched. Unless she was very much mistaken, there were motorcycles coming.

"Any of ours out there?" she asked.

"Nope. Scouting was done on foot." Carol's face was tight, and her hand was on her gun. "The scouts wouldn't be calling in the alert if it were ours either."

"That's what I thought."

The five of them formed a loose blockade across the road. Shannon heard Rebecca on the radio, giving orders to different townsfolk regarding the defense of Watchdog. Shannon didn't bother to pay attention to the actual words. She knew what the plans were, and she trusted Rebecca as much as she could trust anyone at the moment.

A dust cloud formed and grew larger until they could see the bikes approaching. Even at that distance, Shannon thought she recognized the bike in the lead—and the rider.

"Aunt Carol."

"I see him." There was a low undercurrent of fury in the older woman's voice. "Austin. That son of a mouse turd. I had a feeling he was mixed up in this, but I didn't see him at The Spoke, and I thought he might have gotten rolled for his bike."

"I saw him at The Spoke. Just a glimpse."

Carol's scowl deepened. "I get a clean shot, I'm putting a bullet in his liver. See the little drunken cockroach enjoy his gut-rot booze with lead in his gut."

"He won't for long if Bill's been hurt bad," Shannon responded.

The bikes were pulling off, and Shannon realized where they were stopping. "They're waiting at the sawmill."

"Let's go see what they want." Carol growled the words and stalked forward. Shannon put a hand on her gun and followed, with Kim and Lee barely a breath behind and Big Ed bringing up the rear.

29

KIM NAKAMURA

K im wasn't sure her mother even knew she was there, but she wasn't going to say anything and get sent back to safety. She wanted to know what was happening.

The short walk to the sawmill was tense. Kim took the opportunity to study the group waiting for them as they approached. The man in the lead was the one her great-aunt had called Austin. There were four more guys behind him, two in a car and two on motorcycles. Those four looked bored or slightly amused, as if they were in on a joke no one else heard.

Austin, on the other hand, looked a little sick, like he'd eaten bad food or was suffering from a hangover. He also looked uneasy. He kept shifting his weight as if he wanted to be somewhere else and was ready to bolt back down the road.

Shannon took the lead as they came to a stop. "What do you want? Because you have five seconds to start talking, Austin, before I fill your worthless hide full of holes."

Austin winced. "Don't shoot. I'm just the messenger."

"Messenger for what?"

Austin winced again, and his face looked oddly distressed. "Got a delivery for you, from the boss."

"From Andre." Shannon's voice was flat, but Kim heard the fear underneath it. "I don't want whatever crap he's trying to deliver. Take it back and tell him that."

"Can't do that." Austin turned and jerked his chin at the thugs. "Boys, bring up the cargo."

Two of the thugs snickered, and Kim felt her stomach clench as they reached into the car and pulled out a large box. Together, the two men heaved their load forward. One of them bent down and unlatched the box while the other two came forward to help. Then they heaved the box up and dumped the contents into the road.

Kim nearly threw up. Shannon dropped her gun in horror. Carol staggered and dropped to her knees. Lee made a sick, choked-up noise of horror and despair. Someone else behind them vomited loudly. Kim knew she should probably turn to make sure that person was all right or step forward to help her mother and Aunt Carol. But she couldn't move.

The cargo was Bill. One look told Kim he couldn't possibly be alive. If he had been, she might have considered killing him out of mercy, because there was no way she could have saved him. Not with those wounds.

The things that had been done to Bill's body were horrendous. His shirt was gone, and his upper body was a mass of bloody wounds Kim didn't want to see any closer. The way some of his limbs bent indicated broken bones, and his face was wrecked to the point of being barely recognizable.

The horrified silence was broken by Austin's quiet, almost apologetic voice. "I didn't…I didn't do this. But Boss Andre, he was mad, and that guy wouldn't stop talking back. I could have warned him Andre don't take defiance too well. And everything just got out of hand."

Shannon's gaze rose slowly. "You…."

Austin flinched back from whatever he saw in her eyes. "I didn't do it, okay? It's not my fault. It's just that Boss Andre is seriously ticked off, mostly at you." He shook his head. "Look, I get you got your reasons, but you were his old lady. You owe him something. So just… you know, talk to him. Cause otherwise he ain't gonna stop. And things'll just get worse. Just, you know, go see him, before something worse happens. That's all. That's what he told me to say."

Shocked silence fell again. Kim saw her mother's shoulders tensing as if she was about to spring at Austin and wring his neck.

Someone else moved first.

Lee gave an inarticulate scream and hefted his gun—Kim's gun, Dennis's old gun—and fired. His hands were shaking, tears were pouring down his cheeks, and the shot went wild.

Austin yelped and jerked back, then cringed and kicked his bike into motion. Lee unloaded another shot, then another, a wild spray of bullets with no aim other than to drive the men away and vent his grief. He was screaming incoherently, the sound raw and primal and gut-wrenching. Kim felt like joining him.

The convicts turned and ran for their vehicles. One of Lee's shots clipped one man on the shoulder, and he lurched forward. Another grazed a man's leg. Then they were in the car, having abandoned the two bikes, and its engine roared to life. The car backed away in a squeal of rubber and a spray of dust and rocks. It made a sloppy three-point turn and tore off back the way it had come. Austin was already long gone.

Lee kept firing and screaming until the magazine clicked on empty. Then he collapsed at Bill's side, sobbing through a throat that was probably raw.

Shannon was the first to move. She staggered forward and collapsed at Lee's side. Her hand was shaking as it touched his shoulder, and tears poured down her cheeks. At the first touch on his shoulder, Lee flung himself at her. His arms wrapped around her, holding on as if he were drowning and she were a life preserver.

Kim felt like she too was drowning. Or freezing to death. She wanted to offer comfort, but she couldn't bring herself to move closer to the awful sight of Bill's broken body. She couldn't find the strength to do anything but stand there, dry-eyed and breath hitching on her sobs, the same way she'd hidden and cried quietly the day Dennis had died.

The memory of that day stabbed her mind, and Kim's knees gave out as past and present hit her like body blows. Once again, she'd been too late. She hadn't been able to save someone she cared about. And this time, it was worse.

Dennis had died quickly. She didn't think Bill had, and the realization made her sick. Kim's stomach revolted, and she doubled over and puked. The sour smell of her sickness joined the iron scent in the air of blood and the acrid scent of burned rubber. Kim dry-heaved again, unable to stop the spasms that gripped her.

Hands grabbed her, and arms were around her. Leather and motor oil and Aunt Carol's voice. "Let it out, girl. Let it out." Her great-aunt's voice was rough—Aunt Carol was crying too.

Then a hand touched down on her back, and she heard Rebecca's soft voice. "I'm sorry for your loss."

That was the last straw. Kim collapsed onto her aunt's shoulders and let the tears come as her voice joined Shannon and Lee's in mourning.

30

AUSTIN

The screams behind Austin as he rode away were almost as awful as the ones he'd heard in the church. He felt just as sick hearing them. Austin barely even noticed when the car with the rest of the delivery team drove past him.

Sober or stoned, he couldn't find it in him to be anything but horrified by what had happened to the mechanic. What Andre had done to the guy. He knew more about it than he wanted to, for all he'd stayed huddled in the hall the whole time it was happening.

And that made him sick too. The fight at The Spoke had been one thing. This—what Andre had done to the prisoner—that was well beyond anything Austin had ever considered doing to anyone, even his worst enemy.

Cherry had been right. This wasn't the outfit for him. Andre wasn't the leader he wanted to follow. The man was deranged, and the guys he'd recruited from the jail weren't much better. They were all psychos.

Austin was a bad guy, and he knew it, but he wasn't a psychopath. He wasn't cut out for the kind of life Andre and his guys lived. He needed to get out.

The rest of the crew was already gone. It would be so easy to turn his bike down a random road and ride. Maybe go back to Memphis and the Rat Trap. It was a crap hole and life was hardscrabble at best, but it had to be better than hearing those screams and knowing they'd follow him into sleep. If he could ever sleep again.

Maybe he could find Cherry and apologize. Beg her to help him keep the demons away. Right now, all he had was coke and liquor, but it wasn't doing the job anymore.

The idea sounded good, and Austin lifted his head to look for the nearest road sign. He'd take a random crossroad, and Andre would never find him. He'd—

A large figure rose from the ground and came toward him. Austin felt his heart sink as he recognized the smooth, predatory walk. Andre.

The temptation to hit the throttle and run for it was heavy, a weight in his gut and an itch in his hands, but his only choices were to ride toward Andre or back the way he'd come to town. He was pretty sure he'd get shot the second anyone from that little town saw him. If he was lucky, it would be fatal, but he wasn't sure Carol Gardena would be that kind.

He forced himself to slow down and come to a stop on the empty stretch of county road as Andre approached. "Hey, boss."

"Austin. I saw the others were injured."

Austin gulped. He hadn't noticed anyone injured. But then he didn't exactly care, and he hadn't bothered to check their condition when they passed him. He couldn't say that to Andre though. "Yeah. Your ex didn't like the gift you sent too much."

Andre tipped his head. "Whyever not? I was simply sending her friend back to her with a message that I wanted to talk."

Austin's throat felt dry. The casual way Andre talked about delivering the mechanic's corpse to his friends, like it was some sort of joke, made chills go down his spine. "I hear you, but I got the impression they wanted him back alive."

Andre sneered at the words, lip curled in contempt. "Then Sarah should not have defied me and kept running from me."

"Uh, sure." Austin licked his chapped lips. "I hear you, boss, I do. It's just, I've never done anything like that before, and I'm not so sure I'm cut out for that kind of stuff. You know, with the knives and the screams and all. I'm more into recruitment, and maybe a little bit of intimidation. Or supply management. I'm not real comfortable with what went down with the old guy."

Austin half-expected Andre to lay him out flat. He wasn't sure whether to feel relieved or horrified when Andre smiled at him and looped an arm around his shoulders as if they were old friends. "Come now, Austin. Have you forgotten the promise we made when we dealt with those bikers you despised? We are the brothers of the road. Ride or die together. Is that not what you promised?"

He'd been high on victory and drugs, but he remembered it. With a sinking heart, Austin forced himself to nod. "Sure. I remember."

"You wouldn't break a sacred promise, would you?" Andre gave him a grave look.

"No, boss. Not at all." Austin dredged up a sick, weak smile. "Ride or die, prez. You know I swore, and my word's good."

"I do know that, yes. But I am pleased to hear you say it." Andre moved to retrieve his own bike from under the trees at the side of the road and turn it on. Austin fell in behind him, heading down the road to Mt. Sinai Baptist Church.

Ride or die. Ride or die.

The words played like a chant in his head, looping around his skull. With a sick sense of clarity, he realized the truth. It wasn't "ride *or* die." Not with Andre. It was "ride *and* die." Or maybe "ride *until* you die." There was no *or*, no choice. Not once you were in with him.

Austin needed coke and a whole bottle of Jack Daniels. Maybe two. He couldn't handle Andre without it. Then he needed to talk to Chip and Art and Sharp, see if they could find a way out of this mess he'd gotten them into. He wasn't too proud to grovel a little, if that was what it took.

He and Andre pulled up to the church, and he was surprised to see a lot of the bikes missing, including Art, Chip, and Sharp's rigs. He frowned for a moment, then hurried to catch up to Andre. "Hey, boss, you got the boys out doing patrols or scavenging?"

Andre glanced at the empty space. "Not at all." He waved a hand, and for the first time, Austin saw that the knuckles were reddened and bruised, as if he'd been fighting.

"Something happen then, boss?" He hoped he was wrong, but he couldn't stand not knowing what had occurred. If they weren't out gathering supplies or scouting, then there weren't many other places the boys could be.

"There was an argument of sorts while you were on your errand. An associate of yours said I was crazy. An obsessed, weak-minded lunatic with delusions of grandeur, to be precise. I couldn't let that stand."

"I...I guess not." Austin's stomach churned so hard it ached. "So you—"

"I killed him, of course, for his impudence. And I told the others that if they did not approve, they could leave. Of course, there will be a reckoning later, but for now, they seem to have taken my words to heart."

Austin staggered as he realized what Andre was saying. Chip, Art, and Sharp had taken off. All gone, just like Cherry. He could barely manage to ask the next question as he followed Andre through the church doors. "Are we the only ones left, boss?"

Andre gave him a lazy shark's smile. "Of course not. My most loyal men from the prison are still here. Which is quite enough to do whatever we need to do to bring Sarah and her friends to their knees." Andre waved at the men sprawled around the repurposed sanctuary. "They know how to follow orders and how to get their hands dirty. They, like you, are willing to do whatever I require them to do."

Austin's gaze slid from one man to another, hoping to see someone he knew. But there was no one. No Black Rats. No members of another motorcycle club. Just convicts sprawled over the pews or drinking stolen alcohol. He spotted the four who'd gone on the delivery with him, two of them with dirty bandages, celebrating with the drugs and alcohol Andre had promised them. It looked like a bottle of rum and heroin, and Austin wished for a moment he were brave enough to try and take it for himself.

As he looked around again, Austin realized something else. All the men there—they'd helped with the mechanic. They'd been part of what Andre had done to the guy. He didn't know who had done what, didn't want to know, but he was sure all of them had gone in to help Andre torture the man at one point or another.

The horrible truth hit home. He was surrounded by murderers who hadn't hesitated to torture a helpless, bound man. They might even have enjoyed it, the way Andre did. He was the only one who seemed at all bothered by what they'd done.

The guys were right. These men are monsters. And now I'm alone with them.

Austin reached desperately for his cocaine.

31

SHANNON GRAYSON

S hannon didn't know how long she sat there holding Lee beside Bill's body. It might have been ten minutes. It might have been ten years. She didn't care. All she could see was Bill, and all she could hear was Lee's desperate sobbing.

She knew Andre was a monster. Why hadn't she been more careful? Why hadn't she kept her family close? Kept Bill close? Why hadn't she gone after him the minute she knew he'd been taken prisoner and tried to save him?

Why had she ever let him come with her at all? She should have left him back in Oklahoma. Shannon's eyes burned as she remembered when she'd first met Bill, when the supercenter shut down and trapped them all. He'd been a rock of good sense, a steady presence at her back, and a helping hand when she needed it. If it hadn't been for Bill, she'd have died of the wounds Langmaid had given her and never found Kim again.

Why hadn't she at least left him in Memphis once she'd realized Andre was on her tail? He and Lee could have managed. They were both smart.

If it hadn't been for her, Bill would be alive. Her determination to stand against Andre had gotten her closest and kindest friend killed.

Her thoughts wouldn't settle, spiraling around her in a tangle of what-if scenarios, regrets, and grief until she couldn't move.

In a distant part of her thoughts, she knew she needed to get up. There were things that needed to be done, and she was aware there was little time for grief. Andre was surely on his way. She needed to help get Watchdog ready for Andre's next move. But that part of her wasn't in control of her body. The part that was could only sit in frozen, horrified silence, unable to move or look away from the body on the pavement.

Then a hand fell on her shoulder and dragged her out of her turmoil and back to reality. She looked up to see Aunt Carol standing over her. "Come on, girl. You need to get moving. There's things to be done."

Shannon swallowed. Her throat was dry and sore, and Lee was still sobbing quietly in her arms. "Aunt Carol...Bill..."

"I know. But there's little time for grieving right now, Shannon." Aunt Carol's expression was sympathetic, even apologetic, but stern and unyielding all the same. "Andre won't wait for the tears to dry before he comes calling with his thugs. You need to help this town prepare for what's coming next, unless you want to see more of these people joining Bill in the ground."

"I don't know..." Shannon looked at Bill's battered body. She remembered Hank and Noah from the supercenter. They'd both gotten burials of sorts. It wasn't right for Bill not to get laid to rest. "I need to bury him."

"We will. But right now, we've got to get busy." Aunt Carol bent down and took Lee from her arms. The young man went without resistance, shattered by grief, and Kim stepped forward to support him. Aunt Carol reached out and helped Shannon to her feet.

To Shannon's surprise, Sam Simmons came forward. "I didn't know Bill real well, and I'm not sure I know everything that's going on, but I recognized those thugs. They're part of the troublemakers that wrecked our town. Which means we all need to follow the same advice—something I learned in the military."

"What's that?" Shannon asked.

"Bury your dead when you have a moment, avenge them when you can, and mourn them when the fighting's done." The words filled the air between them like the command of a higher power, and something inside Shannon settled at the rightness of the sentiment.

"You're right." Shannon swiped the tears from her face and accepted a water bottle from Sam to wet her throat. Rebecca joined them, and Shannon said to her, "We need to get ready for an attack by Andre and his men. But I also want to see Bill laid to rest. Do we have anyone who can help me with that?"

Sam stepped up. So did Big Ed and David Skinner. "We can put a coffin together and dig a hole for Bill. Maybe even set up a marker stone of some kind."

"Just a small stone for now. I don't want..." Shannon choked on the words for a moment, then forced them through the tightness in her throat. "I don't want any of those beasts to mess with his grave." She wouldn't put it past Andre to defile Bill's grave just to spite her if he happened across it. "We can do proper stones later, just like our mourning."

"Yes ma'am." Sam nodded.

John Deckon came forward. "It wouldn't be anything fancy, but we could see if Jeb would be willing to say a few words, seeing as he's a reverend."

Shannon was surprised the reverend hadn't already come running to denounce them as dangers to the community and call for their immediate expulsion. She looked at the gathered townsfolk, some of whom were still looking at Bill with horrified fascination. The rest of them were glancing at her, or looking away awkwardly, or staring at her and Rebecca as if waiting for directions.

There was no sign of Jeb Butler's distinctive white hair, fake-tan skin, or rumpled suit. Shannon frowned, trying to remember the last time she'd seen the man. She'd glimpsed him skulking about the command post, but he'd never joined in the discussions, so she hadn't given him much thought beyond being glad he wasn't interrupting them while they worked. She couldn't recall if he'd been in the crowd that had come to the edge of town when the alarm went up, but she definitely didn't see him now.

She turned to John. "Where is the Reverend? I don't see him."

John frowned. "I don't know. He was around when we heard the alarm, and I thought he came out to see what was going on with the rest of us, but I don't recall seeing him after the...delivery." John hesitated on the last word.

Grief threatened to engulf Shannon again, but she focused on the more immediate issue. "Rebecca, can we see if anyone knows where Reverend Butler is?"

They'd all been so focused on Austin and his men, as well as the shock of what had happened to Bill, they hadn't been paying attention to anything else. Shannon doubted even the guards who were supposed to be keeping watch had been thinking of their duty, not with the dramatic way Austin had staged the "delivery" and their reactions to the sight of Bill's body.

It would have been easy for another contingent to sneak in and grab a new prisoner for interrogation and hostage. Jeb was an easily recognizable target, and most would assume he was an important member of the community, given that the billboards near New Wren had his face plastered all over them.

From the look on her face, Rebecca's thoughts had gone in the same direction as Shannon's. While Big Ed, Sam, and David gathered Bill's body and the tools to prepare for his burial, Rebecca, John, and Carol began organizing a search party to look for Jeb.

Shannon wanted to stay with Bill, but the unfortunate truth was she wasn't strong enough to do the things that needed to be done. She couldn't carry Bill's body anywhere. She didn't have the skills to build a makeshift coffin of any kind for him. She could dig the hole to lay him to rest, but not as fast or as deep as the men who were already working on that task. As much as she hated it, her efforts were better spent locating Jeb and making sure he hadn't suffered a similar fate.

He wasn't in the command post, where Shannon had half-expected him to be. Nor was he in the childcare center, the medical center, or the Old Grady Sawmill. Rebecca and John checked the house Jeb had claimed as his own and found it empty as well.

Shannon was beginning to truly worry about the man. Jeb Butler had been nothing but a thorn in her side since their arrival, but that didn't mean she wished him ill. She met up with Rebecca and Carol at the command post after searching the nearby houses and under the tractor, in case he'd hidden in fright.

"Where else could he have got to, assuming he wasn't kidnapped?" she asked.

Rebecca huffed. "If we're assuming he wasn't kidnapped, then he could be anywhere in Watchdog. He might have even gone as far as one of the watch posts, though I don't know why he would leave town. He knows it's dangerous out there."

"He wouldn't try to go back to New Wren, would he?"

Rebecca shook her head. "He heard the brigands were there, same as the rest of us did. Besides, I don't think he can ride a motorcycle, and he sure didn't take your truck cab, so he'd have to go on foot. Jeb isn't the sort to put himself to all that trouble."

Just then, Margaret Tarrow jogged up. "We found Jeb Butler."

Relief filled Shannon. "Where?"

Margaret pulled a wry face. "He's at the old, dilapidated church three streets off. And he's—well, I think you'd best see for yourself what kind of shape he's in."

Shannon followed, her heart in her throat. Despite Margaret's unconcerned behavior, she feared they'd find Jeb beat to a pulp, like Bill, or dead with a bullet in his head, like Toad. The thought of having to bury two people in one day made her sick to her stomach.

Jeb wasn't dead, but he was oblivious to the fuss he'd caused. Shannon entered the church to find him sitting on the battered steps to the altar, a half-empty bottle of amber-colored liquid clutched in his fist and his face streaked with tears, snot, and spittle. His hair was disheveled, his eyes were bloodshot, and his suit looked more like something rescued from a dumpster than the expensive outfit it was probably meant to resemble.

Shannon went closer. Jeb was muttering under his breath, nothing she could make out properly. His breath stank of alcohol, and he only stared vaguely through her when she tried to get his attention.

Shannon curled her lip at the picture he made, then went back to the other two women. "Where did he find the drink? Smells strong."

Rebecca sighed. "Could have found it anywhere. God knows I wouldn't put it past old Ed Grady to have set up a moonshine distillery around here somewhere, and he was certainly the type who would drink a brand-name bottle of whiskey or rum dry and reuse it for his own production so he could save money and hide his efforts from the police. And we're always finding this and that in the buildings as we clean them up. Jeb might even have brought the stuff from New Wren, either during the initial evacuation or during the salvage the other day."

Margaret scowled. "Typical Jeb."

"At least he's not dead or kidnapped." Shannon eyed Jeb for a moment, then shrugged. "Might as well leave him to it, I guess. He's no use to anyone right now, and I don't have the energy to waste on trying to sober him up. Too much else to do."

Including burying Bill. Guess someone else will have to speak for him.

Margaret went to call off the search. Shannon went to check on Lee and Kim. She wanted to see how the two of them were doing before she went to check on the progress of the burial team.

She found them both in the Black Rats sleeping area, with Lee sitting on his makeshift mattress, knees pulled to his chest and arms wrapped around his shins. Kim sat behind the shattered youth, her arm around his shoulders. To Shannon's surprise, Aunt Carol was there as well. She looked up as Shannon entered the room and came over. Her voice was low as she spoke.

"Boy's in shock. Kimmy seems to be holding up better, but it's hard to tell. She's got the Gardena stone-face when she wants it."

Shannon nodded. She'd seen a lot of Kim's stoicism over the past couple of weeks. "I don't know if Lee was in any condition to hear us making burial plans. Can you and Kim keep an eye on him, and I'll radio you when we're ready?"

"Sure." Carol agreed. "Anybody find that reverend?"

"Yeah, for all the good it does. Man's drunk as a skunk and near insensible. We'll make do without him." It was difficult to speak the words quietly in the face of her scorn, but Shannon managed.

Aunt Carol made a disgusted face but didn't say anything more. Shannon checked her radio battery, then headed out to the men who were handling Bill's burial.

Someone had donated a pale sheet as a burial shroud. It had been wrapped around Bill's body and stitched closed. Meanwhile, the men had gathered some old pallet slats to form a rough coffin. Big Ed was in the process of giving directions, but he stopped and came over to talk to her when he saw her.

It was hard to talk around the ache in her throat, but she managed. "What's the plan?"

"We were thinking he might like to be buried by the woods. We can also use one of the trees as a marker, make it a little safer from those skunks." Big Ed shifted his weight. "Glenda and Suzie took some time to clean and wrap the body, and we've got a sort of coffin made. Sam suggested we line the grave with sheet metal too, since the coffin isn't as sturdy as it might usually be."

"Will we still have enough supplies for fortification if we do that?" She wanted to just say yes, but she had to think of the town as well as her own feelings.

Ed nodded. "We can get more from the auto shop if we need it. Wood's actually more scarce for the moment."

Shannon considered the matter. "Can we line the grave, and use that as the coffin? Save the wood?"

Big Ed looked uncomfortable. "We thought about that, but honestly, doesn't feel right to any of us. Might be a mistake, but I think we all agree it's better to do it this way."

"Okay." Shannon took a deep breath. "Thank you for thinking of those things. I…Bill was my friend. I don't want to cause trouble for the town, but Bill…"

"Bill deserves the best we can do for him." Ed spoke the words firmly. "I didn't know the man long, but I knew him well enough to know he was a good man."

Shannon nodded. Ed went back to work. In the main square, a few people were setting up for a meal, but no one really seemed hungry. Shannon knew she wasn't.

Slightly more than an hour later, it was time. Shannon called Lee, Kim, and Carol, and the four of them formed a sort of loose honor guard around the coffin bearers. Glenda had provided a stretcher from the medical center to carry the coffin on. Big Ed, Sam Simmons, David Skinner, and John Deckon served as the pallbearers.

Outside town, a large oak tree stood sentinel over a deep hole, the bottom of which had been roughly lined with metal. It was far from a professional job, but Shannon didn't care. Like the cobbled together coffin, it was the thought that counted more than the execution.

The men had rigged up a simple system to get the coffin into the ground. Two ropes were laid on the ground, and the coffin was placed on top of them, with one rope at the head and one at the foot. The four pallbearers took up the ends, stretching the rope across the open grave. Then, using the ropes as a lift, they hauled the coffin across the grass until it slid into the hole. The ropes were used to control the descent, mostly through the brute strength of the men holding them. Once the coffin was in the bottom, the men on the left side released the ropes, and they were pulled free of the grave. There was a lot of grunting and hauling involved, but eventually, they were both free and coiled to one side.

With a start, Shannon realized it was time for speaking. For saying farewell. Her gaze searched the crowd, but no one was stepping forward.

She couldn't ask Lee. He looked as if he was barely able to stay on his feet, tears streaking his face. Kim was standing shoulder to shoulder with him, offering her support.

A hand landed on her shoulder, and Shannon turned to look at Aunt Carol. The older woman nodded. "Go ahead."

"What?"

"Go ahead and say a few words, if you want them said." Aunt Carol tipped her head at the grave. "You knew him best, after all."

Shannon swallowed hard. Just the thought of saying farewell made her throat hurt, and there were so many people—she'd never liked speaking to crowds.

But if not you, then who will speak for Bill? The thought drifted through her mind.

There was no one else. Shannon took a deep breath and stepped forward, Aunt Carol's hand still on her shoulder as a support.

"We're here today to say goodbye to a good man, Bill Wheeler." It was hard to talk, and she forced the words free, no particular speech in mind, just the thoughts in her head and in her heart.

"I met him for the first time the day the world fell apart. We got stuck in a supercenter together. Bill, he wasn't a leader, but he was a rock for everyone else. If we had something we needed, Bill was the one to make it happen, and he always had a smile and a kind word for those around him while he worked. Because of Bill, we managed to get radios working and find out what happened. Because of Bill, we eventually got out of there, and I was able to come and find my daughter, Kim."

She took another deep breath. "I didn't know Bill as well as I wish I did, now. But I know he was kind, he was resourceful, and he was brave. Brave enough to leave behind the place he'd lived his whole life, just to come with me and help me. Strong enough to defend me when I needed help. Dedicated and determined enough to take care of me when an injury I had became infected and I almost died. Kind enough to give food to strangers and give his help to people, even people who weren't always the most welcoming or grateful for it."

Some of the Black Rats in the crowd shifted at that.

"Bill was a good man, and a good friend. He deserved better than what happened to him." Shannon felt tears in her eyes as her voice cracked. "He deserved a lot better. Bill, I'm so sorry. I can't regret having you beside me, but I wish I'd left you in Oklahoma. I wish none of us had got caught up in this madness, and I'm more sorry than you'll ever know that my past cost you your life."

She looked at the gathered crowd, Black Rats and Watchdog residents standing together in silent reverence for the man who had touched their lives so briefly. "There's trouble coming, and I'm sorry for that. But when you get frightened, when you want to run and hide, or shout and fight among yourselves—remember Bill Wheeler. Remember a kind, brave, incredible man who stood against the monsters who want to take over our lives. Remember a man who had the courage to step into the unknown, even in the face of disaster, and offer kindness to others. Remember him, and help me make sure his life, and his death, aren't in vain."

She couldn't think of anything more to say. Instead, she went to a shovel that had been leaned against the marker tree. She scooped up a shovelful of earth and cast it into the grave, then turned and offered the shovel to Lee.

Lee's face was damp, but his eyes were dry, his expression fierce with determination as he cast his own shovel of dirt onto the grave.

Lee was followed by Kim, then Carol, Sprocket of the Black Rats, Rebecca, Big Ed—one by one, they came up and tossed a shovel full of dirt into the grave, a final goodbye. When everyone had participated who wanted to, Ed and David stepped up to finish filling in the hole. When that was done, the crowd began to disperse.

Shannon lingered for one final, private farewell.

Goodbye, Bill. I hope you've joined your wife in heaven, if it exists. And I promise you, the animal that did this isn't going to outlive you for very long, not if I have anything to say about it.

32

KIM NAKAMURA

The day after the funeral, everything seemed to change, and Kim couldn't decide if it was changing for the better or the worse. On one hand, the Watchdog residents had wholly enveloped the Black Rats crew into their community and embraced them as members of the town. The Black Rats, in turn, seemed to have decided that everyone was part of their brotherhood, whether they were members of the MC or not.

On the other hand, the town was gearing up for war. Everywhere she turned, she saw grim expressions and determination to pay Andre and his thugs back for everything they'd done. Anyone who had a weapon was going around visibly armed. In addition to reinforcing buildings, Rebecca and a small group of townsfolk were setting up traps.

There were trip wires, road pits, homemade caltrops—anything that could slow riders down or cause an accident. They were sensible precautions, but Kim didn't like seeing them in what had been a peaceful town.

She knew it was Andre's fault, but she didn't want to navigate a battleground. She also couldn't help wondering how any of them would be able to stand living there, if and when the fighting was over. Assuming any of them were alive to worry about that.

She'd said they needed to take a stand, and she was glad to see that her mother was finally ready to dig her heels in and fight back against Andre's cruelty and tyranny. But the grim reality of living in what amounted to a war zone made her sick to her stomach.

The medical center was as ready as she and Glenda could make it, so Kim excused herself to go check on Lee. He'd barely said two words since Andre's thugs had dumped Bill's body in front of him. The desolate sobbing of the first hour had eventually died away, but there was something sharp and dangerous in Lee's eyes now, and it worried Kim.

She found him out about halfway between the Carlo's Pizza watch post and the main settlement area, sitting with his back to a wall and the gun she'd lent him in his hand. She slid down to sit beside him.

"Hey, Lee."

He didn't answer. After a moment, she spoke softly. "I don't know what you're thinking, but I can tell you from personal experience— whatever it is, that gun won't help heal what hurts inside. Not if you use it on someone else, and not if you try to turn it on yourself."

"Try?" Lee's voice was cracked and broken, hoarse from screaming the day before.

"Try. If you actually turned a weapon on yourself, I'd stop you, and I'd have Aunt Carol sit on you until you came to your senses," Kim stated. "Or Mom."

"Why would they care?"

"Because they care about you—"

"They don't. They don't!" Lee's voice rose as he whipped around to look at her, eyes wild like a wounded animal's. "They only ever tolerated me because of Bill. Bill was the only one who ever treated me decently, who ever actually *cared* about me! And now he's gone." He wrenched himself to his feet. "I should have known better than to trust him."

"Hey." Kim rose too. "He didn't choose to leave you."

"Doesn't matter. I can't trust anyone, and I should have realized that a long time ago. I should have realized the monsters always win."

"They don't." Kim tried to calm him, but Lee didn't want to be calmed.

"Don't they?" His burning eyes met hers. "My dad's a monster, and he drove my mother away. Andre's a monster, and look at everything he's done! And Bill went and got killed by a monster, so doesn't that prove that decent people can't win? That monsters are always going to destroy everything, one way or another?"

"It doesn't. I refuse to believe that's true." Kim stood her ground, raising her chin as she faced him down. "I won't think that way."

"Why? Didn't a monster kill your friend too?" Lee's voice snapped out the words like a whip.

Kim winced as his accusation cut deep, but she refused to give in. "Yes, but I still won't believe what you're saying is true. Because if it's true, then what about Mom, and Aunt Carol, and Rebecca, and all the good people we've met here? If you're right, then we're all going to die or become monsters ourselves. I won't accept that." She stepped closer until she was inches away. "What about you? Do you really want to die or become a monster?"

Lee stared at her for a long moment. Then his expression crumpled as the fire went out of his eyes, drowned in grief and remorse. His voice was barely a whisper when he spoke. "No."

"Then don't. And don't fall into the trap of thinking people like Andre always win." Kim pulled him close, into as comforting an embrace as she could manage. "Don't let your anger and grief make you like them."

Lee made a soft, choking sound and slumped against her. Kim eased both of them back to the ground as he started to cry.

"It's okay to be angry. It's okay to be hurting inside," she said as she rubbed his back. "It's all right to be upset and hurt and wanting to hurt someone or something. But you don't have to act on it. And you don't have to let it twist you up and tear you apart. Don't let what they've done destroy you. Don't let Bill's death turn you into something you're not. He wouldn't want that."

Kim let the words die away, determined to hold Lee and comfort him as long as it took, and to do whatever she could to help him feel the slightest bit better.

Eventually, Lee spoke again. "I hate Andre. I want to kill him."

"You're not the only one," Kim acknowledged. "I think everyone here wants to kill him for one reason or another."

"I want to hunt him down like an animal." Lee's voice was ragged.

Kim remembered Lewis, the way she'd felt after he killed Dennis. She also remembered how Joan had looked after she'd shot her husband. "Not sure that's such a great idea." She paused. "But you know, we do need to hunt. Get some meat for the town to supplement the food supplies. We could do that, if you like." It might do Lee some good to get moving, and to have a target for some of the rage he was feeling. Plus, it had the added benefit of being helpful to the community.

After a moment, Lee nodded and sat up, swiping at his face. "Sure. I'd like that."

Kim went to collect a bottle of water for each of them and tell Shannon where they were going. Her mother made her take a radio, and Kim clipped it onto the least battered of her belt loops. Mutt had been lounging near the map board, but she got up and joined Kim and Lee as they headed back out. Kim ruffled the big dog's ears, grateful for her company.

The walk out to the woods was mostly quiet. Lee tromped along, shoulders tight and expression grim. His hand was white-knuckled around the pistol grip, and he kept glaring at shadows, as if he expected Andre to appear from behind a bush.

To distract him, Kim bumped Lee's shoulder with her own. "What are you thinking? Aside from wanting to shoot Andre."

Lee's breath hitched. "I don't know. I don't know what I want to do now. I was just going along with Bill, and now he's gone."

"You've still got the Black Rats. You're a prospect, so you're practically one of the crew now," Kim pointed out.

"That doesn't mean much. I don't feel..." Lee paused. "I appreciate Carol saying that and everything, but it doesn't feel right. Not much seems to, these days." His shoulders hunched. "I don't mean to sound ungrateful."

"You don't. And you're right. Not much about the world feels right these days." Kim paused to sip at her water. "And honestly, it drives me kind of crazy. Not just that there's so much wrong with the world, but that more people aren't trying to make it right."

Lee blinked at her. "What do you mean?"

"I mean..." Kim hesitated, then voiced the thoughts that had been with her ever since her mother's birthday. "I mean that I want to get out there and help people. I can't leave Mom while Andre's out there, but if he weren't a problem—if it was just us settling down and building new lives—I probably would go on the road. Pack up a medicine kit and some supplies and start traveling, looking for people to help. As much as I hated the place, I might even go back to Humboldt. Or I might go elsewhere, maybe to Oklahoma to see if there's anyone there who knew Bill and might care about his passing."

"You'd leave your family?" Lee looked surprised.

"If I knew they were safe, and healthy and happy? I might. I've thought about it often enough." Kim sighed. "Not right now, of course."

"Not while *he's* out there." The venom in Lee's voice made it clear who he was talking about. He raised his pistol and fired at a tree, and Kim jumped. So did Mutt.

Lee fired again, this time at a bush. Then again at a branch.

Kim managed to recover from her shock enough to grab his arm. "What are you doing?"

"Shooting. Just like I'm going to shoot Andre the next time I see him." Lee wrenched himself free and fired again at another bush.

There was a rustling sound, and a rabbit bolted from the base of the vegetation. With a happy bark, Mutt raced after it.

Kim grabbed Lee's arm again. "You're not going to shoot while Mutt's in the line of fire, not right now. Besides, we can't afford for you to keep wasting the ammunition, not with Andre planning to attack us. You've already lost us four bullets we may need."

Lee looked mutinous, but he nodded and clicked the safety on before tucking the pistol into his waistband. "Okay."

The two of them followed Mutt's trail through the underbrush. The big dog hadn't been at all careful in her passage, and even Kim could follow the erratic path of broken twigs and flattened vegetation.

They found Mutt pawing at the dirt near a depression in the ground, not a rabbit in sight. Kim huffed a laugh. "Come on, Mutt. You're not going to get a rabbit out of a warren." She stepped forward to pull the dog back. "If we want to get any meat, we'll have to move to another part of the forest."

"Wait a second." Lee stepped forward and crouched down to brush some of the dirt away from the area Mutt had been digging. "Kim, look."

Kim bent closer and blinked in surprise. There in the dirt was a heavy metal ring. The metal was so weathered it blended easily into the dirt, but it was clearly part of an underground structure. The depression Kim had originally thought was the entrance to a rabbit warren appeared to be a dirt-covered door.

Guns were in the woods, surrounded by stone. Food in a dry place where nothing could come. Herb's words echoed in Kim's mind. She shared a look with Lee, then reached for her radio and clicked it on. "Rebecca. This is Kim Nakamura, calling Rebecca Holden and Shannon Nakamura."

Seconds later, the radio crackled in answer. "This is Rebecca. What's up, Kim?"

"Lee and I went out hunting, north of the sawmill. We found something I think you'll want to take a look at, but we need some shovels, and maybe a couple of the stronger men." There was no telling how long it had been since the entrance to whatever it was had been shifted, or how heavy it was.

"I hear you." Rebecca sounded intrigued. "Can you give us more precise directions?"

Kim handed the radio to Lee, knowing he was better than she was at guiding people through wooded terrain and identifying natural landmarks they could use to orient themselves. She listened to him with half an ear as she used her hands to clear the space around the heavy ring. It wasn't the most effective method, but she was too curious to sit still while they were waiting for Rebecca and the shovels.

Lee clicked the radio off. "They'll be here in a few minutes." He and Mutt joined Kim in trying to clear as much dirt away as they could.

By the time Rebecca, Sam, and David arrived with shovels, they'd managed to find what looked and felt like a heavy concrete door beneath the ring. With the aid of three more people and shovels, they'd soon cleared away the rest of the door, which turned out to be steel camouflaged to look like concrete or stone. The hinges were rusty and clogged with dirt, and the door was heavy. Sam and David placed rocks in front of it, then rested the hafts of the shovels on them to create improvised levers to force the door open. When it finally creaked upward, Kim stuck another rock into the opening in case it slipped. Then she and Lee helped the other three pull the door the rest of the way open.

There were narrow steps going down into the ground. Sam had a flashlight he'd been using to examine foundations during repairs, and he switched it on. After a moment, Kim took it and started down the steps first. She was the smallest and lightest of them, the least likely to cause the worn stairs to buckle or crumble, and the easiest to rescue if she did fall.

She knew what she was hoping to find, but somehow, it still came as a shock when her flashlight beam cut through the darkness to light up rows of neatly stocked armaments.

Pistols, rifles, machine guns—there were rows of each on the walls, above stacks of the appropriate ammunition. In the very back, there were two things that looked like bazookas, and two larger boxes labeled *Land Mines* and *C4* in red, stenciled lettering.

It was everything Herb had said it would be. Between the steel-lined walls and careful plastic wrap that covered every gun, it all looked to be in good condition. Kim ran a hand over the grip of a pistol. They were old, Soviet era if Herb was correct, but that didn't matter. With this, they could arm everyone in Watchdog and have weapons and ammunition to spare.

She went back to the steps and looked up at the four faces looking down at her. "We need to get my mom and my aunt out here. We've got some plans to make."

33

SHANNON GRAYSON

Of all the things Shannon had expected to see when she joined Kim and the others out north of Grady Sawmill, a cache of thirty- to forty-year-old weapons in pristine condition was not among them. She'd thought the stories about Ed Grady's weapons cache were just fanciful local legends.

She was glad she'd never said so aloud, otherwise she'd be eating her words. The cache was even bigger and better preserved than she'd been led to believe. Her first instinct was to hide the cache and only take out what they needed. Then her good sense reminded her that they weren't sure what they needed, and if they left the weapons where they were, they might not be able to get to them when they needed them.

Instead, she went back down to Watchdog and drafted Big Ed, along with the Black Rats, to help pull the weapons from storage. They were too heavy to carry all the way to the Watchdog town square, so Shannon took the tractor up to Grady Sawmill along with some empty crates for transporting the weapons.

Working together, it took about three hours to get everything out of the bunker and cataloged. It took another hour to get the weapons back to Watchdog and unloaded into the command post, then into one of the few rooms with a door that could be locked. Perhaps Shannon was being paranoid, but she didn't want those weapons to be accessible to everyone, and Rebecca agreed.

By then, rumors were spreading like wildfire, and everyone knew they'd discovered Ed Grady's weapons cache.

Once the guns were unloaded, it was time to decide what to do with them and form a new plan for defending Watchdog.

Shannon was the one to start the discussion among the members of the makeshift council. "Now that we've got weapons for everyone, we need to decide how to distribute them and where we want to station the defenders of the town. Then those defenders need to decide if there's any additional armaments they might need,"

Rebecca nodded. "We also need to figure out how we want to use what we've found for traps. The land mines could be pretty useful."

"True, though I'm thinking the tripwires, pitfalls, and stake traps will still be better. And less dangerous to the kids around town," Shannon said.

"Speaking of kids, our first plan should be what to do with them when trouble comes. You can't have kids on the firing line," Carol spoke up.

"That's right. And not everyone will want to fight anyway," John Deckon said. "There's some too young, some too old, and some who just don't have the nerve for it."

Shannon saw light glinting on Jeb Butler's white hair as he skulked into the council room and settled in a corner. It was on the tip of her tongue to ask the reverend if he'd be fighting, but she had a feeling she knew the answer. She also knew there was no point in suggesting he help guard the more vulnerable members of the community. The man was unreliable at best, and a coward at worst.

She turned her attention from Jeb back to the question at hand. "They'll attack the town most likely, so I'd say we want to have those who aren't fighting gather at the sawmill. They can hide out there, and if everything goes wrong, they can run."

Rebecca pointed to a spot on the map. "Grady Bridge isn't big or well-maintained, but it can be reinforced, and it should be sturdy enough for us to escape across in an emergency. John and I can lead the old, the young, and the pacifists across the river and collapse the bridge if we have to."

That would strand the defenders on the near side of the river, essentially trapping them, but then again, by the time they needed to take such measures, the majority of the more active defenders would likely be dead or captured. Shannon made note. "We'll consider that as a final safety measure."

"What about the town?" Carol spoke up. "Are we going to continue fortifying here, or are we going to move people up to the sawmill?"

"Some of both, I think." Shannon considered the map. "I think we should get the vulnerable folks and most of the supplies up to the sawmill, just to have them there. Then those of us who plan on fighting can set up for battle and hunker down without worrying about noncombatants."

"I like that idea," Big Ed agreed. "I'd prefer to see my daughter and my wife out of harm's way, even though I'm planning on being with the fighters."

"Okay. So who do we want to put on guard while the rest of us move the non-fighters and supplies?"

"Lee," Carol spoke up first. "Lee's a good shot and a steady hand. I say we put him in the farthest watch post, the one up near the lake. Put him out there with a rifle or two and plenty of ammo."

Shannon turned to Lee. "You up for that? You'll be the first line of defense, and the first warning we have."

Lee nodded, his jaw tight and his eyes bright with determination and grim fury. "I can do that."

Rebecca pointed out the second and third watch posts. "I say we put Sam and David out here—Sam on the middle position and David in the pizza place. Sam, you've got enough experience to get back from behind enemy lines, so to speak."

"That I do. And I don't mind, as long as I've got the guns for it. I'll take one of the machine guns, a couple pistols, and some of those mines. I can use the mines to fortify my position, so they can't come at me." Sam's face was grim, but resolute.

"Works for me, so long as you don't forget where you put 'em and step on one," Rebecca replied. There were nods from the rest of the council, and Shannon made another note.

The rest of the planning meeting involved discussing the best place for additional traps and dispersing their fighters. They didn't know how many men Andre had at his disposal, or where he'd attack from, so they elected to have their watchers and their fighters staked on every street, above street level where possible. The heaviest fortifications would be on the road to New Wren, since they knew Andre had men there, but none of them were willing to leave any other road undefended.

As they began to disperse and prepare for the evening meal, Carol took Lee into the back room. Shannon moved closer to the door, unwilling to intrude, but also determined to make sure there wasn't a falling out between Carol and Lee. They didn't need to be at each other's throats on the eve of fighting for their lives.

"You're a good kid, Lee, but you need to get your head on straight." Carol's voice was gruff, but not harsh, and Shannon relaxed. She knew that tone. Aunt Carol had used it with her years ago, when she'd been a newly orphaned teenager with a chip on her shoulder.

"I'm fine." The sullen way Lee responded was familiar too.

"That's a load of bull crap, and we both know it. And don't think I didn't see those bullet holes in the trees, or watch you replacing your ammo. You ain't fine, and you don't need to be. Just need to keep your cool."

"You saw what they did." Lee's voice was sharp and mutinous. "What they did to Bill."

"Yes, I did. And not too long ago, I watched that animal Andre shoot my husband through the head. I've lost friends and family to those monsters and that devil who leads them. I know how bad you're hurting, and I'm not the only one. But that's not the point."

"What is, then?"

"You heard what Rebecca and Shannon said. You'll be the first line of defense. For you to be effective, you need to control your temper and keep your head. If you can't, then it isn't just you who's likely to pay for it. You might miss something critical that means we aren't prepared when we need to be. Or you could do something reckless and get killed, and then we'll be adding you to the list of people we mourn."

"But—"

"Don't pretend Bill was the only person who cared for you. He might have been the first to take you in, Lee, but he sure wasn't the only one. I know for a fact that Kim and Shannon would be hit hard if they had to put you in the ground beside him." There was a moment's pause before the older woman continued. "And I wouldn't be happy either."

"But I helped Andre kill your husband." Lee sounded a little lost, like all the anger had been doused in guilt.

"You didn't pull the trigger. And I know as well as anyone that he can be a silver-tongued snake. You didn't know any better, and you had the good sense to get out when you learned he was trouble. That's better than most."

"I'm still sorry."

"And I'm sorry I rode you so hard early on, made you feel unwelcome. I should have known better. So let's call it even and focus on ridding the earth of that skunk once and for all."

"Yes ma'am." Lee's voice was stronger, and Shannon slipped away. She knew Lee would be all right with Carol having his back. Aunt Carol knew a thing or two about handling troubled teens.

The residents of Watchdog were subdued as they gathered for the evening meal. Everyone was on edge. They knew there was fighting in the near future, and victory was far from guaranteed. It was a sobering thought, and even the children seemed less energetic and excited than usual. Bill's death, plus the discovery of the weapons cache and everything it meant for the community, hung like a fog around the residents of Watchdog, young and old.

Shannon was one of the last to collect her food. As soon as she had it, she sought out Kim. Her daughter was almost done with her meal, but it was clear her focus was elsewhere from the distracted greeting she gave. Shannon nudged her shoulder. "What's on your mind?"

"Him." Kim jerked her head toward a figure who sat on the edge of the crowd. Jeb Butler. The reverend had food, but he seemed preoccupied, and he couldn't stay still. He kept fidgeting, looking around as if he expected someone to jump out of the shadows at him. He usually wolfed down his food and disappeared, but for some reason he didn't have much of an appetite. Of course, that might be a result of getting blackout drunk again.

"What about him?"

"I don't trust him." Kim scowled at the man. "And I've got a bad feeling about the way he's acting."

Shannon's first impulse was to brush that aside, but she'd learned Kim had good instincts. She was smart, even if she was sometimes too helpful for her own good. "What are you thinking?"

"I don't know just yet." Kim made a frustrated expression. "But he was so outspoken about getting us to leave before, and he hasn't said a word since the meeting where we told the people here about Andre. Why'd he get so quiet?"

Shannon frowned. "That's a good question. I saw him at the meeting earlier tonight, and he didn't say anything then either." She knew about men like Jeb Butler. It wasn't normal for them to keep their opinions to themselves.

"There's another thing, too, though I didn't think much about it at the time. When we went on the salvage mission to New Wren, he left the group. He disappeared for hours, and he was really jumpy when he returned. Spooked, almost. I thought it was because Sam told him he'd seen the raiders back in town, but looking back—he was on edge even before Sam told him anything."

"And you know Andre was in town then too. Is that what you're thinking?" Shannon's stomach clenched.

"Yeah. I'm wondering if the reverend knows something we don't."

As if the words were some sort of signal, Jeb stood. He dropped his plate next to one of the other residents—Margaret—and said something Shannon couldn't hear. Then he turned and hurried off into the twilight.

Kim set aside her empty plate and stood as well. "I'm going to go after Jeb and keep an eye on him."

Shannon wanted to protest. She didn't want Kim putting herself in danger. But despite her reservations, she had to admit her daughter was a capable young woman. She was strong, she was smart, and she was always armed. In some ways, she seemed even better prepared for the lives they were now living than Shannon herself.

More than that, Kim was an adult. She was independent enough to know her own mind, and old enough and wise enough to make her own decisions. Trying to act otherwise would only drive her daughter away from her.

Kim was still waiting, and Shannon forced herself to nod. "Be careful. If you run into trouble, remember we'll be moving supplies and non-fighters up to the mill after dinner. And don't forget to use your radio if you need help."

"I won't." Kim smiled, then turned and disappeared down the path Jeb had taken. Shannon watched her go before bending to her food.

Watching wouldn't make her less worried or Kim any safer. And no matter what Jeb was doing or what Kim might encounter, there was work to be done, and far too little time to do it.

34

KIM NAKAMURA

Kim followed Jeb out of Watchdog along the road toward New Wren. The man was easy to trail—he wasn't being at all quiet or stealthy, and he kept muttering to himself. Kim wished she could get close enough to hear what he was saying, but she didn't want to risk giving herself away.

Finally, a little over a mile out of town, Jeb stopped walking. Kim crept as close as the woods would allow and settled in to wait. She didn't have to wait long. Less than twenty minutes later, the familiar sound of a motorcycle engine filled the air, the headlight shining like a beacon as the bike rolled to a stop and a familiar figure clambered off.

In the light of the motorcycle, Austin looked terrible. His eyes were bloodshot, his skin pasty—what could be seen of it under the greasy hair and stubble across his unshaven face. His clothes hung loose on his skinny frame, and his expression was tense and unhappy. His restless, almost jittery movements as he walked up to Jeb suggested he was either high or jonesing for a fix.

Kim edged closer to listen, not that she needed to. Austin's nasally voice was clear enough. "You got anything for me, Reverend?"

"I do. All day I have been listening to those interlopers, those wolves in sheep's clothing, as they plotted how to lead my flock down a path of violence and—"

"I don't need no sermon," Austin cut in sharply. "Just tell me what they're planning, and I'll take it back to the boss, okay?"

"Oh, yes. Of course." Jeb started talking, and Kim felt herself grow cold as he laid out all their plans for defending Watchdog. He might not have all the details right, like the location of the traps, but he knew enough to tell them where the scouting and watch posts were, and what the emergency evacuation plan was.

Crap on a cracker. Kim bit her lip. She wanted desperately to radio Shannon at once to warn her, but the crackle of static would give her away before she got three words out. She had to wait.

Austin listened to everything Jeb told him, his fingers dancing on the grip of the large-caliber gun at his side. When Jeb finally stopped talking, he nodded. "That everything?"

"That is all I know, all they deigned to discuss in my presence." Jeb's hands gestured expansively. "Surely it is enough? Mr. Atkinson will be pleased?"

"Yeah. He'll be pleased, I'm sure." Austin's shoulders were tight, and Kim felt a sense of foreboding as he shifted his weight slightly. "In fact, he told me to give you a little something for your trouble before I left."

"Really?" Jeb sounded hopeful, and Kim wanted to shout a warning. She knew from past experience that Andre's "gifts" were never anything good.

"Yeah." Austin pulled the pistol from his belt and leveled it at Jeb. "Real sorry, Reverend, but Mr. Atkinson don't want any traitors in his outfit. Figures if you turned coat on folks once, you might do it again."

Jeb quailed back. "I wouldn't! I—please, don't! I can do more! I can help Mr. Atkinson! Truly, I can. Please—"

"Sorry, Reverend. I got my orders." Austin's expression was remorseful, conflicted even, but his grip on the pistol was steady, and his aim never wavered. Even from where she was, it was evident to Kim that his fear of Andre far outweighed any misgivings he might have about shooting a reverend.

Jeb saw it too. He turned to run, face full of fear and surprise, as if he'd never imagined he might get stabbed in the back by his new allies.

He didn't get three steps before Austin pulled the trigger. The gun went off with a loud bang, and Jeb's chest exploded in a violent spray of red. The reverend collapsed to the ground in mid stride, dead before his head hit the dirt.

Kim jolted backward, stunned by the casual violence. Despite everything she'd seen, everything she knew, some small part of her had almost hoped Jeb would get away, that Austin wouldn't pull the trigger.

Too late, she realized she'd moved too fast, made too much noise. Austin's head snapped around, facing her, then he grabbed his motorcycle and turned the headlight her direction. Kim had no time to hide before the light fell on her.

Austin cursed. "You!"

If he said anything else, Kim didn't wait to hear it. She took off through the trees, moving in an erratic zigzag pattern like she'd been taught and hoping to lose Austin amid the undergrowth. She heard him crashing through the woods behind her and wished she could run faster. Her shoulders itched with the fear that at any moment she would feel a bullet hitting her in the back.

She emerged into the outskirts of Watchdog and broke into a dead sprint. She could hear Austin still following behind her and sped up, glad that the traps in this particular area weren't established yet. She called out as loudly as she could manage with her aching lungs. "Help! Attack!"

No one answered. Kim cursed in her head as she remembered the plans. Everyone was probably up at the sawmill, taking care of the preparations there. It was only then, as she emerged into the main square, that she realized the tractor was gone as well. Most likely, it had been used to ferry the supplies up to the mill.

She was alone. Kim bit her lip, then ducked into a nearby alley. She pulled the first weapon she could get free of her belt into her hand. She found herself holding her Uncle Bruno's old knife and clenched her fist tight around it.

Austin came running, or rather staggering, into the square, his expression a mix of rage and fear—a trapped animal ready to tear apart anything that seemed like a threat. He looked rabid, the shadows cast by the low light giving his face a sinister cast it normally lacked. Kim thought about ducking further into hiding, but she knew Austin wouldn't stop looking for her. He had to know she would warn the residents of Watchdog that Andre knew their plans. There was no way he could let her get away, any more than he could have let Jeb live.

She held still, waiting until he blundered past her, swearing under his breath. Then she dove out and hammered the butt of her knife into the back of his skull as hard as she could.

Austin staggered, but he didn't go down, and his hand managed to catch her shoulder. "Got you, you little witch!"

Kim didn't stop to think. She spun on her heel, pulling herself free even as she lashed out in a long arc with the knife. She was hoping to hit him again with the butt, but the angle of attack was wrong. Instead, the blade slashed across and opened up Austin's face from ear to cheekbone.

Austin howled and let her go, falling to his knees as he clutched at his bleeding face. Kim slammed the hilt of the knife into his temple, and Austin collapsed into the dirt. Kim stumbled backward, then stood for a moment, chest heaving with exhaustion and adrenaline.

He didn't rise. Kim gulped in air for a few moments, then sheathed the knife and jogged down the road toward the sawmill. She needed help if she was going to hold Austin captive, and Shannon and the others needed to know Jeb had betrayed them.

It was only then that she remembered she still had her radio. Kim sighed, then decided there was no point in wasting the batteries.

She found Shannon supervising the unloading of the tractor. Her mother took one look at her and hurried over. "What happened?"

Kim took a deep breath. The adrenaline was wearing off, and she felt ready to fall over. Her throat was dry, her chest ached from the exertion, and talking was difficult. "Jeb was a traitor. He went and told Austin everything. All our plans. Austin shot him. Saw me, chased me. I managed to get away, clocked him with a knife, but..." Her voice failed her.

Shannon disappeared, then returned with Carol, Rebecca, and a bottle of water. "It's okay. I got it." Shannon's arm went around her shoulders, supporting her as she sipped the water. "We'll go and see if Austin's still there, catch him if we can. In the meantime, you need to rest." Her hand squeezed Kim's shoulder. "You did good, Kimmy. I'm proud of you. Let us take it from here."

Kim nodded. She finished the water, then let Aunt Carol lead her to a makeshift pallet set up inside the sawmill. She was asleep almost as soon as she went horizontal, without even enough time to take off her boots.

She woke some time later to Shannon's hand on her shoulder. She blinked up at her mother, still tired. "What is it?"

"Figured you'd want to know what was going on." Shannon's voice was soft. "We went after Austin, but he must have come to pretty soon after you left him, because he got away. We've been talking, and we have to assume Andre knows what we're planning. We'll be changing plans slightly, but we'll talk about that in the morning. For now, I wanted to give you an update, so you'd know."

Kim nodded. "Thanks, Mom."

"You earned it." Shannon's voice was a strange mix of pride and sorrow. "You were brave, taking him on. And smart to get away like you did. Even smarter to guess there was something up with Jeb. If it wasn't for you, everything we planned would be in vain. Andre'd have the jump on us."

Kim wasn't sure what to say. After a moment, Shannon squeezed her shoulder again. "Get some more sleep. We'll talk about the new plans in the morning."

Kim nodded and closed her eyes, though she wasn't sure she could sleep, not after that. Exhaustion, however, was stronger than she knew, and before long, she was dragged back to slumber once again.

35

SHANNON GRAYSON

D awn was barely past when the alarm sounded and Shannon rolled out of her cot. She was torn between anger at Andre for attacking so early, resignation that fighting was at hand, and relief that it was coming to a head.

At the very least, she didn't have to lie in bed, attempting to sleep and failing miserably, for the most part.

She'd slept in her shoes, her weapons close at hand, in case of a night attack. It was the work of a moment to grab everything she needed, including her radio, and hurry out to the main command post. She clicked the radio on. "What's the situation?"

Several seconds of crackling later, and Lee's voice came through. "We've got enemies in the woods heading for the bridge and the sawmill side of town."

"Same here." Sam's voice came through a second later.

"Same here." From Big Ed, who'd taken a position on the road to New Wren.

"And the same from this direction." Aunt Carol made the last.

"Crap on a cracker." Shannon stared at the red game pieces she'd placed on the map to represent Andre's forces. They were coming from every direction, circling the town. "Any idea of the numbers?"

"More than I'd like, no matter how you look at it." Rebecca's voice came through.

Shannon couldn't fault her. "Might want to start the evac plan now."

"Already on it." Rebecca would gather people together, getting them to head for the sawmill and the evacuation point near the bridge. Watchdog would soon be a ghost town except for the fighters.

That was one worry down. On to the next. "Anyone got eyes on Andre or Austin?" The Watchdog residents wouldn't know who Andre was, but she'd given them a good description of her ex-husband with instructions to sing out if they saw anyone who looked remotely like him.

Big Ed spoke up. "Think I got an eye on the weaselly one, Austin. He's got a crew with him, but he looks like hell. His face is all bruised and bandaged. Your girl did good work on him." Ed sounded grimly pleased. Shannon smirked.

"She's a tough one." By now, Kim would be awake and helping Rebecca.

Several things happened at once. Shouts and shooting erupted in the distance from several directions. Shannon knew that at each major road, the defenders would engage Andre's men, hopefully with more lethal results for the attackers than the Watchdog inhabitants.

There was a muffled boom, and the radio crackled to life as Sam reported in: "Idiot hit one of the mines. They work just fine." Shannon grinned. The mines were so old no one had been sure they'd work, and it was nice to know that part of their defenses was functioning properly.

A loud crunching sound came from the direction of New Wren, followed by Big Ed's voice. "Just had two guys hit the tripwire trap. One of them hit the spikes too. He won't be getting up again. Not sure the other guy's much better off."

That was at least three down, as well as whoever had been shot by the people defending the town.

Big Ed came back on the radio. "They're trying to wreck the buildings by knocking out windows and setting fires to drive out our defenders. David had to abandon the watch tower when someone got a Molotov on it. And it looks like someone's got a brain, because they called the bikers back, and they got two guys with cars coming down the road now."

The tripwire trap wouldn't do much against cars, and there weren't any mine traps on Big Ed's side. Shannon scowled, but the result was hardly unexpected. They'd never thought they'd hold the town without losing any ground. It simply wasn't fortified enough.

"Understood. Do what you can, but don't risk yourselves any more than you need. Fall back to the secondary lines if you're pressed, or join Carol and Sam." Lee and the other distant scouts—mostly Black Rats on motorcycles, like Sprocket—would come in behind Andre's men, as a second wave to take them by surprise. That was the idea, at least.

It depended on how many guys Andre had. At the moment, they weren't sure all Andre's forces were in Watchdog. With no eyes on Andre, there was no guarantee that a second wave wasn't waiting in the wings.

Shannon grabbed her guns. She needed to get out there and see what she could do to help. She wasn't the best shot, but she could still fire a pistol, and she might get lucky. The building across the street from the command post had a ladder around the back she could use to get up high.

Two minutes later, she was on a roof, watching cars rolling down the road. She sighted in on one of the drivers and fired.

Her first two shots cracked glass and pinged off the bumper, but her third hit home, and the car lurched to one side as the driver slumped over. Shannon grinned at the faint sounds of cursing.

A few more shots took out a man who was trying to set fire to various buildings and made the others duck into cover. That slowed their advance, though there were too many for her to handle on her own.

Her radio crackled again, this time with Lee's voice. "We got another crew coming in hot from the woodland side."

"Any sign of Andre?"

"Not yet. But he might be taking a back way," Lee responded.

"He would." Carol's voice was disgusted. "Coward always did like to send people in ahead of him to take the worst hits."

That was true enough. Andre only liked to join a fight when he was certain he could win. Still, the fact that there was another crew coming from the woods brought another concern to mind. "Rebecca, how's the evacuation going?"

Silence, then a low-voiced "We've got a problem."

Crap on a cracker. "What problem?"

"Bridge is gone."

"Sonuva..." Shannon swore.

That was why there was a second wave. And where Andre had gone.

They'd sent one crew over to blow the bridge and cut off the evacuation.

Good thing they'd had a secondary plan ready to go then. "All right. Plan B or Plan C, whichever you think better."

Plan B would be to try and access the storm drains and hole up beneath the town. Plan C would be to try and get everyone into the now empty bunker where the guns had been stored. There were drawbacks to both choices, especially if they were followed, but it was all they had.

"Going Plan B," Rebecca announced.

"Good. Kim, Lee and Carol—go rear-guard." Rebecca would guide the townsfolk through the tunnels to the safe point. Kim, Lee, and Carol, along with whoever else of the defenders could get there, would stand by to make sure no one found the entrance to the tunnel.

"Shannon, I got someone who looks like your man." Ed's voice sounded worried.

Shannon scrambled to the edge of the roof and looked down the road. After a moment, she spotted the tall, muscular form of her ex-husband next to a spindly figure she thought was Austin.

Andre. Andre was dangerous and unpredictable. Andre could change the whole situation—for the worse. If he rallied his men or managed to set up a counterattack of his own, they'd be sunk. It was bad enough most of the defenders on that side had been forced to retreat.

She needed to make sure Andre didn't have time or inclination to think of counterattacking. And she knew exactly how to do that.

She clicked the radio on. "Everyone, find tertiary defense positions. I'm going for the bear bait tactic."

Seconds later, Kim spoke up. "Bear bait tactic?"

She'd hoped to have more time to explain the plan to her daughter, but there wasn't any time if she wanted to get her plans in motion before Andre could start whatever scheme he had in mind. "I'm going to draw Andre out."

"Mom!" Kim's voice was frightened and dismayed, even through the crackle of static. "You can't!"

"I can. And I have to. I need to get him to come after me. If he starts thinking and planning, we're toast. I need him mad and focused on one thing: catching me." The words came out calmer than Shannon actually felt.

"You don't have to. There's other ways to handle that devil than baiting him." Carol was the next to protest, much to Shannon's surprise. "We can find a different plan."

"We don't have time."

"Then we can help you."

"No." Shannon shook her head, even knowing they couldn't see her. "You focus on getting people to safety, protecting everyone in Watchdog. Leave Andre to me."

"But he'll kill you!"

"He'll try. I don't plan to let him succeed, and definitely not without a heck of a fight. But either way, I'll do better if I know my family will survive."

"But—"

"Shannon—"

"No arguments. There's no time. Get to safety and keep yourselves alive. That's the best thing you can do to help me right now."

Shannon clicked off the radio. She hated to do it, but she knew that Kim and Carol would only keep trying to change her mind, and she couldn't afford to let them get in her head. She couldn't afford to be distracted, not if she wanted to have any chance against her former husband.

She readied her pistol, checked where she'd parked the bike she'd claimed from among the spares the night before, then climbed down from the roof. She took a deep breath and stepped onto the road, into full view. "Hey, Andre! I'm here, you son of a halfwit mule, and I'm ready to settle this, once and for all! Come and get me, if you think you have the stones, you weak-minded coward!"

36

AUSTIN/ANDRE

He'd snorted the last of his coke, and his face still hurt like a knife to the gut. But more than that, Austin was aware of a bone-deep urge to be somewhere, anywhere, else. And yet, here he was, leading a bunch of homicidal lunatics, most of them drugged as well, in an assault on the town of Watchdog.

He felt sick. He'd felt sick since the death of the mechanic guy, but it had been worse since he'd shot the reverend. Sure, the guy had been a traitor and hardly a proper man of God, but it didn't sit right with him. Even with all he'd done, there was some little sliver of preacher's son still in him. That part of him had given him nightmares and recriminations all night long that no amount of booze could silence.

He hadn't wanted to be part of this attack, but he didn't dare refuse Andre. The man was completely mad—manic and high on bloodlust and who knew what else. Just like the rest of his murderous crew. Trying to get out of the attack would have been suicide.

Not that attacking was much better. He'd nearly thrown up when he saw the first guys hit the tripwires and go flying, especially when one man hit a patch of sharpened stakes. He'd called the men back and, with some effort, made a new plan.

Two guys had driven cars down the street to trigger any traps. He figured the heavier car frames wouldn't have the same problems the bikes did. The rest of his team started systematically destroying windows and doors and setting fires to see what they could get to burn.

Not much, as it turned out. The buildings were old, but they were sturdier than he would have expected. Still, they did damage and managed to ferret out some of the defenders and send them running— those they didn't kill.

He wondered how the other attacking squads were doing. They didn't have a way to communicate, but he'd heard some explosions and shooting, so he figured they were having trouble too. He was tempted to check on the others, but he knew Andre wouldn't appreciate him deviating from his orders, and who knew when he'd get to town after destroying the bridge.

Shots took out one of the drivers and a few of the other thugs ahead of him, but there weren't a lot of shots being fired. They managed to make their way to the town center.

It was deserted, and Austin scowled. Where were all the residents? They had to be somewhere, especially if Andre had succeeded in cutting off the escape route.

Just then Andre appeared, a manic grin on his face. "Austin! Well done. You've taken the center of the town." Andre surveyed the empty square with satisfaction. "From here, we can finish them off."

Austin nodded, though his heart wasn't in it at all. "How'd the bridge destruction go, boss?"

"It went quite well." Andre chuckled. "The fools are trapped, and it only remains to weed them out and punish them for their foolishness in daring to side with Sarah in defying me."

Austin didn't see it. They hadn't found very many people so far, and even fewer had died. He knew the girl had probably gotten back to her mother and warned her about Jeb's betrayal. That meant the bulk of the town was somewhere else, planning something. But there was no point in telling Andre that. The man was far too insane to listen to any words that might conflict with his vision of how the day would go.

Austin was still trying to figure out what to do next when a shout rang out from only a few yards away. He looked up to see Gardena's niece staring at them, a challenging smirk on her face.

"I'm here! Come and get me if you think you have the stones, you weak-minded coward!" The words rang through the air.

Andre's good mood vanished into anger. "Sarah!" He snarled the word and started forward.

Austin caught his arm. Even knowing it was suicide, he couldn't keep his mouth shut in the face of such an obvious trap. "Boss, wait. Let's think about this for a moment." The remaining men nearby nodded in agreement.

Andre shook him off with a snarl. "I will not stand here while that little witch taunts me!"

"I get it, prez, I do, but we gotta play it smart. She wouldn't be doing this unless she had something planned. It's gotta be a trap. We don't want to rush into it."

Andre backhanded him. "Don't even think about running now. We will catch Sarah, and we will destroy her."

Austin reeled back and stared as blood trickled from his mouth. "But boss—"

Andre pulled out a gun and fired wildly into the air above Austin's head. "Move!"

Austin's already frayed nerves broke. He moved, but not to follow Andre. *That nut's gonna get us all killed!* He scrambled backward toward his bike.

Andre's eyes gleamed with depravity. "Coward!"

Austin didn't care what Andre called him. He turned and mounted his bike, then whipped it around. He was done. He didn't care if Andre hunted him down later. He wasn't going to drive headfirst into an obvious trap for a lunatic like Andre. No chance. Let some other idiot follow the madman on his quest for vengeance. Austin was out.

He revved the bike and gunned it back down the street. He wasn't thinking of anything particular, just his desire to get away. Away from Watchdog, away from Andre and his ex-wife, and away from all the misery he'd dealt with ever since he'd joined up with Atkinson.

He was so focused on running, he didn't see the tripwire across the road, not until just before he hit it. By then, it was too late to slow down, much less stop. As if in slow motion, he saw his front wheel hit the tripwire.

The bike flipped upward, instantly out of control. Austin didn't have time to even think of holding on to his handlebars as he was flung away from the machine. His body flew through the air, limbs flailing wildly. He braced himself to hit the ground.

He didn't experience the bone-breaking impact he expected. Instead, something sharp slammed into his back and his right leg and ran through him. Austin choked and tried to breathe, but his chest wouldn't expand. His muscles wouldn't obey him.

He forced his eyes open, despite the blinding pain, and found himself staring at a spike. One of the spikes from the trap he'd seen earlier. He'd landed on it.

The pain was fading away, replaced by a sort of floating feeling. It was kind of like being drunk. Austin let his eyes slip closed again.

It wasn't so bad. He was probably going to go to fire and brimstone, but that wasn't so bad. At least he was getting away from…Andre…

Andre watched as Austin pinwheeled through the air and crashed into a set of stakes. It looked like he was done for. Andre brushed it aside and turned to his one-time wife. She still stood in the street, challenging him. Laughing at him.

He charged after her, and Sarah turned and ran for it. Andre pursued, his blood pounding in his ears, his nerves alight with anticipation.

He would catch her. And then he would punish her, until she was begging him for the right to die. He would kill all her friends in front of her, burn her supposed haven to the ground, and destroy everything she cared about. And then he would do everything to her that he'd done to the mechanic, and more, until her mind and will shattered.

He could already see it, the bright scarlet of her blood. The way her face would twist in pain and fear when he cornered her. The way she'd cower before him, as she had all those years ago. He would teach her a lesson no one in the entire state—the entire country— would ever forget.

He stalked after her, a devil's sneer on his lips. The hunt was on, and he was already looking forward to the moment he cornered his prey.

37

SHANNON GRAYSON

S hannon dove for her borrowed bike as Andre came closer. Her hands shook, adrenaline pumping through her veins as she climbed aboard, revved the engine, and gunned it. The bike roared out into the street. Shannon took just enough time to meet Andre's eyes and smirk before she took off through Watchdog.

Andre gave chase. Shannon could hear his engine as he started his bike and roared up behind her. She thought she could outrun him, but that wasn't the plan. She didn't want to escape Andre—she simply wanted to control when and where she confronted him.

She tore through the streets, riding hard, but always slow enough for Andre to keep her in sight. Her first goal was to run his machine out of fuel.

They ran through the streets with reckless abandon, taking ninety-degree turns at speeds that would have made her cringe any other time. Out toward the hunting lodge. Back around in a loop toward Big Ed's Auto Barn. Across the streets in a zigzag pattern, careful to avoid the hospital and the childcare center.

Elsewhere, she knew Rebecca and the others were making sure the rest of the Watchdog residents were safe. Sam and Big Ed would be shoring up defenses at the medical center. Just a few more moments and everyone would be safe.

Shots whizzed around her ears. Shannon ducked, then chanced a look at her fuel gauge. Only about a quarter tank. Andre would be down to less, hopefully. Shannon decided it was time to move to the next stage of the plan. She turned her bike toward the sawmill and increased her speed.

She knew the road, but Andre didn't. So she was ready for the curve toward the sawmill. Andre veered wildly around the curve and lost control of his bike. Shannon grinned as he went into a skid off the side of the road.

The grin vanished a second later as Andre gave an inarticulate roar and fired his pistol wildly in her direction. By bad luck, one of his bullets hit the front tire of her motorcycle. The tire blew, and Shannon went flying.

She had no chance to brace herself, no chance to control her landing. Shannon slammed into the ground at an awkward angle. Her left arm hit the ground first, and Shannon both heard and felt it snap. Searing pain slammed through her forearm. The shock rocked through her arm to her shoulder, and the wound from Langmaid's bullet tore open from the impact. Shannon gasped in pain as she rolled across the ground.

Andre laughed. The sound was bone-chilling. Shannon shoved herself into a sitting position and nearly blacked out as pain raced through her like lightning strikes.

"Finally. You can't run anymore." Andre smiled, an expression of pure malice and cold venom. One hand still held his gun. The other held a wicked-looking serrated knife. With horror, Shannon saw that the blade was still flecked with blood, like it might have been used on Bill. She shuddered.

Andre advanced one slow step at a time. Shannon scrambled to try and get up or to get her hand on a weapon. Her gun had gone flying from her belt, and she had no idea where it had landed. Her knife was sheathed in a place she couldn't reach with her left arm no longer functional.

She couldn't get to her feet, too bruised and battered. Fear poured through her as Andre approached. She felt like a mouse cornered by a snarling, feral alley cat.

Five yards. Four yards. Three yards. Andre's grin was manic and vicious as he stalked her. Shannon's heart pounded in her throat. *No, no, no, no, no...*

A shot rang out. For one moment, Shannon thought she was dead. Then Andre collapsed into the dirt, eyes wide in anger and shock as blood poured from a suddenly ruined knee.

"Got you, you scum!" Shannon looked up to see a small knot of people. Kim and Carol were there, but in the lead was Lee, his hands wrapped around a smoking rifle. His expression was grim and triumphant. "That's for Bill!"

Shannon watched as the group approached, her fear slowly fading. She wasn't alone. She had her friends and family at her back.

Another figure emerged from the sawmill: Rebecca. David and John and some of the others also came out, all bearing weapons and all glaring at Andre.

Andre's confident demeanor vanished in an instant as he realized he was alone and outnumbered, exactly as he'd intended her to be. All the bloodlust and meanness ran out of his face as he held up his hands, the knife and gun both falling from his grip as his eyes flashed around the group, seeking an escape.

His eyes landed on Kim. "Kim, daughter. You wouldn't attack your own father, would you? Surely you wouldn't." He cringed as Kim fired a shot into the dirt at his knee. Rocks flew up like shrapnel, cutting into his face, and he gasped in pain.

"I'd shoot you in an instant, if you weren't a waste of a bullet." Kim's voice was cold and harsh.

Andre rallied. "Kim, you can't mean that. Come now, don't you remember when you were younger? When you were a child, and we lived as a family?" His gaze shifted. "Carol, surely you remember what it was like when Black Rats were the kings of the road. We could have that again. We could have it all. A family, a flourishing motorcycle gang. Everything we've ever wanted—we could have it all. You just need to—"

"To tell you to stuff it. Shove it up your tailpipe, Andre." Carol spat the words. "You're pathetic, and there's no one here that's going to fall for your crap and silver-tongued lies."

"Aunt Carol's right. You're full of crap. And I'm not falling for it. Things weren't better or simpler or kinder when I was a kid." Kim shook her head. "I was just too young and dumb to know what you were doing to Mom."

"I..." Andre's gaze flicked from one face to another as Shannon rose to her feet, seeking mercy or some crack he could exploit and finding nothing. Eventually, his gaze came back to her. "Sarah. Sarah, don't you remember what we had? What it was like when we fell in love?"

Shannon snorted. "When I fell for your lies and charisma, you mean. It wasn't ever love. Especially on your part."

"But I took good care of you. I provided, did I not? I was strong enough to protect you. I could offer you that again."

Shannon spat blood from a split lip at his face. It missed and hit his shirt. "Only thing I need protecting from is you."

Shannon turned and looked around. Her pistol was a few yards away. She limped over and picked it up with her good hand, then turned and pointed it at Andre.

His eyes widened. Then a slow smirk crossed his features, and his expression turned condescending.

"Sarah." He shook his head. "Sarah, Sarah. You and I both know you're not going to shoot me. You're not ruthless enough to shoot an unarmed man, especially one who's already on the ground. You're not that cold, so I know you're not going to pull the trigger. You don't have the will to do so."

Shannon was so focused on his face, and so sure he couldn't attack with his ruined knee, that she'd let her guard down. She'd forgotten Andre was pumped up by drugs and pure, unrelenting spite. Kim's warning came at the same time as Andre's sudden lunge upward. "Mom! Watch out!" Shannon jerked backward as Andre slashed out with the knife he'd picked up while he was talking.

Shannon's gun fired, and it was far from the only one. Rebecca, Carol, Lee, and Kim all opened fire at the same time. Red wounds blossomed in a dozen places at once across Andre's torso as he was driven back by the barrage.

Andre staggered, his chest a red-painted ruin. His eyes bulged, his mouth worked with no result as the knife dropped from nerveless fingers.

Andre's body followed it a moment later, crashing to the dirt. Lifeless eyes, still clouded with malice and cruelty, stared at the sky.

Shannon staggered and almost followed him down as her legs gave out from sheer relief. Kim and Carol caught her, and Carol slung Shannon's good arm around her shoulders. "There we go."

Shannon stared at Andre's dead body. Adrenaline drained away, and slow-growing elation started to take its place.

After so long, it was finally over.

38

KIM NAKAMURA

Of course, Andre's death wasn't the end of everything. There were wounds to be tended, buildings to be inspected, damage to be cataloged for repairs, and a lot of terrified people to reassure. There were also the dead to be taken care of.

Andre could rot for all Kim cared. She'd happily burn his body and dump the ashes into a toilet. A heavily used toilet.

The same could be said of all the members of his little gang who'd been killed or injured attacking Watchdog. Kim didn't care what happened to them. She was more concerned with the residents who'd been injured.

Along with Shannon's broken arm and injured shoulder, Sam had been pretty badly hurt. Big Ed had sustained some burns. Suzie Mullen was unconscious, and John Deckon had slipped in the tunnels and gained a concussion. There were plenty of other smaller injuries as well.

Eight of the residents had died, including, to everyone's sorrow, Rufus Holden, Rebecca's father. He'd been caught in a building that had partially collapsed. No one knew if his heart had given out in the excitement or if an attack had been responsible. Rebecca had been quiet and withdrawn since hearing the news, not that anyone could blame her.

There was also the matter of Jeb Butler. He'd been a traitor and incompetent, but he hadn't deserved to be murdered in cold blood, and he didn't deserve to be left to rot.

Kim helped tend the wounded, but her gaze kept going back to Shannon. Her mother's injuries had required Glenda's more experienced touch. She was currently settled on a medical cot, teeth clenched as Glenda gently tugged the bones of her broken forearm back into alignment.

Shannon was amazing. She'd faced down Andre like a champion and survived. She was brave and strong, and over the past week, she'd become a leader. A good leader, of the kind that Watchdog would be proud to have.

Kim was happy for her, but at the same time, it brought to mind an issue she'd avoided thinking about: her own position and plans. She'd always known she couldn't leave her family while Andre was on the loose. That threat was now ended.

She was free to choose her own path. And that reminded her of the conversation she'd had with Lee only a few days before.

Her gaze went back to Shannon. She'd been thinking of leaving, but could she really do it? For a moment, she wasn't certain.

Then she thought about her frustrations over the past several weeks and how much she hated knowing that there were more monsters out there. The world was a dangerous place, but she knew in her heart she had the skills to make it better, as well.

She met Lee's gaze across the medical center. His eyebrow rose and his head tipped toward the door in a silent question. After a moment, Kim nodded.

She finished with Margaret Tarrow's injured wrist, then made her way to where Shannon was sitting, her arm in a sling and bound up tight in a splint.

"Hey, Mom."

"Hey, Kim." Shannon gave her a tired smile. "How are you holding up?"

Kim shrugged. "I'm holding up. And I came out in better shape than you." She smiled. "But you were amazing."

"I was terrified." Shannon grimaced. "I thought I was going to die."

"But you didn't. You got him to chase you, and you managed to hold him in a standoff until we could arrive to help you. It was the most incredible thing I've ever seen."

"I appreciate you saying that." Shannon reached out her good arm for a hug, and Kim obliged.

They sat in silence for a moment, then Kim spoke again. "Watchdog is a good place to settle down. A good place to build a life with friends and a community around you. You and Aunt Carol could be really happy here."

"I think you're right." Shannon hesitated. "It's just—Kim, why do you sound like you're *not* planning on staying?"

No way around it. "Because I'm not. I've thought about it a lot, and I decided that once Andre was dealt with, I'd hit the road."

"Why?" Shannon's expression filled with distress. "We finally have a chance for a peaceful life as a family, Kim."

"Maybe. But I can't settle down, not knowing what the world's like right now. There's a lot of good people in trouble out there. A lot of communities that need help, even if it's just a stranger passing through. I want to be that help, if I can."

Shannon's expression cleared a little. "You're talking about what you said to Carol, back in Memphis. Nomadic helpers."

"Yeah. I still want to do it."

She could see her mother's reluctance—and her fear. Kim waited. She wanted Shannon to accept what she'd said, but she wasn't going to try and argue the point too much. She was going to follow her heart, whether Shannon approved or not. She'd rather have her mother's blessing, but it wasn't necessary.

Shannon swallowed hard. "It's dangerous. You weren't thinking of going alone, were you?"

Kim shook her head. "I could do it alone, but I was actually thinking of taking Lee. And maybe Mutt too."

"Mutt would like that." Shannon looked away for a moment. Her voice was quiet when she spoke again. "You thinking of taking motorcycles, cars, or heading out on foot?"

"I was thinking we could take two of the bikes. They seem the most fuel efficient."

"That's probably as good a plan as any, but the dog might give you trouble, as big as she is."

Kim considered that. "Maybe, but a couple of the bikes are rigged with oversized rear seats or carrier baskets, including at least one whose rider got killed in the fighting. Or Lee and I could possibly get Big Ed to help us cobble together a sidecar for her, or something we could tow." With a start, Kim realized her mother wasn't trying to argue her out of leaving. "Mom?"

"I don't like it. I don't like the idea of you leaving. But if I've learned anything over the past few weeks, it's that you're a grown woman. You can make your own decisions and walk your own path. I might be your mother, but I don't have the right to stop you." Shannon's breathing stuttered a moment. "When were you thinking of leaving?"

"Pretty much as soon as I'm done here. Waiting would just make it harder for all of us." She saw her mother's face contort in grief and felt a pang of regret. And still, she knew she was making the correct decision. Waiting wouldn't make leaving any easier.

Shannon's hug tightened. "I understand." She took a deep breath. "Carol and I are going to stick around Watchdog for a while, maybe set up a new Black Rats chapter here. If you want to take a rest from wandering and come home, you can always come back here."

"I know." Kim hugged her mother back. "I'll be sure to remember that and try to make it back for regular visits."

Shannon nodded. Kim took a deep breath. "I love you, Mom. I love you and I'm proud of you."

"I love you and I'm proud of you, too, Kim."

Kim pulled away carefully. There was nothing more to say. She supposed she should say goodbye to Aunt Carol and the rest of the Black Rats crew, but that was sure to be awkward. It might be easiest to simply slip away.

"Go. I'll take care of Aunt Carol. You and Lee get going, unless you want to debate your decision with everyone in the motorcycle club." Shannon's voice was sad, but certain.

"Hey, Shannon," Rebecca called out as she walked over, "we need to make a plan for repairing the buildings that were damaged in the attack."

Shannon met Kim's eyes and nodded, then turned her attention to Rebecca. She began to look over the list the other woman had compiled, seemingly immersing herself in the discussion. Kim knew her mother was watching her out of the corner of her eye, but if Shannon wasn't going to stop her, then the least Kim could do was make good use of the opportunity her mother was offering to slip away clean.

Kim stepped back and called out softly. "Here Mutt." The big dog loped over, tail wagging.

Kim met Lee's eyes, and the two of them moved toward the doors and slipped outside.

Kim took a deep breath. "You ready to go?"

"More than." Lee nodded. "I've got my supplies by my cot. Never really unpacked."

"Neither did I."

The two of them headed over to the command post. The building was deserted, and they made their way to the cots. Then they stopped short.

There on Lee's cot was a jacket with the Black Rats logo crudely stitched onto the shoulder. There were also two sets of keys for motorcycles. Kim blinked back a sudden stinging sensation in her eyes. "How'd they know?" She hadn't said anything to anyone else, and she didn't think Lee had either.

"Maybe they didn't, and just wanted to give us these to show we're part of the family. Or maybe your Aunt Carol figured us out. She's real smart." Lee's voice was thoughtful as he picked up the jacket and stared at the logo.

Lee slipped the jacket on and settled the denim across his shoulders with a look of satisfaction. They shared smiles, then grabbed their packs and went outside to the motorcycles. One of the bikes had been fitted with a large basket for Mutt, and Kim coaxed the dog into place before she clambered into the seat and started the bike. Mutt woofed. Her basket wasn't exactly the roomiest space for a dog her size, but at least she wouldn't fall off the bike every time Kim took a curve.

Twenty minutes later, they were on the road, riding into the unknown and whatever awaited them in the world beyond Watchdog.

EPILOGUE
KIM NAKAMURA

Iowa road, two months later

The sun was hot with the beginning of summer, even though it was still morning, and Kim swiped at her brow as they rode along at an easy pace. Beside her, Lee grimaced at the cloudless sky and fiddled with the makeshift headband he'd tied across his head to keep his hair out of his eyes. They were going slowly enough for Mutt to lope along beside them. With no destination in mind, speed didn't seem as important as conserving fuel and watching the road for anything of interest.

There wasn't much of a breeze, but that was all right. Summer wasn't in full swing just yet. In the meantime, Kim was enjoying the chance to get more of a tan.

"Hey, Kim?" Lee pointed at the road further ahead and pulled his bike to a stop.

Kim stopped as well, then squinted against the sun and shaded her eyes. After a moment, she saw what Lee was pointing at. A distant figure was standing beside a vehicle.

"Stranded, do you think?" he said.

"Can't hurt to ask." Kim grinned. "It's only one person, so we're safe enough." She hesitated. "On the other hand…"

"Can't hurt to be careful." Lee nodded. "What's the plan?"

Kim loosened a knife in its sheath and the catch on the strap for her pistol. Then she swung off the bike and kicked the stand down to hold it. "I'll go with Mutt to say hello. You stay back with the motorcycles and keep your sights trained on them."

"Works for me." Lee swung his rifle into position.

Kim beckoned Mutt closer and put a hand on her back to steady the dog. With a final look to Lee, she and Mutt set out.

They strolled closer, and the figure resolved into a young man about Kim's age. He was wearing battered jeans and a polo shirt that had seen better days. Brown hair fell in shaggy waves around his face, which bore signs of a heavy sunburn fading into a healthy tan. He wasn't wearing a hat, and Kim could see the sheen of sweat on his forehead. He looked up at their approach and offered them a friendly wave. "Hey."

Kim waved back. "Hey."

Mutt made an inquiring noise, and Kim shushed her with a hand on her head. "Easy girl." She faced the stranger. "I'm Kim. And this here," her hand ruffled Mutt's ears, "is Mutt."

"Rick Corman." The young man said. "Nice to meet you."

"Nice to meet you." Kim eyed the young man. "Mind if I ask what's up? You look like you might be having a spot of trouble."

Rick grimaced. "You could say that. I was on the road, and my truck crapped out on me. It's old, and it wasn't in the best of shape when I got it, but I don't know how to fix it."

315

Kim grimaced sympathetically. "I hear you. Afraid I don't know much about engines. Still, I have a bike back there with a friend of mine. We could give you a ride to wherever you're headed."

Rick chuckled and rubbed the back of his head, a sheepish look on his face. "It's actually kind of funny, but I can't say exactly where I'm headed. I was going to see my family, but they weren't home when I got there, and I have no idea where they could be, so I've just been roaming aimlessly."

Kim's heart went out to the guy. "That's some rough luck."

"Man, you've no idea. Ever since that crazy disaster hit, life has been weird. I can't say if my luck's been good or bad, the way things have been going." Rick shook his head. "I'm just glad my broken arm healed."

"Yeah. I can see how a broken arm would be an inconvenience." Kim thought a moment, then turned and waved, giving the "all clear" signal she and Lee had worked out at the beginning of their journey. "Hey, why don't you let me introduce you to my friend, and we can talk?"

"Sure." Rick shrugged and reached into the truck to fish out a duffle bag that bulged with various items, probably food and basic supplies.

Kim led Rick back to where Lee was waiting, with Mutt bounding back and forth between them. She made quick work of introductions. "Lee, this is Rick. Rick, this is Lee. We travel together. Lee, Rick's car went bust."

"Yeah? Where you headed?" Lee asked.

"Nowhere. Or everywhere, really." Rick shrugged again. "I don't really have a destination." His expression turned sheepish. "Honestly, I'm just looking for some company. Talking to myself gets kinda old after a while."

Lee and Kim exchanged a look. Rick didn't seem like the bad sort, and even if he turned out to be dangerous, they had him outnumbered. From the look of him, Rick wasn't carrying a weapon, which meant they had him outgunned as well, in a worst-case scenario.

Lee offered Rick a small smile. "Well, it's not much, but we've got some room on my bike and supplies enough to share. You could come along with us until you decide you're done with life on the road."

Rick's smile held more than a little relief, and Kim had the suspicion he'd been alone for longer than his easy response to Lee indicated. "That sounds great actually. I was working in a superstore when the power went out, if you can believe it. I'll try not to cause you too much trouble."

"No worries. We'll find another bike for you somewhere." Lee held out his hand. "Welcome to the crew, Rick."

"Thanks."

Together, the four of them set off again under the rising sun.

END OF FINAL DAYS
AFTER THE END BOOK 3

Trapped Days, August 7, 2024

Fractured Days, September 4, 2024

Final Days, October 9, 2024

PS: Do you like disaster fiction? Then keep reading for exclusive extracts from ***Toxic Tides*** and ***Erupting Trouble.***

THANK YOU

Thank you for purchasing 'Final Days'
(After the End Book 3)

Get prepared and sign-up to Grace's mailing list
to be notified of my next release at
www.GraceHamiltonBooks.com.

Loved this book? Share it with a friend,
www.GraceHamiltonBooks.com/books

ABOUT GRACE HAMILTON

Grace Hamilton is the prepper pen-name for a bad-ass, survivalist momma-bear of four kids, and wife to a wonderful husband. After being stuck in a mountain cabin for six days following a flash flood, she decided she never wanted to feel so powerless or have to send her kids to bed hungry again. Now she lives the prepper lifestyle and knows that if SHTF or TEOTWAWKI happens, she'll be ready to help protect and provide for her family.

Combine this survivalist mentality with a vivid imagination (as well as a slightly unhealthy day dreaming habit) and you get a prepper fiction author. Grace spends her days thinking about the worst possible survival situations that a person could be thrown into, then throwing her characters into these nightmares while trying to figure out "What SHOULD you do in this situation?"

You will find Grace on:

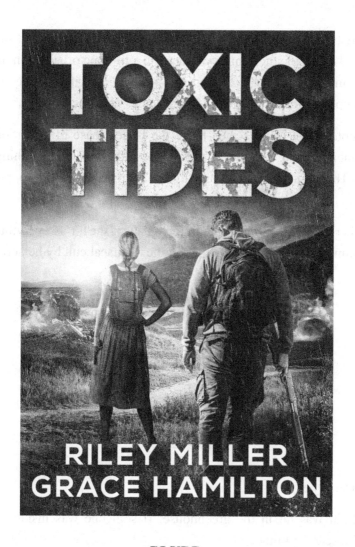

BLURB

In a world ravaged by drought, family is all that matters…

Eighteen-year-old Hazel refuses to become another wife and brood-mare to the prophet of the Wellspring cult. She's determined to find a safe haven for her younger brother, Caleb, in a world where 80% of all fresh water has been contaminated by an algae bloom. But if they're going to survive, they'll need help.

Scientists Emily and Sam, and wilderness guide Bash, might just be the kind of people they can count on. But a lifetime of isolation makes it near impossible for Hazel to trust outsiders. Even if they may be her only hope of breaking free from the prophet's clutches.

A remote forest cabin seems to be the perfect base of operations to plan their escape. But when the cult's soldiers come searching for them, Hazel must draw upon all her strength and skill to protect Caleb.

With her brother's life hanging in the balance, she'll risk everything to save him - even if it means taking on the maniacal cult by herself.

Get your copy of *Toxic Tides*
Available February 5, 2025
(Available for Pre-Order Now!)
www.GraceHamiltonBooks.com

EXCERPT

Chapter One

The light was on in the greenhouse. If someone was inside, Hazel could lose everything.

She hesitated, crouched by the edge of the dining hall. Her knees shook holding the awkward pose. To keep her balance, she leaned on the handle of the collection basket sitting at her side.

Tilting her head as if that would help her hear better, she strained to make out any sound from the brightly lit building. Outside of the soft yellow light from the greenhouse, the night was pitch-black. It was the new moon, and wisps of cloud hid the stars from sight.

Lights out was long past, and everyone in the compound was in their beds. Or at least, everyone should be.

But the greenhouse light was on, and all of Hazel's carefully laid plans were in jeopardy. Was the greenhouse empty? Had someone forgotten to turn the lights off after their shift? Was an insomniac prowling the orderly rows of vegetables, just waiting to sound an alarm at the sight of two children creeping past the translucent walls?

Hazel felt a sharp, insistent tug on her belt and glanced behind her. She knew her younger brother was there, but Caleb's features completely disappeared into the night.

"What's wrong?" He kept his question to a whisper, but even so Hazel felt a cold squeeze of fear on her heart. She took an unsteady breath and pressed a finger to where his lips might have been.

They were so close. The forest was barely a hundred feet from where they were crouched. All they had to do was sprint past the greenhouse, make it through the gate in the palisade, and disappear into the tree line beyond.

If they were forced to give up and try again another night, they wouldn't have the safe darkness of the new moon. And in less than two weeks Hazel would be eighteen, and it would be too late for Caleb.

She wouldn't give up now—they had to risk rushing past the greenhouse and hope that no one was inside to see them.

She touched Caleb's head, soothingly, then rose from squatting. She felt him rise behind her. She could hear his even breaths.

He trusted her—and she prayed that trust was well-founded. It all came down to this. If they got caught…

If she was honest with herself, she had no idea what Prophet Saul would do to her for trying to flee. But she had a few ideas, and fear made her dizzy when she thought about them.

Hazel took a deep, steadying breath. Her mother had taught her to breathe through the pain of cramped knees during long vigils by the wellspring. Breathe in slowly over a count of four, hold for four, and release.

She did that twice, then crouched a little lower and started the slow, agonizing creep toward the well-lit greenhouse. The path ahead was dark, at least, and bushes provided some cover.

Soon she and Caleb reached the front side of the greenhouse. Hazel paused again, calculating the distance. The greenhouse was only sixty feet long. Sixty brightly lit feet, light pouring through the plastic walls, where every step could mean exposure.

She and Caleb could cross the distance in less than thirty seconds. But those thirty seconds could lose them everything.

Twisting both hands in opposite directions on the handle of her basket, Hazel reminded herself why they were doing this. *I'll never let them take you away,* she silently promised her brother. *Whatever it takes.*

Pushing those thoughts from her mind, Hazel let go of the basket with one hand and reached back to squeeze her brother's hand. Then she started the torturous creep past the greenhouse.

As the light sliced across her face, she crouched even lower. She couldn't believe, after all her careful planning, how exposed they were. The light cast their long shadows against the bunkhouses across the way—anyone awake inside would see the flicker in the darkness.

She realized she wasn't breathing anymore, just holding her mouth firmly closed and moving as quickly as stealth would allow.

Five feet. Ten. Twenty...

In the greenhouse—a glimmer of motion. She froze, dropped to the ground, and felt Caleb struggle to keep hold of her belt as he copied her.

The light hadn't been mistakenly left on. The Wellspring prophet himself was in the greenhouse.

He was tending to the fresh shoots and leaves of what would become the fall harvest. Hazel watched him, her eyes wide, afraid to even blink in case the movement gave her away.

Saul was a tall, gaunt man in his late fifties. He had a long, carefully tended beard and equally long hair that he kept clean and brushed. Hazel had known him her entire life, but lately he had been acting with a feverish intensity that felt new.

Seeing him with his hands among the greens, she felt a pang of remorse. How would he react to her and Caleb disappearing? Would he be worried about them? Angry? Disappointed?

It didn't matter. She'd made her arguments to the commune's leader, and her pleas, and they had fallen on deaf ears. There was no rescue from that quarter. No, as far as she was concerned, Prophet Saul was the most dangerous man in the world. His will was the way here.

The Prophet's newest wife, Anna, shuffled into view. She said something to him, smiling nervously, and plucked a leaf from a nearby plant. He shook his head sharply and slapped her hand, not in anger, but as if he was chastising a naughty child.

They weren't facing her but weren't quite facing away, either—she and Caleb would be at the edge of their peripheral vision.

Was it more dangerous to move and risk catching their eye? Or to wait, hoping that neither turned this way?

Hazel bit her lip. They couldn't just stay put, waiting for discovery. It was now or never.

She pushed up onto all fours, and Caleb let go of her belt. Her collection basket slapped into the ground, and Hazel winced. Had anyone heard?

Had anything fallen out? She touched around the ground to check, but she didn't feel anything. There was no time to be entirely sure.

Moving as fast as she dared, trusting Caleb would be right behind her, Hazel scurried past the bright greenhouse walls, scraping her knees on the gravel even through her long dress. It hurt, and she felt herself slowing down. *Keep going! Don't stop.* Thirty feet. Forty.

A sound shattered the night stillness and she froze. Was it the Prophet raising an alarm? No, it had come from her right, not her left. A cough, or maybe a footstep scraping on gravel. From inside, or a nearby building?

She couldn't tell. Either way, she had to keep moving. She couldn't stop here, in the light.

Doggedly she moved on, ensuring Caleb was behind her all the way. Fifty feet. No sound of pursuit, but the gravel under her knees felt as loud as gunfire. Sixty feet, and they were past the greenhouse. Another ten feet farther and they were hidden in shadow again.

She stood up quickly, then helped Caleb to his feet. Her heart thudded against her ribcage. She held him for a moment against her chest, as her eyes tried to pierce the darkness. The shining greenhouse had destroyed her night vision. There was no way to know what had made the sound. No way to tell how much farther they had to go.

Gritting her teeth, Hazel took Caleb's hand and ran.

Her long ponytail slapped from side to side as they dashed toward where she knew the compound wall would be. She couldn't see it, invisible as it was in the darkness, but it loomed in her memories. The wall that had kept her trapped inside every day of her life.

Putting out a hand to keep from running smack into it, Hazel made contact. In daylight, from a distance, the wall looked natural, like trees planted in a neat, tight row. But the bark-covered posts were reinforced with thick wooden braces, creating a sturdy wall all around the wide compound.

There were two gates, one at the front big enough for trucks to pass through for those rare occasions when community members traded with the outside world, and the other, the gate Hazel was now feeling for in the dark, opening into the forest. This was the gate they used when they went out foraging for plants that didn't grow inside. Rarely had she ever been able to slip through the perimeter alone to spend some time away from the constant observation that was her daily life.

Hazel ran her hands over the rough wooden posts in front of her. Her pulse hammered loudly in her ears. Was someone following them? That eerie moaning query had to have been an owl, right? A person would have shouted.

There. She found it. She ran her hands slowly up the gate and found the smooth metal handle. Gasping in relief, she yanked. But the door didn't shift. Someone had dropped the lock bar in place.

The gate was secured with a huge horizontal lock bar that she would have to push into its vertical position. Hazel handed her basket to her brother and gave the bar an experimental shove. It was heavy and high enough up that she struggled, clenching her teeth and feeling the pressure build behind her eyes, as she heaved.

Earlier that day, Hazel, fawning and as sweetly as she could, had asked her betrothed to open the gate so that she might collect flowers to make into a crown for their wedding day. His eyes had narrowed in that sinister way that sent jitters shooting up from her gut, and he insisted old May accompany her.

When she had come back from foraging, she deliberately left the bar open, hoping no one would notice.

But someone had. It barely budged. If she used sheer brute force, it would make an unholy noise. She'd have to open it slowly.

She crouched and got her shoulder under the bar, then slowly straightened her legs. It shuddered against the wooden door, letting out the soft beginning of a truly awful shriek. Hazel locked her knees, panting, and paused. Her head felt like it might explode.

Holding the bar in place was even harder than pushing it up, but she couldn't risk a sound. Not when the Prophet was so close, with nothing but a few sheets of plastic separating them.

Slower this time, Hazel rose. Inch by incremental inch, the bar levered up.

"Hurry," Caleb whispered, but Hazel knew that she couldn't. Panic could get them both caught. And she was at the limits of her strength.

Her legs straightened, and the bar just passed halfway. With a small grunt, she reached overhead, took it in both hands and turned, bracing the weight with her own. Her arms trembled. She pushed up, giving it everything she had, and the bar rose higher and higher.

Finally, just when Hazel thought she might drop the terrible weight, the bar locked into place upright. Suddenly relieved of its force, she tumbled forward into the gate, scraping her forehead against the rough-hewn planks.

With a deep breath, she gathered herself, pushed the door open a foot, motioned Caleb through, then followed. Her arms were shaking. She touched a fingertip to her forehead but felt no blood. She wished there was a way to drop the bar again, but there wasn't. Not without making way too much noise.

When people came after them, it would be obvious which gate they had escaped through. Their only chance was to put as much distance as possible between themselves and the Wellspring commune.

Taking Caleb's hand again, Hazel hurried them through the woods. They stuck to the well-worn path for the first few minutes—she didn't want to make too much noise breaking a trail through the crunchy scratchgrass and dried pine branches, and she wanted to move fast. Going off-trail at a gallop could mean twisting an ankle, and that would be deadly.

They were only a few hundred feet away from the compound wall when Caleb tugged on her hand. "Hazel, wait," he whispered.

"What's wrong?" She turned back and felt for her brother, touching his shoulders. "Are you hurt?"

"The water," he whispered. "We have to use the water."

Hazel bit back a growl of frustration. He was talking about the dangers outside of the compound they'd been taught about: the sin of others was infectious, like a terrible disease. Only the blessed waters of their wellspring protected them.

Every time they'd left the compound, even for short foraging trips, they were made to bathe in the water to shield themselves. Hazel didn't believe a lot of what they had been taught—not since the community had shown it cared more about its rules than her family. But Caleb clearly hadn't moved on the way she had. He was younger, more impressionable.

"We need to save it for drinking. Besides, there's no one bad out here," Hazel told her brother. "We're fine."

"No! We need to do it," Caleb insisted. He grabbed her arm and felt for the basket.

"We have to *go*," she said, tugging the basket out of his reach. "Do you want them to catch you? Do you want them to take you away from me?"

"Please, Hazel," Caleb whispered. "I don't want to be bad."

Hazel blinked back sudden tears. He was just a kid. He'd never been out of the compound at night. He was being so brave, following her out into the unknown world. She was so proud of him.

"I'm sorry. Of course we can. We just have to be fast." She crouched down and felt around in her basket for the waterskin. Quickly, she popped open the top and squirted a little on Caleb's head. "The wellspring protect you and keep you pure," she whispered, rubbing her wet hand down each of his arms.

She handed him the waterskin, and he did the same for her, only he squeezed a little too hard and soaked the whole top of her head.

"Caleb!"

"Sorry! Sorry!" But he was giggling. "The wellspring protect you and keep you safe."

He rubbed water on her arms, then capped the waterskin and handed it back. She shook her ponytail over him, splattering a few cool drops on his upturned face and making him laugh quietly.

"Okay. Ready to go?"

"Ready," he promised.

BLURB

He'll get his ailing father home…

Matthew Riley wants to believe people come together in times of struggle, but as chaos sets in after a massive EMP event, he discovers the only people he can trust are family. His father, an Army vet, has skills to survive this dark new world, but with no medication for his heart, keeping him alive may prove an impossible task.

She'll protect her daughter and reunite her family…

Kathleen Riley doesn't share her husband's optimistic view of humanity. When the power goes out during a visit to her brother in prison, she and her teenage daughter must find a way out before starting the long trek back to their family.

They'll defend their home…

With the rest of the Rileys away from home, it's up to Ruth and her grandson, Patton, to keep their hotel safe for the family they know is coming back. But food is running low, and some see an elderly woman and a preteen boy as easy pickings.

In a broken civilization, there is strength in numbers. One family is determined to survive, but will they be able to defend themselves against desperate survivors?

Great news! *Erupting Trouble* is even better than before - it was expanded & republished in February 2024!

Grab your copy of *Erupting Trouble* (EMP Catastrophe Book One)
eBook
Paperback
Audiobook
www.GraceHamiltonBooks.com

EXCERPT

Chapter One

From his spot in the cashier's line of Wilson's Antiques, Matthew Riley smiled at the gorgeous expanse of blue sky that he could see outside the shop's windows. It was turning out to be a beautiful day, and not just because of the spring Wisconsin weather: he'd junk-hunted through rickety wooden chairs and strange metal plush seats from the '60s, and had found the perfect set of green velvet chairs. They'd be perfect decor for the hotel's summertime grand opening. Even his daughter, Allison, would think them retro-cool instead of outdated-gross. The ticket to claim and purchase rested in his palm.

"If this line moves any slower, I might keel over," David grumbled beside him. His father wasn't wrong—it seemed a lot of people had the same idea of taking advantage of the weather to hunt for trash turned to treasure. They were near the back of the line, and up ahead, the cashier was doing her best to keep the line moving.

"We have nowhere else to be," Matthew told his father. "You can consider this mission a success. We found everything we came for here."

"And some things we didn't expect to find. What is this thing, anyway?" David asked, gesturing to the items in the basket Matthew held.

"It's an old-timey coffee grinder," Matthew said.

"Could just buy a new one," David responded, peering at the squat wooden box with a rotating handle. "Looks like a Jack in the Box. Remember those toys?"

"It's about the aesthetic. The River Rock Hotel is a rustic resort, and that's what our guests will expect. We're not going to use it, but doesn't it look cool? People will imagine what it was like to explore the wilderness and find ways to get their morning joe while watching the sun come over the hill."

"Should've kept my coffee grinder from when I was a young man. It might not have had the same *aesthetic*, but at least it worked and looked old. You could've used that for free instead of paying twenty bucks for something that cost fifty cents back in the day."

"Fifty cents then might've been the same amount as twenty bucks now," Matthew said. The lights above flickered, almost as if someone was playing with the light switch. "It's called inflation, Dad."

David snorted. The lights continued to stutter, casting a dim flickering glow over the customers. With a sudden bright surge, as if the bulbs had been pushed to their max, the store fell into darkness. Around him, the customers in line murmured.

"Sorry, folks," the cashier said in a loud voice. "Looks like we lost power. Again."

A collective groan rose.

"We'll just wait for it to kick back on, and then we'd be happy to give you all a 10% discount for your patience and understanding," the cashier finished. She pushed a straggling lock of hair off her forehead with the look of a rabbit caught in a trap.

"I can't wait for you to get your store back in order," one woman near the front said. "You should be prepared for this. It's Madison, for goodness sake. The electricity is always unreliable in the spring."

"It figures," a young man said to his friend just in front of Matthew. "These kinds of shops aren't investing in tech or updating their contingency plans in case something happens. Something like this could send them under. You need to take steps to ensure you aren't losing your customer base just because the electricity goes out. The winter ice must've done a number on their infrastructure."

Some of the customers rolled their eyes and pulled out their phones as the grumbling continued. Matthew sighed. He understood why everyone was frustrated—the world was a hustle-and-bustle kind of economy, where listless time meant money lost or accomplishments not achieved. Still, the poor cashier looked flushed and stressed, and Matthew tended to have a strong, soothing personality. If everyone just understood that they were in the same boat, things would calm down. Sometimes it just took a little nudge for everyone to remember that. He opened his mouth.

"Don't even think about it," David said to him under his breath. Matthew gave his father an irritated look. The two of them were so similar, yet their experiences had shaped them into two very different men.

"I wasn't going to do anything," Matthew said, but even he could hear the lie in his voice. "While we're waiting, I'll check in on Kathleen." He pulled out his phone and dialed his wife so she'd know they might be late.. She'd been on his mind all morning. He knew today would be hard on her.

"She's inside a prison," David said to him gently. "I bet neither she nor Allison can answer. Especially during visitation hours."

Matthew kept the phone to his ear, but he couldn't hear anything. The phone was eerily silent. He ended the call with a frown. His battery was fully charged. Why wouldn't the call go through? "It's not that. The call doesn't even go anywhere."

David shrugged as he pulled out his much older cell phone. "This old building probably has too much concrete blocking the signal, plus the electricity is out. Maybe a tower's down. I don't have signal either."

"It's all right. I just wanted to check in with her. It's tough for her, seeing her brother locked up. I feel bad not being there with her."

"You can't be in two places at once. She'll be all right," David said. "Plus, the hotel is like having another child. You were needed here."

Matthew swallowed the lump in his throat and nodded, steering the conversation back into familiar territory with a joke. "At least it's a child we're raising together."

"The most time-consuming money-sink of a child I've ever had."

Matthew smirked, knowing his father liked to pretend the hotel hadn't given him some purpose in his retirement. "You fuss over the place more than I do."

"Never thought I'd be a retiree," David mused and scratched at his temple. He had the same sandy-blonde hair as Matthew, only his was cut military style and had been for decades. "In all honesty, opening this hotel together will be as good for me as it is for you."

"It's been Kathleen's and my dream for a while now. It's about time we took the steps to make it happen. I'm glad you and Mom decided to be part of that dream too." Matthew paused. "I know we told Mom we'd be back early this afternoon to help her and Patton clean up the rooms, but they'll understand why we might be late."

David grinned. "Patton's probably driving Ruth up the wall."

"Hey, he elected to stay behind and help clean." Matthew held his hands up, palms out. "Sometimes I don't understand that child of mine. I wouldn't be caught dead having to clean, especially on a nice day like this."

"Oh yeah, as opposed to shopping, which has always been something boys enjoy."

"Ha. Ha. Very funny."

Up ahead, the cashier held her hands around her mouth. "Hi there, valuable customers! Since the power doesn't seem like it's coming back on right away, we are going to ring out customers with cash purchases only. If you have a cash purchase, please form a new line to the right."

"Are you serious?" the woman near the front yelled. She walked out of line and around the numerous displays, leaving her pile of things in the middle of the store. "You've just lost my business."

"I'm with her," another man seconded as he abandoned his items.

"I'd be more than happy to put your purchases on hold until tomorrow," the cashier said, her face crumpled with distress.

"You think I'd ever come back to a mismanaged establishment like this?" The bell above the door jingled as the woman stormed out.

"That's uncalled for," David said, his gruff voice low. "No need to be rude."

"They're just frustrated." Matthew released a sigh and looked down to his basket. "I don't have much cash on me. Not enough to get the chairs, that's for sure."

David bit his lip as most of the customers left their items strewn about the store or dumped on displays. "Maybe we should come back when things aren't so hostile."

"Yeah, this poor lady has enough to deal with. Let's go put our things back. The furniture hasn't been pulled yet." Matthew ran a hand through his short, wavy hair, and placed the coffee grinder back on the shelf.

He turned a watchful eye on his father, who was placing a few art deco hinges and doorknobs back, and searched for any signs of distress. It had been a couple of hours, after all.

"This whole thing has been a bust," he said to David. "Feel like heading home? We can try again another day." He shouldn't push his father to keep going and explore the other antique shops in Madison.

"You read my mind." David rubbed his gnarled hands together as if to warm them. His eyes skittered around the shop, always taking in his surroundings. Old habits died hard. Matthew nodded, and together they walked out into the bright sunny day.

The warmth hit Matthew's face, dispelling his worry over his wife and daughter. It was hard to be upset on a day like today. Together, David and Matthew headed to Matthew's silver truck—a couple years old, but still up to date. They hopped in the truck's cab, and Matthew clipped his seatbelt before reaching to start the car by hitting the button.

Usually, a green light flashed at him when the car started up and his phone connected to the Bluetooth. Now the light flashed yellow. With a frown, he pulled out the key fob from his pocket and held the angular piece to the button. The button flashed green, indicating the key was near, but when Matthew tried to turn the car on, nothing happened. "C'mon," Matthew said, pressing the button again. "You have to be kidding me."

"I'll go check it out." David laughed, opening the truck door to get out.

"There's no way," Matthew said, holding the fob closer to the button, only now no colored light flashed to even acknowledge the key was present. He didn't hear any clicking or whirring indicating that the system knew he was in the car. He followed his father out of the cab and popped the hood.

David lifted the hood up and hooked it open. Matthew bit back the admonishment to be careful. Ever since his heart attack, his father had been sensitive to Matthew's hovering. David poked at the looping wires bundled along the engine, checked a few things that Matthew had no idea what they did—a master's in business did not a mechanic make.

"What's it look like?" Matthew asked.

"I can't see anything wrong," David said slowly. "Probably left an interior light on that drained the battery. Happens to the best of us. You're low on washer fluid."

"What should we do?" Matthew looked around and saw that despite the exodus of people from the shop, a lot of cars still filled the parking lot. "Call a tow?"

"If you have signal. Honestly, we should go back inside and see if anyone can give us a jump."

"Good idea." Matthew smiled at his father. "I'm sure someone will help us out."

David patted Matthew on the back, and together they turned to head back inside Wilson's Antiques.

Grab your copy of *Erupting Trouble* (EMP Catastrophe
Book One)
eBook
Paperback
Audiobook
www.GraceHamiltonBooks.com

WANT MORE?

WWW.GRACEHAMILTONBOOKS.COM

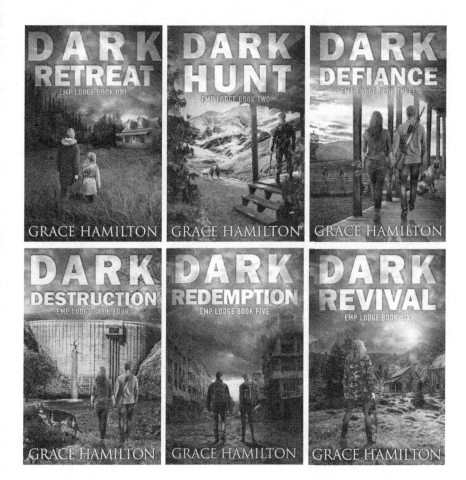

Made in the USA
Monee, IL
19 October 2024

68258747R00197